Elizabeth Brown

Montefiore's Goddaughter

MONTEFIORE'S GODDAUGHTER

written by

ELIZABETH BROOKS

First published in 2010 by M P Publishing Limited

12 Strathallan Crescent, Douglas Isle of Man IM2 4NR
www.mppublishing.co.uk

Book and Cover Design by Maria Smith,
Original Artrwork by Elizabeth Brooks

A CIP catalogue record for this book is available
from the British Library.

ISBN: 978-1-84982-099-8
10 9 8 7 6 5 4 3 2 1

I am grateful to all the people who have helped me to produce this book, in particular my husband Chris, Katherine Reed, Maria Smith, Mark Pearce and Christine Pearce

In memory of Rachel

The Vulture Man

here do you go at night, once you have turned out the light and snuggled down under the blankets? Do you worry about yesterday and tomorrow, until you are so worn out with worrying that you fall asleep? Do you try to turn your mind into a vacuum, believing that the best sort of rest is blankness?

Or do you slip away into a world that is all your own?

When I was small I went to an oak wood with Boris, my bear (he was limp, loose-limbed and already balding). It was a dark place of green-black shadow, though there were clearings where the sunlight or moonlight sometimes crept in. The trees were wider and taller than they are in the Waking World, and one of them was my night time home. It looked just like any of the neighbouring oaks, but it was entirely hollow, and underneath it, among the roots, there was a room, where I lived.

The Tree People lived there too, and they lived there always – that is to say, they were not obliged to re-enter the Waking World every morning as Boris and I were. The Tree People were my companions. I expect that you know some of them, or people like them. There identities chopped and changed depending on where my thoughts were tending at the time, and what I was reading. I remember that a blond-haired boy called Prince Constantine was a great favourite of mine as this story began, and that I had a penchant for fainting gracefully at his feet and observing his concern through half-closed eyelids. There were many others besides him though, and they drifted in and out according to whether I wanted them or not.

There was an owl as well, with a wing-span as wide as a dragon's.

He was the guardian of my oak, since he had lived in its shelter all his life, and he was many, many years older than me. His name was Eyes.

The tree was a proper home. Somebody had always made the place comfortable in anticipation of our arrival: the kettle was on the boil, and the fire rustled complacently. Constantine was a clever teller of frightening stories, and once we had settled down with a hot, sweet mug, and maybe a slice of toast, he would regale us with his tales. If the weather was particularly stormy then I would run around the wild, wet wood for a while before settling myself at the hearth. The weather was frequently violent in my night time world, because I am the sort of person who likes to batten down the hatches.

I hope you don't think our pleasures were staid? On the contrary, even our most peaceful moments were enlivened by the proximity of danger. You see, we shared the wood with a tribe of giant cannibals. Eyes often saw them as he glided through the trees; the rest of us heard them smashing through the branches and roaring for our flesh. They, in turn, knew of us because they could smell us, and because we left our footprints on the muddy paths.

They caught me once – only once. I was four years old when it happened, but the memory is vivid.

I remember that I was running from them, running through the rain, when I slipped. I tried to scramble to my feet, but a hand closed round my neck and lifted me from the ground. The other cannibals caught up and gathered round in an admiring crush. I kicked and choked, and this amused them. A female leaned over to pinch my plump arms. She shouted her appreciation, and slapped my captor on the back.

He parted from the other hunters and took me home. I remember that his family were very noisy: the children singing tunelessly at the tops of their voices and quarrelling with one another and crying, while their mother – the loudest of all – called for quiet.

There were squeals of appreciation when their father appeared in the clearing, dangling me by my plaits like the tasty morsel I was. The youngest child made a hungry grab at my legs, but I was whisked out of reach, bundled into a wire cage and hung from an oak branch. This cage served as their larder, I presume, for besides me it contained a pile of pungent cheese rinds and a turquoise bird's egg.

As he locked the cage door I saw my captor's face. There was no malice there, as he looked me over, only appetite. He had fat, moist lips and smiling eyes.

I watched as the family began their preparations for dinner. The smoky fire was forced to blaze, and a man-sized saucepan of water placed over the flames. The woman peeled onions and slid them into the pot with a handful of wild garlic. Then she knelt on the grass with a wheel-shaped grindstone and a carving knife. She began sharpening the blade, testing it every now and then against the soft pads of her fingertips. Her husband, in the meantime, laid plates and cutlery on a makeshift wooden table, while the children constructed a posy of primroses and violets, and placed it in a cup at the centre of the table.

The water had come to a rolling boil. The woman was wiping her hands on her apron and advancing purposefully towards me, when rescue came at last. Eyes the owl plummeted through the sky like a meteor. His piercing scream sent the cannibals scurrying for cover, their arms wrapped over their heads. In a trice he had unhooked the cage and he carried it home in his beak. My friends wrenched the door off its hinges and I was freed.

So long as we stayed inside the tree we were safe, though we had to keep our voices down. The cannibals were not imaginative and it would never have occurred to them to investigate the interior of a hollow tree. Besides, the entrance was protected by magic. Anyone wishing to enter had to murmur an unguessable mantra, like *Ali Baba* and his *"Open sesame"*. No, it was only while we explored the woods that we were in danger of meeting the man-eaters. Often (at least once a night) the ground quivered and swathes of foliage crashed nearby and then, if we were outside, we knew we must race back to our tree like lightning. Those cannibals gave our happiness just the edge it needed.

I would never have described all this to you in my secretive childhood, but it is easy and even pleasant to talk about it now that I am old.

Now I will tell you about the night when my adventures began.

I remember that it was a winter night in my imaginary world; that there was a fine mist suspended from the trees and that the wood was cold, dank and still. Our fire threatened to die out during one of Constantine's chilling tales and though we were reluctant to venture into the murk, we were agreed that a blazing fire was an essential accompaniment to the story. After a short squabble, Boris bear and I volunteered to venture outside in search of fresh firewood.

My tree stood at the edge of a clearing and it was across this crackling carpet that we began our quest. Sticks were plentiful here, even dry, grey sticks, if you kicked aside the covering layers of forest debris. So here we were, in the clearing, stooping and shushing our way around the edges, when (and the sensation came upon us gradually) we began to feel a faint, rhythmic drumming along the forest floor, and to hear dead leaves swish-swish-swishing beneath the beat. We looked at one another questioningly, because we had never heard sounds like these in our wood. I was sure that they were too light and fast for a cannibal's footsteps. Yet how could I be perplexed by the identity of a presence in my own imaginary land? Curiosity and a vague, thrilling hope of something wonderful, overcame our fear, and instead of scrambling back to the tree we lurked in the shadows to see what it might be.

As the sounds drew nearer I finally recognised them for the rushing hooves of a horse. Immediately a rider galloped out of the mist and the silhouetted trees and reared to a halt in the centre of the clearing. Boris and I gasped and clung to one another. Boris's golden fur gleamed in the leafy moonlight, so I hid him beneath the folds of my green cloak and backed into the shadows as noiselessly as I could.

The horse was as sleek as a wet, black stone. I am no judge of horses, but I know that I have never seen such an imperious animal in the Waking World. I have met ponies, whom I have patted and fed and sat on. They were always either submissive or else sweetly stubborn. This stallion, with its tossing head and fiery yellow eyes, seemed arrogant and sneering. Its body was all bone and quivering muscle and it was very tall – its shoulders the height of a man's head. It was never still, but shifted about perpetually from hoof to hoof and blew great clouds of steam from it nostrils. It seemed to eye me through the shadows and, when it drew its lips back to whinny, I could have sworn that it was laughing.

Still, it was the rider, not the horse, that frightened me most. When I chose them for my world I thought that giant cannibals were the most horrible creatures imaginable, roaring, lumbering and slavering for flesh. Now I realised that a thing could be still and silent, yet too malign for my immature imagination.

The rider was male – I knew by his square shoulders – and like me he wore a cloak, only his was hooded and very full (it covered him from head to foot and draped itself over the horse's rump). It was made of black velvet. Embroidered onto the cloak, across his chest, there was a curling, silver crest. He kept his reins in one gloved hand; in the other he held an empty net that dangled down among the leaves. I could see little of his face, but what I saw made my soul shrivel. For a bird's beak protruded from his hood, yellow and cruelly curved, like a vulture's.

Perhaps you think the idea of a bird-man comical? But imagine that he is towering near you, breathing hard after his gallop, and turning that hooked blade this way and that, as his hidden eyes search and search. I could hear blood banging between my ears, and my breaths shuddered as though I too had been racing through the night.

All of a sudden his gaze jolted against me. Surely I was invisible, crouched so small and green and silent among the low leaves and branches?

But: "Come here," he rasped, and I saw the glint of eyes, as black as coals, from deep inside the velvet hood.

I did not move. Then he thrust his beak towards me and screamed a harsh, piercing scream, which brought me to my feet. He beckoned me nearer. Slowly, slowly I approached the restless horse.

"What are you doing in this wood?" he demanded.

"I live here." I stuttered.

"You live here?"

"Yes. At night. In the day I live...somewhere else."

"Do you live here alone?"

"Yes." I lied quickly, as Boris clung to my cloak-lining.

"I have permission to kill trespassers," he continued mildly. "But I will let you go on condition that you never set foot in this forest, or in any part of Traumund, ever again. It does not belong to you and you are not welcome here."

"But...surely...this wood can't belong to anybody," I said, my voice trembling like a violinist's vibrato, "because I made it up in my head."

"This forest belongs to the King of Traumund."

"The...Who?"

The beak almost touched my nose. The air between us was unbreathably acrid. "You heard me, little Insolence. Scurry off home to your Waking World and stay there. Return to Traumund, and the king will have you eliminated." He lowered his voice to a hiss, and I could not help smelling the stale meat on his breath. "We will find you." He drew himself up to his full height. "Do I have your word?"

I knew I would say 'yes', and that my 'yes' would be a lie. I wondered whether he would see through my 'yes'. The possibility made me hesitate. The hooded body took my hesitation for defiance. It stooped once again. The net twitched.

"What is your name?" he asked.

"Abigail Crabtree." I answered.

He changed at once: lightened and loosened and excited. "Ah!"

he wailed, as though gratified by a flash of comprehension. "Indeed? Abigail Crabtree! How strange! How...odd. I'm afraid you will have to come with me after all. The king will be delighted."

As he blurted that last word he made a grab at me, and to my horror I felt gloved talons pricking my forearm.

At the same instant I forced my leaden legs to move. They leapt through the undergrowth and hurled me, tripping and tumbling, at the hollow tree. The Vulture Man whipped up his horse, but the foliage was too dense for the animal and it made little progress. I heard a whistle and a slap against my ears and glimpsed the rider's net falling slackly over a clump of ferns, just inches from my feet. Then – bruised and gasping – I touched my tree. I breathed the magic words into its kind bark, and it folded me into itself. Boris tumbled from my cloak and we lay amongst our friends, speechless.

We all froze as the horse and its rider thrust through snapping branches and brackens and passed by our home. In my mind I saw the horse's nostrils flicker as it came close to us, and I saw the roll of its fretful, yellow eye. But the Vulture Man urged it forward into an unfathomed woody darkness.

Boris and I told our tale in cautious whispers. We asked one another, uselessly, how, or where, the Vulture Man had entered the wood. What was Traumund? Who was its king, and why did he want to possess my imaginary land? We speculated, but to no avail, since none of us had the least glimmer of understanding. For much of the night we sat still in troubled, broken silence. Constantine never resumed his tale and the fire cooled to a dusty white.

As waking time approached Boris said, "Abigail...I'm sorry...you didn't make it all up, did you?"

"No! Honestly, no."

"Then how, in heaven's name, could he have been here, in your imaginary wood?"

"Boris, truly, I don't know!"

One of the tree people - an Edwardian girl - poked at the dead fire with a stick. She wore blue ribbons in her hair. "Will you come back again?" she asked timidly.

I drew shapes on the dusty floor with my finger and made no reply.

"It would be better, perhaps – safer – if you didn't."

I looked at Boris and we glowered lovingly at one another. "Of course we will come back." I said.

We made our way up the trunk and into the Waking World. The

morning light was gleaming safely round the edges of our curtains. I lay in my pyjamas, a mute bear in my arms, and I wondered.

The Institute

t was summer in the Waking World: a hot, purple-skied August. I remember lying on my stomach in the garden at home, three or four weeks after the Vulture Man had appeared in my wood. I was sweltering and enjoying my idleness with such enthusiasm that it was no longer idleness, but energetic joy. I watched the hypnotic scurryings of ants among the short grasses of our lawn, and thought what a spindly, sky-scraping city they lived in. I thought, too, that the sun on my neck felt blood-red and that the tree-shade across my legs was a pale, soapy lilac. I wondered how these physical feelings could have become colours in my head. I felt inspired, but by too many things and with too much dizzy glee to be able to create any meaningful response.

My mum came out of the kitchen with a letter in her hand.

"Abigail," she said, "Come inside. Your dad and I want to ask you about something." I hauled myself up and traipsed into the house.

Green spots floated before my eyes in the relative darkness. I sat down at the kitchen table and yawned. Dad leant against the sideboard, frowning at the letter that my mum had handed back to him. Mum sat down and began shelling peas into a bowl. They didn't speak, so eventually I said,

"What, then?"

"Well," replied dad slowly, turning the letter over, reading it to the end and finally looking up at me, "We've had a letter from your godfather, Ludovick Montefiore."

I had heard of Ludovick Montefiore, but I had only seen him once and that was at my christening when I was two months old. I knew nothing about him, except that he was a friend of my mother's family.

I also knew that I liked his name.

"He wants you to go to St. John's School…The Institute, I should say," said mum. "He's a governor there and he says he'll easily be able to wangle you a place."

"But I can't go away," I answered anxiously. I was loath to leave home. "You always said that boarding school would be too expensive."

"Well, but Ludovick wants to pay your fees. He insists. In fact, he's already paid next term's," said my dad.

"What I can't work out," mused mum, as she vacantly nibbled on an empty pea-pod, "is why he seems so anxious for her to go? I mean, he writes…persuasively"

Dad shrugged. "He is her godfather. Perhaps he feels it's only fair, with Dominic having had the opportunity, and so on."

· My elder brother Dominic had won a scholarship to St. John's School. He had excelled in art and now he taught drawing and painting in Paris. Since his time (he was seven years my senior) St. John's school had become *The Institute of Social and Personal Advancement*. The head teacher and most of the staff had been replaced. This did not bode well. But my parents wanted the best for me, and Ludovick Montefiore had written persuasively.

"What do you think?" asked mum, her eyes searching my face for doubt.

I looked at the table and chewed my hair thoughtfully.

"Dominic loved it there," she added. We all thought, "Yes, but it wasn't called The Institute of Social and Personal Advancement then", though none of us said that.

Dad piped up, "Your godfather seems to think it has an excellent reputation – well, everyone says the same, don't they? He seems to think it'll suit Abigail down to the ground." We all thought, "But the last time he set eyes on her she was two months old," though none of us said that either.

"If I go to school," I asked eventually, and weightily, "Will I be able to learn French?" Learning French was the great goal of my life at the moment, since Catherine Lorimer, who used to live a few doors away and personified everything I ever wished to be, had read French at Edinburgh University.

"I would imagine so." Dad shrugged.

"Well in that case," I said, and a rush of courage straightened my spine as I spoke, "Perhaps I'll give it a go. I can always change my mind later on."

So my parents wrote back to Ludovick Montefiore, informing him that I accepted his offer with thanks.

On an overcast afternoon in September I stood before the main entrance to The Institute of Social and Personal Advancement. I clutched a small green suitcase in one hand and Boris bear in the other. I suppose I looked childish for my age, but I did not know it – yet. My courage had wilted long ago: I felt utterly bereft. My parents were gone because I had begged them not to prolong their goodbyes and now I wanted them with a depth of wretchedness such as I had never known before. To make matters worse, the people who streamed in and out of the front door all seemed to me - miserable me – loudly and self-lovingly happy. In (it seemed) deliberately cruel contrast to my crushed state, they exuded cleverness, poise and impossible glamour. One girl bumped into me; she was chatting on her mobile and failed to notice me. She stopped for a second and peered into my face from beyond layers of make-up and clouds of expensive perfume. "Ugh!" She shrieked at the sight of my faded coat and wan, streaky cheeks. She drew back and laughed sharply. "Oh my God!" She flashed past.

I tucked Boris into my inside breast pocket (he was a compact bear) and wiped my nose across the back of my hand, leaving a snail trail over my knuckles. I had read enough to harbour vague pre-conceptions about boarding school: there would be foggy lacrosse matches, I thought, and forbidden midnight feasts and dingy wooden desks. I expected the details of my pre-conceptions to be incorrect, but the girl with the mobile made me feel that the very spirit of my ideas were not misplaced.

Then a low voice near my ear said, "Are you all right?" and I turned to find a fellow mismatch standing beside me. He wore thick glasses and an exquisitely tailored suit that he pulled and picked at in relentless discomfort. He was glaring at his shoes and scuffing them on the gravel. I was neither afraid nor ashamed to answer him, at any rate.

"No," I moaned with a gurgling sniff. "I'm not all right. I'm going to go home. I'm going to walk home now, on my own." Home was two hundred miles away.

At this he looked up. He stopped fidgeting and studied my snotty pallor intently.

"You really don't like the Institute, do you?"

I had not even entered the door yet, but I replied without hesitation, "I hate it. I'm not staying here."

He made a vicious grab at my arm and then, to my astonishment, embarked upon a rapturous, whispered plea: "Please don't go. Please stay. You've no idea how much I need the company of someone like you: somebody scruffy and ungainly, whose nose runs and whose hair doesn't stay in place. It's so lonely here."

I frowned and pulled my arm away. "I'm not ungainly."

"I know you think I'm being rude," he went on. "I don't mean to be…But it's so hard…What I mean to say is that you look as though you're still real."

A gang of teenagers (I noticed later on that almost everyone survived within gangs here) jostled the boy. "Ooh, Four-Eyes has got himself a girlfriend!" they screamed in unison, then one of them made a swipe at his glasses and dropped them into a muddy puddle. They swaggered away, crowing. Three adults – teachers, as I presently discovered - were loitering in the doorway and saw what happened, but they shrugged at one another, smiling. I retrieved the boy's spectacles; the lenses were intact. He snatched them hastily and polished them against his expensive suit. He affected to be unmoved by the incident, though he couldn't help blushing.

"My name is Joachim Larrouse," he continued in his peculiarly intense manner. He held out his hand and I shook it formally. "I am very pleased to meet you Miss…?"

"Abigail Crabtree," I smiled, despite myself.

"Miss Crabtree. And I really would appreciate it if you didn't run away from school…not just yet anyway."

"I don't know…all right."

A tremulous grin almost broke across his face. Then he frowned and shrugged self-consciously. "I suppose you'd better go and see Anna. You may as well get it over with."

"Who's Anna?"

"It's my name for the headmistress, Miss Konder. Sometimes I think of her as Anna, and sometimes just The Snake."

"Hello, Darling," hissed Miss Konder, and made as though to kiss me on either cheek. Her flesh never actually touched mine, but I felt as though cold water were trickling down my neck when she came close to me. "We don't need you, thank you very much Larrouse," she added, and Joachim slunk away. I sat down before her stainless steel desk and glanced around at the whitewashed, breeze-block walls. Like the corridors through which Joachim and I had passed to reach her office, the room was bare and uninteresting. There were no books or pictures; even the blinds and the wastepaper bins were sleek and bland. Besides the desk and two chairs, the Snake's office contained a metal cupboard and a shelf piled high with glossy magazines.

"Well Darling and you are...?" she asked, glancing down at her register.

"Abigail Crabtree."

"Oh yes. Mr. Montefiore's protégé." There was a pause as she looked me up and down. She was tall, thin and crisp, with short hair, long nails and not a trace of physical softness. "Well, well, we are in a mess, n'est pas?" she smiled brightly. "You didn't think to spruce yourself up for day one?"

"Um..."

"Never mind. You're not the first. Now then." She swung my little suitcase onto her desk and clicked it open. I protested with a murmur of shy alarm. She glanced blankly at my forehead and my protest withered away.

I watched as she rifled through my precious possessions. First a much-mended woolly jumper. I used to wear it when I was climbing trees at home. Mum had packed it saying, "You'll need something rough for playtime."

"My goodness me, Abigail Crabtree!" Miss Konder exclaimed. "That will have to go!" She dropped it into a black bin-bag. I did not protest, because I had no courage in my indignation, as my mum would have done. What were my feelings beside Miss Konder's expertise?

All my clothes went in the bin bag and, to my horror, two new notebooks, a pencil case and a pocket English dictionary. Then she picked up my battered copy of *The Wizard of Oz*.

"Oh no! Please let me keep that!" I cried as she studied the cover with uncomprehending disdain.

"What, *this*?" she said, dangling the book in front of my anguished gaze. "What do you want this for? We don't read books at the Institute – especially not old, messy ones like this."

"No books?" I was astounded.

"Oh no," she replied breezily as *The Wizard of Oz* flopped into her rubbish bag. I winced to see the cover bend back against the sides of the bag, the pages creasing under their own weight. "This is a forward-thinking institution. You will only study things that are relevant and useful. You want to be able to leave school as a presentable money-earner, don't you? That's why Mr. Montefiore is paying for you to have such an excellent education. Well then! How exactly is a story book going to contribute, do you think?"

I didn't answer, because I was busy thinking what a hateful man my godfather must be. Miss Konder took my silence for submission, so she patted my cheek with her cold-blooded fingers and murmured, "Good girl!"

"Will I learn French?" I asked hopelessly.

Miss Konder was writing something on her clip-board against my name. She wrote slowly and with a great effort of concentration, which surprised me and made me fear her a little less. She answered absently, "Oh yes, you'll do a bit of French."

I felt so deprived of good news that her welcome words excited me to volubility. I said, quietly and quickly,

"Oh good! Oh, I really want to learn French! You see at home I have – used to have - a baby-sitter called Catherine Lorimer and she baby-sat when my parents went out, and she did French at university and she wrote a sort of thesis or something on this French poet called Verhaeren, although actually I think he's Belgian but he writes in French. And she told me about this poem called The Mill, only in French it's called Moole-Anne I think…"

"Abigail, Abigail, Abigail!" Miss Konder was shaking her head and smiling thinly, with her lips. There were no smiling creases around her eyes. "You have a very great deal to learn!"

"I know," I replied timidly, "I know, I was just saying…"

"You won't be learning frivolous things like poetry while I'm in charge of your education. What practical purpose would that have? Mmm? I meant that if you were very good and very clever, you might learn a little bit of social French. When you're entertaining, for example, it's useful to know words like vol-au-vent and hors d'oeuvre."

I stared at her stonily.

Miss Konder caught my eye and bent to write something vehement against my name. Then she looked up with that same loveless smile. "Now, have I seen all your possessions? No toys I presume?"

I could feel Boris's friendly bulk against my chest. Thank God I had thought to put him inside my coat. "No!" I squeaked with a desperate sort of carelessness. She focussed her suspicious snake-eyes on my lying face and paused before saying, "Good. Money?"

"Oh, yes!" I said eagerly, glad to divert her attention. "In the side pocket of my suitcase. Dad gave me twenty pounds pocket money."

"Is that all?" She sneered, as she extracted my twenty pound note and fastened it to her clip-board. "Try and bring a bit more than that next term. Especially if your parents are expecting the school to kit you out with clothes and make-up."

She stood up and unlocked the metal cupboard. I could see that it was piled high with small plastic boxes and cellophane packages. Miss Konder mused, rummaging for a while before turning to me with an armful of clothes and a pink box.

"This will do to start with." She said. "One pair of high-heeled shoes. One pin-striped trouser suit. Two silk tops. Three sets of underwear. Inside this box you'll find hair-brushes and straighteners, foundation, eye-shadow, mascara, blusher, lipsticks…Anything vital that I've forgotten?" I did not reply. "Ah! Nail varnish!" She returned to the cupboard and produced a vibrant red bottle. "We'll sort you out properly in a few days time, as I say – but this will keep you going in the meantime."

I stared at the pile in my arms and my scruffy, ungainly, real self quailed. You might think there was nothing so terrible in Miss Konder's determination to smarten me up; to dress me in pinstripes and mascara. But you would be wrong. This was no giggly dressing-up game – it was a serious, permanent imposition, so I felt crushed and ashamed. My real self was to be obliterated and I had no will to resist. I could not even be sure that the obliteration was wrong. I only knew that, daubed with lipstick and tottering about on high-heels I would feel an incommunicable loneliness. I would look ridiculous to anybody whom I loved and since they could only see my made-up body, they would assume that my mind and soul was ridiculous too. For a nightmarish moment I imagined my parents staring at me without comprehension, then laughing at me.

"Now, finally, your timetable."

Miss Konder handed me a sheet of paper and I took it dazedly.

"We rise at eight-ish; there's a bell at eight o'clock. Lessons begin at around nine-thirty tomorrow morning. I see that your first class is Hair Care, so try and get yours straightened before you turn up. You've got Relationships in the afternoon and a bit of preparatory reading won't go amiss, so I'll give you the June copy of Hey,Guys! – there's a really good article in there by Candy Feckle who was, I am proud to say, one of our own…there you go, can you manage?" She placed a colourful magazine on top of my cellophane pile. "Now, off you go, Sweetie!"

Joachim lurked outside. I think he had been listening at the door. He smiled conspiratorially as I emerged, and this encouraged me. I was about to speak, but The Snake marched into the corridor, smacked him hard over the back of his head and rasped, "Get…out…of…my… sight…Larrouse." We were obliged to leave in opposite directions, and I did not see Joachim again that evening.

Boris and I made our way to the imaginary wood that night. I felt I would rather face ten-thousand Vulture Men and Kings of Traumund than suffer another moment at the Institute.

"What will you do?" asked Prince Constantine as he folded a roomy quilt round my shoulders. A girl called Dorothea stirred a pan of cocoa over the fire; I watched the flickering of her plaits and her faded gingham dress with a yearning watchfulness, as though she might fade from my sight in a moment.

"They'll run away, of course," she answered scornfully. "Why wouldn't they? What's there to stay for?" She turned to me. "Just tie some bed-sheets together, climb out of the window and walk home. Only, make sure you walk at night – you've to hide in woods and behind hedges in the daytime, in case Anna Konder has a search party out."

Boris slurped his cocoa and glanced at me. I looked into the fire. Eyes the owl sighed moodily.

"What?" demanded Dorothea.

"The boy, Joachim," Eyes intoned.

I beat my fist against the floor. Tears sprang to my eyes.

"I don't even know him! I hadn't even entered the building before he made me say I'd stay! I'm not beholden to him! Well, I'm not, am I?"

"I don't know," murmured Prince Constantine and Dorothea in tones of quiet distress.

Eyes the owl and Boris the bear were silent.

I spent the rest of the night wondering, crying, resolving to stay and resolving to go. My friends did their best to comfort me, and I was thankful, but their kindness made it even harder to tolerate the prospect of an imminent return to the Institute. We returned nonetheless, Boris and I, at dawn. Radiators hummed around the room and the air might have been insufferably hot, only the window over my bed was ajar.

I knew I must hide Boris from Miss Konder and her staff. I thought of putting him inside my pillowcase, so I felt cautiously (for the surrounding beds were occupied by potentially hostile girls) for the opening. There was something already there, inside the pillowcase: a hard, rectangular object, like a book. It had not been there yesterday evening. I knew that because I had, very incompetently, made up the bed myself.

It was a book. I drew it out surreptitiously. It was my *Wizard of Oz* – bent, injured but intact.

A slip of paper floated onto the mattress as I turned its beloved pages. I read a pencilled message by the feeble light from the window.

"Dear Abigail – I retrieved your book as a token of my friendship for you. I know this is your bed because I saw you struggling with sheets and pillowcases when I was taking a stroll in the 'garden' earlier. Do you have a bear, or something of that sort? I know you told Anna you didn't, but maybe you do. If so, then loose floorboards are good hiding places. I could come and loosen one in your dormitory at an opportune moment, should you so wish. Will you meet me at lunch break tomorrow? We could talk then. I know French – I could try and teach you. Please don't run away. I'd run with you, only my parents will send me straight back - Your friend Joachim Larrouse."

I sighed and closed my eyes. Moist air drifted through the window and cooled my flushed face. I lay wide awake and waited for the eight o'clock bell.

Joachim Larrouse

We can't run Abigail, we can't. They will laugh at us; then they'll tell The Snake and then she'll kill us." Joachim paused and added stiffly, "It's quite out of the question."

I looked at him and nodded, but there was a sly joy in his eyes and on his lips. I felt the corners of my mouth quiver with laughter. We looked again at the strip of turf that wove among the empty flowerbeds, glowing like white gold in the winter sun. Our feet sweltered and pined in their expensive shoes.

One more glance at Joachim's face, but not another word: we stripped our feet bare and raced down the dewy lawn. We dared not laugh aloud or scream, but our hilarity was all the more exquisite for being suppressed.

I was sixteen years old now and I had been a student at the Institute for three years. I could totter steadily in my stilettos now, apply make-up without a thought and straighten my chemically altered hair. They deflated my mind day by day and wrestled to kill my childhood, but at least, thanks to Joachim, I was sufficiently self-aware to know it and to resist it in silence (or at least to desire to resist it).

Joachim had saved me; there was never any doubt about that. He kept my soul alive. If I was homesick or sad, he would leave a comforting note under my pillow. If I was bored he would talk me out of it. He taught me French as we ambled round the school grounds at break time. They were furtive, whispered lessons – nevertheless I was fluent within two years. He was always passing cartoons and witty poems to me during class (at great risk to us both), for no other reason than to see me smile.

On my fourteenth birthday Joachim arranged an escapade. He saw
to it that we both fell 'ill' at seven o'clock in the evening and were sent
to our respective dormitories. Twenty minutes later we were scurrying
through town, hand in hand, breathless with laughter and fear. He took
me to an Italian restaurant and we hid at a dark table in the farthest
corner. I remember there was a candle in a Chianti bottle. I blew it out,
but the waiter immediately relit it and this seemed like the funniest
thing that had ever happened to either of us. We ate nothing but a side
order of garlic bread, since it was all we could afford. We were too
scared to enjoy it anyway. But the memory of that evening – for we got
away with it, somehow or other – was a source of unending pleasure
and solace during those dark years at the Institute, though we never
dared to repeat it. It was our great triumph.

Other than that, our rebellions were quiet and discreet. Only today,
during the last lunch-break before the Christmas holidays, we decided
to run a bare-foot race.

As we neared the steps where they lounged, flicking their silky hair
and screeching, I glanced back at Joachim. I was an idiot to lose my
focus, but I was afraid of them and I wanted the reassurance of his
complicit face. Of course, I lost my footing. I skidded across the grass
and crashed into the bottom step. My school bag burst, spewing its
contents at their feet: magazines, biros, purse…and Boris. I almost
cried out when I saw him roll from his hiding place. He lay just beyond
my dazed grasp, his pale fur ruffled and mud-stained.

Joachim, red-faced and mumbling, was trying to shovel everything
back into the bag and pull me away when I saw him catch sight of the
bear. He lunged at Boris, grabbed a paw, but he was too late. A boy
slid idly off the top step and clamped his own manicured hand around
Joachim's wrist. With the fingers of his other hand he lifted Boris,
delicately yet irresistibly, high above our heads. Everybody gazed up
at the dirty, dangling creature and there was a taunting silence. Then
one of the girls said:

"That is *so* sad!"

Another girl moaned in a fragile tone: "It's disgusting. I mean, it's
all dirty and, like, manky? Oh my God, I think I'm going to throw up!"
She buried her face in her hands.

The other girls glanced at her enviously and concurred. Fingering
their earrings weakly they declared themselves overcome by

incomprehension and nausea. At this the boys began hurling and catching the bear, laughing manfully at their game and at the girls' admiring shrieks.

"Don't!" I stamped and Joachim clutched my hand as they suddenly stopped.

"*Don't!*" mimicked a boy with greased orange hair and small eyes. The others giggled, so he sang "*Don't! Don't! Don't! Don't! Don't!*" in a voice whose pitch rose with every word. Then he clenched his fingers in my hair, rammed the bear into my face and rubbed the muddy fur round and round. I could not breathe as wispy bits of dirt clogged my eyes and throat. I heard Joachim shout, and then there were blows, an intake of breath and then nothing. Feet shuffling in the gravel. It was light again. I looked up. The group were standing still, smiling awkwardly at something behind me. Joachim groaned faintly.

Miss Konder had arrived on the scene, as stealthy as a predatory reptile. Today she wore a shiny green suit, glossy lipstick that was dark red – black, even, like dirty, clotted blood - and there were jewelled clips in her thin hair. She glittered.

"Hi guys!" she began.

"Hia!" responded our tormentors, who believed in her affability and liked it.

"So what's going on?" she smiled. Then, arching her pencilled brows she asked, teasingly, "What have you got there, Bruce?"

Bruce, the gang's pet joker, was eager to explain. "This, Miss Konder", he said, holding Boris aloft like a guillotined head, "is what I believe one calls a '*teddy bear*'. Not that I'd know. It was discovered among the possessions of that...*child*. I was just explaining to the child and its grubby little Friendy-Wendy, that this Institute forbids running, bare feet, teddy bears, grazed knees (Miss Konder glanced coldly at my legs which were beginning to trickle) and immature things like that. But I'm sure you can put the point better than I can, Miss Konder." She smiled at him with a show of coy approval, as she smiled at all the older boys whom she liked.

"Thank you, Bruce. Oh and I suppose I'd better take that." She took hold of Boris's left ear between the silvered nails of her thumb and second finger, her upper lip curling theatrically. I bit my lower lip. My mum had made Boris during the months before my birth.

Turning to me, Miss Konder said,

"I think it's time we had a little chat, Abigail. Would you pop over to my office after assembly?"

I nodded, as though I had any choice in the matter.

She could not prevent her friendly mask from slipping as she turned to Joachim. She hated him, as I loved him, because his very existence was an innocent subversion of the Institute's ethos. He was incurably blithe and clumsy, musical, plain and kind. She bent down until her face was level with his, then pinched both his cheeks hard, bruising the skin and distorting his lips. For a while her malevolence was lost for words, and she merely stared at his lowered eyes. Then, moving his face slowly from side to side, she hissed, "What a horrible…stupid… ugly bit of filth you are."

The others laughed and out of the corner of my eye I could see that Joachim squeezed his lips together tightly.

I missed most of the assembly, since I needed time to repair my appearance. After a hurried bath I donned a new set of expensive underwear and tights, a white satin top, a tight pink skirt and a pair of white high-heels. I did my face and hair poorly, with trembling, angry hands. I was frightened for Boris. I wondered how I would save him from The Snake's black bin-bag. I dared not imagine that I was already too late.

Joachim required grooming as well, so we arrived outside the school hall simultaneously. He wore a slick black suit, a garish tie and he looked as gloomy as I felt. We smiled wanly at one another and sidled into the back row.

A Mr. Wells-Wilton was presenting the prizes this year. He was doubtlessly a successful businessman and a governor. Teeth, rings and cufflinks flashed as he shook hands with the prize-winners. Sometimes, with a waggish smile at the audience, he would pat a girl on the thigh as she left the stage, raising an appreciative chuckle. I glanced at Joachim and we laughed too, but our sniggers had their own elite significance.

Miss Konder stood behind a lectern, announcing the awards in a tone of delighted incredulity.

"This year the Best Turned Out prizes go to…Lily Pinnington and Ollie Schwartz! Well done, guys! Great stuff! You deserve it!"

And, "The Gillingham Memorial Prize for Achievement in the Arts goes to… Shane Carter! …for his inspirational final year project: 'Calming Colours for Waiting Room Walls'. Absolutely brilliant! Let's have a big hand for Shane, everyone!"

Then, "Now for a new award that we've never handed out to anyone before today! I think most of you are aware that there is a very special young lady in our midst...where are you, Patricia Cass?!" (There were whoops and cheers as an elegant sixth former tottered onto the stage, into Miss Konder's congratulatory embrace. Mr. Wells-Wilton licked his sausage lips.) "Now then, guys and gals," Miss Konder resumed, with one hand on Patricia's shoulder, "as you all know, last April Pattie wrote an article on nail care that was published by none other than...Hey, Guys! magazine!" (More cheers from Patricia's friends. Miss Konder threw them an indulgent smile and held up her hands for silence.) "And it is in recognition of this outstanding academic achievement that the governors and I have created the new Award for Excellence that Mr. Wells-Wilton will now present! Well done, Pattie!"

Miss Konder kissed her pupil on both cheeks, then Mr. Wells-Wilton took his turn. His kisses were not so light as Miss Konder's and, as he planted them, he clutched the girl's waist with his sausage fingers.

The applause was fervent. So was Joachim's groan. Mr. McBain, an inarticulate teacher who liked to inflict pain, dragged him up by the collar and carried him off without a word. Joachim barely had time to hand me his thick-rimmed spectacles. The last time Mr. McBain had beaten him, they were irreparably smashed. I slipped them inside my bear-less bag.

The assembly ended shortly after Joachim's untimely exit. I made my way to The Snake's office and waited. I could see Boris through the frosted glass. He was perched on her stainless-steel desk, the blurred posture of his body exuding disdain and discomfort. Well, at least I knew where he was.

On the other side of the corridor I could look down on the garden where Joachim and I had run our doomed race. It was the last strip of green in the Institute, and I supposed they would tidy it away soon. My brother Dominic once told me that when he was a pupil the whole place was a wilderness of apple trees and crumbling red brick. Now it was made barren by concrete and steel.

I thought about the prize-giving with a guilty wistfulness, wondering how long I could remain a misfit within such a persuasive environment. For a moment (I had experienced such moments before) I wished that my better self would allow me to conform; to become devoted to fashion, or paint-chart design, or nail care. But every holiday I returned to the heart of an arguing, book-loving family that loved me despite the ways in which I had changed. And every term I re-discovered Joachim Larrouse, whose determination to withstand the lures of "The

Zombie Factory" (his invention) was stronger than mine, and kept mine nourished.

I found it difficult to comprehend the strength of character that allowed Joachim to maintain his originality. The Institute had given up on him long ago and so, unlike me, he was never soothed or flattered by the teachers. They realised he would never bow to their system, therefore they bullied and mocked him and wished he would go. So far he had escaped expulsion because his parents, who were wealthy, influential people, preferred him to stay. During my first week at the Institute Joachim had told me, with a strained sort of indifference, that his mother and father did not object to his maltreatment, because they did not love him.

"But you said they run charities and stuff," I had objected, naively. "Of course they love you."

"No," Joachim insisted. "They love people when there are millions of them, all starving and suffering from wars and things – they get really cut up, and then they go off and found charities and make speeches and all that. But that doesn't mean they have to love an ugly thirteen year old with thick glasses and 'poor socialising skills.'" (This was a reference to Miss Konder's latest quip.)

I laughed, because his manner of speaking tickled me. Then it was that I asked him how he found the courage to remain true to himself, despite his school and home life. There was a long, wary pause before he said,

"You won't laugh or tell…you know that if you did, I would never speak to you ever again."

This was clearly a dispassionate statement of the obvious, so I did not bluster or protest. I just shook my head.

"Well…at night…when I'm in bed…I suppose when I'm asleep…I go away somewhere."

"To an imaginary place?" I asked excitedly.

"Sort of imaginary. I suppose I invented it once, though I'm not sure. It seems – it feels as though it is bigger and older than me…so it must be independent of me, mustn't it?"

"What's it like?"

Joachim paused again and blushed.

"It's a wooden house in the middle of a sprawling forest. The house belongs to me, and nobody can find me there."

"And you are all alone there?"

"Yes, but I'm not lonely. Sometimes I just sit, all snug and warm, listening to the wind in the trees. And sometimes I play my violin."

"But you don't know how to play the violin." I objected.

"I've heard music though – snatches of it here and there – I know what it is. And there, in my hut, I can play the violin. I can play it… quite brilliantly actually." He smiled at his own smugness, and at the thought of his secret place.

"It's like me and my tree," I whispered happily. "I have a hollow oak tree, and I go there every night just like you – only I take Boris with me. We hide there, you see, from the cannibals who live around our part of the wood. They want to kill us, but so long as we're quiet and careful, they can't find us…"

I would have gone on, only Joachim was nodding at me with an expression of such solemn understanding that I laughed and took his hand. I realised then, with a flush of exhilaration, that Joachim would save me from the blandishments of the Institute. I remember wanting to honour him for his valour, and for his likeness to me, so I said: "Perhaps your hut and my oak tree are in the same forest. The Forest of Traumund."

"Traumund?"

So I told him about the Vulture Man who had tried to capture me in my own wood and take me to his king. Joachim listened carefully. His expression was troubled.

That conversation had changed our friendship, establishing a nervous sympathy between us so that I could not keep still just now, three years on, knowing that Mr. McBain was walloping him and roaring hoarsely into his ear.

I turned away from the window to see Anna Konder bearing down on me, her hard face creased into a caricature of forgiveness. I felt Joachim's wry distaste for her, and I tilted my chin and narrowed my eyes, as he would have done.

"Come on in, Miss Crabtree!" she smiled, so I shuffled into the office and sat down, scraping my chair forward so that I was within reach of the bear.

"Oh. Please. Do sit down," said Miss Konder, eyeing me coldly. She seated herself behind the desk and interlocked her snaky fingers. "Now then. Are you going to tell me what all this is about? Because you're not really a naughty girl - not at heart – but you've obviously been having a few problems lately. Where did you get this 'teddy-bear' from?"

I did not reply.

"It saddens me, Abigail."

I glared unsympathetically at her silver nails and shrugged my tense shoulders.

She lowered her voice to a confidential murmur. "If you're worried about your appearance, your dress-sense, your hair – we're all here to help, you know and we've all been through those sorts of anxieties…"

I shook my head curtly.

"Boyfriend trouble?"

"I don't have a boyfriend." I managed to sneer through my hot embarrassment.

"Precisely!" She retorted snidely and leant back. "You know, don't you, that you never will get one – in fact you'll never get anything or anywhere in life - if you don't start to care about the things that matter? I mean, look at you. The way you're slumped there, hiding behind your hair, chewing your nails, fidgeting with those lovely white shoes, rubbing your sweaty hands all over that skirt…you look as though you ought to be running wild, like an animal! And your work is poorer than ever – Miss Dixon even tells me you've been skipping her Eye Make-Up class. Is that true?"

I shrugged again.

"I just don't understand you, Abigail. True, you're not naturally pretty and neither are you…well…particularly bright. I'd say you were just average. But that's OK – with a little effort, a little goodwill on your part we could help you to become satisfactory. Aim high, be ambitious – what's to stop you from achieving? With your imagination you'd be a great…I don't know…assistant of some kind. All you need is a bit more easy charm, a bit more willingness to please…and the world's your oyster. It's not asking much, is it?"

It was as though Joachim prompted me. "Miss Konder, you're right when you say you don't understand. You *don't* understand. I don't want to be charming and pretty. I don't care about my nails or my hair or my figure and I don't want to spend my life wearing tight pink skirts in a bid to impress some lecherous-"

"Abigail!"

"-some lecherous, mindless nobody like Mr. Wells-Wilton."

Miss Konder had always taken me for a demure mute, so she was taken aback by this wordy bombardment. Her eyes and mouth widened with pain when I insulted Mr. Wells-Wilton – when, I should say, I blasphemed against one of the Institute's tutelary gods. She observed a minute's silence, then continued tightly.

"Abigail. How, precisely, do you propose to spend your life?"

"I…I don't know. I want to understand things and have ideas about things…" It was my turn to flounder. I hated the Institute, but was there any real alternative to its deadening spirit? Perhaps my family, and Joachim, and I, with our immaterial imaginings and wonderings, were as ludicrously unjustified as Miss Konder would have me believe. Miss Konder's ethos was made and upheld by authority. Ours was apparently supported by nothing but our own perverse inclinations.

"Well, I want my bear back anyway." I finished lamely.

"You can't have your 'bear' back. He's going straight in the bin where he belongs. Items like that are for silly children who don't live in the real world. We will not let you degenerate any further in that direction, Abigail."

I sat up, trembling. An idea had come to me in my desperation, but it was a weak one and I trembled as I lied:

"My godfather gave me that bear, and he would be extremely angry if he knew that you had stolen it. In fact, he would probably have you sacked."

I still had not met Ludovick Montefiore and knew no more about him now than I had done three years ago. Perhaps The Snake knew him well (he was on the board of governors), and would realise that he was an unlikely donor of teddy bears. I expected her to toss my deceit aside with a sarcastic laugh. Instead she hesitated. She was pink with anger at being defied, yet, glaring at me suspiciously, screwing her hands into tight fists, she said quietly,

"No doubt your godfather has his own laudable reasons. You will please remove the…thing from my desk and never let me catch sight of it again."

I promptly scooped Boris into my bag, trying to restrain my glee.

She continued, "There is a packet of antiseptic wipes beside your chair. Remove one wipe from the packet and apply it to the area of my desk, which that…*object*…has contaminated."

I obeyed her.

"Now sit down again, and…yes…I will inform you how your difficulties will resolve themselves after our return from the winter break."

Suddenly, and for the first time during this interview, I was afraid, because I saw that she had contained her rage. She seemed newly calm and malicious.

"Abigail - Is there anything here, anything or anybody, that brings you pleasure…makes you happy."

"Joachim Larrouse." I answered promptly, proudly and then I hiccuped with misgiving jerking my hand against my mouth. Miss Konder nodded, smiling through her sparkling snake eyes.

"Because I'm afraid Joachim will not be here when you come back after the holiday." She said. "He is a very troubled child and The Institute is not equipped to deal with the profound behavioural and mental disabilities that he exhibits. He needs specialist care and I have recently discovered an educational institution in the north-east that will suit him perfectly. His parents will co-operate, they have confided in me…"

I cried out with such an anguished wail that she was startled into silence. I held my head in my hands for a long time, then I looked up at her. My wet eyes were snake-small now, like hers. "You're jealous of him." I spat.

"Jealous? He's utterly stupid!" She laughed languidly, glancing at her watch and then at my forehead. She would not meet my glare.

"But he thinks…"

"If one is stupid, like Joachim, then thinking is a dangerous waste."

I wept at her, all the more wrathfully because she was made of steel and concrete:

"He's my only friend! You can't take him away from me – "

"Abigail," she said gently, her poise contrasting finely with my spluttering woe. "You will be so much happier, so much better off without him. I know you can't see it now, but he's holding you back. What sort of lifestyle can you hope for when you've got a friendship like that dragging you down?"

"Lifestyle?" I spat. She sighed and looked at her watch again.

"Look, I haven't time for all this now. Just…believe me…you'll be better off without Joachim Larrouse. Now off you go." She looked at me distastefully. "And wash your face before your parents see the state you're in. What will they think of us?"

So I left.

Two hours later there were hundreds of cars and buses hovering in the forecourt. I spotted my parents without even meaning to – they had parked up and were leaning with their backs against the boot, their raised faces soaking up the last of the evening sun. They waved when they saw me, and dad turned to unlock the car. I ignored them because

I had to find Joachim.

I found him queuing for the London coach. He turned around as I touched his arm.

"Abigail?"

He spoke questioningly because he could barely see me; I still had his glasses. I rummaged for them in my bag and hooked them over his ears. He looked pasty and shocked.

"I got Boris back." I said.

"Oh good...Abigail?"

I tried to smile, but the effort made my sadness feel heavier.

"What?"

"I've just seen The Snake and she said...she said I'm not to come back. She said she'd phoned my parents and they've agreed to send me away to...some sort of an...an institute for...for...a...um..."

He petered out and gulped. I thought he was going to cry and, because Joachim was so noble and heroic in my eyes, I'm afraid the prospect made me feel embarrassed. In a heartless effort to stall his collapse I piped,

"You should be glad. It can't be any worse than this place!"

I had never sounded so childish in my own ears as when I said this. The queue began to move, the crowd jostling around us for a while before Joachim asked in the smallest of voices,

"Abigail – you're not glad I'm going, are you?"

At this my face crumpled with self-reproach and at the same time he was hustled up the steps and into the coach, the automatic doors hissing and shutting behind him. He found a seat and I saw his face disintegrating through glassy lights and shadows as the engine began to growl.

Suddenly I saw him clearly again, as though a panicked inspiration had made him shine. He tore a piece of paper and a pen from his school bag, and scribbled madly for several seconds. His teeth were clenching his tongue, his shoulder was jerking with fury. The coach began lumbering towards the road; I ran alongside as he pressed his message to the window:

"*WRITE. DON'T address JOACHIM but MR. WELLINGTON-GRUB, 26 WOODBINE ST, PUTNEY, LONDON.*"

I slowed down and let the coach overtake me. I didn't wave, but I stared at the pale blur of Joachim's face until I no longer knew whether it was his, or somebody else's, or a flash of white sunlight, or an illusory light inside my own eyes.

I trailed back to my parents, stumbling in my shoddy high heels. "Mr. Wellington-Grub, 26 Woodbine St, Putney, London." I said dully. They stared at me and I snapped, "Write it down! Quick! Mr. Wellington-Grub, 26 Woodbine St, Putney, London." As I spoke I wrote it onto my arm with a biro, in large haphazard letters. Then I collapsed across the back seat of the car, pregnant with a fat, unmoving rage, unable to cry.

The King Henry Hotel

y parents let me lie there for a long time. I could sense their anxiety, as they glanced at one another and then at me, longing to comfort and interrogate me, yet not daring to speak. I felt so bruised by the day's events, indeed by the whole three years at the Institute, that I luxuriated in their concern and in the fact that I could cause them pain merely by feeling sad. I had never told them the truth about the Institute: now I no longer understood my own silence. They imagined that I learned things from the teachers here – real things, I mean - and that my pseudo-adult clothes and posturings were forms of self-expression. This had saddened them, as it had saddened me, but they had left me alone. They thought that I was drifting from them by my own free will, when really I was tightly trapped, yearning inarticulately for rescue.

Now I found that I wanted to tell them everything in the most vivid terms: about the way the Institute made us dress and act, and its distaste for the good things in life; about Miss Konder's treatment of Boris and her "little chat" with me today; about the prize-giving and, most dreadful of all, about Joachim's expulsion. So I released a storm of words whose uncontrollable tearfulness shocked me. By the time my tale was told, fully and colourfully, I was tired, almost to the point of sleep, shaking under a succession of dying sobs.

Everybody was silent as mum stroked my shuddering back and dad drummed the steering-wheel. Suddenly dad spat:

"I can't believe…What…Why have you never told us?…Is it really true?… 'Eye-make up class'?…Really?" He began thumping the steering wheel gently with his fist. "Do you mean to tell me you don't study anything worthwhile? No English, or Maths or Science or Art?"

"No."

He looked at me in furious disbelief. "Music?"

"No."

"Latin?"

"No."

"Tuh!" He thumped the wheel, accidentally sounding the horn. Mr. McBain, who happened to be marching past our car, yelped and jumped, then turned a pop-eyed glare upon my unapologetic father. I smiled despite myself. Then, out of the blue, my mild, matter-of-fact mother said, "She's certainly not going back."

I whipped round to face her, open-mouthed. I gripped my skirt and tried to breath slowly. Dad agreed with her, but his eyes were surprised, his tone cautious now, not angry. "No. No, she's certainly not going back."

Mum voiced their joint thoughts firmly, "I am not going to allow my daughter to waste any more of her life in that dump. Montefiore or no Montefiore."

"But what will we tell him?" Dad asked, loosening his tie.

"We'll…just tell him." She managed to suppress the quaver in her voice. "We'll do it together. He'll be in London at the moment – he always is over Christmas. We'll drive down now and tell him. What can he do, after all? Abigail is our daughter, not his."

"Could we not just write?"

"It would be better to see him."

"He'll be beside himself." Dad murmured. Then, straightening his shoulders he said more confidently, "But you're quite right. She's our daughter. You're quite right." He started drumming his fingers against the steering wheel again.

There was a tap on mum's window. Miss Konder eyed us through the glass, like a specimen of something cold-blooded hunched in a jar of vinegar. Mum wound the window down languorously. "Yes?"

"I'm Miss Konder…How do you do?…Lovely to meet you at last…Since you are still here, Mr. and Mrs. Crabtree, I wonder whether you would like to come to my office for a little chat about Abigail's progress…?"

"You two stay here," my mother commanded. Then, stepping out of the car, she turned to Miss Konder. She spoke coolly, but I could see that her jaw was stiff with rage. "I would like nothing better, Miss… What did you say your name was?."

"Konder," The Snake huffed.

"Then come along, Konder, we don't have all day. Some of us have lives to lead"

That evening, as billows of October rain swept over London, Boris and I sprawled across my plump hotel bed and wrote a letter to Joachim. Mum sat reading beneath a yellow lamp, and dad snoozed on their double-bed, digesting his dinner, smelling warmly of coffee and alcohol. The joy that had swelled up in me that afternoon was as large and distracting as ever: I felt bloated with it. Every time I breathed in it pressed against my lungs. I wrote guiltily:

My dearest Joachim,

Firstly, you know I'm not glad to lose you – you do know that don't you? It's horrible without you. You are my best friend and you always will be, and it's only because you were there that I could bear the Institute at all. I will write to you everyday, and send the letters to Mr. Wellington-Grub in Putney, and that way we won't lose each other. One day, somehow, I'll rescue you from your parents and your new school, and you can come and live with us. I hope you can cope till then. Do please try to, although I know it's hard for you. You see, the second thing is that I'm all right now. Or rather, I would be if you were here. My parents have taken me away from the Institute and they're going to let me stay at home for good. Only, you know my godfather? I've told you about him; he's a governor of the Institute and he pays my fees. Well, we've got to tell him that I'm leaving. He won't be pleased because for reasons best known to himself he's very keen for me to be there. I'm writing this in a London hotel, because he's staying in London too and we're going to see him tomorrow to tell him.

That's all my news at the moment, except that my mum gave the Snake a right earful this afternoon. She won't tell me what she said. I wish she would because I bet it was strong stuff. She tried to look nonchalant when she came back from the Snake's office, but she couldn't help smiling in a victorious sort of way.

What are you doing for the holidays? Do you have grand dinners to attend this time and will you get much chance to escape? I hope you do. But there's always night-time and you-know-where, however bad things are. I wish your parents would let you come and live with me. I'm so sorry, Joachim, about everything.

All my love,

Abigail.

I showed my letter to mum, and it made her sad. She had never met Joachim, but she loved the idea of him, and her love – like mine – was made painfully present, and maternal, by her pity for him: by our intimate seclusion inside this room and the lovelessness of the vast, rainy world that gaped at its windows. I sealed the letter and addressed it to Mr. Wellington -Grub of 26 Woodbine St, Putney.

At the Institute girls were not allowed to eat breakfast because it was considered bad for their figures. This morning I ate mine hungrily: grapefruit, toast, bacon, egg, sausage, tomato and coffee. Mum pushed hers dolefully around the plate. Dad seemed to have difficulty swallowing. I prattled on, still tipsy with excitement, about everything and nothing: Wasn't this a wonderful hotel? Would Dominic be home for Christmas? When would I have to start school? Did they think it might snow? They answered distractedly. The first time either of them focussed their eyes or thoughts was when a waiter approached.

"Excuse me sir, madam. A gentleman has just telephoned our reception desk in response to your earlier call."

My mum swallowed her toast with a gulp. My dad set his coffee cup down with a quivering clatter. They glanced at one another and then dad asked,

"Was there a message?"

"Yes sir. The gentleman required me to inform you that he will be in his rooms all morning and that he looks forward to welcoming you at whatever hour is most convenient for you and your family."

I gaped admiringly at the long-winded elegance of his sentence. He raised his left eyebrow at me very slightly, then glided away smoothly, as though his feet were on castors.

"So," said my mother, heaving a sigh.

A black cab drove us to the leafy boulevard where my godfather awaited us and our unwelcome news.

My first thought, as we stood in front of The King Henry Hotel, was that it was a thousand times better (more refined, more warm, more poetic) than the bustling hotel we had left behind. I had praised ours over breakfast, but I now realised that it was not wonderful in its own right. I liked ours only because it had provided a backdrop to my new happiness. The King Henry was wonderful even despite its foreboding associations (for my parents' anxiety about the forthcoming meeting had at last penetrated my delight, and my heart quickened uncomfortably as I watched our taxi drive away). It was an old, white, expansive building, exuding richness and solidity. The golden leaves on the pavement outside it had fallen from distinguished trees and they had been brushed into banks all the way along the road. There was nothing fresh about the place – its white was not pure, its black iron railings were tinged with orange, its windows were dim and warped - yet neither was it down-at-heel. Its dignified old-age enhanced its beauty better then fresh paint and new glass could ever do. I guessed, correctly, that it housed leather armchairs and faded Persian rugs and deep-toned Grandfather clocks.

A woman as quiet and mild as a curator of such a place should be, led us up and down dark stairs and crooked corridors, past ten or twelve numbered bedrooms, until we reached a door that was slightly larger and grander than the others, that bore no number. She tapped lightly, and a faraway voice cried, "Come!" My father felt for my mother's hand and she squeezed my shoulder. The woman opened the door, then a further inner door immediately beyond it (this would account for the distant quality of the voice, I thought), and ushered us into the presence of Ludovick Montefiore.

The room we entered was so inviting, as though the spirit of the King Henry Hotel had been condensed into one small space, that I did not know where to look first. Then, despite itself, my roving gaze was paralysed and for several minutes I was unable to look away from the most captivating pair of eyes that I had ever seen or would ever see in all my life. Captivating, yes, that's the word; there was really no escaping them because they inspired such a desire to look.

Stories often mention a character's eyes, because they are supposed to be the windows to the soul. I had never really understood this convention, because most people's eyes, most of the time, are veiled by a polite blankness. They are coloured balls, no greater then the sum of their parts. But these eyes…to look at them was to look down the barrels of a firing gun. They shot at me with an intrusiveness that I was almost unable to bear. They arrested, questioned and judged me as soon as I stepped across the threshold of the hotel room and, strange to say – perhaps because of the grand beauty of their oceanic blue – I felt honoured by the inquisition, as well as diminished.

It was my mum who broke the spell when she advanced towards him, pecked his cheek and said shyly, "Ludovick?" My father held out his hand, greeting my godfather brusquely. I think he felt annoyed by his own timidity.

It was difficult to age my godfather precisely, but he was certainly not old: in his mid-thirties perhaps, or his early forties. He had a great deal of wild, black, curly hair, that made his head seem even more large and forbidding than it already was. His mouth contradicted the deep seriousness of his eyes: its default expression was a mixture of amusement and disdain. He was odd but undeniably handsome. He was unsettling.

"How are you?" asked mum in a gentle tone, as though she anticipated a despondent answer. This confused me at first, for he was a bulky, strong-looking man – surely not an invalid. Then I looked more closely at his skin, which was pale and clammy, and at his hands, which shook as he sipped from a china cup. He brushed my mother's enquiries aside with a politeness that seemed to smile at itself ironically. I wondered whether he was very ill.

As they spoke their opening civilities I studied the room, though I could not do so attentively at first since my eyes were still reeling from his stare. I noticed, however, that it did not feel like a hotel room, because none of its contents looked impersonal or temporary. The walls were lined with shelves of thick, leather-bound books and these helped to calm me. I could not decipher any of the titles yet I did not dare cross the room to inspect them more closely, since this would have meant inviting (and, much worse, seeming to invite) his scrutiny. However, I noticed that my godfather was holding a volume loosely on his lap, his left thumb serving as an absent-minded bookmark. I managed to spot the word Atlas on its weathered red spine. Then those eyes shot a new round at me and he slid the book out of sight, between his leg and the arm of the chair.

There were three sash windows, all down one wall; three white shafts of sunlight streamed through them and pressed against the rippling wooden floor. There was a fireplace in the opposite wall, where a pile of orange coals smouldered. As mum talked, Ludovick Montefiore rested his eyes on the embers. Sometimes he stirred them with a poker. The morning light was so bright and warm that the fire seemed unnecessary to me, even unattractive. He must be ill, I thought.

There was a small cabinet behind my godfather's chair. I had just enough time to think it – or rather its contents - curious, before my contemplation was cut short. To begin with, its mirrored door was ajar, and inside I saw a dull-gold plate of something that had been covered over with a square of muslin. Around the plate there were six or seven bottles - some made of coloured glass, some apparently of clay. They looked a little like wine or spirit bottles, though none of them were labelled. Secondly, and still more intriguingly, I saw a box on top of the cabinet. It was a cube, about seven inches long, wide and high, made of a black-red, highly-polished wood. There were two ornate handles on top of it, and its corners were reinforced by a reddish metal. Curious, geometric patterns had been cut from pieces of the same metal and nailed all over the box by way of decoration. I call this cube a box, but I suppose that implies that it opened and yet, from where I stood, I could see no opening at all.

"Are you not going to come and say hello to me, Abigail?" said a gentle voice from the fireside chair. For a moment I did not believe that my godfather, with his beetling brow and square frame, had really addressed me, so womanly and lilting was the tone. Mum took me by the shoulder, propelling me into his presence. I looked at my feet, and then, with a consciousness of delicious excitement, such as you feel when you are throbbing with heat at the edge of an ice-blue pool, I raised my eyes to his. But a fly buzzed across my line of vision, my eye-lids floundering confusedly until the insect steered itself away and settled on the arm of the chair.

He didn't speak. This was terrible. I had never felt such shyness as disabled me now. My tongue turned to lead in my mouth, and my brain ground down to a sickening sluggishness. One part of my mind examined the buttons on his shirt and mumbled slowly to itself: "White buttons with four holes sewn on with pale blue cotton." Another part of my mind scrabbled in slow motion, crying, "Concentrate, you idiot! Wake up! Say something - something intelligent!" Only my heart actually quickened, and rose up in my chest like joy.

"No. Obviously you're not going to say hello to me." He laughed: whether genially or slightingly I could not decide, and this troubled me at once. I managed to say, "Hello," and he laughed again. Then turning to my parents he said, authoritatively, "I would like to have a word with Abigail on her own. Perhaps you could wait outside?" I was glad to see them leave the room because I wished to choose my words well before offering them to Ludovick Montefiore, and an audience would only distract me.

"So you're too good for The Institute?" he began. They had already told him the reason for our visit then, while I was scrutinising the room. I was surprised. I had been led to expect a scene: threats and long pleadings and tears.

"Not too good..." I answered. I had spent the last three years believing in my own superiority to the Institute's ethos, so this piece of self-effacement was dishonest. I felt very small however, standing before his chair.

"Yes, yes - too good," he insisted. "You have a brain, a mind, an imagination - and you want to use it. Am I right? You don't want to file your nails and read the horoscopes all day, everyday? Mmm?"

"Well – no..." I said, gathering courage from his tone. He had pronounced the words "file", "nails" and "horoscopes" as though placing them between inverted commas.

"Are you sure? Absolutely sure?" he responded with a sudden earnestness. "There are wonderful "lifestyles" to be had doing all that sort of stuff, you know. You could have a thoroughly shoe-shopping, fake-tanning, cappuccino-sipping existence if you worked hard at the Institute."

Although he spoke seriously he could not disguise his sympathy for me. We were smiling at one another as he concluded his speech. I shook my head slowly from side to side.

"I thought you approved of the Institute," I felt obliged to murmur. "Being a governor...and you were so keen for me to go..."

He stopped smiling and frowned at his hands, which lay limply on his lap. He thought for a while before he spoke. "There are a great many governors. How much authority can a cranky old invalid expect to wield? Besides, I didn't know how bad the place had become till your mother and father told me." I was afraid to ask further questions because he seemed irritated. Then he drew himself up, sighed, and said,

"Go to the cabinet behind my chair and open the mirrored door. You will see a gold plate inside. Please bring it here."

The door was already open, of course: I had been peering beyond it a moment or two before. I brought him the gold plate. He removed the muslin square to reveal a heap of chocolate truffles: black-brown and muffled in cocoa. He took one himself, then gave one to me. We ate them slowly, in a peculiarly intense silence. I barely tasted mine, because I felt so nervous, although once it had gone its bitter flavour lingered on my tongue and the insides of my cheeks, making me want another.

Ludovick Montefiore turned back to the fire.

"I know all about you," he said. "Your past, your present, your future, and all that goes on in your head."

I opened my mouth as if to speak, and then shut it. I laughed timidly and inappropriately. I blushed.

The eyes stabbed and twisted. "Yes, I do. Did you know you had a destiny?"

"A..?"

"A destiny. It's an over-used, sentimentalised word, but I am not using it in a twinkly way. You have a life-mission…a fated purpose…a destiny."

"Oh." I said, inadequately. My mind was still half-occupied by the sweet darkness of those truffles. But Ludovick Montefiore wished to talk about my destiny, so I tried to engage myself with his madness. "Could you…Do you know what it is, at all?"

"Do you not know, yourself?"

"No. I didn't know I had a destiny till you mentioned it just now."

The conversation was going all wrong, and the fault was certainly mine, even though – or, more probably, because – mine was the voice of sanity. He motioned me to sit down on his footstool. I sat close to his knees and he bent his head so close to mine that his dark hair prickled against my ear-lobe. I heard my father coughing theatrically in the corridor beyond the double door, and then Ludovick spoke with a hard urgency,

"Listen to me, Abigail. You may think I'm a mad man, and you may be right to think so. But this is the truth: you have a hard, hard mission ahead of you. It will be dangerous." He paused and added with difficulty. "It might…you might well die."

My head jolted awkwardly as he said the word, and my nose banged against his cheek. He stood up and walked to the third window. He leant on the sill as I watched him writing hastily across a piece of thick parchment. My father coughed again and shuffled noisily. Ludovick took my fingers and closed them tightly around the parchment. "This is the address of my house in the country," he said. "I am never in London for long. I will do my utmost to protect you. I beg you, should you be in need, to come to me." Then he released my hand. "Put it safely in your bag," he ordered. As I obeyed he unlocked the doors.

My parents breezed in, embarking upon wordy thanks, apologies and farewells, but Ludovick Montefiore barely replied. A tense intelligence seemed to unite the two of us, and to exclude them, as though he had dragged me, unresisting, out of their enclosure and into his. I needed them to fail to notice this new arrangement. I looked around the room for inspiration, and my eyes fell, once more, on the open cabinet. I said brightly,

"Have you seen this box on top of the cabinet, mum? Don't you think it's…interesting?"

We all stared at the black-red cube on the cabinet. Ludovick

Montefiore picked it up and stroked its shiny wood.

"This is my mah-jong set," he said. He slid one of the sides upwards to reveal five slim draws, all made from the same dark wood and each with a hinged metal handle. He opened the top draw,

"Look, Abigail," he said.

"May I look too?" asked dad crossly. We all crowded round. The draw was lined with ivory tiles - about forty of them. A couple were blank, but most were numbered and decorated with strange designs: circles and sticks and Chinese characters. One showed a stretch of empty green sea, another two tiny boats on a grass-lined river. Ludovick Montefiore pulled open the next draw to reveal a similar array of tiles. He removed one and handed it to me. I held the little oblong in my hand. The front of the tile was ivory as I had already noticed, but the back was made of a pale wood. This one showed a bird, with long orange legs, flame-like green wings and a fanned tail with peacocks-eyes. "That's the Rice Bird," my godfather informed me. I handed it back, and he shut the box again. "Mah-jong - it's a Chinese game," he explained. "I'll teach you how to play…if we ever meet again."

I wondered whether I should kiss his cheek, as I might when saying goodbye to my other, ordinary, godparents. I held out my hand instead, and he shook it with (perhaps mock) solemnity. My parents left the room ahead of me. As I followed them, Ludovick reached out and pulled at my sleeve. He did not speak, but I turned my frightened face towards him for a second, in a gesture of assent, and then I hurried from his room and from the crooked corridors of The King Henry Hotel.

"That was surprisingly straightforward," said dad as we stepped into the day.

We left London the following morning. As our car crawled through the traffic I caught sight of a signpost to Putney. This brought Joachim to the forefront of my mind for the first time since yesterday morning. I repented of my forgetfulness, and by way of reparation I said,

"We're only a couple of miles from Putney, look. I could deliver Joachim's letter by hand to Mr. Wellington-Grub."

My announcement prompted a short argument, but in the end we agreed that we had time to call briefly on the go-between. Dad turned the car around with a few muttered curses and, ten minutes later, he parked carefully in dapper Woodbine Street.

To my delight, Mr. Wellington-Grub's door was opened by a butler. I knew that Joachim moved in grand circles, but I had never thought to imagine butlers. We were led to a pretty sitting room. The door was open, and inside I could see green, floral wallpaper and thin, elegant chairs – though no Mr. Wellington-Grub. The butler tapped lightly on the open door. There was no reply.

"A young lady and her parents to see you, sir," the butler intoned. Still no response. The butler was unperturbed,

"If you would care to go straight on in? Mr. Wellington-Grub will be happy to receive you." He bowed and disappeared. I entered, warily. My parents lingered in the hallway.

A young man, in his early twenties, sat before a piano with his back to me. He had floppy blond hair, small round spectacles and a very bad, drooping posture. He wore a silk dressing gown and held a bowl-shaped brandy glass in one hand. I advanced into the room and asked tentatively,

"Are you Mr. Wellington-Grub?"

Instead of turning to face me he sounded a chord on the piano and then drawled, "Seems an odd time of day to be paying visits. I've barely finished my first cup of tea."

"Tea…Oh." I mumbled apologetically. "Well, it is ten o'clock. Or nearly ten o'clock."

"Quite," he replied, running his fingers down the keyboard and tossing back his brandy. "Don't you know it's just not done to go calling on people at such unearthly hours of the morning?"

Still he did not turn around. I could not decide whether I found him more amusing or irritating. He continued to run his fingers up and down the piano keys, so I said,

"Are you a pianist?"

He snatched his hand away. "Lord no, what d'you take me for? I just play for amusement's sake, on occasion."

I shrugged. He continued to ignore me until I said, "Well anyway, I'm here because of Joachim Larrouse…" at which point he turned round and deigned to notice me.

His face was handsome but his features drooped with boredom. With his lank hair, sullen pout and heavy eyelids he looked bored even when, as now, his interest was aroused.

"Little Joachim Lawwouse?" he said, his indifference drifting into a smile.

"Yes, we are – were - at school together. He was my best friend. Only now we've both left school, and we've no way of keeping in touch. I think his parents open his letters you see…" I stopped cautiously; presumably Mr. Wellington-Grub belonged to the Larrouse social circle. "Anyway, Joachim suggested that I write to him via you. If you are Mr. Wellington-Grub and if you've no objection? And so I've called with a letter for him." I held out the white envelope and Mr. Wellington-Grub took it slowly, as though distracted by a difficult thought process.

"So Master Lawwouse named me? He thought of me as the twustworthy sort of fellow who'd help a chap out? Well, well, well." He stared at the letter dazedly and repeated, "Well, well, well. So it was me he thought of". He placed the letter carefully on top of the piano, then shook my hand limply. With a slight, though rather endearing smile he said, "Forgive my earlier wudeness. Wupert Wellington-Gwub. Pleased to meet you, Miss?"

"Abigail Crabtree."

"Miss Cwabtwee." He placed a black cigarette holder between his teeth and lit up with a louche flick of the wrist. Then he winked at me in an almost animated fashion. "You may wely on me Miss Cwabtwee," he said.

Shadows

hen I left the Institute for good, I felt certain that the most serious troubles of my life were over and done with. I felt so free and so sure that I would be filled with a golden glow for evermore. But after a couple of weeks I became acclimatised to my freedom. My joy subsided, to be replaced – certainly not with unhappiness – but with more complex sensations and thoughts.

My home seemed strange to me – that was the worst thing. It disturbed me very much. I do not mean to say that the house was physically altered in any way. On the contrary, it was much the same as it had ever been, but its homeliness seemed skin-deep now.

In the past, if I had ever been disturbed by a sense of the eerie and odd, one glance at our cul-de-sac with its trim front gardens and solid, red-brick houses, used to satisfy me that my world was essentially concrete and mundane. Everything else was "just in my head" and therefore safely unreal. But now, this Christmas holiday, all the familiar details of our semi-detached house – the creamy, wallpapered walls and the bowl of fruit on the kitchen table and the yellow candlewick cover on my bed – all refused to sooth me. It was as though they looked right back at me and said, "Are you sure all the strangeness is sealed safely inside your head? Are you sure that you have a refuge here? Are you sure that you are safe?"

I did nothing at all during those winter weeks. I had decided, once I escaped Miss Konder's clutches, that I would immediately embark upon a great journey of learning and creativity; that I would read every book on my parents' shelves and begin the composition of those plays, poems and short stories that would, one day, bring me renown. But I did nothing. I sat on the end of my bed and gazed at the back garden.

Every time the hedges and shrubs shuddered against another December gust, I felt my heartbeat quicken for no good reason. I was frequently alone. My parents always seemed to be out somewhere during those strange and troubling days.

I often watched Mrs. Lorimer's comings and goings. Mrs. Lorimer was a neighbour: her garden backed onto ours, and I could see through her kitchen window. I used to be fond of her when I was little. Her daughter, Catherine, used to babysit when my parents went out, and sometimes Mrs. Lorimer came too. She was spry in those days, and rather glamorous, and though she never spoke much she had a one-sided, confidential smile that flattered and pleased me. Also, she used to bring rough-cut cubes of vanilla fudge in a paper bag.

But now Catherine had left home and Mr. Lorimer (if there ever was a Mr. Lorimer. I have no recollection of him) was dead or otherwise departed, and Mrs. Lorimer had gone to seed. She had become the sort of woman who, centuries ago, would have been burned as a witch. Her collection of cats (she used to keep one or two) had multiplied beyond reckoning and taken over the house. I could see them, poor, skinny, dirty creatures, stalking round the sink and reclining across the kitchen table. All Mrs. Lorimer's glamour had ebbed away. She never seemed to change her clothes at all. She always wore the same grey trousers and blue cardigan that were spotted with spilt food and other unwholesome marks. Her hair, once so glossily sculpted around her head, hung in lanky grey strings.

My mother worried about Mrs. Lorimer and talked sadly of her decline. I shared these feelings to some extent but, this Christmas at any rate, my compassion was complicated by a new unease. I would watch her hobble around her kitchen floor, her chin lower than her humped shoulders, her crooked fingers feeling for food or crockery beneath the sprawling cats and I would think how vacant she had become; how pitiably mad. But then, all of a sudden, a crafty smile would seem to pass across her face and my mind would turn to burning witches again. Then I would have to draw the curtains or take myself off to a different part of the house.

The weather contributed to my suspense by its unusual stillness. It was tremendously cold and the days were dark, as though a grey blanket had been spread out between the earth and the sun. And then, three nights before Christmas, the blanket drifted down from its moorings and we had snow.

On the twenty-second of December, I ran down to the garden as soon as I was dressed. Blades of grass poked through the thin layer of snow, speckling the pure white. Everything – the bird bath, the hedges, the empty flowerbeds – looked vivid against the white. When I had seen, from my bedroom window, that there was snow, I had wanted to feel it, stamp in it, play with it like a little child. But now that I stood on the edge of it I did not know how to act. I shivered in my coat and turned back to the house.

Then I stooped, peered and knelt down by the back door. I removed my gloves and touched the snow where it had been compacted; I touched the band of lilac shadow that had caught my attention. With my fingers and my eyes I traced the outline of a shoe-print, and I frowned.

The shoe-print was a woman's: the toe was pointed and the heel must have been high because it had left behind nothing but a dot. My mother did not wear shoes like that. I did not wear shoes like that; not anymore. I looked along the ground to my left and to my right. The prints paced back and forth, lingering untidily beneath windows, where – presumably - their wearer had peered through the glass and fingered the latches. I stared at the prints for a long time, then straightened my back and entered the kitchen. I locked the door behind me.

It snowed again the following night and fresh, high-heeled shoe prints appeared in the morning light. But then, on Christmas Eve, the snow turned to grey slush, so if the intruder had called again on Christmas night I was none the wiser.

On Boxing Day I sat on my bed and thought: life was never like this before. Why has it changed? Life's excitements used, almost always, to be sunny and easily articulated. There was never this addictive feeling of joyful terror; this objectless sense of anticipation; this feeling of being dangerously seduced. Seduced into what? I had no idea.

But I knew well enough when the seed had been sown. Everything dated from that meeting with Ludovick Montefiore. It was because of him that I took notice, and it was thanks to him that my throat contracted whenever I pictured those high-heeled shoes circling our house at dead of night. Perhaps he was right and there was a real danger pending. Perhaps his words had simply infected my imagination. Whatever the truth of the matter, it was he who had altered my world, making its commonplaces dark and alluring.

I did not tell my parents about the footprints in the snow, because I felt that a full discussion would, eventually, involve Ludovick Montefiore and his cryptic confidences in the King Henry Hotel. I couldn't bear to witness my parents' careless demolition of his mystique. They would say he was unhinged and self-dramatising, and once the thought had been voiced I would have to agree with it. I hated common sense. I still do.

That afternoon I found a green-black magpie feather beneath the pear tree. I sharpened it and turned it into a quill pen and from then on, when I wasn't following the movements of Mrs. Lorimer and her cats and worrying about witchcraft, I would sit at my desk with a pot of ink, signing his name over and over with exuberant loops and curls: *Ludovick Montefiore, Ludovick Montefiore, Ludovick Montefiore.*

Two holiday weeks had passed when my solitude was broken by a letter from Joachim. The very sight of his handwriting warmed me, and brought me to myself again, however briefly. The contents of his letter were of great interest too and, though imbued with their own darkness, at least they redirected my thoughts for a while and brought me into contact with a warm-blooded human being; a friend.

My dearest Abigail, he began, in mock-pompous style.

Hearty thanks I render unto thee for thy several letters. I beg you to accept my most sincere and regretful apologies for having failed to reply until now. I have been up to my ears in dismal dinner parties and 'Social Skills' coaching (yes indeed, I deceive you not. My beloved and despairing parents have acquired a 'Social Skills' coach for the purposes of torturing me during the holidays. Imagine a male version of Miss Konder. But don't dwell on it).

I will be seeing Rupert Wellington-Grub tomorrow evening, I hope, whereupon I shall endeavour to pass this epistle to him. He's been very good about the whole go-between thing – very careful and discreet with your letters. He is an odd kettle of fish, you're right there. He's incredibly idle in a somewhat stylish, silk-dressing-gown-and-chaise-longue way. But he's driven to it, you see, a) by similarly idle and elegant people who egg him on and b) by over earnest people like my parents who irritate by trying to alter him.

I do miss you, Abigail – more than ever, since I know that I will not see you next term. These holidays are so tedious that I'm almost looking forward to starting at my new school in mid-January. Not that there's much to look forward to as – guess what – this new place turns out to be another Institute. An "Institute of Social and Personal Advancement" of all things. There must be loads of them all over the country – a sort of chain of Institutes. Makes you shudder, doesn't it? This one's somewhere near Durham.

Anyway, I'll stop grumbling or this will turn into a boring letter.

Thank goodness for you-know-where. I often think of you when I am there, in my house, sawing away on my violin and listening to the wind in the trees. I wonder whether you are close by. I mean – you know – somewhere in the same forest. It's a silly thought, I know, but a comforting one. I often think about your Vulture Man as well. What a strange thing that was. I wonder whether he will ever return to your oak wood.

Your godfather sounds like quite a character, judging by your brief description. But why – Oh bother, must go. Gong's just gone for dinner. Will resume tomorrow.

So far Joachim's handwriting had been its usual steady, rounded self. But his second entry, written the following morning, was all jagged and tangled with excitement. I was barely able to decipher it.

Abigail, Abigail! Listen! Last night I went to the wooden house in the forest as usual and I SAW A VULTURE MAN! A Vulture Man, just as you described him. Listen, I'll tell you what happened.

I was standing in the doorway, flicking through my collection of sheet music. I hadn't opened the violin case yet. It was a beautiful night, cold and still. I looked up at the black trees that towered around my house, as clear and straight as javelins against a jade sky and a pearly moon. And then I heard it. No, I felt it first, thundering through my feet and coursing though my whole body: the rhythm of galloping hooves. Then I heard it; then I saw it; then I turned and ran.

Of course, there is a hiding place inside my house, since frightening things will happen in dream worlds. I have had intruders before, though on those occasions, like you, I invented and therefore anticipated them. So I scrambled into the loft, two feet and one hand racing up the rungs of the ladder and one hand clutching the violin case. All the time I could hear the pounding of hooves across the soft forest floor. They came closer and closer until the horse halted, with a bellowing whinny, just yards from the door. I pulled the ladder up after me and swung the wooden trapdoor shut as quickly and carefully as I could. I was comforted to remember how perfectly camouflaged it was from below, amidst the uneven grooves and bumps of the surrounding ceiling.

I lay flat on my face, with one eye to a crack between the floorboards. I needed air, but I dared not draw a full breath, lest I be heard.

The rider entered my house with a jangle of spurs and, as his eyes whipped round the room, he snarled, "Come forward, in the name of the King of Traumund!" Oh, Abigail, he was exactly as you described him! He was tall, and draped from the top of his head to the soles of his boots in a black velvet cloak, which bore a royal crest, and he trailed a huge wire net from one of his clawed hands. As soon as I felt the thunder of his approach through my feet I half – perhaps fully – expected that your Vulture Man was on his way. He is the only dream intruder I ever heard of, and the truth is that he is always at the back of my mind. But oh, I might have been expecting him, but I was not prepared for the horror of being close to him and seeing him in the flesh! It was horrible, horrible! He – it – was so almost-ordinary, so almost a man, yet that hideous beak protruded from his hood like an over-sized, discoloured cut-throat razor. And the smell! Like rancid chicken – I had to draw back and retch. And (I'm sorry to disgust you with such detail, but it does haunt me so), as he strode about my room, turning over chairs and rooting through cupboards, he kept reaching into his pockets and pulling out chicks (dead, thank God, but still yellow and fluffy), and nibbling on them.

He turned everything inside-out. He seemed bored and irritated: he kicked my things and slashed at them with his net. When he thought he had checked every conceivable hiding place he stalked out. I heard him mutter, "Nothing!" and then he made a clicking noise with his tongue. I heard him remount his horse and gallop away.

What does it mean, Abigail? That you or I should be visited in our own dream worlds by something that was not brought there by our own imaginations, is strange enough. That we should BOTH be visited by the SAME (or very similar) creature is stranger still. But that this THING wants to harm us, and in the name of a king…this terrifies me.

One thing I am glad of: that this adventure unites us, though we are many miles apart.

I hardly need urge you to write soon my dearest friend.
Joachim.

I lowered the letter and leaned my head against the window pane. This was the third time that I had read it since its arrival that morning. I did not look out at the darkening afternoon, but with my mind's eye I watched the Vulture Man pick distractedly at his snacks, and the spot of light on Joachim's eyeball as he peered through the crack in the loft. I wondered and puzzled, as Joachim did, but to no avail. Then, by the rapid, flickering light of her television, I saw Mrs. Lorimer forking cat meat from a tin as the brood surged and jostled against her arms, and I hastily turned away from the window.

I wandered through the upstairs rooms, trying to speculate on Joachim's letter so that I could respond to it later that night. I did not necessarily seek a solid theory or a plan, just something other than the obvious exclamations of horror and surprise. But my skittish mind would not dwell on the Vulture Man. As my fingers fidgeted with Joachim's envelope, I thought about Mrs. Lorimer's fingers caked in meaty jelly, and I remembered Ludovick Montefiore as he brought his prickly head close to my ear and whispered. I looked at the sky over the street, and noted its solidity, like a sheet of slate: we would have snow again. I wondered when my parents would be home: I wanted them. The road was so quiet. In the summer there had been children criss-crossing the pavements on bikes, and people pottering in their gardens, but now there was nothing; nobody.

And then, all of a sudden, there was a woman. She walked past our house hurriedly, her slim body wrapped in a full-length black coat; her face hidden under a veiled hat. It was really a strange hat; I leant forward so as to study it more closely, and as I did so the invisible face whipped round and up, as though it could feel my gaze like a touch of the hand. She stopped abruptly. I felt her eyes contemplate my naked face from beneath their black shroud, and menace me at their leisure.

I drew away from the window and listened to the drumming blood in my ears and the ticking of my parents' alarm clock. A long minute elapsed before I could muster enough courage to sidle back to the window. She was hurrying away now, through fast flakes of snow, as dad's car turned into the drive. It was still sufficiently light for me to notice her boots. They were sharp-toed, high-heeled, black leather lace-ups.

Tea with Mrs. Lorimer

I could not sleep that night. Ordinarily I would have abandoned my bed and perched on the windowsill, the curtain draped over my back. Tonight the air was clogged with snow, and with the eerie silence that accompanies snow. I would have liked to sit and watch, but I was too afraid of finding myself watched, so I lay between my sheets, hot and uncomfortable.

The streetlamp that shone over Mrs. Lorimer's back-gate, and across our garden, bled a menacing orange light into my curtains and my walls, and this frightened me as much as any of my godfather's words, or my confrontation with the veiled woman, or my mental picture of Mrs. Lorimer burning at the stake. I was being bombarded by such a grotesque amalgamation of fears that I could no longer distinguish between the fanciful and the real. For all I knew, that light, made thick by its passage through the falling snow, was the one true portent of that danger which Ludovick Montefiore had foretold.

My head hurt. I had to see him. I sat up in bed and said it out loud: "I have to see him". Only a proper interview with my godfather could put an end to this tortuous unease. I would talk to him, and discover that he was merely odd, in the most ordinary sense of the word, and a little pathetic, and then the world would regain its former, cheery colours, and that would be that.

Or maybe (since I did not like that scenario) I would talk to him and discover in him a great, heroic and fantastical soul such as the Waking World has never before produced, and he would reveal to me, in full, the mysteries that I was now glimpsing through the corner of my eye. Perhaps, through him, new worlds would open up.

In other words, Ludovick Montefiore, and he alone could put an end to my predicament, or else develop it in interesting ways. I hoped for the latter.

Of course I would have to travel to his house; I could hardly summon him here. For one thing, he was not the sort of person whom one might summon anywhere (nor was I the sort of imperious person to whom summoning would come easily). For another thing, I would not wish to see him in suburbia. I feared (since my faith in his "great, heroic and fantastical soul" had not yet gathered pace) that suburbia would diminish him.

I reached across to my desk, opened the bible that sat beside the lamp, and retrieved a square of parchment from between its leaves. Though I could barely read the words in this light, I knew them by heart:

Ludovick Montefiore,
Boughwinds Abbey,
Nr. Boughwinds Village,
W. Yorkshire.

I knew how to reach him: almost the first thing I had done on my return home had been to locate Boughwinds Abbey in the road atlas. It was well and truly in the back of beyond; it was five or six miles from Boughwinds village, a hamlet that was, itself, fifteen miles from the nearest station. Nonetheless, I had already planned my (hitherto hypothetical) journey in detail. I would catch a train to Leeds; at Leeds I would change for Keighley; at Keighley I would change onto the branch line that would take me within fifteen miles of the village. At that point I presumed there would be a bus or a taxi, or if I had to walk then at least I had committed the sparse tangle of lanes and dirt tracks to memory, and I was not very likely to get lost.

No, I could find him easily enough. The difficulty lay in persuading my mother and father to let me go. I had not completely lost my hold on reality; I realised that they were unlikely to be enthusiastic. The abbey was remote; its owner was alluring after the moody, Byronic model. He was also quite likely to be insane. With all the blinkered recklessness of adolescence I was unable to share their qualms, but I could foresee them. I decided to lie.

I lay thinking for hours, but eventually my brain grew heavy. I dreamed I was sitting on a grassy bank amidst the ruins of an ancient abbey. A monk and a cat walked round me, in ever decreasing circles. The monk's face was concealed by a cowl. I followed the pair with my eyes, and tried to explain to them about my lie. I had to shout, because my voice was drowned by the rhythmic clatter of a train that never appeared and never departed. Neither the monk nor the cat spoke to me, or even glanced my way. Their circuits became so small that the monk's cowl and the cat's tail brushed against my knees. At their touch I awoke.

"Mum?" I began, as she drove gingerly down our street the following afternoon, through daubs of dirty slush.

"Mmm?" She turned onto the main road, and we were heading for town.

"I think I'll visit Joachim for a bit. That'd be fine, wouldn't it?" I frowned at the clumsy mixture of indifference and anxiety in my tone.

"You sound as though you expect me to say no."

"No I don't!" I was too defensive now. I strained to achieve insouciance. "I thought you'd be fine about it actually. Are…are you not?"

"Oh…yes…it sounds fine, in theory. I thought you said his parents were a bit funny though? They never sounded very nice to me."

"No, they're not. But I wasn't going to visit his family, in London. I was going to go up to Durham. He's started his new school there by now, I think."

"You think?"

"No, I mean I know. He is up there, in Durham, but term hasn't started yet, and he's allowed to have friends to stay."

"At school?"

"Yes, at school. Because term hasn't started yet you see, so there's loads of room, empty dormitories and…"

"I see. And where exactly is this school again? What's it called?"

"It's…I can't just remember off hand. I'll tell you before I go. You are all right with it though, aren't you?"

Mum was perplexed by my ill-concealed urgency, and this made her want to keep questioning me, though she must have known she had not found the right questions. Eventually she shrugged her doubts away.

"You'd take the train up, then?"

"Yes…in fact…I was thinking I might as well buy my ticket now."

She took me to the station. As we pulled up outside I ran my eyes along the grimy Victorian façade and at the people meandering or scurrying beneath its massive white-faced clock. I could hear the rush of a through train and the echo of a platform announcement. Here at last was adventure and life, and it swept me up in a gush of romance. It was as though I was in a film, and all my actions were taking place to the accompaniment of rapturous music. I wished that the world and I could look the part: there ought to have been steam trains, and I should have been dressed in an Edwardian gown and a neat, tilting hat. I wished that I could be truly free to go where I pleased, without having to lie in order to preserve my parents' peace of mind.

"When will you be going, anyway?" Mum called as I slammed the car door shut. I smiled and waved as I walked away; it was easy to pretend that I had not caught her question.

Once I was standing at the ticket booth I did not dither. Any doubts were swept away by the nebulous romance whose air I breathed. I decided that I would pack tonight and leave tomorrow, the fourth of January. I only felt fear for one moment, and that was when the woman behind the counter frowned and said, "You want to go where, Love?" and I had to spell out the station name twice before she was able to print my ticket.

When I reached into my shoulder bag to find money, I was surprised to discover Boris bear inside, squashed up against my umbrella. He must have been there since my return home. I wondered why I had not missed him, these last few weeks and why we had not visited the oak wood since our escape from the Institute. A precious orange ticket, which was to take me to the home of Ludovick Montefiore, slid under the screen. "I have grown up" I thought serenely. I reached inside the bag and touched Boris's head by way of an apology.

I knew that Mum would be in the library at five o'clock, should I wish to cadge a lift home. We had made no definite arrangement, however, so I decided to make my own way back. I wanted to be alone because I was reluctant to hear any new allusions to my supposed Durham trip: the lie was justified in my mind, but I still disliked telling it. And anyway, I needed solitude if I was to properly exult in my purchase. Mere awareness of the ticket, its silent presence in my bag, filled me with feelings that left no room for thought. I already knew the pleasures of secrecy, but it was the first time in my life I had ever revelled in power: the power to act (and act dramatically) in consultation with nobody but myself.

I walked home in the gathering twilight. As I rounded the end of our street I stepped out of my romance and into a place of dread, as simply as though I had stepped over the border of one country and into another. The sky was a bruised, yellow-grey behind the serried ranks of houses and trees. These had lost all their individual colours and forms, and become murky, misshapen hulks. They seemed unnaturally tall and bulky, and they leaned towards one another across the way so that the street (though I knew it to be a wide, grassy cul-de-sac) felt like a gorge. And it was silent yet again: there were no cars, no people, and the few lighted windows glowed with baleful oranges and reds. I wished that I had met up with mum after all. I was frightened. I ran to the house, fumbling in my bag for the front door key.

There were no lights on in our windows either. Dad was not home then? No, his car was not in the drive. I stumbled across the snow, my throat tight. I remembered where the veiled woman had passed yesterday, at a similar hour, and I could not look round for fear that she was there again. The sight of her would surely paralyse my feet. I had the key ready in my fingers; I plunged it into the lock with one single stab and twisted. The few seconds it took were an agony. I hurried inside, whisking the bunch of keys back into my fist as I did so, and I slammed the door shut with the whole weight of my back and shoulders. I closed my eyes and let out a shuddering sigh. I smiled wearily, able to mock myself now, and then I opened my eyes.

She was there, inside our house. She stood right in front of me, in the kitchen doorway. She ought to have been camouflaged by the dusk, but her deep darkness was as strong as light. A tall, featureless pillar she was, and yet, somehow, certainly female. She wore the veiled hat again: cloudy black lace where her face ought to be; where her face was, studying, from its place of privacy, my noiseless scream. I covered my open mouth with both hands and instinctively stepped backwards in retreat, but there was the door behind me, firmly shut. With a scrambling motion I yanked at the catch, of necessity turning my body towards my escape yet unable to keep my eyes from the apparition. She moved as I moved, stepping forwards and grasping at me with her leather-gloved hand. Terror, I suppose, lent me dexterity and speed and I managed to fall out of the door. I ran, slipped, righted myself and ran again. I could barely hear her footsteps over my pounding and panting, but I knew that she was close.

But where to run? There were no lighted windows at all this end of the street; everyone was gone; where had they gone? On every side I met with fixed, glassy stares: not one of the houses saw me; not one cared to see. And, oh God, I was running the wrong way down the cul-de-sac, making for the dead-end instead of heading out towards the

main road. I was cornered. One hundred yards more, eighty, sixty…
and I would have to turn round and give myself up.

I dashed through heaps of dirty snow and tripped against the buried
edges of paving slabs. I moved as quickly as I could, but the air felt
like syrup. I pictured those coiled fingers close to my neck, poised to
pounce, and this made it almost unbearable for me to keep running with
my back to her. Almost unbearable. To turn and face her would have
been worse.

And then, to my right, I saw a beacon. It was Mrs. Lorimer's
television set, lighting up all her downstairs rooms with its rippling,
aquatic gleam. And Mrs. Lorimer herself: I saw a wispy figure crossing
the hallway, fractured by frosted glass panelling. She was at home. I
pounded across the hillocky grass in a moment, fell and smashed my
knee on her pot-holed path and flung myself at her front door with a
wail, thumping at it with my fists and rattling at the handle. It opened
immediately and I fell, trembling and crying, into the old woman's
arms. She shut the door and held me.

"Oh dearie, dearie, dear," she crooned into my ear as I came to. "Oh
dearie, dearie, dear." She started to stroke my hair, combing through
the strands with her skeletal fingers. I tried to extricate myself, but
her embrace, though fragile, was determined. I was afraid of hurting
her arms if I struggled; they encircled my shoulders like dry twigs. So
when I spoke my voice was muffled by her woollen cardigan.

"Mrs. Lorimer, I'm sorry…I need to use your phone. I need to ring
my dad."

The crooked comb swept over my scalp more rapidly and harshly
than before. Mrs. Lorimer did not answer my request, but her sing-song
"Dearie dears" fell silent. I was about to repeat my question when she
said,

"You've been watching me from your bedroom. What do you think
of me, then? Am I a mad old witch?"

I wriggled free as gently as I could. She let me go and her darting
eyes sought mine.

"Am I a mad old witch?" she repeated sharply, and then she laughed
and waved her sharpness away. She started singing again, as she led me
through to the kitchen. She breathed through loose lips in short, noisy
puffs. "I'm a mad old witch," she sang tunelessly, "and whose fault's
that? I'm a mad old witch, and whose fault's that?"

I sat down and gripped the edge of the kitchen table with my fingertips. There wasn't much room for my fingertips amidst the grimy cups and mould-encrusted plates, and the cats. One of them, a stinking tabby, pounced onto my lap and settled himself there, a ring of gristle and fur. It was cold and damp in here, and as usual the blinds were open. The television blared and flickered on a sideboard. It was her only source of light

"Please can I use your phone?" I asked, imperatively this time.

"My phone?" She thought solemnly for a moment, her fingers drumming on the stove, her uplifted gaze reflected in the inky window.

"Yes. Please."

"I don't have a phone," she said decisively, breaking away from the stove and lifting a cat off the bread board. She draped it round her neck like a stole. "But. But, but, but. I do have tea. Plenty of tea. Have a cup of tea instead."

"No!" I cried, standing up.

"Yes!" she retorted, and for a moment I thought she was mimicking me, but then I saw real tears starting in her red eyes and I sat down again, shamefaced.

"Thank you" I muttered.

The doorbell rang. "Oh please, please, don't answer it!" I screeched, as Mrs. Lorimer meandered into the hall. I saw her hesitate before she puffed her way back again. She filled the kettle.

"Quite right, quite right." She started her sing-song chanting again. "We're not ready yet, are we? We're going to have a cup of tea first."

Mrs. Lorimer opened a cupboard and, to my surprise, extracted a clean, elegant tea set: glossy red china patterned with swirling gold. I watched her scoop three spoonfuls of tea into the pot and cover them with scalding water from the kettle. She stirred with a long spoon for a good three minutes, puffing and muttering all the while, and never taking her eyes from the teapot. Then she poured, and set the cups down on the table: two exquisite still-lifes amid the mouldering clutter.

I sipped. It was delicious: like liquefied Turkish delight. Or rather, on the second sip, like bitter chocolate. Like roses. Like the smell of the sea. I blew across the surface impatiently, and drank again. The kitchen was warmer now. I was no longer afraid. Had I been afraid? I drank and drank, and Mrs. Lorimer refilled my cup, although she had not tasted her own yet. When my fingers slipped limply from the handle she took my hands, smilingly, and wrapped them round the cup. When I could no longer lift the cup to my lips, she lifted it for me. When I had finished, she poked inside the cup with her forefinger and smeared the thick dregs across my mouth. My head fell onto the table with a bruising bang as the doorbell sounded again.

I was still conscious, though the world was sluggish and strange, like a silent film in slow-motion. Mrs. Lorimer was far away from me, at the other end of a foggy tunnel. I wanted to speak, but I could not formulate sentences in my mind, let alone with my tongue.

I saw a woman standing next to Mrs. Lorimer, her head and face hidden inside a dark grey cloud; a snow cloud. An American voice cried out from the television with sudden clarity, "You can't do this to me, honey. You just can't do this." The woman and Mrs. Lorimer exchanged whispers. Then the woman approached the table, and the snow cloud drifted down towards my face. I felt the first flakes brush my nose, and then there was darkness. I remember nothing else.

The Trains

y first impression upon emerging from the drug-induced sleep was that I had not been asleep at all. At least, I had succumbed for no more than two or three seconds, and there was still time to resist and run away into the snow, if only my leaden arms and legs and eyelids would obey the command. I think it was the energy of my resolve to escape that actually woke me in the end, though I sank back into drowsiness again. Then, gradually, though not in unison, my senses returned to me.

First I was aware of a rumbling noise, whose rhythm matched the slight jolting of my nerveless body. The noise, a repetitive, metallic drumbeat (ta-tum-tee-tum-pause-pause), was familiar and not unpleasant. My brain leafed dreamily through the pages of memory until, with no sense of surprise or even interest, it was able to inform me that I was on a train. I let the knowledge seep through me, like water through a dry sponge.

It was dark: I assumed it was night time. I opened my eyes and shut them again straightaway, dazzled by the searing light of day. I tried again and again, blinking and squinting, until my sight could bear the dull clouds that spat stringy raindrops across the glass. The train raced through brown, snow-streaked fields; past bare hedges and trees.

I turned my aching neck from the window and scanned the rest of the carriage. I suppose I ought not to have been surprised to find one other seat, and one alone, occupied. But my struggle back to consciousness had been such a solitary effort, that I had come to believe that I was alone, and I could not help feeling shocked, as well as horrified, at my renewed proximity to the woman with the veiled hat.

I opened my mouth to speak, but the drugs had left my mouth so parched that I released nothing but a sigh. The woman did not hear, and her face was turned away from me - aggressively turned, I thought. I looked at her (what I could see of her) sitting so neatly across the white Formica table, her gloved hands folded in her lap. I thought she should look ridiculous in that outmoded hat, but she didn't, she looked elegant. I was outraged by her self-possession. My dread gave way to an inexorable tide of anger, and my helpless sigh gathered itself into a croak.

She turned to me at last, though slowly, and without a word. Then she knelt down and removed a clear bottle from the bag beneath her seat. She stood in the gangway, unscrewing the lid. I tried to shake my head, but this made me dizzy. She held it to my lips and I pursed them furiously. Then she spoke, but her voice was so soft that I could barely understand her.

"It's water."

I choked on my scornful laugh, and grimaced at the bitter taste of my own poisoned saliva. I took a sip of her water, and then a gulp. It tasted tepid, but pure. Soon I felt I could speak again. I breathed fast with renewed fury as she returned to her place.

"Who are you?" I seethed. There was no reply.

"Where are we? What's happening?"

No reply.

"What day is it?"

No reply

"Answer me! Please, answer me! What day is it?"

No reply.

I don't think I have ever felt such an urge to kill as I did then, when my shrill panic crashed so pitifully against her silence. It scares me to think that, had I possessed my natural strength, and a gun, or a knife, I would have destroyed that insensible block with enthusiasm. And it scares me more to remember how I imagined tearing away her stupid hat at the crux of the extermination and finding an expression of surprised pain on her face, and how the sight of this stirring of sensibility did not act on me as a suppressor but, on the contrary, allowed me to finish the job with a rush of pleasure.

But my murderous rage only made me feel dizzy again. As it passed, I said feebly, and with little hope of any response, "Where are we going?"

To my surprise she deigned to reply, albeit with a question.

"Where would you like to go?"

It was some comfort to be able to answer her with the same silent disdain with which she had treated my inquiries.

"I mean," she added, qualifying her unexpected question (with, I hope, some sense of embarrassment), "assuming that you can't go back."

Nowhere, I thought to myself. There is nowhere I want to go; nowhere I can go; no one to whom I can turn for help. And of course, as soon as I had assured myself of my absolute aloneness a name flashed into my head and gave me such a frisson of relief that I said it out loud without meaning to: "Boughwinds Abbey." It was as though I had been treading water all alone at night, in a volume of ocean that swelled for miles around me and beneath me, when suddenly I felt – from far away – a lighthouse's golden arc swing across my face. I would still sink and drown, no doubt, but I preferred to sink and drown with that light in my sights.

A moment later I regretted pronouncing the name out loud. I wanted it back, safe and secret behind my clenched lips and teeth. The woman leant towards me slightly. I unfocussed my eyes, and she became two-dimensional – a black, oddly-shaped silhouette against the colourless walls and windows. She leant back again and we relapsed into silence.

Minutes passed. I smiled at her with a feeble attempt at sarcasm – that is to say, with eyes unsmiling and face slightly tilted to one side. Then I stood up, on legs that felt like jelly. "I'm going to the Ladies'."

"You'll find it in carriage H, which is behind you," she replied, without so much as a twitch of alarm at the prospect of my leaving her sight. "But before you go, there are two things that I ought to tell you.

"Firstly, this train will not stop until it terminates in Leeds, and that won't be for another two hours, so you can't jump off anywhere in between unless you want to kill yourself. Secondly, you and I are the only passengers."

Perhaps you imagine that she spoke these words in a cruel tone. Perhaps you think you can hear a catlike smile playing across her lips. But it wasn't like that. She spoke, as she had spoken all along, in a monotonous murmur, as though she was explaining a series of tedious circumstances that she could not help. She was only half listening to herself. She did not move a muscle as I stepped over her bag with some dizzy difficulty, squeezed past a folded wheelchair, and escaped into the comparative freedom of carriage H.

I found the cubicle, locked myself in, and promptly vomited into the lavatory.

After this I felt a bit better, though my mouth tasted even fouler than before. I closed my eyes, and after a few seconds of welcome blankness, plans began to form in my mind of their own accord. They were vague and chaotic, but not entirely implausible. They centred on the train's termination in Leeds. The station would be thronged with people: Leeds was a place for swarms. Surely I could secure somebody's help? I could shout out loud. She might grip my arm as tightly as she liked: somebody was bound to interfere when they heard me, and saw me struggling.

I was not adept at planning for such adventures – for example, it never occurred to me to imagine the point of a knife pressed against my back, or a crowd of co-conspirators hustling me away from the train. The confusing influence of drugs is only half an excuse for my muddled thinking. I must confess that my imagination had already skipped the uninteresting details of my escape and sped off to Boughwinds Abbey in search of Ludovick Montefiore. I pictured his loving welcome, and the speedy competence with which he would punish the woman with the veiled hat. At the prospect of my happiness so romantically restored, I burst into tears and sobbed hopelessly for a good five minutes.

I felt in my bag and found a fragmented tissue, with which I mopped my slimy face as best I could. I also found, and brought forth, the precious train ticket that was to have taken me to Boughwinds Abbey, and I wondered whether I had bought it yesterday or weeks ago. There was no way of knowing how long my stupor had lasted; I had lost all sense of time.

I sat on the lavatory for a while, breathing as slightly as possible through my mouth and thinking. It smelled in here, but at least I could lock the door. After five minutes I returned to my captor. I would gladly have sat in a separate compartment, but I could not bear the thought of her searching down the train and sniffing me out like a sleek ferret. So I sat as far from her table as I could, and stared out of the window. Two hours went by, and then the fields gave way to red, terraced houses and road bridges.

I was thirsty, and the mingled taste of poison and sick in my mouth was driving me mad. I spent each second dreading the necessity of swallowing, and every time I did swallow I felt my face contort as though I had sucked on a lemon.

Our train pulled into an ill-lit bay at Leeds. There were no crowds; only a man who leant against the sooty brick wall and smoked and another who sat perusing a grubby newspaper. As our train sighed and stopped the first man spat on the ground, while the second man licked his middle finger and turned a page. I wondered if this was some sort of a pre-arranged signal for my captor. But neither man looked up as we disembarked, and the Veiled Hat took no notice of them. She glided from the train, her head down and her hand looped round my elbow.

She made her way out of the grimy shadows, where we were dwarfed and deafened by trains, and brought us into the concourse, where metallic grindings and hissings were banished by the tinkle of small change and coffee spoons. We strolled across the square side by side, arm in arm, keeping pace. We must have looked as thick as thieves, and just as furtive. There was I, casting about for my escape-route with frantic, sidelong glances. And there was she, her face entirely concealed by an archaic headpiece.

Actually, I was surprised by how little notice we (especially she) attracted. I expected comments from passers-by, or, at the very least, peculiar looks. This was rarely the case, however. I suppose her hat, with its sombre colour and neat size, was a discreet oddity. Though weird, we were not a flamboyant pair. And anyway, I am sure she altered with her environment, like a chameleon. At home her statuesque solidity had shocked me; she had been tall and implacable, like the black queen in a giant game of chess. And yet here, in the station concourse, amidst the clattering cafes and shops, she had somehow become unassuming: a petite spinster with quaint sartorial tastes.

I peered at her from the corner of my eye. I could easily dislodge her hand from my arm, and I could probably out-run her too. The question now was whether I should take the risk.

There was the departures board: a massive square slab teeming with rows and columns of yellow figures, which clacked briskly as the trains came and went. It was too high up for me to read in secret. Even when I rolled my eyeballs as high as they would go, so that they strained at the roots, I was unable to read without simultaneously tilting my head. So I looked up as rapidly as I could, and the words I was yearning for leapt out at me as though mirroring a picture in my brain: KEIGHLEY: 14.25: PLATFORM 3. In the same voracious glance I took in the clock: twenty-three minutes past two. The date: the fourth of January. The date on my ticket.

I drew a sharp breath and ran.

A guardian spirit seemed to run at my side, directing my feet to platform three and blocking off false turns. It shepherded an aimless crowd into the space between me and my captor; it pointed out the waiting train as it hummed and grumbled for the off.

She kept pace with me though; I was always in her sights if not in her grasp. As I reached the first door of the train she drew close. The complicit spirit must have abandoned me because my feet were hindered by a pile of suitcases and an embracing couple; my pursuer glided round them like a stream of dark water. And then something peculiar happened.

There was a further delay as, in my confusion, I pushed at the door instead of pulling it open. She caught up and stopped. There was no one near us; nobody watching. I whipped round; better to surrender face to face than with my back to her. There she stood. She could have got me; of course she could. She even made a half-hearted mime: lifting her hands as if to seize my sleeves. But her arms were loose; her fingers limp. It was barely even a gesture. She hesitated and halted. I stumbled into the train and the hefty door clanged shut between us.

She did not endeavour to reopen it. Her hands dropped and clasped one another lightly, and she stepped backwards. She stood near the edge of the platform and watched as the train slid away. Her secret mission, so urgently pursued, so ruthlessly executed, was abandoned with barely a shrug.

We watched one another until a curve in the track bore the train away.

The Witch's Broom

he afternoon tumbled into premature night. *All the Christmas* snow had dripped away now; I stepped from the train into a dank gloom. I waited an hour at Keighley, my feet juddering with cold as I sat. Despite the calm with which she had abandoned the chase at Leeds, I could not believe that I had seen the last of the Veiled Woman. She would appear, I thought. Indeed, once or twice there was a black mark at the edge of my vision, but it must (I concluded) have been put there by my imagination. She did not materialise.

I stepped from my second train into a proper nocturnal darkness that swirled and swarmed with wind and wet. There were no lights here; no station bustle; just a shelter with a corrugated iron roof that rattled beneath the downpour. As the train shuffled away I explored further. There were no waiting buses or taxis, and there was no telephone. I pushed through the picket gate. No lights and no houses; only a narrow, pot-holed lane, bordered on either side by over-grown verges and stone walls. I told myself resolutely that I knew this lane. I did know it, albeit as a thin white line in my parents' road atlas. I swung my bag over my shoulder and started to walk.

The moon was bright that night and intermittently veiled by masses of wet, drifting grey. I had been walking for five hours and it was gone ten o'clock when, at long last, a small, off-white rectangle gleamed faintly at my side. I walked past it before registering its presence. Then I retraced my steps and realised it was a road sign. *Boughwinds Village,* it said.

"Oh!" I made some such exclamation and stared stupidly, my mouth agape. I think I was semi-delirious by this time; cold, wet, famished and still sick with the remaining traces of Mrs. Lorimer's poison. I remember feeling surprised that minute after minute went by without the road sign fading away in a dreamy mist, or swelling up into some monster, or a veiled hat, or Joachim's head. I touched it. The whitened metal was cold, like my flesh. The lettering was obscured by rusty flakes and mud splatters and dribbling raindrops. I pressed my numbed fingertips against the lower edge of the sign, and when I took them away and held them before my eyes I saw that a purple line had formed across the soft skin. I began to shiver violently, and my teeth chattered as though I was being shaken hard.

A car whirred up the road behind me; the first vehicle I had seen since stepping off my train. The driver did not observe me (at least, he took no notice of me), as the water from the bumpy track spurted up from under his wheels and drenched my legs. I saw rain fall like slow-drifting dust in the cones of light from the headlamps. I watched the red brake-lights glow as the car passed me and slowed, and I saw an orange light flash on-off-on-off as the car turned right and briefly illuminated a shabby, whitewashed wall. I saw the driver run from the car, hunched, with his coat-collar pulled up high against the weather and I saw him enter a long, low building whose windows were dimly lit, as though by firelight. A sign swung above the door. It creaked irregularly as the wind slapped it back and forth.

I took one more look at my road sign. *Boughwinds Village*. I read it out loud and then set off for the inn in a tipsy zig zag. It was difficult to make out the name on the flapping board, partly because of the darkness and the wild wind, and partly because the lettering was flamboyantly gothic in style. I deciphered it eventually, as I stood beneath it. It read: *The Witch's Broom*. The picture was weathered, but I thought I could make out a gnarled hand and a spray of twigs.

I leant against the whitewashed walls, trying to shake off my dizziness before making an entrance. I peered through the diamond-pane windows. It was difficult to see clearly, since the wet glass was old and warped. However, I discovered that The Witch's Broom was not a meeting place for the youth of the village. A few old men sat around, leaning both elbows on the bar or staring into their drinks. The air was cloudy with pipe smoke and a low fire smouldered on the hearth, dying in a glow of delicious, lingering warmth. I threw my weight against the door and tripped across the threshold.

You have no doubt seen one of those westerns where a stranger enters a saloon bar and all the swearing, laughing, chatting, kissing, glass-chinking, music-making chaos gives way to a hostile hush? Well, my entrance was a low-key version of that scene. Murmuring quietness, rather than noisy conviviality, gave way to silence as I stood dripping on the black stone flags. The men looked up blankly or suspiciously. They were mollified, perhaps, by my limpness. I did not twirl pistols around at hip-level, or slam my hand down on the bar and call for whisky.

The barman - a hulk of a man, whose face comprised an unpleasantly random amalgamation of stubble, grease and flab – seemed the most averse to my appearance. He leaned across the bar and eyed me sourly, his puffy lids half closed. To my surprise he said,

"Reckon we've been waiting for you."

"Er..." What did he mean? The heavy heat of the room was contending very strangely with the goose-pimpling cold of my body. I felt I must be behaving stupidly and I feared I might be sick. A green pallor fought against my blushes as I stuttered confusedly. "You... know who I am?"

"I reckon I know, but I'm not about to tell you, 'cause you're about to tell me! Well? What's your name then, Miss Mumble? Miss Not-quite-with-it-at-the-present-moment-in-time?" The barman looked round for a laugh, but nobody obliged. One of the men at the bar, a powerful looking man with a bushy white beard, shook his head. "Knock it off, Gibbon," he muttered.

"My name's Abigail Crabtree."

"Well that's all right then," Mr. Gibbon retorted defensively, with a glance at the bearded man. "'Cause it's Abigail Crabtree we're expecting. Right, now get yourself sorted out. These clothes," (here he drew a bulging cloth bag from underneath the bar) "are the dry ones what were left here for Abigail Crabtree. I don't know what all this is about, and I'm hoping you'll have the courtesy to tell me, but I'm doing exactly what I was told to do – to the letter - so nobody, nobody (here he glared round at the assembled drinkers) can't accuse me of being an unhonest nor an unhuman nor an unpitying man." The drinkers nodded and mumbled their assent.

I stared at the bag, astonished at first and then comforted. I knew what this meant. My godfather was expecting me. He knew that I might come to him at any time of the day or night, in wind and storm, and he had provided for me. Did this not prove that I had reached Boughwinds, at last? That I was safe in his protection, at last? My anxieties melted away, leaving a weak, sleepy tenderness. I had my hand on the bag, but Mr. Gibbon pulled it away sharply. He brought his face close to mine and snarled, "You got proof of your identity then?"

Fortunately my face blanched as he spoke, and he realised I was about to vomit. I saw the reddish whites of his panic-stricken eyes as he flung the bag into my arms and shouted, "Up the stairs you little baggage! First door on the right! Go on! Up the stairs! Now!"

I made my way up in time. I found myself in a mean little washroom with a lino floor, damp- blackened walls and a tiny window that would not shut. I was shivering uncontrollably now and wanted nothing more than to curl up before the fire and sleep. But I was a mess: I smelt of sick and sweat, and I was drenched to the skin. So I stripped – my skin so tenderly cold that I felt as a potato might if it were forced to peel itself – and turned the shower on. There was a juddering in the pipes, and the shower head spat a bulge of brown water onto the cubicle floor. It then paused, as I stared despairingly. At last a clear, steady trickle pattered down. I stuck out my hand, gingerly. The stream was tiny, but hot, so I plunged underneath it and danced about, grim-faced, until I was wet and lathered and rinsed all over. The soap was bright yellow and smelt like disinfectant, which was not very alluring, but probably just as well. I had to wash my hair with it, since there was no shampoo.

Only when I had turned the dribble off did I remember that I had no towel. I looked around, and saw a pile of thin, paper hand-towels on the basin, so I patted myself dry with about fifty of them. Then I spilled the contents of the bag onto the closed lavatory seat. This was a pleasant surprise; everything new: boots, trousers, underwear, a long-sleeved T-shirt and a thick, soft, red jumper that belted at the waist and looked as snug as a dressing gown. A blast of wet wind wriggled through the half-open window and slapped me between the shoulder blades. I bundled everything on.

Mr. Gibbon did not even glance at me as I sidled back into the bar. He was deep in discussion with one of his drinkers and did not choose to hear me creaking down the stairs. I wondered, with some embarrassment, what I should do. I looked towards the fire of course, having not quite plucked up courage to cross the room and warm myself before it, when I saw a little old man lean forward from his fireside seat. He smiled a surprised smile, and nodded as I caught his eye.

"Warm yourself," he suggested as I neared his seat. His voice was like his face and smile: kind yet distracted.

I hunched over the embers and closed my eyes as the heat flooded over me and then began to seep through my body. My feet and hands tingled with pain as they rapidly warmed. My blood began to throb again, as though it had been blocked by ice floes. For a few minutes everything was subordinate to this exquisite billow of pleasure. Then Mr. Gibbon poked my shoulder.

"Oh you've appeared, have you? Well, please just sneak across to the fire and hog it from everyone else! Let poor old Toby here freeze to death, why don't you?" He nodded in the direction of my faded friend, who turned his unseeing eyes on us. He made vague gestures of reassurance and murmured, "Mr. Gibbon, don't trouble yourself. It's no bother." I shifted my stool a little distance from the hearth.

"Now look here," Mr. Gibbon continued, ignoring Toby altogether, "Don't you go telling me that I'm not more human (I think he meant humane) than most, 'cause this is not a pub what serves food, so I might have said no when I was told to feed you and I'd have been within my rights, but here I come bearing soup and bread for your ladyship." He slammed a tray down on one of the tables. I did thank him, but I don't think he heard me above his mutterings about "… *demanding people…*", "*…this day and age…*" and "*…does it look like a bloody soup kitchen?*"

My recent experiences of poison ought to have taught me caution, but nonetheless I wolfed the tomato soup and used the bread to mop up every drop. The portion was ungenerous, but at least it was wholesome. As I ate, I eyed Toby without much interest. He didn't notice me; his grey eyes, which were pale and watery, seemed to look inward all the time, as though they were watching sad memories play themselves out in his mind. His eyes fell on me once though and on my soup bowl and he brightened briefly into wakefulness. "Five twenty-pound notes," he said. "Five. I saw her count them out. For half a tin of soup and a slice of plastic bread." I smiled, and then my smile froze. He had said her. It was a woman then, who had brought the clothes and paid for my food? Not Ludovick Montefiore? And then I reassured myself. Doubtless there was a whole household of servants at Boughwinds Abbey. I could hardly expect my godfather to see to everything in person.

"Is this really Boughwinds Village?" I ventured dreamily before Toby sank back into himself again. However, despite that flash of conviviality over the soup, Toby was neither eager to make conversation nor sharp of hearing, and, by leaning forwards and cupping his hand to his ear (his eyes glazing over all the while) he signalled that I must repeat myself. I was forced to speak so loudly that my inane question

– after a crescendo of repetitions – was broadcast to the whole room.

"Oh good Lord, what have we got here?" sneered Mr. Gibbon. "Where'd you think you'd landed love? Buenos Aires?" My short experience of Mr. Gibbon encouraged me to ignore him. At least my question was answered.

"Who was the woman, who paid for my food and brought my clothes?"

"Ah, the beautiful stranger!" The room burst into laughter as one man simpered in a high-pitched voice, "Oh, Mr. Gibbon!" The laughter became bolder. "He liked her all right did our Gibbon!" another man guffawed. "She knew just how to deal with him! Went all quiet he did, couldn't do enough to please, eh Gibbon? Not that she'd much to say, herself."

"It helps though," added someone else, "when a woman showers you with twenty quid notes! Sort of…brings you round, I imagine?" Mr. Gibbon growled incoherently and purpled like a misshapen beetroot.

"That's enough questions from you, Baggage," said Mr. Gibbon, transforming his embarrassment into annoyance and directing it at me. "I reckon it's us that's due an explanation. What's a snotty-nosed kid like you doing out on its own at this time of night? Up to no good, I know that much."

I drew a long breath, wondering what on earth I could say. I looked into his stone-hard face and shrugged wearily. "I'm trying to find somebody…a relation of mine."

Mr. Gibbon twirled a finger around the side of his head. The man with the bushy white beard said, gently,

"Your…relation live round here then, love?"

"I think so. His name is Ludovick Montefiore and he lives at Boughwinds Abbey…"

I was looking into the fire as I spoke, unaware at first of what I had done. But then the silence hit me, and I turned round to discover that the room had changed: it had lost its easy, careless air. Nobody talked, or if they did they sounded so forced and unnatural that they quickly tailed off again. Nobody looked at me, except with quick, sidelong glances. There was a general polishing-off of drinks and a buttoning-up of coats and over-hearty expressions of surprise at how late it had, all of a sudden, become. Then the bustle died down and everyone turned to Toby and eyed him nervously. I followed their eyes, of course and found that my friend had risen from his chair like a spectre from its tomb - his colourless eyes staring, his thin arms feeling for balance. A passion (was it anger or terror, or merely the excited recognition of a long unspoken name?) lent his voice a new decisiveness.

"Boughwinds Abbey? Who is going to Boughwinds Abbey?"

I answered as mildly as I could through my tensely self-interested curiosity, "Me. I'm going to find Ludovick Montefiore at Boughwinds Abbey."

"No! Shh!" someone hissed at me, flapping his hands. "It's all right, Toby," he shouted, "Nobody's mentioned…anything. You must have misheard. You've been asleep."

But his reassurances came too late. Toby was gripping my arm now and to my dismay I saw tears coursing down his yellow parchment cheek-bones. He gave my arm an emphatic twitch with every word he spoke, though he was weaker than a blade of dry grass, the effort was so pitiful that I almost cried as well.

"Why did you have to say the name? Why did you have to…wake it up again?"

"I'm sorry." I said. "I don't know anything at all about it. I didn't mean to hurt you."

"Never say the name again!" He ordered, a shudder – a thrill – in his voice. "It is a *terrible* name! Terrible, terrible, terrible!" He shook his head and lowered it until his chin touched his chest, his tears falling vertically to the carpet.

"…Why?" I asked timidly, to a chorus of exasperated groans. But can you blame me?

Toby's grip tightened. It was like being grappled by a moth.

"The devil. Montefiore. He took my Sylvia. My girl – my granddaughter. She went down there for her education and she never came back. He murdered her – that devil, Montefiore, murdered my Sylvia!"

Toby's mumbly sobs overcame his efforts to speak. He released my arm when one of the men came to lead him away. "Come on now, Toby old fellow. You put it all out of your mind. Let's get you home and it'll all look brighter in the morning."

Toby did not look at me again. The two hobbled away without another word, their coats folded over the stronger man's arm and after a minute or two (for nobody had spoken yet), we heard a car rev up and drive away.

I stood still, my head hanging, weighed down by a strange and heavy feeling – what was it? Dread fulfilled? Excited desire? No, no, I assured myself it was neither of them. It must be self-reproach. Yes, it was self-reproach. To have laid bare the morbid obsession of a frail old man was bad enough, but then to probe it for the sake of my own idle inquisitiveness…I had been brutal, for nothing but a story that didn't ring true. I could trust Mr. Gibbon to make me feel worse.

"Well, that was beautifully done, Miss Baggage. Scare my best customers off the premises why don't you…?"

The landlord was clearly limbering up for a heavy onslaught, but he was interrupted by the kindly white beard.

"I think you'll find the young lady has been your best customer this evening, Gibbon. So why not throw a few more logs on the fire and find her something to sleep on, instead of keeping on at her? She's done you no harm – far from it."

"Yes, John Fogle, sir!" replied Mr. Gibbon, sarcastically polite. But for all his irony he did as he was told, lumbering about with armfuls of blankets and pillows and firewood, while John Fogle turned to me with a down-to-earth smile.

"Don't worry about Tobias," he said, as he fastened his scarf. "This isn't Transylvannia, and I don't suppose Mr. Montefiore is the Count Dracula neither. No, Tobias is a nice old boy, but he's a bit…you know. He did lose his little girl there…at the abbey…but it was nobody's fault I'm sure. We don't mention the place in his hearing."

"No. I see." I smiled wanly. Then as John Fogle turned to go I added anxiously, "How do I get to the abbey? I don't know the way."

"Well, don't you go trying to get there now, Gibbon or no Gibbon. You'll need the daylight." He took me to the door and we stood under the porch. The rain had stopped, but the darkness was so intense that it seemed to press against us like a moving wall. I shuddered.

"Go on up the road," he said, "and pretty soon you'll see a stile, and a muddy track that'll take you left, over the fields. Follow that on and on - don't be put off by the distance, it's a good few miles – and you'll see the abbey in a valley bottom. You won't see it 'til you're almost upon it, it's that hidden by the hills and woods."

I thanked him. He nodded and walked away from me. Within seconds he was swallowed by the noiseless night.

Boughwinds Abbey

When John Fogle had gone I strained my eyes against the darkness. I took a few steps forward into the road, hoping, uselessly, that I might see the stile he had described. "I can't believe I'm here," I whispered. "I can't believe it." But I was lying. I believed, all of a sudden, with exuberant relief, that my face really was turned towards Boughwinds Abbey; that I was within a few miles of my godfather; that I could walk to him now, if I chose, and be in his presence before the end of the night.

I took a few more absent-minded steps, and as I walked I felt a bitter-sweet taste rise up in my mouth from underneath my tongue – as though I had just tasted something better than chocolate. It was so wonderful, and yet so tauntingly vague, that I desired, with a childish, foot-stamping impatience, to know what it was, and to gorge myself on it. And though it was only a taste, it seemed to be appealing to my head, my heart and soul, as much as to my taste-buds and my stomach. I wondered whether I was remembering food that I had eaten in heaven, before I was born.

The seductive taste was strange enough to stop me in my tracks for a few seconds. But then I found that the joy of it was making me walk, then jog, and then half-run (I would have raced had I been able to see an inch before my eyes) towards the stile. The longing for this heavenly taste and the longing for my journey's end merged into one, and I felt I must not waste another moment in my quest for Boughwinds Abbey. I was sick of strangers who cared for me very little, or not at all, or because they were paid to care. How stupid of me to think of wasting a whole night amongst them, when Ludovick Montefiore was so near. He is not a stranger, I said to myself in my restless longing. So I rushed on through the slippery roadside mud.

But moods – especially exultant moods - burn themselves out. I fumbled my way over the stile and onto a hillocky, gorse-bordered sheep-track that led me steeply downwards. After a few yards I was forced to shuffle, my arms stretched out and my fingers groping in the black void. Presently I stopped and stood still. There was a prickling chill in the air: yet more rain was on its way. I was as blind as a mole in his deepest, narrowest tunnel, feeling stupid and scared. John Fogle was right: I should have waited until the morning.

I looked up – uselessly, for there were no stars or moon anymore. I guessed, by the creaking and rustling and dripping over my head, that I was standing among trees. In my oak wood, I thought, there was always a sun or moon or lightning flash by which to see. In my oak wood I was never far from the secret tree, where my friends waited in a dim, fire-lit circle. I remembered that Boris bear was inside my bag, and that I had left my bag in The Witch's Broom.

My dithering deteriorated into miserable panic. After all, how could I know, without my eyes, that the sounds above my head were the sounds of wind-swayed boughs? Perhaps I heard giant skeletons stalk in a tightening circle, leering with their rectangular grins and empty eye-sockets. Perhaps spectral women in dark, Victorian skirts trod with them, breathing evil sighs and looking me up and down as though, in their dead sight (since night is day for ghosts), I stood beneath a blazing noonday sun. The wind moaned, but I heard the hungry complaints of wolves as they loped leisurely across the hill, faster than I could ever run. I pulled my outstretched arms back against my body, in case something grabbed them: something bony, cold, sharp and strong.

I stood rooted to the spot, with a fear of the dark that was new to me. I was used to feeling that the night hid me from danger. Now I felt that it was against me and that it hid my danger from me.

There was a screech, as though somebody close to my ear had been struck with a knife and then I felt a whirring weight in my face. It disappeared instantly. I think, now, that it was an owl. I was too frightened of the blackness to reach into it, even with a scream. I scrambled back to the stile without drawing a single breath and ran, gasping, until I arrived back at The Witch's Broom.

Mr. Gibbon stood behind the bar, totting up his takings. Thank God he had not locked up and gone to bed. He scowled as I burst through the door, and he maintained his surly silence. I wonder what he would have thought had he known how gratefully I blessed his ugly, fleshy face, and his bulky, grumpy, prosaic realness.

When he had gone I lay down by the fire, my tremblings gradually easing, and I murmured, "Oh God, please just let me sleep. Please: no dreams or visions or imaginings. Shut me down as though I was a machine."

I repeated this mantra over and over and then slept till morning.

I woke at ten o'clock. Mr. Gibbon was lumbering about the room, slapping beer mats onto the round tables and brushing white ash onto the floor with the back of his hand. It occurred to me that if I could work up a pretended self-assurance, then he might be more accommodating, as he was towards John Fogle last night. He was the sort of person, I surmised, whose aggression is provoked by timidity.

I sat up, gulped, counted up to three in my head and said with a strained sort of severity,

"Mr. Gibbon, I would like a cup of tea."

Mr. Gibbon turned and glared at me.

"Please." I added hastily.

His expression wavered between astonishment and scepticism. I managed to meet his eye and hold it steadily, though this was as difficult as holding a massive weight high above my head: I had to strain to prevent my gaze from plunging to the stone flags. Mr. Gibbon gave in first. He shrugged and muttered, "One cup of tea for Lady Muck," before trudging out to the kitchen. Soon there issued a clumsy, bustling racket: water gushing, cupboards slamming, switches flicking and china clinking. I stretched and smiled complacently.

It was a raw day, following a raw night, and I wrapped my fingers gratefully around the mug, letting the steam cloud up into my face and condense there. Mr. Gibbon had redeemed himself a little by making a very hot, very brown brew. I stood slurping in the doorway, surveying what I thought of as my godfather's landscape.

It was a bleak corner of England, that was for sure. Across the track, and beyond the dry-stone wall, a moor rose up, like a solidified swell of mid-Atlantic water. Just like the colours of the sea, the colours of this earth-wave mingled and shifted as clouds drifted across the white sky, turning red bracken to brown and grey stone to black. Flecks of briny foam bleated and nibbled among the rocks, which stretched out like clutching fingers.

The scene was silent, but for a wind that blew off the hills with a low, constant moan: so low and so constant that I thought I was listening to silence, until I turned back to the inn and shut the door behind me.

There was a telephone in the vestibule, a solid black object festooned with wires, dating from another age. I knew that I ought to ring my parents, but I feared their anger, and I feared having to lie again. Would they really be worried; wouldn't they just assume I had gone off to see Joachim? No, I answered truthfully after a brief meditation, they would really be worried and the last thing I wanted (my wants had priority over every other consideration, of course) was to be the object of a clamorous, nationwide search. That would scotch all my dreams.

And beneath these anxieties was the terrible prospect – half-buried by my conscience – that they would not be there at all. That something bad had happened to them.

The telephone rejected my coin on the first couple of attempts, but finally I was able to dial, hearing a crackling burr as it started to ring. My dad answered immediately, as though he had been waiting with his hand on the receiver. I yelped with relief.

"Dad? It's me. Are you all right?"

"Oh, good God! Abigail! Where are you? (It's Abigail, Love...I don't know...hang on.) Abigail? Where are you? What on earth's happened? Are you all right?"

I rolled my eyes at their frenzy of anxiety. I found it irritating because it dampened the charms of my solitary adventure.

"Dad, I'm fine. I don't know why you're fussing! I told mum I'd be going away."

"So that is where you are? You're with Joachim in Durham?"

"Yes! Obviously!"

"Not obviously! As far as we were concerned you just vanished into thin air."

"I said I was going away! Mum even dropped me at the station!"

"Yes, to buy a ticket! You never said anything about boarding a train!"

This exchange of exclamations continued for some time and I was almost out of small change before they were pacified. I think they were so relieved to hear my voice that they forgot to ask awkward questions (When would I phone again? When would I be home? How was I managing without a suitcase? Etc). I replaced the receiver with the feeling that I had got off lightly. They were content now, therefore I was at liberty to forget them.

I went back inside, thanked Mr. Gibbon for the tea and placed my empty mug on the bar. We had nothing more to say to one another, so without further ado I rolled my old clothes into a bundle, crammed them into my bag and left The Witch's Broom behind.

It was not quite noon by the time I reached the stile but there was already a bluish deadness about the sky, the landscape was fast becoming monotone. Daytime, it seemed, barely existed in this place. I walked as quickly as I could beneath that line of tall trees that had terrified me last night, trying not to hear the eerie wind starting up in their branches. I kept seeing – or half-seeing – a stooping figure that scurried and ducked from tree to wall to heather-clump. I heard things too: twigs snapping and dead leaves rustling, as though crushed by a light foot. Sometimes the noises were clear and the sightings almost certain, but I kept telling myself to remember last night and so (because I didn't like to think of myself as an hysteric) I kept a lid on my mounting fear. Once or twice I did spin round, but the phantom always evaded me.

The sheep-track never widened into a more substantial path, but I followed it with ease. Sometimes I squeezed between knee-deep walls of rocky earth and bracken; sometimes I found myself exposed on a bleak hill-top, chilled through by the blasting wind. I had walked for hours and a bright night had fallen on me, when I found that I was coming steeply downhill, the trees were thickening and that their breathing was becoming heavier over my head. Soon they were crowding and hissing so close to me that my fear was ready to burst again. But then, without warning, I emerged into the open and had my first sight of Boughwinds Abbey.

It sprawled across the flat valley floor like a sleeping monster; like an old dragon, with all its harsh angles and spikes, its hundred glinting windows, veined arches and smoking chimneys. It slept amidst lawns and sweeping gravel walkways, boxed into its valley on all sides by high, hilly woods, such as the one from which I now emerged. I stood for a moment, breathing deeply and staring, and then I walked on. I was transfixed. I don't know why it is, for that evening was clear, but when I look back on my first sighting, I see the abbey swathed in a magical mist. Sometimes I imagine that it was wreathed in smoky dragon-breath, enchanted dragon-breath that filled my lungs, my head and my blood as I approached, and bound me to the place forever. There was nothing by which I could identify it as a part of my world. There were no telegraph poles or electric lights; no whirring traffic, no aeroplane-trails way above my head. Only a fat white moon hanging low, lighting my way across the night-grey grass to my godfather's front door.

I reached the porch. Now that I was close to the walls I could no longer see the moon for I was blinded by the building's dank, mossy darkness. I felt all across the massive door – its width was at least twice my height - for a knocker. At last I felt something cold and heavy that shifted reluctantly beneath my hands. I stood on tiptoe and lifted it as high as I could, then I let it fall. An almighty booming crack dizzied my ears immediately and then thudded through the house. My legs vibrated with the noise, as though I had detonated a subterranean cannon. The succeeding stillness was profound.

Five minutes must have gone by, but I dared not knock again. At last I heard the faint slap of footsteps, faraway across many draughty stairways and corridors. They seemed closer and then they seemed faraway, then close once more. They disappeared altogether, though I was straining after them. Then, suddenly, there was somebody there, on the other side of the door. A key rattled in the lock. Chains were drawn and bolts shot back. The door opened and as it did I felt a gust of stone-cold air against my skin: colder than the night wind and not so alive.

The door opened and the Somebody stood before me. I could see nothing but a guttering candle that hovered in the dark mid-air and then moved roughly across my face, singeing a strand of my hair. I gasped, screwing up my eyes against the flame. The flame moved back inside the door, which began to close.

"Clear off," said a voice that seemed neither male nor female. "There's no room for more pupils."

The door was an inch from shutting, but I pulled myself together and shrieked, "Wait!" The door stopped moving. I put my foot between it and the frame and said, quietly, "Please wait". With just a little pressure from the other side that great portal could have crushed my foot like a dry biscuit.

"Please," I continued. "I'm not a pupil. I've come to see my godfather, Ludovick Montefiore. I've come so far to see him, I'm in so much trouble and I've nowhere else to go. He told me to come."

I heard a sighing sound from the other side of the door. It was a sound as enigmatic as the sound of Tobias's passion and I still wonder what it meant. Was it a sigh of resignation perhaps, or of sorrow, exasperation or comprehension? At any rate, the door opened and I was allowed inside. Then it closed again, softly, like a muffled drum.

I could see no more of my surroundings now than I had done on the porch, as the single, sputtering candle was still our only source of light. I felt that I was in a vast room: higher, wider and longer than The Institute's substantial assembly hall. From the lofty echoes that resounded when we walked and spoke and the chill that oozed into my bones as I stood there in the dark, I knew that this hallway was built of stone.

"The master is away on business," said the voice from the face that the light did not reach.

Ludovick Montefiore not here? My heart sank. I could feel it plunging down through my stomach like a dead weight. "When will he be back?"

"I don't know," returned the Somebody with sardonic emphasis. "Five minutes? Five days? Five years? He's a law unto himself."

"What shall I do?" I moaned, to myself, to the cold, stone house, and to the cold, stone Somebody.

"You will stay here until he comes."

"But…five years? What if he really is away for five years? I need him to help me. I need him now. He said he'd be here." I clenched my fists in frustration and stamped on the knee-jarring floor. The sexless voice continued, relentlessly cool.

"You will stay here and do as you are told. If you disobey me then the master will be angry when he does return. Now. Follow me."

I followed the candle up and down through mile upon mile (so it seemed) of tomb-like air until I heard the rattle of a key and a door handle and I was drawn into a closer space, that seemed carpeted and curtained. A second candle was lit from the first one, then the voice said.

"You may sleep here tonight. Tomorrow I will ensure that you have a bed made up in the school building, like the other pupils. Lessons begin at eight o'clock. You will not be late." Then the first candle, and the Somebody disappeared. The door slammed and the lock rattled. I was imprisoned in my room, but I did not have enough sunken heart to protest.

I sat down on the edge of my bed (I discovered later that it was a four-poster, but I noticed nothing at all that first night). All my griefs and longings seemed to take physical shape and, emboldened by the darkness, leapt all about me and over me: hurting me, like malicious monkeys. Fear yanked at my hair, disappointment bounced heavily on my bowed back, belated homesickness – worst of all – stamped about on my insides, until I felt more broken than I had ever felt in my life before: as broken as a dry biscuit against the great abbey door. I lay face down and cried out "Ow! Ow! Ow!" as though I was being kicked. It was not a very appealing noise and you might have laughed an embarrassed laugh if you had heard it. But I was too wretched even to make my wretchedness attractive.

I wonder how long I lay there. I don't think it was very long: half an hour or so. I was as inert as a dead body now, my eyes open against the quilt. All at once I felt a movement underneath my jumper. It was as though a warm animal was wriggling around at my side and slowly moving towards my head.

"Ugh!" I leapt up and drew away from the bed sharply. "Not a rat?"

"Abigail? It's me." A small gruff voice came from the centre of the bed: a voice whose dear tones were redolent of wood-smoke and autumn leaves and dry soil; a voice that I had only ever heard before in the other world: in the oak wood. My breath quickened and, keeping my face turned towards him, I reached dazedly for the candle.

"Boris?"

"Long time, no see," replied the bear composedly from the centre of the quilt.

"Boris!"

"C'est moi," he continued, swaying a few times from side to side. "Nice springy mattress."

"What are you doing here?" I whispered, somewhere between joy and surprise and a peculiar sort of horror.

"I was in your bag."

"Yes I know, but I mean, what are you doing here…alive…talking to me? You know what I mean."

"Ah. Well. Normally I wouldn't dream of it. But this time I have two very serious reasons." He stood up tall and crossed his arms. "You clearly need your oak wood, you Truant." I looked down, guiltily. "And the oak wood certainly needs you. It needs you like never before."

Traumund

oris and I lay talking awhile, and then my long walk and my hard crying took their toll. Warmth suffused my body from my feet. I thought that the quilt, sheets and pillows rose up and encircled me in a winding column. The light was dim but I could see billows of white linen stiffening, darkening and expanding and I could hear a crackling noise, as though hordes of tiny people were jumping up and down on dry twigs. The light went away altogether and I smelt a leafy, outdoor smell. I realised I was falling because I heard myself gasp and felt my feet trying to push against nothingness. My terror lasted for half a second and then I was there, on the ground inside my hollow oak. I had not fallen after all, I thought with relief, though my heart was beating fast as though I had.

I was inside my hollow oak, but my hollow oak – my home – was not as it should be. I did not hear the furtive welcome of a dozen whispering, laughing voices. As I sat up, I did not see the smoky lights of our fire play amongst the tree's black hollows and stringy, hanging roots. I did not inhale that magical air which, till now, had always filled my lungs like a breath-stopping, inebriating dust-cloud. The air I breathed tonight was slimy and cold.

The Tree People awaited me: I could see black shapes against the black-grey walls. But nobody moved to greet me or uttered more than a subdued, "Hello". They looked like prisoners chained to the spot: prisoners going mad for lack of daylight and exercise. And in fact, it struck me, this was only to be expected. My tree was nothing but a stuffy, windowless cell. A dismal little madhouse in the middle of a dismal forest. Claustrophobia made manifest. How poor my imagination must be to have created this dank hovel as its refuge; it's heaven.

"Light the fire, somebody," I snapped. Prince Constantine obeyed me promptly, but with a sigh and I watched him as he knelt before the hearth. I had never disparaged him before, not even in my heart of hearts, but now I saw that he was just a sulky teenager whose courtly manners and clothes made my toes curl with irritation.

"Where's Eyes?" I asked nobody in particular.

"You'll find out soon enough when he gets back," somebody answered tartly.

Nobody spoke. We were all painfully conscious of every creaking chair-leg; of the ticking clock above the fireplace; of our own noisy need to cough and swallow.

We must have sat like this for half an hour before there came, at last, a feathered flurry from the top of the tree and Eyes burst down the hollow trunk. He landed heavily and greeted us with a wan hoot. His muscular wings drooped, weighed down by rain and weariness and troubles. He shook himself before taking a canvas satchel from his shoulders and laying it down near the door. Prince Constantine offered him water, but the owl refused with a curt shake of his head and began to pace round and round the room. We all watched surreptitiously as his great eyes darted from me, to the others, then back to the thoughts inside his head.

"Where've you been, Eyes?" I asked eventually.

"That's a long story," he replied mysteriously.

I tutted pettishly and said, "Well I wish you would get on and tell it. I can't be bothered to sit around in here all night. You're all so miserable."

Eyes glanced at me with a frown and then, for the first time, he noticed how slumped and sulky we all were.

"What's the matter?" he rapped.

I said nothing. Somebody said, "I don't know." Somebody else said, "Nothing."

There was a crash like falling timber as Eyes slammed the sinewy weight of his wings onto the table top and screeched. "Screech" is an undignified-sounding word, though it is the only one that will do. Remember that Eyes was an owl: his rare screeches were both dignified and terrible. We all looked up at him. Eyes towered over us, his wings outstretched. When he spoke, his voice was quiet, but it quivered with weight.

"The oak wood is in danger. We are all in danger. If we do not act against our enemies then we will certainly die. Abigail, you must do something, otherwise we, with the whole wood, will perish and you will have no foothold here. You will be condemned to live in the Waking World always and forever. So please shake off this lethargy: listen to our story and then decide what you can or cannot be bothered to do."

"All right," I muttered, embarrassed by his intensity. "Go on then, tell me everything. I'm listening."

There were no cosy preparations for this tale. One of the Tree People brought food and wine for the weary owl. We pulled our knees up to our chins and followed him with our eyes and ears as he paced the sooty hearthrug.

"I shall begin my tale," he said between gobbles (again, "gobbles" doesn't do Eyes justice, because it makes him sound inelegant, and he wasn't), "with the second visit of the Vulture Man. Or rather, Vulture Men. This happened, Abigail, shortly after your last visit to the woods; that is to say, towards the end of your time at the Institute.

"We were sitting inside the tree one evening, talking and dozing and wondering whether you would visit us later on that night. The cannibals were rampaging noisily, so we could not go outside. Prince Constantine, I seem to recall, was cooking up some plot for your escape from the Institute. He had worked out a rather unconvincing scenario involving the entrapment of Miss Konder inside a shed or a sewer..."

"A sewer." Constantine interrupted. Eyes hesitated and glowered.

"A sewer. At any rate, Constantine was detailing his silly scheme, when all of a sudden he fell silent. I woke up with a start. We all sat as stiff as statues, only our lowered, staring eyes told that we were listening – strenuously listening. Had we really heard it? No...Yes! Almost before we had time to doubt our terror, there it was again: Knock, knock, knock."

I gave myself up to the Owl's melodrama – with fear, of course, but with more disinterested pleasure.

"Somebody was hammering against the hollow wood of this very tree.

"The knocking continued for half a minute. We dared not move a muscle. We covered our mouths to muffle the noise of our own breathing, feeling the air around us shudder gently at every blow. With my heart in my gullet I edged to the fire and reached for the poker. It was the nearest thing we had to a weapon.

"The knocking stopped. This was worse. Now we could not know whether the...the thing...was still near us or whether it had moved away. So we stood a while longer like dummies, our limbs beginning to tingle and our heads to turn dizzy, until one of the Tree People raised her finger and tilted her head in a listening gesture. There was the knock, knock, knocking again. We all heard it, but it was further away now, as though whoever-it-was was hammering on another tree. I stole to the peep-hole and looked out.

"Though the night was black I could see what I needed to see. Two tall, hooded figures lurked underneath the young oaks on the other side of the clearing. One of them had a burning brand of wood. He held it up high as the other one took a scroll of parchment from a pouch at his hip, unrolled it, and nailed it fast to one of the trees with an ugly curved hammer: knock, knock, knock. Together they moved on to the next tree, and then the next, until they had posted squares of parchment on all the trees around the clearing. When they had finished they came towards us again and for the first time I saw a flicker of beak and beady eye in the wavering torchlight. I watched as they remounted their horses (both steeds as black and silent as the night; they had been grazing among the trees all this while and we never noticed them), and trotted away, into the wood.

"We moved again and breathed freely, and whispered at one another excitedly. The riders had been gone a good half hour before any of us dared venture forth -" (here there was a murmur of protest from my valiant Constantine) "– into the night. Eventually I glided into the clearing. Prince Constantine was anxious to go in my place," added Eyes magnanimously, "but that was considered too dangerous, on account of his having no wings. We wished, of course, to remove a notice from one of the trees and read it together.

"It did not take me long to discover that all the parchments were identical. So I tore one down (not the one posted on this tree, for fear of drawing attention to our hiding place) and then I flew back as quickly and noiselessly as I could."

"What did it say?" I asked breathlessly.

"Have a look for yourself," replied Eyes. He shuffled over to the fireplace and I saw that a roll of thick parchment lay on the rustic mantelpiece. I took it from Eyes' outstretched claw, unrolled it and read these words, so beautifully written in curling swirls of red ink.

The King of Traumund issues Greetings to His Faithful Subjects.
It is the King's pleasure that a Tour of Inspection be
conducted through this Forest, over the Winter Season.

*It has come to the King's notice that the Traitor & Usurper of
Lands, ABIGAIL CRABTREE, & her Confederates,
remain at large within these Royal Territories.
The King commands that ABIGAIL CRABTREE be speedily sought
out & brought before his Royal Person ALIVE. Her adherents must
also be found & ELIMINATED, before the Royal Tour can continue.
The King warns that if these Traitors are not HASTILY
PROCURED then this domain will be
RAZED & BURNED without compunction.
GOD SAVE THE KING.*

I looked up. The others were watching me intently, so I tried to seem
airy and unflustered.

"It's the same sort of stuff that the Vulture Man said that first time,
only it's written down. But so what? They'll probably leave us alone
for another three years now."

The Tree People looked at one another meaningfully. Eyes sighed.
"I'm afraid this isn't the end of our tale."

"What else has happened?"

Eyes wiped his brow and took a generous slug of wine before
continuing.

"The next day we went out into the clearing and counted over a
hundred of these notices defacing the trees. The morning sunlight made
us feel less afraid and more indignant than we had done during the
night. With one accord we began tearing them down and ripping them
to pieces: making it clear what we thought of them.

"Well, we had worked our way through twenty or so, beginning
(thank heaven) on the far side of the clearing. That is to say, fortunately
we had not yet stripped this tree. We still haven't."

"Why not?" I asked impatiently. "I thought you said that all this
happened weeks ago?"

"Wait!" exclaimed the owl. "Let me finish! As I was saying, we had
stripped away twenty-odd notices, when a couple of thrushes rushed
down and warned us to get back inside your tree as quick as lightning.
They were in a terrible fluster and we did as they said without wasting
time on questions. On our way we met rabbits who thumped their feet
and gabbled at us, their ears all a-tremble: 'Hurry, hurry, go on!'"

"We were lucky; we reached the tree in time to catch our breath and
settle ourselves at the spy-holes before four (four this time) Vulture
Men came surging through the trees, sweeping every inch of the forest

floor with their nets.

"I remember that one of the Tree People whispered in my ear, 'They must have an encampment close by, don't you think Eyes? Perhaps they heard us out and about, tearing down their notices?'

"'You may well be right,' I replied. 'At least let's hope that there are no traitors amongst the forest-creatures...'

"But the truth is, Abigail, that we have lived with that fear ever since I voiced it. I know that we have always been discreet about our comings and goings, on account of the cannibals, but I can't believe our home is an absolute secret. The woods are teeming with birds and animals."

I pinged the coal scuttle glumly and repetitively with my index finger. Then I leant back with a sigh. "Well, nobody has betrayed us yet. Carry on with your tale, Eyes. What did these four Vulture Men do next?"

"They must have been expecting us to desecrate their notices or to do something of the sort – fools that we were – because they came armed with axes this time. Great axes, with blades as broad as dinner plates and sharp as razors."

"Axes?" I asked faintly. I already knew what came next.

"Axes. And they chopped down all the trees that we had stripped of parchment. Chopped them down, one by one. So now you know why we left this one well alone."

For some minutes nobody spoke. I rose and put my eye to a peep-hole, but it was too dark to see the white stumps of my slain oaks. "My poor, poor trees," I said sadly, and then angrily: "How dare they? How dare this 'king'...?" I had never felt proprietorial about the wood before. I had called it mine, but never seriously thought of it as such: after all, I had never done anything for it, except love it, or asked anything of it, except its nightly presence. But now I found that I had subjects and enemies who would uphold or fight my ownership, so I felt newly jealous and queenly.

"You've not even heard the worst part yet," said Constantine. He struggled to suppress that unintentional smirk which people often wear when they are narrating grim news. "They've been capturing animals and torturing them: trying to force them to give you – and us - up. And when the animals refuse to speak, then the Vulture Men kill them and mark them with the sign of the King of Traumund."

"Is this true?" I said, though everybody knew I did not disbelieve the Prince.

"All too true," replied Eyes. "We have found four bodies so far: a rabbit and two blackbirds were discovered in the clearing a few weeks ago. And I found another as I returned home tonight."

He fetched the satchel that he had brought back with him and laid by the door. We crowded around the dying fire as he unstrapped the bag and pulled, from its depths, the sodden body of a grey squirrel. I laid it down tenderly in the low light and we all stared. I did not know what to say.

"Look," whispered Eyes. "Look at the fur on her breast." I bent close to the dead animal and saw that her fur had been marked in blood with the same device that Joachim, Boris and I had seen in glittering silver thread on the black cloaks of the Vulture Men. "It's horrible," I breathed, staring in fascination at the poor squirrel. "And you think she died protecting me?"

"It seems likely that she died for failing to answer questions about us and our whereabouts. I can't think of any more probable explanation."

I sat at the table and watched (or seemed to watch, though my eyes were glazed) as the squirrel was washed and wrapped in a sheet. I heard somebody telling someone else that they would bury it tomorrow, alongside the other three. Eyes poured a large tumbler of wine and offered it to me. I took a long draught.

"I feel as though I've so many questions; there are so many things I don't understand in this terrible business. Like...well like Traumund. What is Traumund? Where is it?" I turned to Eyes. "I mean, here we are at war with the king of somewhere I know nothing whatever about."

"Ah," Eyes intoned sagely. "You reach the crux of the matter with those questions. What is Traumund? Where is Traumund?" He closed his eyes.

"Do...you know the answers?" I inquired after several minutes had gone by.

Eyes nodded slowly. "I believe I do, Abigail. I believe I do. If you had asked me the same questions a month or two back I could not have answered you with any certainty. I could have recounted a legend; nothing more solid than that. But now, through my own exertions (which you will hear about shortly) the legend has solidified. I know what Traumund is. Or rather, I begin to grasp what Traumund is, which is as much as anyone can ever say."

"Go on," I urged.

"Traumund is...To put it simply, Traumund is the universe in which we find ourselves now. It is quite separate and different from the universe you know about in the Waking World, though the two are inextricably linked. Legend says that Traumund is globe-shaped, though I am unable to verify that. It is not important.

"What does matter, what defines Traumund, are the infinitely varied lands...worlds (I don't know how to describe them most accurately; it's not as though there is a word for them in common parlance...not yet anyway) that constitute it. These worlds are...well you know what they are." He stopped and looked at me searchingly.

I hesitated, afraid that my ready answer would sound stupid.

"Are they...imaginary places...like this wood?"

"Precisely!" He was pleased and excited by my reply. "Traumund is a universe made up of imaginary worlds; millions upon millions of imaginary worlds: vast, wealthy kingdoms and modest hideaways and everything in between. Worlds that are the secret domains of a billion human souls; the nocturnal retreats of a billion human brains; vast, rich, weird, wonderful, terrifying, dark, bright, beautiful creations brought together in an infinitely extendable patchwork -"

"- and the patchwork; the quilt," I interrupted, fired up by an inkling of the scale of our subject, "the quilt as a whole -"

"– is Traumund!"

"Yes! I see!"

I was standing and the owl had raised his wings so that he seemed to fill the room. I could see my glowing face reflected in his eyes. My mind raced.

"And so the man who calls himself the King of Traumund...My God...he is...How can anyone pronounce himself king of all those worlds? All those worlds that he has had no hand in; that are not his?"

"He is a megalomaniac." Eyes agreed.

"A megalomaniac of epic proportions!" I exclaimed. "A...isn't there a word that's more expressive than megalomaniac?" I sat down, and my friends and I fell silent in our efforts to comprehend the magnitude of the "king's" presumption.

"So...what shall I do?" I asked at length.

"What shall we do." corrected Constantine, reassuringly.

Nobody answered for a while. Then Boris asked me, rather unhelpfully, as people always do in these quandaries, "What do you think we should do?"

I almost answered, "I don't know, what do you think?" but then I remembered that, as their figurehead, I ought to make a more decisive response. So I started fiddling with the ring at the top of the poker and said, "I think I should find this 'King of Traumund'."

"And what then?" said Boris.

I floundered. "...Um...I don't know. Argue with him. Fight him. Kill him." I laughed nervously at the very sound of such words issuing from my unheroic mouth. Nobody else laughed, but they didn't cheer either. Eyes studied me closely as I sat with my chin in my hands. Eventually he spoke,

"Find the 'king' by all means, but remember that you are practically powerless. We already know that he has at least four Vulture Men, and he is likely to have many more than that. Armies of them, probably. And you...you have us and perhaps a few squirrels and blackbirds."

"And a poker," I added. Again, nobody laughed. Eyes refilled my tumbler.

"Alone, you are powerless," he repeated.

"What do you think I should do, Eyes?" It occurred to me that for some time now he had looked like an owl with an idea. I was right.

"I think you should venture out of your land and into Traumund, and gather a band of allies."

"You mean I should go into other people's lands?"

"Yes."

"But I can't do that. Surely it's too intrusive...it's wrong...It's what the Vulture Men do."

"I know, I know," said the owl, shaking his head and clenching his eyes. "It's barbarously unconventional, to say the least. But you must! You have no choice! Your land has been violated by a ruthless power, so have other people's: so has Joachim's – yes, Boris told us about Joachim's letter. You are weak. Joachim is weak. Every land in Traumund is weak while it stands alone. You must unite if you are to defy this self-styled 'king'."

I thought for a while, my fingers drumming excitedly on the coal scuttle. Then, despite myself, as though gravity had forced the idea from my brain to my lips, I cried,

"I wish I could discover Ludovick Montefiore's land! If I can't find him in the Waking World then perhaps I can find him here? He would help us; he would know what to do!"

Eyes sighed. "Abigail, you forget the dimensions with which we are dealing. The prospect of finding a particular land is well-nigh impossible. Which makes my news all the more remarkable."

"News?"

"I have – I think – already found one ally."

"Who's that then?" I asked, trying to wrench my mind from its own impractical stratagems.

"Joachim," answered the owl.

"Joachim?"

Eyes surveyed my face, flattered by its open-mouthed attention.

"At least, I seem to have discovered his land and his painted house. You remember how he described it to you and you described it to us – in strictest secrecy of course. I never thought to make use of his confidence. I only hope he will forgive us..."

I brushed all that aside. I couldn't remember what there might be to forgive.

"But how, Eyes? How on earth?"

"Purely by chance. Remarkable chance. Or fate. You see, I have been turning this scheme around in my head for some time – the idea of gathering allies to your cause. Ever since I tore that insolent notice from your tree and read it, the idea has been gathering strength. There was no harm in proving the legend and scouting around other lands while you were away, watching people on the quiet to judge their suitability. I flew out night after night (and Traumund nights are long), covering mile upon mile of land (and Traumund miles are boundless), but even so (and this proves how amazing Joachim's proximity really is) you must understand that if Traumund were a palace then in all this time I have barely traversed the width of its smallest keyhole.

"My journeys became longer as the weeks wore on and the night before last I flew further than I had ever managed before. Land after land fell away beneath me and I scanned them all – lingering over some, wheeling away high and fast from others. I was just about to turn for home when I felt the touch of semi-recognition, as though somebody too far away had waved and bellowed my name, although there were only trees (that same vast swathe of forest to which your land belongs) and night breezes beneath me. I flew lower and saw colours gleaming between the branches. I flew lower still and saw that it was a brightly-painted house, its windows and doors flung open to the night and there was music stretching out sinuous arms from every opening to pull me down. So down I came until I could see through the open window. I did not show myself to him; I thought it best if you... There was a boy there, playing on a violin... "

"That's him! It must be! That's Joachim!" I cried. I was so excited by the thought of my friend's proximity that I chafed at my inability to reach him at once. I stood up and walked in circles. People began to move and chatter around me. Eyes laughed.

"Wait!" he said. "We can't go now. The journey is relatively short, but it is also longer than you can possibly imagine. We need time to prepare…"

"But I will go?"

"Yes you will, but -"

"Tomorrow night then!"

The owl hesitated. "I agree with you that we must not waste time. After all, Joachim is only one ally and we must gather many more. And who knows when the Vulture Men may return? But have you considered - "

"Eyes!" Delay seemed to me to be a physical impossibility. "I leave all the practical arrangements to you. We leave here for Joachim's land tomorrow night."

I gloried in my new forcefulness. It shocked them. I liked to shock them.

The owl nodded slowly and answered, "Whatever you say. Tomorrow night, then."

Mrs. Veals

The thought of the coming night's journey saved me from despair when I woke, that first morning, in my bed at Boughwinds Abbey. Since Traumund demanded all my attention, and since Ludovick Montefiore was absent, I felt distanced from the Waking World. My fruitless journey to the abbey, with its various encounters, was a story that I thought I could break away from, like a book that I put down with tired eyes, meaning to take it up again shortly.

At first I thought I would spend the day in hiding, watching the clock and waiting for the night to come with its adventures. But the longer I lay, the more my mind dwelt upon Ludovick Montefiore. At least I could wait for the night here, in his abbey. At least I could look around my room – his room – and down from his window over his grounds. Perhaps I would see him gallop up the drive on his horse and then I would lean from the window. He would look up with a smile and everything, everything - in this world and the other - would be resolved. At this I rolled over in bed and laughed at myself for imagining his horseback gallop, when of course he would arrive in the back of a taxi or at the wheel of a car.

This room, though, this room was the room of a man who drove horses, not cars. It was old, creaking and cold, its draughts imperfectly stopped by carpets and curtains whose once-rich colours had faded into a pink-brown monochrome. I let myself down to the floor and pulled my coat on. The furniture – four-poster bed, fire-place, armchair, wardrobe and chest of draws - was unapologetically massive and dark, with were patterns and stories carved along legs and sides, whose exoticism seemed at once forbidding and (after the superficiality of life at the

Institute) friendly. Above the unlit hearth and opposite the window there were framed oil-paintings, screwed fast to the wall. These were so very dark and shiny that I had great difficulty in making anything of them, but I think I deciphered a mastiff's snout and a cavalier's white cheek-bones and black ringlets. The walls – what I could see of them between the paintings, the wardrobe and the curtained bed – were unevenly darkened by centuries of soot, but I curled my lip at Miss Konder when she appeared in my mind's eye with a roller and a tray of fresh emulsion. This was the abbey of my imagination: a place where hooded monks must have lived once and surly squires and doomed lovers.

I pulled the curtains back from the window and gasped with a fresh sense of expectation fulfilled. There was the sweeping drive that my mind had drawn a few moments ago. There were rose gardens and a maze and a green-brown, tree-shadowed pond. There to my right was a stable-block and a paddock, where muscular horses grazed and snorted and chased against the morning breeze. The landscape was dark, because the sky was a level grey and because the woods were crowded so close and high about Boughwinds' grassy basin. The darkness signified something to me though: a sort of fullness and promise, as though the landscape were a sponge, soaked and darkened by its own history and on-going intrigue. I shivered and wrapped my dirty coat around my shoulders.

I was just thinking that I could happily wile away my day in the gardens or (since rain was beginning to fleck the arched window) in exploring the house, when I heard a key in the lock and the door opened abruptly. My expanding spirits shrank at the noise. I snatched up my bag and turned to face the door quickly; nervously.

I was sure, almost at once, that the person who stood in the doorway was the one who had let me in last night: her movements, her smell and soon her voice, confirmed it. I was sure, just as quickly, that I disliked her. She was one of those people who are so inherently unattractive that it is difficult even to pity them. I do not mean that she was ugly, though she was certainly plain enough with her large, square limbs, long, flat breasts and sparse, grey hair. Nor did she say or do anything to me that marked her out as a monster. In fact all she said was, "School begins in half an hour. Breakfast is laid out in the dining-room," that, you will argue, was innocent enough.

But, you see, her eyes were dead. She looked at me – alone and lost and friendless – with as much sympathy as though I was a fly struggling on its back, half-dead. I felt she would look at me like that whatever I did or said. She would look just the same whether she passed me a slice of toast or brought an axe down on my head. She was not redeemed by the appearance of any faint, excusing charm, such as self-doubt or shyness. Even a superficial grace would have been something, would at least have left me wondering, as I used to do (at times) over Miss Konder when I envied her self-possession and guiltily desired her approval. With this woman there was no doubt: she filled the doorway like a stone monument to heartlessness.

I flashed an uncertain smile at her dead eyes, despite my immediate dislike. They were large, mud-brown eyes, like jars of pond-water and when they met mine I was inversely reminded of Ludovick Montefiore's sea-blue scrutiny. When he had looked at me, I had felt uneasy, but my uneasiness goaded me forward, prompted vague longings, made me expand, somehow, inside myself. When she surveyed me I shrivelled defensively.

"My name is Mrs. Veals," she barked, as I followed her along the freezing gallery. "I am the housekeeper here at Boughwinds Abbey. I also run the school. When you have finished your breakfast we will remove to the school building, where you may as well try to fit in, until your godfather's return."

"Really…" I stammered huskily, for my throat was dry, "I'd really rather amuse myself. I'm sure Mr. Montefiore wouldn't mind."

Mrs. Veals made no response. I shrugged; my eyes rested on her mannish lace-up shoes. Upstairs, downstairs, through passages and hallways we marched, until we arrived at the dining room. The air had a fragile touch of warmth in it at last, for a young coal fire – still shiny and black - had been lit in the grate. It was a high, airy room with a bay window whose light whitened the polish on the long, mahogany table. I would have liked to pace around the table, listening to the wealthy, leisured sounds of my steps upon the wooden floor, the spitting of the fire and the ticking of the grandfather clock. As it was, the housekeeper pointed me to a chair, took a ladle to the silver tureen that stood on the sideboard and presented me with a bowl of cold, gluey porridge.

I waded through it, with the assistance of a small wine-glass full of water. Mrs. Veals sat down opposite me, her dead features suddenly animated by a smile. She leaned forward in her eagerness to watch. It was a surreal and sinister meal, which I recall with uncomprehending shame. Her eyes followed every spoonful from bowl to mouth and back again. She breathed a private laugh through her nose when I retched.

I tried to push the unfinished plate away but her glassy eyes narrowed and she made as though to rise, so I pulled it back and continued. With every mouthful I loathed her more, until it seemed to me that my loathing had taken on material form and become porridge.

At last, when I was sick and thirsty and full of hatred, I let my spoon clatter onto my empty plate. I had been strangely humiliated and therefore I did not look up. I wondered whether Mrs. Veals had a special aversion towards me,or whether she was generally sadistic and, if so, why my godfather employed her.

"Now," said the housekeeper, in a satisfied tone, "It's time we removed you to the school building. I hope you haven't left anything in the bedroom."

"Can't I sleep there tonight?"

"Certainly not! We don't allow pupils in the main part of the house. You will sleep in the dormitory, with Fay."

"Fay?"

"Follow. Quickly now."

I followed my jailer through the ground floor to the back of the house. We passed many dark doorways and curving staircases and I wondered whether I should make a dash for freedom, especially when I glimpsed a library, with ladders on wheels and row upon heady row of books, but I considered it would be a poor sort of freedom when Mrs. Veals knew the house so much better than I. Besides, I was too cowardly to risk a more explicit hostility.

We stepped out of a backdoor, into a yard, where the winter air was scarcely colder than the abbey's own indoor climate. Across the yard, behind a row of smart black railings, I saw what I least expected to see: horribly familiar; horribly incongruous with my surroundings. I looked up at Mrs. Veals with distrustfully, but she was calm and did not notice my dismay.

"…Institute?" I said.

Mrs. Veals looked down at me. "Yes, it's our little Institute," she replied expressionlessly. "The Institute of Social and Personal Advancement," she added, reading out loud the notice that I had already seen attached to the smart railings and read twenty times over in uncomprehending haste. "It's a lot smaller than most Institutes of course – a lot smaller – we only have two pupils; three counting you. But it's run along precisely the same principles. Mr. Montefiore is devoted to the education of young people." She lifted the bunch of keys that clinked from a string at her waist and began to sift through them.

"My godfather has nothing to do with this," I declared, as I stood stock-still in the drizzling yard.

Mrs. Veals placed a mannish hand upon my shoulder and thrust me into the school building. As I tottered through the doorway I heard – at least, I'm almost sure I heard – the sound of hooves, galloping fast at the front of the house and scattering the gravel on the driveway. Half mindful of my earlier daydream, I knocked the housekeeper's hand from my shoulder and ducked back into the yard. But nothing could take her by surprise. She lunged at me, grabbed my arms and twisted them behind my back. Then she picked me up, as though I was a wriggling hen and she a chef, lugging me into the school building. I heard the front door click shut. She battered my head and torso against two more inner-doors, that swung apart as I hit them, then flung me down upon a concrete floor.

After a moment's pause I lifted my face and tried to flex my bruised arms. I know this room, I thought, though I had seen nothing more than the concrete beneath my nose. I know this metallic light, the smell of cheap detergent, the murmur of radiators sending out their swampy heat-waves. When I look up, I thought, I will see bare white walls, and slick blinds and book-less shelves: soul-dead brutality posing as stylishness. I looked up and found that I was right.

Perhaps it was rather melodramatic of me, but I could not persuade myself to move until I heard a childish snigger and realised that Mrs. Veals was not the only witness to my prostration. I rolled over and pulled myself into a sitting position. Mrs. Veals said, "It would be more polite to stand up," so I stood up. It was as though I had no recourse to an inner dignity: my sense of self-worth simply bowed to her judgement because she was stronger than me.

"Abigail, this is Fay and Marcus. They are brother and sister; they live on a farm in Boughwinds village, though they board here during term time. And this is Abigail Crabtree, who joins us somewhat unexpectedly…"

"How long for?" whined Marcus, a greasy ten year old with bad teeth. It was he who had sniggered.

"We don't know," replied Mrs. Veals.

"Until my godfather gets here," I ventured.

Fay crossed her legs and rocked back in her chair with a sigh (Mrs. Veals did not make them stand up I noticed resentfully). I wished, with all the vehemence that seethed behind my face, that Fay could be greasy and yellow-toothed like her brother. But she was beautiful in the Institute style, with long, firm, brown limbs; regular, blue-eyed features and a mane of blond hair. She reeked of perfumes and sprays. When she spoke, she looked at her glittering nails, not at me.

"Your godfather…?" she murmured, so bored by the effort of framing a question that she barely seemed to notice whether or not I answered it.

"My godfather owns Boughwinds Abbey and this building and everything," my tone was imprudently defensive, so I tried to alter it and mould it, instead, on Fay's coolness. "He doesn't like me to attend classes like yours…Institute schools are…well, they aren't very academic are they? They're for unacademic people really, that is fine… only they're not for me."

Fay tilted her head and bit her thumb nail. Her burnished lips moved lazily, but the look she gave me was more like a slash than a smile. It punctured all my inflated hauteur and my gaze slumped.

"Don't chew your nails, Fay." Mrs. Veals commanded. "No, Abigail, you must stay standing at the front," (I had sidled into the plastic chair next to Marcus). "I will need you as a model during maths. We will begin with maths this morning."

This was not quite like the Institute then, where the word 'maths' was unknown, let alone taught, under any guise. I wondered whether the difference could be put down to the character of Mrs. Veals, who seemed to hold sole sway over this mini school. I knew already that her malevolence was real, but it was not Miss Konder's stylish brand. She had none of Miss Konder's ease in her role as Institute mistress - how could she when her own clothes were dull and shapeless; when she did not wear nail polish or perfume; when (I smirked shamelessly) she had cropped her hair by herself, and done away with all the nonsense of beautification? Had she been left to herself, I thought, she would have taught with a battery of grammars and long division sums and lists of dry facts. She would have kept a supply of dunces' hats and smacked our heads with a wooden ruler. Who made her teach the slick values of the Institute…? I began to ask myself this question, but I did not like it, so I pushed it away vigorously.

"Take your coat off, Abigail," continued Mrs. Veals. (Mrs? I could not believe she had ever married. What sort of man, in what conceivable circumstances would have married such a monster?…My silent backchat, the cattier it became, sustained my flagging spirits.) I obeyed again. At least I was glad to take my grubby coat off - the heat in this bunker was stifling and besides, I could see Fay surveying it. My palms were pink and damp, my fingertips leaving a mark on Mrs. Veals' chrome desk as I touched it in passing. I felt Fay's slit-eyed scrutiny and my hot cheeks boiled.

"Take that big jumper off as well." Once again I did as I was told, though more slowly and uncertainly. Was this woman going to make me strip naked? After the porridge incident I could almost believe it. But no.

"Right, that'll do. I don't think we want to see all of Abigail Crabtree!"

Marcus tittered. Fay gave a liquid sniff that – issuing from her nostrils – managed to sound chic.

"Silence," growled the housekeeper. She took a green chalk from one of the capacious pockets that bulged around her grey smock. Then she turned to the black board at the head of the tiny classroom and proceeded to draw the crude outline of a human being. The character, though roughly drawn, was represented wearing jeans and a long-sleeved t-shirt. It had haystack hair, a dirty face, a peculiar slouch, one long eyebrow across the forehead and an expression of drunken bemusement. When Mrs. Veals had finished (and this took some time, for she kept adding afterthoughts: a few spots on the face; a bit more width around the hips...etc) she wrote in capital letters over the head: ABIGAIL CRABTREE.

Marcus burst into uncontrollable giggles - or rather, he worked hard at making them seem uncontrollable. Fay picked at her thumb nail.

Alongside my portrait, Mrs. Veals drew two columns. The first one she headed: CHANGES REQUIRED. The second one she entitled COST OF CHANGES. I noticed with disgust that while she was concentrating she stuck her tongue between her teeth and pulled her lips apart to reveal a row of greying gums. They looked like slivers of rotting steak.

"Now!" she resumed, closing her mouth and then licking the dryness away from her lips. "Today's maths challenge is an interesting one. Abigail," (here she struck my skull with a rolled up copy of Hey Guys!) "has been invited to a formal dinner, that will be attended by lots of important, beautiful and well-dressed people."

Marcus pretended that the fist that he had planted inside his considerable mouth was no longer a sufficient stopper against his bubbling mirth. He let out a snorting whoop of derision. Fay pulled her left shoulder up to her neck and turned away from him with an expression of disdain. She was sitting sideways now, gazing at the blinds.

Mrs. Veals ploughed on. As she spoke she flashed glances at me from the edges of her eyes. I tried to seem unmoved, but my cheeks were turning from pink to purple and I could not stop my hands from trembling.

"I want you, Fay and Marcus, to outline all the changes that will be required in Abigail's appearance before we can let her loose in such society. And when you've done that, I want you to work out the total cost of Abigail's transformation. But we will begin by filling column one....Yes. Marcus."

Marcus's hand had already shot up as though he was straining to touch the ceiling. I think his bottom left the seat as he answered breathlessly, "She needs to lose weight, to buy some clothes that actually fit, to get some new moisturising cream, to have her hair styled, to get -"

"-that will do for the moment, thank you Marcus." Mrs. Veals interrupted as her chalk raced across the black board, jotting down all his suggestions. "Fay? Have you got any ideas?"

"No," replied the girl, tossing her hair back lightly and pulling it into a pony tail.

Mrs. Veals swiped Fay's cheek with the rolled up magazine. "That I do not accept," she snapped. "You will make a full contribution to this class, Fay Price, or...I shall cut your hair off."

I don't know how Mrs. Veals withstood the glacial blast from Fay's eyes, but it passed through her as though it was nothing.

"OK." Fay murmured, addressing a smile to her superior inner-self. "Well?"

Fay surveyed me, as though I were an accessory that she might or might not buy.

"Actually her hair is kind of nice. And her coat is cool."

Mrs. Veals stooped until her face was inches from Fay's and rapped the desk legs with her magazine-baton. Fay drew back with a supercilious lift of her pencilled brows.

"And her skin? Her size?"

Fay shrugged. "Whatever."

Mrs Veals sprang into huffing, puffing action. "Right," she snorted quickly, clenching and unclenching her fists and rapidly smoothing her dress. "Right. I've had enough. I have wanted to do this for a long, long time, Fay Price. Those goldilocks are coming off."

The three of us watched, speechless, as Mrs. Veals rummaged in her desk draw and produced a pair of scissors. No not scissors; shears: they were as long as my forearm. She held them open in front of Fay's face and then snapped them shut. They made a grinding, rusty, slicing sound. Fay's complacency showed its first fracture. She said nothing, but her eyes were wide and her mouth was slack. She pulled her long hair against her neck and covered it, as far as she was able, with her hands.

Perhaps I felt a servile fealty to Fay on account of her hauteur. Perhaps I glimpsed the possibility of an alliance against Mrs. Veals. At any rate, I felt an unexpected desire to rescue the blond ponytail.

"I think," I gabbled, "that that would be against the whole spirit of the Institute. Cutting hair like that, I mean. Short hair is fine -" (Fay darted me a look) "- I mean, it's not. It's not fine. But it might be if you went to a proper hairdresser and had it done properly. But this isn't how they cut hair at the Institute. Honestly, I was at one for a while and they didn't use gardening shears, ever. Never, ever. It's - "

Mrs. Veals snatched the yellow rope from Fay's grasp, yanking it so hard that she was pulled from her chair. She shrieked with pain.

"-it's probably not a good idea," I continued rather pathetically, hopping from one foot to the other, "I don't think it's fair...Ow!" Mrs. Veals brought a clumpy heel hard against my shin. I felt as though I had been kicked by a cart horse. The shin is such an aggravating place to be hurt: somehow it makes you feel taunted as well as physically pained. My fury had a free-reign: I clung onto Mrs. Veal's arm and cried,

"LEAVE HER ALONE!"

Mrs. Veals brushed me off like a cake crumb. For the second time that morning I crashed face down upon the concrete. As I tried to rise I heard a rasping click and I saw an airy mass of yellow hair drift down to the floor. Some strands passed near my face, forming matted strings in the blood that was dripping from my nostrils.

For half a minute the room reverberated with a shocked silence, as though the scissors had cut through a mounting shrillness. Then Marcus started tittering again and Fay relaxed into muted sobs. Mrs. Veals stood breathing heavily, her rusty blades still poised.

Then, quite unexpectedly, the stillness was shattered.

It was shattered by a thunderous hammering, as though a giant had emerged from the woods to beat against the building with his club, or if the classroom had been carried off inside a thunder-cloud, or the winter raindrops were turning into rocks as they hit the low, metal roof. It was a tremendous noise: I squinted up at the walls and ceiling, half-expecting a blizzard of plaster.

For a moment we were united in an attitude of puzzled alarm. Fay stopped crying. Mrs. Veals was galvanised so far as to turn towards the door. Marcus shrank into his seat and asked, in a tiny voice, "What's that?"

Dazedly I said, "It's…I think…is somebody banging on the outside door?"

I was right, but nobody heard me. As I spoke the front door crashed open under the pressure of all that wrathful pounding. We heard quick, heavy steps in the passageway. Four pairs of eyes were glued to the classroom door as the feet paused outside it. Then the door smashed back against the wall to reveal the figure of Ludovick Montefiore, his face and hands white and clammy with sickness and anger.

Mrs. Veals and I moved simultaneously: she stepped forward, spreading out her palms in a pleading gesture; I raised my head with a shout.

"Get back!" exclaimed my godfather as Mrs. Veals advanced. He pushed against the air with his hand, as though to strike her or cast her into the corridor. "Get out! Go! Now!" I heard a clicking sound in her throat and then she scuttled away, like an over-sized beetle.

Fay and Marcus watched as Ludovick Montefiore knelt down by my head and said, "Abigail," though he could still barely catch his breath. I was so proud, that I looked up, not at him, but at them, as he spoke. Then he helped me to my feet, gently wiping the blood from my nose and chin with a handkerchief from his own pocket. He did not spare a glance for the others.

The Watercolour Painting

udovick Montefiore whisked me out into the drizzling yard, and then back through the old house. I say that he whisked me, even though I am not certain that he lifted me or even touched me at all, because I do not remember walking. I felt as though I was in a dream where nothing was solid, not even my feet, nor the wet concrete and polished floorboards they trod. My eyes seemed to have moved from the centre of my face to the tips of stalks on top of my head and so I watched myself beneath my own gaze, floating through the passageways on dithering insect wings.

Ludovick Montefiore brought me to a room at the front of the house. Like last night's bedroom and this morning's breakfast room, it belonged to the Boughwinds Abbey of my imagination. Two bay windows towered over the front garden, looking like hinged screens of vivid, trickling greens and greys. Paintings hung all around the walls and a shabby writing bureau crouched inside an alcove. There were various chairs and low stools ranged around the fireplace, which comprised a stone cavern approximately equal in size to a garden shed. Inside the cavern a hefty pile of logs, enough to fuel a respectable bonfire, bellowed and spat their thick, golden rods of fire.

"Come here, rest on this sofa Abigail. Lie back." As he spoke he pushed with his knees against the back of a yellow plush sofa, rolling it closer to the hearth. I perched stiffly on the edge of the seat, as I was too self-conscious to abandon myself to real comfort.

Beside the fireplace there hung a bell-rope. It was made of pink and gold silk spirals and it ended in a short fluffy tassel. Ludovick Montefiore fingered the tassel for a moment in silence, then suddenly he grasped it and tugged sharply. Almost immediately I heard an answering clangour within the bowels of the house. Ludovick Montefiore pulled the rope again and again and again and by doing so he seemed to feed some inner fury, so that each pull was more violent than the last one and seemed to follow on more rapidly.

Seconds after he had first touched the bell-rope I heard flat shoes slapping along the passage and Mrs. Veals entered breathlessly. "Yes, Sir?" she inquired between gasps, her hand pressed against the place where her heart should be.

My godfather continued his assault on the bell-rope. Clang, clang, clang, answered the hysterical bell, somewhere far beneath our feet. As he pulled he stared at the housekeeper with a menacing lack of expression. I was afraid of, even embarrassed by, his resolute demolition of her composure, but I could not do anything to stop him. I told myself that I need not wish him to stop.

Ludovick Montefiore let go of the rope abruptly and it whipped up the wall before dropping beside his shoulder, where it bounced from side to side as though recovering its breath and whispering to itself, Calm Down, calm down, …calm…down. My godfather let the bell itself fade into stillness, before he broke the new calm with bullet words.

"Warm, salted water. Cotton wool. Coffee. Toast. Now!"

"Yes, sir," murmured Mrs. Veals, stooping at the shoulders and turning to leave. Then, pausing, she asked (whether through genuine opacity, or else a brave, residual aggression),

"Will that be coffee and toast for two, sir?"

As Ludovick Montefiore took a step towards her, his pasty cheeks took on a pink tinge, while his knuckles whitened even against the white of his fists. His words were so soft that at first I could not hear their bite.

"Am I to understand that you, Mrs. Veals, would like to join us? That you are proposing to bless Abigail and me with your charming presence? That you were hoping to provide coffee and toast for three?"

"No, sir, I - "

"No. Then it will be coffee and toast for two, Mrs. Veals."

The door clicked shut. He shivered and pressed his fingers to his temples. A minute or two passed before he spoke. His eyes were closed against the warmth of the fire and his face was invisible to me.

"Abigail, I am so terribly sorry. I don't know what to say. If I had only been here, if I had only known you were coming…You were quicker than I thought…"

"You couldn't have known," I replied, tripping over the words in my eagerness to reassure him. "You see, I couldn't warn you. I wish I could have warned you, but you see - "

"But that woman! How dare she treat you with such disrespect! No...with such cruelty! How dare she?"

Perplexities that had half-awoken earlier and drifted back to sleep, stirred again and made me ask timidly,

"Why do you employ her?" My question hid the assumption that Ludovick Montefiore had only just recognised his employee's depravity and that he would, he must, immediately dismiss her. He replied vaguely however,

"Why indeed? For no good reason. Because she's always been here."

My perplexities, unsoothed, wanted to know more.

"And why is there an Institute here at Boughwinds?" I murmured.

He looked at me with his mouth slightly open, perhaps hesitantly, perhaps bemusedly.

"I mean," I explained, "An Institute of Social and Personal Advancement. That's what the notice said outside the schoolhouse and she – Mrs. Veals – said that it might only be small but it was still run along the same lines...and everything."

My godfather kicked one of the logs thoughtfully. Sparks glowed and then blackened beside my shoes. I shifted my feet.

"I always liked the idea of running a school here," he replied, "and I always thought that Mrs. Veals would make the perfect school ma'am. But she's got out of hand. I've been away a good deal, so I know little - nothing - about the school except what she chooses to tell me." He kicked the log again as his moodiness melted into enthusiasm. "She's never spoken to me about turning the enterprise into an Institute. Never! Where on earth has she got her ideas from? If I'd only known...!" He kicked the log ferociously and leapt back with a sudden laugh as it tumbled forwards onto the hearth.

Mrs. Veals re-entered with a tray. Ludovick Montefiore pointed to a green baize card table and she set it down. She scuttled back to the door, my godfather allowing her to set one foot in the passage. Then he fired languorously.

"I hear you've taken it into your head to start running an 'Institute of Social and Personal Advancement', Mrs. Veals?"

"Sir?"

"You must regard yourself as a rather glamorous girl?"

"Sir, please, I only - "

"Not now, woman! Do you think I want to hear your blathering now? I shall allow you to speak in my own time. Clear off."

"Sir." The door shut with barely a click.

Ludovick Montefiore rolled up his sleeves and dipped a wad of cotton wool into the salted water. Then he wiped my wounded face, cleaning it more thoroughly now than he had been able to do with his dry handkerchief. I noticed that his fingers were long and clean and that, judging by his slowness, by the faint smile on his face, he took pleasure in musing as he squeezed hot water from the white fluff. I also noticed that he expressed no involuntary distaste as he wiped the clotting stains from my nostrils and upper lip. In fact, though he worked efficiently over my face, he did not seem to register it. He looked through my increasingly bold stare, as though his thoughts were far away.

"There!" he exclaimed as he finished. Now he smiled broadly at me and I quickly lightened my own expression. "Now, is coffee acceptable or are you in need of something stronger? Brandy? Wine?" He laughed as a repulsed expression broke through my shyness; wrinkling my nose and making me smile. "Ah ha! You sneer at my offer of spirits, do you? Hmm, well, let's just wait a few years and we'll see…we'll see. In the meantime, coffee. I'll pour and you help yourself to toast. The beauteous Veals will bring more of either if you haven't enough. Milk?"

I was half-inclined to feel shocked by my godfather's verbal brutality and by his housekeeper's frightened submission, but I reassured myself that his victim was Mrs. Veals. At that thought I forgave and applauded him. I was flattered too, by the contrast between his harshness towards her and his kindness towards me. It added a dangerous element of gratitude to my love.

"Milk?" he repeated patiently.

"Oh…milk…er…yes, please."

"Sugar?"

"No thank you."

We settled back with our cups and plates, Ludovick Montefiore on one side of the fire, I on the other. Then he said, "So…?" I hastily swallowed my mouthful of toast.

"I'm sorry, I forgot. I haven't told you what happened."

"I hope you are not in great difficulty or danger? But I suppose you must be. I expected it, I'm afraid, as I told you last time we met. Tell me everything."

"I think I am in danger. The strangest things have happened to me since I was in London. But all the same, I'm afraid I haven't anything satisfying to tell, because I don't understand anything."

"I don't see why that should spoil a good tale," he remarked.

Then I told him about the woman in the veiled hat, how I had escaped her clutches and made my own way to Boughwinds Abbey. As I talked, Ludovick Montefiore stared at me. He never took so much as a sip of coffee. His eyes were wide and unselfconsciously excited by the twists and turns of my story. I wished that I was skilful enough to turn my narrative to my own advantage: to make the heroine more admirable than she really was and to make him fall in love with her. But it was all I could do to voice the amateurish words that came to my tongue.

He sighed as my story drew to a close. "And I was away on business in London," he said gloomily. "I really am so sorry, Abigail."

"Please don't apologise anymore," I pleaded, not just because it seemed the polite thing to say, but also because I was genuinely appalled that this man, who crushed demonic housekeepers under the heel of his shoe, should demean himself, however slightly, before me. "I think she is around here somewhere, the woman with the veiled hat. I'm sure she was lurking among the trees as I walked from the village to the abbey. Who do you think she is? And why do you suppose -"

"I don't know," he interrupted, as though the question was beyond consideration. I was surprised: judging by his interest in my story I had expected him to mull it over at length, however fruitlessly. "I'm sorry, I've absolutely no idea. But don't be afraid of her anymore. You are safe while you are with me."

"And do you think my family will be safe from her?" I asked, clutched all of a sudden by a new fear.

"Oh yes," he replied, reassuringly airy this time. "It sounds as though you and you alone, were the object of all this interest, don't you think?"

"I don't know...I suppose so..."

"I'm perfectly sure of it," he declared, and that was that.

Our coffee cups were as small as egg-cups and as delicate as egg-shells. I thought them pretty: they were white and green and the painted people who pranced around their sides wore high wigs and vast skirts, or knee-breeches and three-cornered hats. The cups did not hold much coffee though and, thanks to our absorption, we had forgotten to refill them. Ludovick Montefiore pressed one palm against the tall silver pot.

"Tepid," he said. He rang the bell - just once this time and faintly. Mrs. Veals was soon to be heard lumbering towards our sitting-room.

"Fresh coffee," ordered Ludovick Montefiore, pointing at the pot and strolling over to one of his windows. My twinge of shame was soothed once again by his authoritative coolness. I caught Mrs. Veals' eye and moved my lips in that mockery of a smile that I had so often seen Miss Konder make. Then I summoned all my audacity and strolled to my godfather's side. I imagined her impotent glare like a phantom knife in my back.

"May I look at your pictures?" I asked at his elbow. "Of course, my dear!" he replied, complying with my obsequious tone: perhaps because he understood that my object was to bait Mrs. Veals. She backed out of the room carefully, with the pot of wasted coffee.

There were more portraits in here: powdered women who sat amidst spaniels and moist-lipped children; a man who held his wild-eyed horse on a prominence overlooking the moor and returned my studious gaze with a savage glare. These paintings, like the ones in my bedroom, were grimy with age and massive. I had to take several steps back and strain my neck in order to take them in. There was another painting though, whose trim freshness caught my eye.

It hung above the shabby bureau that stood in an alcove near the door. I needed to scrutinise it closely in order to make any sense of it.

This is what I saw, after I had peered and thought for some time: a framed watercolour on heavily-grained white paper or card, brightly coloured and in a Chinese style, depicting a simple river scene. Green and blue jabs indicated the flowing current of water. Two boats, formed from five or six lines of blue and orange paint, sailed across the river. Beyond the boats there were two narrow, reedy banks and above them a hollow red sun emerged from a green cloud. In the top right hand corner there was a green '4' and in the top left hand corner a Chinese character. This last detail, above all, elbowed my memory but I could not think why.

"That's a copy of a mah-jong tile."

Ludovick Montefiore stood at my shoulder. I hope he did not see me start at his words. He was a high, broad man, but he could move as stealthily as a cat.

A mah-jong tile. A what? I thought and then I remembered the box that had caught my attention at the King Henry Hotel and the tiles inside it.

"Did you say it was a game?"

My godfather did not answer and I discovered, when I looked around, that he was standing by the window once again with his back to me.

I shot the picture a farewell glance and this time I saw something I had failed to see before: a faint, pencilled inscription on the bottom right hand corner of the paper. The writing was round and confident – rather childish – and it said,

"To my dearest Ludovick. All my love, Allecto."

My cheeks turned warm, then the warmth flared into a jealous heat and I asked, with a petulant urgency that shocked me,

"Who is Allecto?"

"What?" He turned and I tried to meet him with a commonplace expression. I touched the frame tentatively and he frowned. "She is nobody."

Mrs. Veals sidled in with a fresh pot of coffee and I forgot the little watercolour.

We settled by the fire again with our coffee cups and all at once I was overcome with an incredulity because it seemed that the impossible was happening to me here and now and that my fantastical dreams were being properly fulfilled: translated, that is, from the world of my imagination to the world of my senses. To be welcomed so kindly in this house, by this man! My happiness really did resemble intoxication. I felt that I could talk and talk, and then I felt that I should talk and talk in order to make sense – profound and beautiful sense - of myself.

"There is something else I want to talk to you about…if you don't mind. If you've time." My words made me faint with excitement: it was as though I had grasped his hand in a brilliantly executed access of emotion. I felt he would be touched (as I was) by my needy plea and shaken (as I was) by my demanding tone of voice.

He answered with querying eyes, and I had a fleeting recollection of those same blue eyes in London, which was accompanied by a fleeting urge to clamp my lips together and say no more. But it was too late. Besides, hadn't I promised my friends that I would seek his help?

"Do you know of a place called Traumund?"

My godfather leaned forward slowly. He set his cup and saucer down with a rattle, almost as though his hand had trembled. Instead of answering my question he said,

"Sit closer to the fire."

I shuffled forward, and he pulled his own chair closer to the flames, and to me. My right cheek was a plane of hot red.

"Now," he resumed. "What do you wish to tell me about Traumund?"

"That it is in great danger from a man who calls himself its king."

Ludovick Montefiore hesitated. Then he tilted his head, questioning my reply. "But how? There can't be a King of Traumund, can there? It would be like being a king of...of not just the universe but of many universes."

"But this man calls himself the King of Traumund. He has servants who look like men, except that their heads are like vultures' heads and they ride black horses and they have been in my land trying to make me leave it. I don't think it's just me and my land. I think the 'king' wants to possess all of Traumund."

"How?"

"Well, at first the Vulture Man just told me to go back to the Waking World and stay there forever. But then he changed his tune. They want to bring me before the king - I mean the so-called king – himself. They have posted notices everywhere, that say that the wood will be razed unless I am given up … My part of Traumund is a wood, you see and my friends and I live inside a hollow tree."

I confessed this last part with a shamefaced eagerness. I felt that I had burnt all my defences now; that there was nothing left to shield me from Ludovick Montefiore's total comprehension. Of course, I had already told Joachim about the wood, but that was different because it was a shared confession. Ludovick Montefiore neither spoke, nor smiled, nor frowned. He just sat there, sphinx-like, listening and watching me. Though I had finished speaking, I did not dare move, on account of his thoughtful gaze. My cheek was so hot that I imagined it sizzling like a slab of meat on a spit. I half-expected my hair to explode in a blaze. But I did not move.

At last he stood up and moved even closer to the flames, his forehead resting against the high mantelpiece. I felt free to lean back and massage my face.

"This is very serious, Abigail. Do you have any idea what you will do?"

I told him about Eyes' plan, that we were due to execute that very night. This involved telling him all about Joachim, of course. "Just by luck – perhaps luck – Eyes discovered that Joachim's world is close to mine. So we are going to find him and start an alliance against this king. Despot."

Ludovick Montefiore sat down again, nodding his head. He leaned the fingertips of his left hand against those of his right, pressing his chin down onto his outstretched thumbs, so that his mouth was completely hidden from me.

"I think your plan is a good one," he said at last, and I was both pleased (because I treasured his approval) and disappointed (because I had expected him to outline some vastly superior idea of his own).

"Do you have a land in Traumund?" I asked. After all, I had laid my own self bare. For the first time that morning I shrank from a rasp inside his gentle voice.

"Yes, I have a land in Traumund."

"...Sorry." I felt as abject as I sounded.

"What for?" he replied, briefly touching my cheek with his thumb. My heart rose, like a balloon, back into the giddy heights of my seventh heaven.

"I...we...wondered," I gushed with renewed enthusiasm, "Whether somehow we could find you and your land? If you could join our alliance? Lead it?"

"Of course, if you can find it. But how? There aren't any maps of Traumund and you know how unknowably vast it is. Or do you? Do you know what an incredible and unlikely achievement it was to find Joachim's land? And to find that it's a mere night-time's flight away? That's a chance in a million. It's not likely to happen again."

"Hmm." I felt dejected.

"I will think about it and see if I can't find a way. I promise. I'll make every effort."

"Thank you." We lapsed into a reflective silence.

"In the meantime!" he exclaimed suddenly, standing up and clapping his hands against his thighs. "You are to make yourself at home here. Mrs. Veals will no longer trouble you, you may be sure of that. Go wherever you like – explore the gardens and the house and make sure you come to have dinner with me every evening at eight o'clock."

"Thank you," I said again, no longer tipsy with joy, but rolling drunk.

"There is only one place that I would prefer you to leave well alone, and that is my library."

Oh. My smile faltered a little and then resumed with a glassy veneer.

"It's just that we are re-ordering it at present – re-classifying, you know – and there are papers and books all over the place, that mustn't be disturbed on any account."

"Of course."

"Listen," he said amusedly. He bent his head so far down that his chin touched his chest and he had to raise his eyes in order to look into my face. I felt very childlike. "I shall send some books up to your bedroom – so many of them, and such exciting ones that it will be like having a library all of your own."

"Thank you," I said, yet again. I realised that this was a dismissal. I went to the door. "Thank you," I said, blushing at my own robotic repetitions. "Goodbye." He nodded, smiling. Then, as I closed the door, I saw him reach once again for the bell rope.

I had not gone far before Mrs. Veals passed. She paid no attention to me. I stared at her though, noticing how her face was stripped of all its arrogance. I also noticed the anxious way in which her body, unaccustomed to hurrying, huffed and jogged towards my godfather's door. I no longer felt any pity for her though – not the tiniest scrap.

I removed my clunky shoes, so that I could feel the cold, stone flags through my socks. Then I turned and followed her. Why? Because I wanted to hear my praises sung? To hear her snubbed again? She entered the sitting room and shut the door fast behind her. I crept up and bent my face to the key-hole.

For a while I heard nothing but my clamorous pulse. I was about to scuttle away, when I heard my godfather's sharp voice saying, "Sit down, Constance." Then more silence. I wanted to clear my throat, but I did not dare: my silence had been so perfect up until now.

The door whipped open. Ludovick Montefiore stood before me and stared at my astounded face. I stared back, not from defiance of course, but because I was transfixed.

This was how I felt when I returned his stare. I felt as though I was dangling from an overhanging cliff, many hundreds of feet above a churning winter sea. Nobody was near me and I would certainly fall and die. The light was fading from the sky and through the grey dusk a few, dismal shards of rain were falling over my face. I wondered how everything could be so real: the crumbling soil in my failing fingers, the half-hearted rain and blustery wind…as though this was an ordinary moment. The black and white sea rumbled and roared beneath me and I could feel its booming echo in the vibration of my hands that were still alive and pink with cold.

That was how I felt when I returned my godfather's stare. So I tore my eyes away from his face and ran, leaving my shoes in the passageway.

Fay and Marcus

I ran through the house like a frightened cat, until I found a dark, dusty space beneath a flight of stairs. I crouched there for a long time, panting and hiding from who knows what. I cried and pushed my eyes hard against my fists and swore at myself in vicious whispers. I wondered whether I should return to the sitting room and fling myself at my godfather's feet and beg his forgiveness, but I restrained myself (from timidity rather than self-respect). After two or three hours I sloped up the stairs, intending to locate my bedroom.

I tried several doors unsuccessfully: they were either locked or else they opened onto curtained, dust-sheeted rooms. As I turned yet another corner in yet another unfamiliar corridor and wondered whether to invent a more methodical method of searching, or whether to start crying and cursing again, I walked headlong into Fay. She was looking round furtively as the collision occurred, so I startled her even more than she startled me. She yelped and her hand shot to her mouth.

"Oh my God!" she whispered, pressing her hand against her chest. "Oh my God! You gave me such a shock! I'm not supposed to be here!"

She leant against the wall, shut her eyes and breathed deep, suffering breaths, although her real panic had died by now. All her hauteur had vanished.

"I was looking for my bedroom." I whispered too, since she obviously thought it politic. My eyes wandered over her head and I saw that she had hidden her cropped hair underneath a maroon silk scarf scattered with yellow daisies. Her half-closed eyes followed mine, opening wide with consternation as I studied the scarf. I think she read disdain where there was only self-absorbed detachment.

"I know," she exclaimed, as her hands flew to her head, "It's hideous. But I didn't know what to do. I stole it from Veals' room, partly because I needed something to cover my ruined hair, but mostly to get back at her. It was the prettiest one she had. Honestly. I mean, can you believe it? I can't believe what she did to my hair though. I'm going to cut it, obviously, but I've only got nail scissors. You don't have any bigger scissors do you?"

She looked at me searchingly, then a blush rose up her face and she scowled at the floor as though she was furious with it. She still held a defensive hand across her head. I warmed to her because she was born to be effortlessly beautiful, yet found herself humbled by the loss of her pony tail and drawn into communication with the likes of me. I expect she had never looked odd before.

"No. How do you know where Mrs. Veals' room is?"

Heaven knows, it would have taken more than an embarrassed face peering out from under an ugly scarf to make me smile just then, but she could not know this and she seemed relieved that I could ask a straightforward question without suppressing sneers. She tried to sound as indifferent as I did, but her fingers gave her away: they still twitched at the edges of the scarf.

"I know this place like the back of my hand. I'm always exploring? Though I'm not supposed to, obviously. Marcus and me aren't allowed anywhere except the school buildings but hey! I'm not going to be told what to do by that psychopath. There is nothing else to do in this place, believe me. Welcome to the Headquarters of Tedium. Unless you like old buildings and views and stuff."

"Where is Marcus?"

Fay curled her lip with such vigour that it almost touched her left nostril.

"Swotting? He's scared of Veals. I mean…why?"

After a second's doubt I decided that the question was rhetorical and passed it over.

"Do you know where my bedroom is then?"

"Oh my God! So you don't have to sleep in the dormitory?"

"No, of course not," I replied coldly, shooting a glance at her scarf. "He's my godfather."

The Institute had conditioned me to fear people like Fay; people whom the Institute had conditioned to despise me. I was enjoying the tentatively cordial power-shift that came with this new environment. Now that we were (just) beyond the clutches of the Institute, instinct told me not to submit to Fay, or fawn, or apologise, in case she should lose her hesitancy. I had to be gruffly unimpressed by her, or her blue-eyed poise would have the better of me, and we might as well be masterminded by Miss Konder.

"What's your bedroom like then?"

I described last night's room. She wrinkled her nose thoughtfully and said, "Mmm…yeah. There are a couple like that. Looking out over the drive? Yeah, I think I know the one."

We stole through the house. Fay's stealth was fast and nervous; she glanced about and sped like a hawk. We did not meet anyone. We did not talk either, until we stood outside the door. I said it might look familiar, but that I wasn't sure. She asked whether she could have a look. I nodded and crossed my fingers. Fay turned the handle and pushed, peering into the emerging sliver of light. I heard a sharp intake of breath and then a silence, then she pushed the door open wide and swaggered in with an admiring, "Oh my God! Is this your room?"

Probably not, I thought, if it has inspired such an admiring response from Fay. I wished she would whisper again. But I followed her all the same.

Yes, it was my room. It was, I concluded with bewilderment, because the pictures and the view were identical. But it was not my room, I concluded afresh. It was not my room as I had left it this morning.

For one thing it was warm, because somebody had lit a pile of sweet-smelling pine cones in the grate. Beside the hearth there sat a basket that brimmed with chunks of pale wood. The furniture – the same furniture that I had slept amongst last night – shone in the flickering light, and smelt glowingly of beeswax. There were thick, creamy rugs across the floorboards and fluffy blankets across the bed.

The wardrobe door stood open. Fay approached it with greedily outstretched palms and began to rifle through dress after dress; heavy, old dresses that rustled with silk and velvet and stiff embroidery.

"Cool!" breathed Fay. "Well, not exactly cool cool, but you know what I mean. Are they yours?" I did not reply.

Over the mantelpiece there stood an extravagant vase, a bucket-sized vase of glossy green holly boughs, all showered with bright red dots. There was a dressing table near the foot of the bed that had not been there last night. Hairbrushes and pots of ointment were laid across it in neat rows, and there stood a bowl and a porcelain urn full of faintly-warm water.

I touched the water's surface with my fingertips as though

hypnotised. Then I backed away with an uncertain sigh. "This isn't my
room. It's just in a very similar position. Or else, it was my room last
night but they've moved me. Maybe Ludovick Montefiore has decided
I should go to the dormitory with you, after all." I felt the corners of
my mouth plunge as I said this and all my misery came flooding back
with such force that I sat down on the bed. Meanwhile Fay flew from
window to bedside to wardrobe without a thought for my self-pity.

"Look at this….Oh that is well cool…Is this really all your stuff?…
You are sooo lucky…I wish I had someone like him…What's that?
Abigail? On top of the book?"

"Where?"

"It's a letter addressed to you. Can I open it?"

"No!" I exclaimed fiercely, slamming my hand down onto the yellow
parchment square that she indicated with an elegantly outstretched
forefinger. She watched with interest as I took up the letter and
examined it. My name was, indeed, scrawled across the folded sheet.

"I expect it's from your godfather," she said casually. She could not
have known how all my bones liquefied at the prospect of a message
from Ludovick Montefiore, whom I had offended so deeply just three
hours before.

My dear Abigail, I read.

*Soon after you left me this morning, I came up to make sure that you
were happily installed in this room. During our interesting conversation
I'm afraid I omitted to enquire whether you would be comfortable here,
all alone, and whether you (who are so shy, and, I'm afraid, a good
deal better mannered than I) would be sufficiently confident to demand
of Mrs. Veals whatever she can procure for your enjoyment, such as
lunch, fresh linen, a hot bath…etc. I discovered that you were absent
so I took the liberty of entering, and I was horrified to find your room
as cold, dusty, un-aired and altogether ill-prepared as, undoubtedly,
you found it on your arrival last night. I apologise most sincerely for
yet another lapse. Whatever will you think of me and of my hospitality?
So I set Mrs. Veals to put the place to rights, and I took the liberty of
choosing a small selection of books from the library. You will find them
underneath this note. I hope they meet with your approval. If not, I will
gladly change them for you.*

I looked up at the bedside table and saw, through a golden glow, a
pile of three, solid, leather-bound volumes. They were: Jane Eyre by

Charlotte Bronte, The Magician's Nephew by C.S.Lewis, and Ghost Stories of an Antiquary by M.R. James.

You will note that there is also a large school bell on the dressing table. You are to ring this loud and clear whenever you require anything – ANYTHING mind, however small. Mrs. Veals is your servant now, as well as mine and she knows she must treat you with the utmost respect.

I look forward to seeing you once again at dinner, if not before.

Your loving godfather,

Ludovick Montefiore.

My loving godfather. Somehow, marvellously, my indiscretion had been forgotten. I almost kissed the letter, but I felt Fay's eager gaze, so I put it aside and said,

"Yes, it is my bedroom. I arrived so unexpectedly last night that they didn't have time to do it up, but they have had time now."

"Oh you are so, so lucky!" repeated Fay, as ingenuously thrilled as a child (or as Abigail Crabtree, though I worked furiously for a deadpan expression). "I have to live in this – ugh – concretey, empty, dormitory thing. It's so...Oh look, you've got a bell! What's that for?"

"That? Oh, that's for summoning Mrs. Veals if I want anything."

Fay's poise completely collapsed.

"Oh my God!" She shrieked. "Oh you are so lucky! I would so love to order Mrs. Veals about! Oh Abigail, ring it now! Go on! Please?"

"But...what shall I say?" I asked. "I don't want anything just now."

"You might not, but I do. I'm starving. We only got cabbage soup and melon balls for lunch."

"Won't she tell you off if she finds you here?" I asked.

"All right, so I'll hide inside the wardrobe," Fay answered impatiently, squeezing between the antique gowns and pulling the door to. I stood alone in my room, clenching one fist after the other in my uncertainty. I was angry with Fay for bossily spoiling my new-found peace.

"Go on then!" There came a muffled hiss from behind the wardrobe door. "Don't be too long about it; there isn't much air in here."

So with a jutting-chinned resolve that turned, slowly, into a malevolent grin, I took the bell and swung it from side to side, until it almost split my head in half and shattered the uneven old windows. Through the dying, whining echo I caught the slap, slap, slap of flat shoes.

"She's coming!" crowed Fay, unnecessarily. The anticipation made me so faint with fear, that when the footsteps stopped outside my bedroom door I almost staggered into the wardrobe myself. But when Mrs. Veals stood before me, beetroot-faced and shaking under the pressure of her enforced subservience, my fear fled and I felt a sense of power that was wonderful to me. It was as though I stood on the stage inside a famous theatre, only all the doors were locked and I was utterly alone, so that in that most public of places I could scream the ugliest, rudest sounds I liked without being heard. I would feel a thrill of abandonment as I yelled at the watching, listening seats and at the same time I would feel reassured by their emptiness. That was the sort of freedom I felt.

"You took your time," I said, unjustly. She did not reply, but looked at me with an intensity that was almost undisguised loathing.

"I said, You Took Your Time," I repeated peevishly, stamping my foot.

She was silent, her lips pursed so tightly that they must have hurt. Then they burst open and emitted three muted, yet bullet-hard words: "I'm sorry, madam." Then she snapped them shut again, as though her mouth was a mousetrap.

"I want a large plate of sandwiches, and some ripe pears, and some chocolate cake, and a jug of lemonade. Do you think you can manage that?"

She nodded her head once.

"Then get on with it! And this time, don't dawdle."

As soon as her footsteps had faded into the house, Fay burst from the wardrobe doubled over with laughter. I jumped a little, having all but forgotten her in the excitement of my actorly abandonment. My hands were trembling and I was grinning and giggling like a clown. She praised me: "That was brilliant, Abigail! That was so cool!"

We ate Mrs. Veals' tray of food by the fire. Fay became shy all of a sudden when I told her to help herself. Then she broke her own awkwardness with a half-hearted joke: "Hey, she won't have spiked it will she? With arsenic or something?"

"As if she'd dare!" I replied, smiling boldly as I bit into a slab of deep, dark cake. Fay nibbled away hungrily, yet still bashfully. I knew by the way she glanced at me whenever she took a sandwich and by the way she dabbed at the corners of her mouth between each small bite and by the way she went quickly quiet if ever I spoke, that she had become, unresentfully, my subordinate. Circumstance had led her to overlook my ordinariness.

"So," I said, flushed by the series of weird new pleasures and freedoms that I had gained since the early morning, "You know your way around well?"

"Yes, you don't know Boughwinds at all do you? Shall I show you round? Do you want to see anywhere in particular?"

"I'd like to see the garden before it gets too dark."

"Come on then!" Fay leapt up enthusiastically; she seemed more at her ease when we were on the move. Then her hands crept up to her head. "Only...you haven't got a hat going spare in that wardrobe of yours, have you? I can't believe what that cow did to my hair! I mean, I don't mind it being short, but styled short, you know? And Marcus is no help, he just thinks it's funny. Little brat. Don't have a brother if you can help it."

I found an off-white fur hat with a matching coat. Fay removed Mrs. Veals' scarf and thrust her scarecrow scalp inside the new hat, so that even the edges of her hair were hidden and her fine, bony face appeared in a wholly new frame. She thought it very elegant ("Oh cool! I look, like, Russian, or Eastern European or something?"). I thought her hairless head looked strange. She was like an undernourished baby haloed by a monstrous dandelion.

I found a coat too and when we were ready we made our way through the house to the main entrance hall. We still whispered as we had done before, but we strode along more solidly and on one occasion Fay broke into a fearless laugh.

When we reached the hall I made straight for the front door, but Fay touched my elbow, murmuring, "I'd better go and get Marcus. Do you mind? I know he's a boy and an absolute pain in the backside, but I promised mum that I wouldn't let him work too hard and I'd make sure he got plenty of fresh air – etc, etc; blah, blah, blah. He is such a swot," she continued as we made our way towards the backdoor and the schoolyard that I had crossed under duress that very morning, "it is so sad, but I suppose he is my brother. More's the pity."

We sauntered into the unlocked school building and I experienced something of that liberating empty-theatre feeling again, because this place had lost its brief hold over me. We walked past the classroom and up a short staircase. At the end of the landing there stood a pair of doors, one of which was labelled, "Girls' Dormitory and Study Rooms". The other was the boys' equivalent. Fay barged into the latter without knocking.

"Get up, child!" she barked. "You need fresh air. Pwah! And so does this room! Boys!"

I hardly needed to sweep my eyes around this room; it was all so familiar, just as the classroom had been, from my years at the Institute. There was nothing to describe except blankness.

Marcus glowered at his sister, then pushed his magazines to one side and rummaged in a cupboard for his coat. Fay swept through the room, holding her nose between ostentatiously pincered fingers. She flung the window open and turned the radiator (which was flogging the small room with wave upon wave of heat) off.

"It'll get cold," moaned Marcus, weakly.

"Yes!" replied Fay in a tone of starry brightness as she patted his cheek, "And won't that be an improvement?"

Marcus did not look at me directly, though I felt the occasional sidelong glance sweeping hastily up and down, from my head to my toes and back again. I suppose his hostility lacked courage in the absence of Mrs. Veals, especially since Fay was on my side.

We wandered into the garden to the accompaniment of Fay's animated emphases. Marcus was wrathfully shy. It occurred to me that I knew nothing about them, and that they knew nothing about me, but that I was too bored to ask for their story (since it would be boring), and much too bored to begin telling mine (since they could never understand me; special, little me). That's the sort of mood I was in.

The garden was beautiful in its wintry starkness. Everything – trees, bricks, bushes, grass, stones, sheds – was ancient, therefore it was all sprawling and soft and richly festooned. I wanted to idle there alone, or else in the brooding company of Ludovick Montefiore. But Fay twittered on like a budgerigar: "This is the pond – it's really stinky – Marcus paddled in it last summer when it was boiling hot - he smelt gross for days afterwards. That, by the way, is not unusual…This is the greenhouse, obviously…Rose garden…Rude statue of somebody. Venus maybe? Somebody like that…Kitchen garden…" I tried to nod every now and then. Marcus half closed his eyes.

Even Fay's flow of words lapsed after a while. We wandered further from the house and entered a wilder part of the garden, which closely bordered the wooded hillside. The grass here was thick and waterlogged. There were no more paths or flowerbeds or trellises. We passed a small stone building that was clearly as old as the abbey itself, only it was run-down and forgotten. Its high windows were black with bars and ancient grime. The tired grey walls were embraced, right up to their splintering roof-tiles, by the brown skeletons of clinging, climbing plants. Three crumbly steps led up to the wooden door that hung slackly from one hinge and was striped by long black holes.

"What's that?" I asked.

"Oh, that's the chapel," replied Fay. "Not that they use it; it's dangerous."

We walked on, the wet grass clinging round our ankles now, soaking our feet. All of a sudden I noticed that Marcus was leading now and that Fay was walking closely by my side. I also noticed that her chatter had waned again, while Marcus's eyes were bright and darting. We entered a grove of yew trees and Marcus stopped. He smiled at Fay maliciously and whistled through his teeth. Fay, who never did look upon him kindly, darted a significant frown and said sharply, "Let's go back. I'm cold."

Marcus shifted his piggy eyes to my face. He was looking at me directly now, though there was still something slanted about his gaze. He shuffled his feet. His whistling shifted to a higher and yet more grating key. He clearly felt that I must ask him what the matter was before long, so I didn't. Instead I turned in a deliberate way to Fay and asked,

"How long has there been an Institute here?"

Fay sighed at me and rolled her eyes. Then she replied softly, as though bidding me to be soft as well, so that Marcus wouldn't overhear,

"About five years. Slightly longer."

"Hmm." Marcus bounced between us. "And we all know what happened five years ago on this very spot. Don't we Fay?"

Fay struck her brother's arm. "My God, Marcus!" she spluttered, "I don't want to think about it, thank you very much!"

"It happened right here," continued Marcus in a spectral tone, "On this very branch. Of this very tree." He pointed and we all looked up. We could not help it. Two or three feet above our heads there stretched a sturdy branch, as thick as a horse's neck. It burned a vivid black against the twilight blue of the sky.

"What happened right here?" I asked, despite my reluctance to gratify Marcus.

"I'm sorry," he replied with too much pleasure and haste, as though he was winning a word game, "But I can't tell you!"

I should have known better than to ask. As I sighed with irritation, some inspiration brought yesterday's encounters to the tip of my tongue.

I turned my steps towards the abbey and said, in a bored sort of a way:

"I suppose you're talking about Sylvia, are you? I know; she died a few years back while she was a pupil here."

Fay and I walked away with long, matching strides. Marcus started to follow sulkily, before trumpeting,

"Ah! Yes! But how did she die? I bet you don't know how she died, do you?"

I was wise to Marcus's tactics now, so I just shrugged. This pleased Fay, who found the subject genuinely distasteful. My inattention infuriated Marcus of course.

"Well, I'll tell you then, since you don't even know! She hanged herself. On that tree we were standing under. I mean, I know it's awful, but apparently she was a bit of a weirdo. Everyone calls her Suicide Sylvia. Or we do anyway and so does Mrs. Veals. And apparently, right, she haunts the abbey. Actually I saw her once - or I really nearly saw her, anyway…"

Fay hurried on and I hurried with her. This time I cold-shouldered Marcus with no ulterior motive. I was not interested in how he might have "really nearly" seen a ghost. I felt sick of him and sick of poor Fay. We were in the dark now amidst those creaking Boughwinds trees and I had that frightened feeling that has often come to me in winter: the feeling that death is close and desolate; that it is as ghoulish as a nightmare.

Suddenly Fay flung her arm out, stopping us in our tracks. We stood still, united in a breathless hush.

"What?" murmured Marcus.

Fay tipped her head forwards and we followed her gaze. I screwed up my eyes, peering through the blue-black gloom. A mannish figure was striding from the woods, and crossing the lawn to the house.

"Mrs. Veals?" I whispered, and Fay nodded.

Mrs. Veals clutched a bundle to her chest and she walked quickly, looking neither to the right nor to the left.

"What's she doing?"

Fay shrugged.

When the housekeeper had gone we emerged from the long grass onto one of the gravel paths that led back to the abbey. That great dragon of a house was suddenly before us, blacker than the black sky and scattered with scales of square orange, wherever a lighted room overlooked the drive. Marcus chattered on blithely about his almost-encounter with "Suicide Sylvia". In the vain hope of drowning him out,

Fay launched into an elaborate curse upon brothers and Mrs. Veals and unstyled hair.

I remembered that I was to have dinner with Ludovick Montefiore in a few hours time and I sighed in grateful anticipation. I felt as though my head – my soul - had been grotesquely clogged with stale, sweet things that afternoon. I hoped – I believed - that the coming reunion with my godfather would cleanse my palate, like a deep draught of some pleasingly bitter and unfamiliar solution.

The Flight by Night

It was late when I returned to my room from dinner. The state of confused urgency in that I had been living over the last few days had fizzled out, for the time being, under a fug of contentment. I was delighted, as I made my way back to the bedroom, by every click of my courtly heels and every rustle of my sweeping skirts. I could not scratch my nose without feeling a glow of regret for the artists of the world who were not present to capture the moment. I was drunk on novelties: wine and dresses; adoration and self-belief.

I sat down at the fireside and rested my chin on my hand. In admiring my own stillness I ceased to be still: my eyes roved greedily over the spread of my green velvet dress, the drooping curve of my wrist and the unexpected curl of my long hair. You know that I was unused to feeling beautiful. And now – just imagine it – I felt I was more singularly beautiful than a blossom tree growing alone in the middle of a wasteland. This evening was so strange and new that I shook, and my teeth chattered, as though I was cold.

I nearly told you that I lost track of time, that I could have sat there forever, but that is not quite the case. It is true that I was mesmerised by my sense of well-being, but there was a part of me that was restless as well. That part of me wanted to leap across the abbey rooftops from turret to chimney to archway. It told me I could run across the whole of Yorkshire without shortness of breath; that I could take on a hundred Vulture Men and win; that I could swing from tree to tree, my feet never touching the ground, until I had encircled this valley twenty times over.

"Abigail!" Boris was leaning over the end of the bed, motioning me sternly with his outstretched paw. "Abigail! It was you who wanted to travel tonight. Eyes is waiting. Come!"

I undressed and climbed into bed. But hours went by before I left the Waking World behind.

There was a good deal of whispered bustle inside the tree. It stopped for half a second when we arrived and I heard Eyes drawl, "Well thank goodness! At last!", and then it continued at a yet more frenetic pace. I took no part, since I could not tell what everyone was doing, why, and how I might fit in. I allowed myself to be wrapped in a warm, dark coat, a woolly hat and a pair of gloves so chunky that my fingers felt as thick and stiff as carrots. A scarf was wound around my neck and head: round and round until I was half-smothered and only my eyes showed over the top. "You'll be flying fast and high," one of my friends assured me, as he pulled a securing knot tight at the back of my neck. "It'll be freezing." I was unable to nod, so I blinked at him instead.

"Now," said a plump voice, as the bustle subsided and an excited stillness gripped us, "I know you don't want to be weighed down, but you'd better take a few provisions all the same: a hot flask, a few sandwiches and what-not." The woman buckled up a satchel as she spoke, then looped the strap over my head and under one of my arms, as if I were about to trot off to school.

"Mmm mmm," I thanked her from the depths.

Prince Constantine stepped forwards shyly. (When was he ever shy? Shy with me?) "I've got a gift for you as well. It isn't much. I made it myself. I hope it works all right."

He handed me a stick and a bundle and for a few moments I was glad of my gag, because I did not know what on earth they were for or, therefore, what I should say. Then I turned to one of our sputtering lamps, and found that I was holding a fine bow – long, slender, taut - and a quiver of arrows. It was only now that my Waking World drunkenness left me and my mind properly engaged with the seriousness of our quest. I'm afraid that my seriousness was born neither of strength, nor determination, nor offended dignity, but merely of timidity. What was I doing, venturing out into Traumund, journeying through places I ought never to see, in order to do battle with a maniac tyrant? What was I doing? Me? Abigail Crabtree? This was a job for somebody brave and debonair: not me. Not me. I wasn't even sure how a bow and arrow worked.

Though my drunkenness had left me and the quest to find Joachim loomed large again, Ludovick Montefiore still overwhelmed my mind.

He was not there as an object anymore, but rather as a colour. Imagine the whole universe of your mind dyed through and through with a dark, inky blue.

"Mmm mmm," I repeated, blinking at Constantine. Then I shook the bow and arrow in a rather timorous gesture of valour.

"Well," he said lamely, with a sad smile. "Bye then."

"MMM?" I struggled out of my gag. "What d'you mean? You mean you're not coming?"

He shook his head. "Just you and Boris. Eyes could hardly be expected to carry more."

I opened my mouth to speak, but what to say? I might beg him to come after all: Eyes would manage. Or, if not, then now was the time to make a laboured farewell. Now was the time to say, "Prince Constantine, my childhood's first hero, my first beloved, though I lose myself forever in this universe of dreams, never, never shall I…"

I closed my mouth. Then I said, "Oh…OK. Well, we'll be back soon, anyway. So. Bye." I kissed, quickly, his soft, pink cheek and he kissed mine in return.

I turned to Eyes, who was all eagerness to leave. Perhaps he was already on his way: his face twitched with thought, as though he was replaying last night's journey in his head. He barely replied as the others bade him farewell. "Hmm…Indeed….Right," he muttered.

"Abigail?" Boris was at my side. "I want to give you this before we are airborne. I want you to wear it around your neck."

Between his paws he held, with absorbed carefulness, a small terracotta bottle, tightly corked, and hung with a thick loop of string. I took it with a querying glance at his face.

"It's called - " He stopped and lowered his voice to a whisper, "It's called Euthusoteria. It is very rare – very rare indeed – so you must use it with great discretion. That bottle contains just one dose."

"Use it…when? What does it do?"

"If you are ever in urgent need of a route into or out of Traumund, then drink it. It will bring you here, or take you back to the Waking World, in the blink of an eye."

"Is that all?" I asked, disappointed. "But I travel back and forth all the time: every night and every morning."

"Yes," Boris explained, patiently. "But that's in the natural order of things. Have you ever tried journeying through mere willpower?"

"…I suppose not," I answered reluctantly and as I spoke I clenched my fists surreptitiously and tried to force my way back to Boughwinds

Abbey. I might as well have tried to will myself onto the surface of the moon.

"Quite," said Boris, with a supercilious glance at my fists. "In the normal course of things the journey is a drifting process. You need a sharp, swift magic if you wish to travel the sharp, swift way. Look after it."

I shrugged, unconvinced, and tucked the bottle inside my scarf.

"Are we ready now?" murmured Eyes sarcastically. "Are we sure? Please don't rush, anybody. I should hate for you to feel rushed. Perhaps we should have a cup of tea before we amble forth…?"

One of the Tree People made an uncertain movement towards the kettle, but with an impatient flurry of feathers and an owlish growl, Eyes hustled us up the inside of the hollow tree: Boris first, then me, and Eyes himself last of all.

It was not a comfortable climb, partly because it was dark; partly because Boris lost his foothold several times and jammed a furry back-paw into my face and partly because the trunk narrowed dramatically as we got higher. I was beginning to feel giddy with claustrophobia, like a juvenile chimney-sweep inside a Victorian chimney, when we emerged onto a bough near the very top of my tree. The night was fresh and I stretched my arms out wide for the sheer pleasure of feeling mile upon cubic mile of empty space.

Clouds flashed across the moon and stars like flocks of scraggy, grey witches, but still I could see more of the wood than I had ever seen before. I could see the dimpled spread of trees and the shape of the earth from which they all rose. My tree stood on the side of a gentle slope, but there were steep hills and mountains on the horizon. I wanted to fly fast and low: I almost believed that I could do so on my own.

"Right," said Eyes briskly. "I shall make a circuit of the tree; you and Boris must leap onto my back when you feel I am beneath you. It's safer that way; I'm not having you clambering around and trying to climb on – not at this height."

"When we feel you are beneath us?" I repeated faintly as Eyes melted into the night.

"How do I…what do I hold on to?" I called urgently, wishing that I had given the situation a good deal more thought before Eyes became so businesslike and impatient. Boris was scanning the treetops anxiously. He had no ears for my belated panic.

I followed his gaze uneasily, but I could see nothing at all. Then I did see my owl on the wing, but the vision was so strangely unsustained by any other sense that I could not trust my eyes. So silently that my bated breath seemed to rattle the tree-top in comparison with its flight, a grey shape, just half a tone darker than the night sky, glided over the treetops and brushed my cheek with its wing-tip. Then it sank back into the gloom.

"Abigail, Boris, you missed!" he bellowed. "Listen, when I hoot you jump, all right?"

"All right," sang my frail voice.

"I won't let you fall, I promise," he added and his voice was behind me now. Then I heard a short, sonorous note, like the low cooing of a clarinet.

I dared not disobey him, but still I felt foolish as I plunged out of the tree and hurtled towards my death with Boris bear in tow. How ridiculous, I had time to think with a pang of grief, to die by my own act, yet for no purpose and in violation of all my instincts. The forest floor, when at last I hit it, was so luxuriously comfortable that I really believed, since there was no pain, that I must be dead. Then I felt the ground rise up rapidly beneath me and I heard the clarinet say,

"We're off! Grip tightly, Abigail - you won't hurt me. I've got enough feathers to fill all the pillows in Traumund."

I did as I was told, and gradually I began to find my bearings, so that after a good five minutes of confusion I understood where I was – by and large - relative to the sky, the earth and Eyes. He was roughly the size of a sizeable horse, and I crouched forward on his back as though I was galloping around a racecourse. I had no control; no means at all of altering our course or our speed. I could only cling tightly, wrist-deep in downy feathers, watching the universe of Traumund as it unfolded many miles beneath me.

It took me a while to comprehend our velocity, since Eyes' flight seemed so stately and grand, like the flight of an aeroplane from the perspective of a passenger, who is leaning her forehead against the lozenge-shaped window and watching the continents roll past, field by tiny field. But I understood our dashing, flashing speed when I tried to raise myself into an upright position, and had my head pushed backwards by a juddering stream of icy air. What I saw of Traumund for the first half hour or so I saw imperfectly, my frozen face cautiously tilted and my vision obscured by a screen of frantic, fluttering feathers.

Nonetheless, I could see the whole width of the forest from this great height. It snaked beneath us like a vast, black river, many miles wide, and of an incalculable length. To this day I do not know where it begins and ends; all I know is that it merges darkly into the hills and mountains that then lay ahead of us.

To the left of the forest lay a gentle, dreamy landscape of rolling meadows, isolated houses and streams that glittered white and black in the moonlight. I begged Eyes to glide nearer the ground so that I could see this new area of Traumund more closely. I peered around as he fell through the clouds.

The pasturelands felt pretty and safe, so as we glided across them we chattered and dawdled (in as far as Eyes would permit it) and pointed and exclaimed. The land was scattered with wild-flowers, as though it was a mirror laid out to reflect the starry sky, the air was abruptly warm, and heavy with sleepy, summery smells. Animals moved amongst the flowers: horned, fleecy creatures in the main, that looked a little like sheep, a little like cows, and a little like neither. The animals wore deep-toned bells around their necks and they were free to wander wherever they wished, though they tended to cluster about the human dwellings that sprang up here and there, like larger, stiffer flowers.

Many of the herds roamed around log cabins, which were ringed by roomy balconies and bolstered by stores of logs - rather like houses I had once seen in Austria. Others grazed in the shelter of white, slatted buildings that were protected by flimsy picket fences and wide verandas. On one of the verandas I saw a naked man. He was dancing happily and rather clumsily, singing as he munched on an apple. I looked away in embarrassment and made a facetious comment that nobody caught.

I saw cottages, windmills and a red and white striped lighthouse, with its white arm of light swinging benignly round and round, though we were far from the sea. But the strangest and prettiest house of all was one that sat snugly and firmly in the boughs of a cherry tree. The tree-house was almost invisible under a shower of pink blossom but Eyes spotted it and we circled it once, peering silently through the tiny, unglazed windows. We saw a woman inside: the sort whom, in the Waking World, I might have written off as a run-of-the-mill old lady. Her hair was stiffly permed and she wore pearls in her ears and a woolly skirt with clunky shoes. I could picture her Waking World self so clearly: the clean tissue up her sleeve; the large-print library books stacked by her bed; the plastic headscarf folded neatly inside her handbag in case of rain. Only here, in Traumund, she lounged in a comfy armchair with her back leaning against one of the arms and her legs draped over the other. She held an empty shot glass in one hand and a half-empty bottle of whisky in the other. She gripped a fuming Sherlock Holmes pipe between her teeth and as we flew past one window I heard her growl, "Go on, Pinkie, go on. And have a drink while you're at it. It's good stuff." She was addressing a flamingo, who stood near her chair, wobbling on one leg, his eyes half closed. As we loitered past the second window I heard the flamingo replying politely: "No, really Betty. No more. Thank you. I was saying…I was saying… how indebted we are to Matisse. Or rather…" - and we were gone. I think that is what he said. I think that is what I saw.

"Eyes! Up! Now!"

Eyes rose obediently at Boris's command, quick and quiet, like a feathered elevator.

"What did you see Boris?" I called when we were high among the chilly clouds again.

"On the edge of the forest…a camp…wigwams and fires and Vulture Men…about ten of them…and the horses…" We flew on in grim silence. My anger against the self-styled King of Traumund was re-kindled, and I felt the rattling quiver on my back with a sense of frustration at my own incompetence.

The moon was high over the long, river-like forest before Eyes gave in and admitted his need for a short rest. We found a tree whose boughs were more than strong enough to bear his weight. There we sat for ten minutes or so, passing the thermos cup back and forth and munching on kipper pâté sandwiches.

Boris, having had his fill of tea and food, clambered along our bough and leapt cautiously onto the branch of a neighbouring tree. I lost sight of him for a few seconds before he reappeared and beckoned me to follow. Eyes was snoozing, so without a word I climbed after Boris until we were three or four trees away from our original perch. (I ought to acknowledge, by the way, that this was not such a gymnastic feat as it sounds. The trees were high, but their branches were as wide and dependable as the man-made bridges and pavements in a city that is gently warped with age.)

"Look," murmured Boris, pointing, "Do you think we should do something?"

I followed his paw with my eyes and eventually, through the leafy gloom, I discerned the figure of a man. He was sitting on a bough, just as we had been, only he was all alone and he was hunched forward so that his head hung lower than his shoulders. He was shaking violently, though silently: at first I thought he was laughing, but then he spoke to himself and I realised he was crying.

"Bella, Bella, Bella, Bella, Bella," he groaned as his shoulders shuddered, "Bella, Bella, Bella. I'm going mad. Where are you? Where are you? Where are you? How can you be dead? How can you?" He shouted the last question angrily, then buried his head in his hands and sobbed. The sobs sounded like squawks. His whole body shook and rattled.

I watched him for a moment. Then I murmured in Boris's ear, "We'd better go. He might not like us to be watching him."

The bear nodded and we were just about to turn our backs on the poor man, when I noticed that the sky around the moon was changing from black to blue: a warm, painterly, royal blue light that swelled and burst towards us, turning, as it burst, into a shower of blue and white carnations. Then the moon emerged from the midst of this blue-white bouquet and became a woman. Or a woman stepped out of the moon. I am not quite sure how it was, though I swear I can picture it all in my head and it makes my heart sing to remember.

The woman was beautiful and she glowed with a pale gold light, like an angel, only her face was homely and affectionate, not celestially superior. She strode through the sky towards the man, who was staring at her and staggering to his feet like some comedic drunk. "I'm here!" she said, quietly. It sounded as though they were at home and he had called up the stairs for her because he had wanted to show her something, or ask her a trivial, practical question and she had come up behind him (because she wasn't upstairs anyway, but with him all along) and said, "I'm here."

I saw them as we glided from our tree some minutes later. They were sitting with their arms round one another. He was laughing as she kissed him over and over again.

We continued to fly down the length of the forest. I spent long, puzzled minutes trying to decide what was that grey, shifting, white-specked mass that lay on the right hand side of the snaking forest. But then my nostrils breathed a damp, briny gust of wind and I exclaimed, "The sea! Oh, Eyes, why don't we fly over the sea for a bit? Please, Eyes, it's hardly out of our way at all." So we did, swooping low over the heaving waves and racing with the nimble white gulls who screamed exultantly through the blustery wetness.

"Oh no," gasped Eyes's rich, woody voice all of a sudden. "Abigail, shut your eyes. Don't look."

"Where? Why?" I replied, looking diligently up, down, left and right.

"We're at somebody's borders. Peculiar things – disturbing things – sometimes happen at the very edges of these lands. It's not for us to look…please don't, Abigail. I know that's irritating…"

Before he finished speaking I saw, and cried out.

In a bay beneath our path I saw circling shark fins. I glimpsed just a few at first, but then I kept spotting more and more until it seemed that the sharks were swarming beneath us as thickly as flies over a rotten carcass. A young woman knelt on the beach beside the deadly, squirming waters. She was kissing a baby and dropping tears all over its tiny body and its outstretched hands. As she wept she tied the baby to a flimsy raft with a length of rope. When the baby was secure she picked up the raft and carried it tenderly across the sand. Then she pushed it out into the hungry, foaming waters.

As soon as the baby had floated beyond her reach, the woman let out a heart-rending wail. She tried to wade after the child but the waters were so deep and savage that she was forced back to the shore.

"Oh God, oh God!" I cried, and I'm not sure whether I was cursing or praying. "Eyes, what shall we do? We have to save the baby! If you swoop down low enough I can snatch it up with my hands!"

Eyes seemed strangely withdrawn. Instead of obeying me he picked up speed and muttered angrily, as if to himself, "I told you not to look."

I was outraged. I kicked the owl hard with the heels of my shoes and screamed in his feathery ear, "I command you to do as I say! If you don't…well!" My threat petered out unconvincingly.

Eyes obeyed me, though as he did so his body seethed with revulsion, just as the sea seethed with sharks. He turned so sharply that I almost slipped into the ocean of jaws myself. Then he dived like a bomb. I stretched and screamed and gritted my teeth as we plunged towards the sea. Just as it seemed we must crash amongst the fins, that cut the water like fast black yachts at some nocturnal regatta, we were up again, safe among the stars. I held the raft and the baby - unscathed.

"You want to return the baby to the woman?" enquired Eyes.

"Of course!" I replied, smug in the expectation of its mother's gratitude.

Eyes seemed to shrug his muscular shoulders. He glided to the beach where the woman stood and watched our approach with an upturned face that was as calm as the full, white moon. I leant over the side of my winged charger and delivered the child to its mother. But my knightly thrill was chilled by her continued calm. She said nothing, though she took the raft from my hands and kissed her wailing child. She stroked its wet limbs and murmured soft nonsense until it smiled into her face. Then she ran back to the shoreline and cast the raft into the breakers all over again.

. Eyes raced away, flapping his wings frenetically as though they were possessed of too much energy. "I've seen it before, Abigail!" he thundered. Very soon I could no longer hear the woman's piercing cries or the baby's hysterical despair. Nobody spoke a word during the remainder of our flight.

Clocks don't work in Traumund, so I don't know how long our journey took from start to finish. It seemed to last many nights rather than many hours. Eyes was obviously and deservedly weary, but Boris and I became sleepy too. Boris told me later that he had begun dreaming dangerous dreams about plump, white beds, from which he awoke several times with that horrible, tumbling-over-the-edge-of-a-precipice sensation. I remember fearing that my body might stiffen completely and slip to one side in its current, inflexible posture and that I would tumble out of the sky like the statue of a jockey, unable to respond to my fall with even a gesture of resistance and fear.

All I know is that the sky was infused with that grey echo of light that marks the approach of dawn, when Eyes (who was powering along like a fish in a sea of treacle) hooted faintly, "Here! I remember!" Though his wings were failing his saucer-eyes were indefatigable. He scanned the grey-green treetops (Joachim's forest, unlike mine, was dense with needly evergreens. I love to see my trees turn scarlet in autumn and then skeletal black in winter), reading them, and the humps and hollows from which they projected, like hieroglyphs. The prospect looked hopelessly uniform to me, but Eyes steered us purposefully, neither his wings nor his eyes ever dithering.

Suddenly he stiffened; his whole body seemed to focus upon some indistinguishable point among the trees. He stopped forcing his way through the viscous air and allowed himself to drop in a gentle curve towards his invisible marker. Only as we landed did I see what Eyes had seen half a mile away: that the densely dark forest gave way, just here, to a lighter tint, which was Joachim's clearing.

Eyes steered his way through the close-knit, horizontal branches. Then he landed near Joachim's door and tipped me, as carefully as he had caught me in the very beginning, onto the dry, prickly ground.

I hobbled to my feet and rubbed my tingling legs. I knew that this was Joachim's house straight away, because it fitted, not only his description, but also him. I would have recognised the place as Joachim's had he never described it and had I stumbled upon it by accident, just as I would have recognised his photograph, his voice, or his inky, varnished smell. I was unnerved by my lack of doubt. I was also shocked by the one element of Joachim's land that I had not been able to foresee: it's realness and particularity; the fact that the soil dusted my shoes, as soil does, and that the trees whispered in the dawn breeze, as trees do; that the gloss paint on the wooden house had dripped a little near the bottom of the windowsill and blistered slightly around the door handle.

The colours of the house were restrained in that they were few (I counted blue, green, gold and scarlet, not counting the pale cream of the wood itself), but each was more vivid than any earthly thing I have ever seen: brighter than peacock's tails or meadow-grass or butter, or blood on a white cloth. It seemed as though a starry light shone through each stroke of paint, so that the blue, for example, reminded me of that blue that Boris and I had seen when Bella and the carnations burst from the moon. The paintings (which ran helter-skelter over the door, the walls and the windowsill) were all mysteriously narrative, rather than abstractly patterned and the figures were bright, solemn, naïve figures: stiffly holy, like the creations of a medieval mystic. They ran riot over the little building, so that it seemed to shimmer with light and music and movement. There were crowds waltzing in a snowy market place; stars exploding over an onion-domed church; chickens scratching in farmyards and horses galloping through corn-fields; men drinking from shiny black bottles; lovers flying like banners over smoking chimney-pots and wooden roofs. Over the portal I discovered, as I concluded my inspection, a dancing violinist, with a crooked smile and a shabby coat.

Below him the door had opened and Joachim stood before me, gripping the door-handle with a white-knuckled fist. He smiled a fixed, desperate smile as my eyes wandered from the violinist and settled upon his face. As soon as I saw this smile and his fingers spreading out over the walls in a futile gesture of diffidence, I felt purple blushes flowing across my face, like the waves of a hot sea against the head of a panicking swimmer. He was kind, of course; he tried to hide his displeasure.

"Joachim," I murmured. I stepped forwards, intending to embrace him, but suddenly I shrank from him. I looked around me and then at my feet. "Please forgive us for intruding. I know it's wrong…it's so wrong. Oh dear. I didn't know it would be like this."

"It's all right," Joachim came to my rescue because he felt sorry for me. "It's all right, Abigail. Honestly. After all…I've imagined you coming here often enough…it seems silly…"

"Maybe," I said more confidently, taking advantage of his good heart. "And you know we wouldn't unless we had to."

Joachim ushered us all inside. Boris and I sat down at a roughly-hewn wooden table. Eyes perched in the corner with his head against the ceiling. As Joachim abandoned himself to the bustling demands of hospitality (urging Eyes to drape his wings as comfortably as he could and fetching food and drink for us) I sat and watched.

The word "sorry" went round and round inside my head and I felt that I should be saying it out loud, over and over. I ought to have said, "I'm sorry, Joachim, but tomorrow evening I will sit at dinner with Ludovick Montefiore and I will describe all this as vividly as I can, until he knows as much about you and your home as I do. I will betray your holiest secret. I'm sorry, I'm sorry, I'm sorry. I'm sorry as many times as you like, but I will do it all the same. I can't help it. I can't help myself."

Of course I said no such thing.

The colour of my soul had been changed that evening. Even as we flew I felt it turn richer and deeper and darker.

Mah-jong

*Y*ou didn't enjoy your dinner tonight?" asked Ludovick
Montefiore as I laid down my knife and fork with a resonant
chime. The dining room echoed like an empty church.
Mrs. Veals removed my plate.

"Oh...it was lovely. I'm sorry I've left so much..." I had often
wished that I might feel moved (whether by happiness, misery or
excitement) to lose my appetite, since I believed that such a loss would
make me seem profound and feeling. I despised myself for never
having lost it properly before. There had been periods of affectation,
for example at the Institute when I had found myself falling in love
with some floppy-haired Adonis, but these were always belied by my
rumbling stomach. Even when my granddad died and the rest of my
family became forgetful of their meals, I was as guiltily hungry as ever.
Only now, at dinner with Ludovick Montefiore, did I know what it is
like to be incapable of swallowing. I felt as though I had been packed
with bubbling lava from the pit of my stomach to the door of my throat.
I was proud of my incapacity, hoping it made me look as frail as I felt.

"Well, if you're sure you've finished, shall we retire to my study for
coffee? I don't believe you've seen my study yet and we don't want the
servants flitting in and out while you're trying to tell the rest of your
story."

I had not seen any servants, other than the omnipresent Mrs. Veals.
She served and waited at all our meals, but Ludovick Montefiore never
addressed a single word to her. I thought that if I was Mrs. Veals, this
impersonal reference to "the servants" would hurt me like a punch in

the jaw and (though I, too, often overlooked her presence as though she was a robotic nonentity) I stole a glance at her face as we rose. I realised, with a shudder, that her face was not robotic at all, but densely, tightly, emotionally still. She stood against the wall to my left, her eyes fixed upon a painting that hung on the wall to my right. She was watching the doe-eyed ancestral youth like a Doberman, as if waiting to leap up and cry blue murder should he slip from his frame. I lowered my own eyes quickly.

Ludovick Montefiore snapped an order for coffee and cigars. Mrs. Veals scuttled through one door, while my godfather and I lounged through the other and made our way to his study.

Joachim's solemn voice kept speaking, as it had spoken years ago when we first shared our Traumund secrets. "You won't laugh or tell," it urged. "You know that if you did I could never like you again."

I wished I could forget the promise that I had given him so readily, but of course I could not. I did not even try to justify my treachery.

The eagerness with which Ludovick Montefiore absorbed every particular of my description (he even told me to slow down in order that I might detail more fully Joachim's exquisite wall-paintings and the solid realness of the sky and the earth that had struck me so strongly on landing) disturbed my conscience still more. I could not but respond to his enthusiasm - all the more recklessly as my betrayal of Joachim grew (I told myself) too comprehensive for reversal. Besides, the part of me that was in unsteady charge at present, the flighty, joyous, tipsy part that I mistook for my whole self, said it was right to tell Ludovick Montefiore everything, since to leave anything out would be an act of betrayal against my love.

The interior of Ludovick Montefiore's study did its bit to drain my mind of clarity and conscience. The room was candlelit (like the rest of the abbey), so that everything I saw – even the most trivial things like the wicker waste-paper basket and the tartan draught-excluder – was saturated with gold. There were dull, shadowy golds and light, resplendent golds that seemed to ooze from the objects themselves, as though liquid light and liquid darkness were mingling within them and seeping out in oily droplets. The place was like a dusky version of Joachim's house, with magic dormant in every particle of dust.

The darkness was accentuated by the bookshelves, that were full to bursting and lined almost every inch of wall. Where there was no longer room for the books to stand upright they were piled up horizontally and squeezed across the tops of others. There were book-heaps on the floor, the desk, the chairs and the mantelpiece. Wherever I turned my sluggish gaze I saw fine, old leather tomes, whose spines were filled with an indecipherable gothic script. There were, I noted, no creased paperbacks, such as overwhelmed our shelves at home. But I knew that his books were well-thumbed, because they covered the room in such an earnest profusion and because (of the ones I could see) they were more swollen than new books.

There was a welsh dresser against one wall. As well as the inevitable volumes, I saw that my godfather kept a collection of old weapons on dusty display here: I could see axe-heads and daggers, blow-pipes (I think) and arrows and a long, grimy, silver sword. In the glass-panelled cupboard underneath, I could make out a collection of mysterious bottles in stone and coloured glass. I had seen similar bottles at the King Henry Hotel.

Against another wall there stood a mahogany desk. As well as a pen and a bottle of ink (and the inevitable books), the desk held a gold plate piled high with chocolate truffles, just like those we had eaten together at the hotel and the mah-jong set. I leaned against the desk and ran my fingers over the mah-jong box, whose wooden sides glowed a resinous red-gold. Ludovick Montefiore said, "I'll show you that properly when you've finished your story. Now help yourself to a chocolate and then come and continue. What did Joachim say? Did you make any plans?"

I perched on a foot-stool at my godfather's feet, while he basked before the fire in a high, leather arm chair. He seemed a colossus to me: his head far away among mists and impenetrable clouds. I would talk to please him, of course, though I would rather gaze in silence. I rolled the chocolate around the roof of my mouth. As I did so my reserve, and the dregs of my guilt, dissolved into a sweet desire for confession.

"It became bearable after a while – thanks to Joachim really – he's too kind to let me suffer for long, even if I deserve it."

"But why did you deserve it? I don't understand why he made you feel guilty in the first place."

"No," I agreed in some confusion. I could recall my embarrassment on our arrival at the house, but I could not re-imagine it and it made no sense to me now. "Well, he didn't exactly make me feel guilty. I don't know…."

"Anyway…"

"Anyway, so he gave us all a long drink and some food as Boris told him all about our journey. That, more than anything, helped to rid us of any awkward silence. And…what else…well then I told Joachim why we'd come, and he said he understood, that he'd have done the same, and that he'd help. After that we both felt better, and we said hello to one another properly, he even seemed pleased to have us there…I don't know. And then…well, then it was dawn so we had to separate. We left Eyes resting in the house and promised to rejoin him tonight and that's all."

"You didn't form a plan then? You didn't talk about the King of Traumund?"

"Oh yes." I replied sleepily. "Yes, we did. We decided that when Eyes had rested we would send him out to find a Vulture Man – Joachim says the forest is crawling with them - and track it in the hope that eventually it will lead us to the king." I recalled our plan gloomily, though it had seemed satisfactory at the time. "It's a stupid plan, I know." I apologised "I mean, they live in camps, the Vulture Men. They might never return to their headquarters. And even if they do and we find it, what are we going to do then?"

I looked at my godfather apprehensively, expecting him to toss our juvenile plans aside with contempt and replace them with something bold and methodical. Instead, to my joint relief and disappointment, he appeared to be thinking far inside himself and when I repeated my questioning complaint, "It's a stupid plan, isn't it?", he merely shook his head and replied with unthinking kindness, "Not at all, not at all".

As I sat there in dozy perplexity, wishing he would speak, yet not daring to demand access to his thoughts, there came a tap at the door. Ludovick Montefiore's head whipped up and he stared at the door in dismay.

"It'll be Mrs. Veals with the coffee," I reassured him.

"Mrs. Veals is it?" he said, and as he spoke his eyebrows contracted angrily. I tried to feel amusement, though actually I felt fear, in my expectation of some new humiliation for the dutiful Doberman.

The tap came once again and the door opened, unbidden. A faint buzzing noise – like a blue-bottle - floated across the room and disappeared into the black-gold shadows. I saw a tray enter, laden with cups and jugs and so forth…but the shoulders and the face hovering over the tray did not belong to Mrs. Veals. They belonged to someone quite new to me.

She was a small woman, with a face that was enviable because, though carelessly tended (unlike Fay's) it was arrestingly beautiful. It was a face that said, you will not question my intelligence, my sensitivity, my superiority. Later I told Joachim that I found her face expressive. He said, "Expressive of what?" I said, "I don't know, just expressive!" But being obliged by Joachim to consider my words, I added, "Expressive of fear, that first night, but also – more fundamentally - pride. Conceit."

"I'm so sorry," she said quickly, addressing my godfather and darting a startled glance at me. "Mrs Veals led me to understand you were alone…Sir." Then, with a glance at the tray, she added. "Your coffee and so forth…"

Ludovick Montefiore neither looked at her nor spoke, so with something like a defiant shrug she said, "I'll put it on the desk shall I?" She made a couple of hasty strides into the room, placed the tray on the desk and retreated. She closed the door firmly and we heard her receding footsteps break into a run.

"Who was that?" I asked, for it seemed the only possible response to this apparition. I was about to add, "She didn't act like a servant," but I found that my godfather was looking at me in surprise, laughing as though I had asked an endearingly dim question. "One of the servants, of course," he said. I bit my tongue and kept my observations to myself. Ludovick Montefiore fell upon a new topic quickly.

"I promised to show you the mah-jong set!" he declared brightly. I nodded, though I was not in the mood for a game. I felt sure that I would never understand the rules, and that I would make a fool of myself.

I brought the box to my godfather, who leapt from his chair and knelt down on one side of the fire. I knelt on the other side and watched while he slid away one of the sides to reveal the five draws that I had seen once before, in London. He pulled out the top four draws, which were lined with coloured tiles. Then he tipped the tiles out onto the floor and began to line them up, face down, until he had built four walls, each wall two tiles high, which met to form a square. As he bent over the walls, constructing each section with intense care, I noticed that his hands were trembling with excitement and that his breath was thick with the smell of alcohol.

"What's in the fifth draw? I asked, reaching out and opening it tentatively, afraid I might ignite his unpredictable displeasure. There were ivory sticks inside, resembling the spatulas with which doctors depress your tongue when they want to inspect your tonsils, and a tiny box which I opened (since my curiosity had not been reprimanded) to discover four tiny dice, each the size of a child's tooth.

Ludovick Montefiore looked up from his work, distractedly. "Those? I think you need them if you want to play mah-jong. I don't know – for scoring and so forth."

"Oh…." I said, and then, as though my words were setting out across a thinly frozen pond "…is that not what we're doing? Playing mah-jong?"

Ludovick Montefiore looked at me and I was shocked to see a sort of fanatical joy in his blue eyes. During my brief acquaintance with him he had always seemed like a compressed spring, full of pent-up life and vigour, struggling to hold himself in. I feared that the spring had burst from its restraints tonight and I moved back to my footstool. "No, no!" He exclaimed, laughing from his belly. "What, did you think I brought you here to play parlour games? No. no. No, I wanted you to see this, Abigail! My gateway to Traumund!"

Every time I spoke to him tonight I hesitated with fear. "Gateway… to Traumund? What do you mean?"

"I mean that I reach Traumund by stepping inside the mah-jong square. DON'T disturb it (as I inadvertently moved my foot within an inch of the nearest wall) now that the magic is done. The walls must stay absolutely whole and intact."

I drew my legs away slowly, my eyes fixed upon the magic square. Ludovick Montefiore's eyes were fixed on me, like points of scorching light. He wanted to hear my questions.

"Don't you get to Traumund just by…drifting off there?"

Ludovick Montefiore smiled a sad, sardonic smile. "Like you, you mean? No. Not anymore. I used to, but I lost that power when…well… let us simply say that Traumund is a place that is driven by a great mind; a will of its own. That will, the soul of Traumund, turned against me. It didn't want me in its bounds. Whereas once I could drift into Traumund without even registering the drift, now I was blocked, frustrated, met at every turn by black oblivion. That was when I first became ill; when my pulse began to falter and my blood discoloured…"

If my mind had consisted of anything more than infatuated mush I would have asked why. Why? Instead I interrupted with a trusting lament: "But that's not fair! That can't be! Surely Traumund is for everyone, there are no limits…" My protests faded. Ludovick Montefiore looked so sad, all of a sudden, with his head hanging and his eyes resting on the fire. He was like a grand allegorical sculpture called Sorrow, stony yet touching, beyond the reach of counsel or comfort.

"Traumund rejected me," he repeated firmly, "but I couldn't live without Traumund. Imagine, Abigail, a world where there was no escape from consciousness."

"The Institute would call that heaven," I mused.

"Yes," he replied with a glancing smile. "Precisely. If 'heaven' and 'hell' are concepts permitted by Miss Konder et al."

He resumed his tale. "Traumund banished me, but I refused to accept exile. I would rather die. I had to find another way in, a secret, illegal route. So I forced my way back to Traumund by magic. I won't – I can't explain to you how I did it – it took years and years of study and experiment and thought. You only need to know that at long last I found the key to my return in this mah-jong set."

"Why? Why the mah-jong set?"

"It used to be my grandmother's and I played with it as a child: not the game itself, you understand, since there was nobody to play with, but my own imaginary adventures. Marches, encampments, castle-building, wars against the dragons: the tiles were my battlements, my soldiers, my weaponry, my spoils, my cities. The Rice Bird (do you remember seeing the Rice Bird in London?) used to be my ally, my advisor. And I used to go inside the landscape tiles as well...you remember that watercolour painting you were looking at the other morning?... I used to pretend that those rivers and hills were parts of my kingdom; that they belonged to me.

"After searching long and hard through all these books and all my lifetime's knowledge, I discovered that this childhood land of mine was my one and only route back to Traumund. So I wrapped each tile in a web of incantations and spells and made them live. Each tile is necessary for the construction of my gateway, my lifeline; each tile is more precious to me than life itself. And now, every night, I construct the walls as I have shown you. Then I step inside the enchanted square, as though through a door, and thus...thus I take myself home." Now I knew that he was drunk, by the slurred emphasis of his speech, the absent-minded blanks and by the way in which he leant into my face, so that I breathed the brimstone fumes from his lungs. I wondered whether he would tell me any of this if he were sober.

"But doesn't...Traumund...mind?" I asked.

He shrugged and flashed me a sly smile. "There's nothing Traumund can do against my magic."

"So..." infatuation had whisked my mind away on a new, fantastical flight, "could I go through the square with you, into your land?"

He looked up with a piercing frown, as though the question had jolted him. He hesitated, as though he was struggling to find a polite way of refusing my request. This surprised me, because I thought my godfather was above such trivialities as politeness.

"You could," he said slowly, "you could". He started to dismantle his wall, nonetheless, in an absent-minded manner. "Maybe that would be a good idea. But, then again, what would become of Joachim? You would have found a new ally in me, only to have lost him and Eyes, and so you would have gained nothing."

"Oh, Joachim!" I muttered dismissively. The prospect of seeing Ludovick Montefiore's imaginary land was infinitely more exciting than a return to our useless plans, to that same old house, which (however fine it was) I had already seen. The existence of my first loyalties irritated me beyond measure at that moment. But of course Ludovick Montefiore's opinion on the matter was what mattered.

When I emerged from my resentment, I realised that the mah-jong set had been packed away and returned to the desk. Ludovick Montefiore was pacing back and forth across the hearth rug, and I noticed once again what I often forgot: that he was ill. His face was cream-coloured, clammy like the breast of a raw, plucked chicken, and he shuffled like an old man. He was talking to himself in a nervous murmur, and I noticed with surprise how his hands trembled and gestured in response to his thoughts. I made out a few cryptic phrases: "I don't know, I don't know. Is it possible? If only...If only..."

I watched him with all the painful pleasure of adolescent love and fantasised that I was the subject of his agitation.

He paused before the dresser and poured a cupful of something black and viscous from one of the stone bottles. He drank this quickly in one, long grimacing gulp. Then he took the silver sword down from its shelf and turned to face me. He stood there in the semi-darkness, leaning with both hands upon the hilt, like an old man with a walking stick. I remember thinking, with an unreal sort of anxiety, that the blade tip would make a hole in the rug.

"You love me, don't you Abigail?" he then asked in a mild, matter-of-fact voice, as though he had asked me, "You like chocolate cake don't you?"

Adolescent infatuation constantly constructs imaginary scenarios like this, but it is too stupid and too tongue-tied to conduct a coherent love-scene in reality. I knew the many things that a dream Abigail might say and do in response to this turn of events, but I lost all her dream-induced assurance when I found myself caught by his question. I managed a hoarse little "No", then a hoarser, "Yes," as I stared at him with an expression and a feeling that were more like dread than love.

Ludovick Montefiore continued. His tone remained quiet and careful, as though I was the expert in some obscure science, and he was my pupil. But as he spoke he stared into my eyes – right through my eyes and into my mind - with menacing intensity.

"Do you think you will always love me?"

I cleared my throat. "Yes." I tried to sound as baldly factual as he did, but I expect my efforts were all too plain.

He took a step towards me. "How can you be sure?"

"I don't know, but I can."

He took another step. He was so close to me now that I could feel his breath on my forehead.

"In that case" he began, "there are things you should know about me."

My terror was like a crowd of icy hands that hovered over every part of my body - my skin, my organs, my limbs, my scalp – and waited to fall and clench with vice-like rigour. His preamble was over, I waited for the great outpouring; the explanation with which I was to be shackled and honoured. My godfather bit his knuckles as though forcing himself to utter something truly terrible. Then, all of a sudden, he relaxed, with a shake of his head.

"But perhaps...not yet," he said. All the intensity had left his voice and I no longer felt afraid. I already felt sorry that I had not played my part well; that I had not made him comprehend the extent of my love and my eagerness to help him.

"Take this," he said, as he placed the silver sword in my hands. "Take it with you to Traumund. It won't fail you."

I took it and barely thanked him.

He cleared his throat briskly. "You'd better get on now," he said, "they will be waiting for you. Don't worry about...anything I said. Don't worry about anything."

Suicide Sylvia

he first thing I noticed on my return to the bedroom was that Mrs. Veals had laid a freshly laundered night gown on top of the pillow. Of all the bizarre happenings whirling through and around me, this was hardly the most startling, yet I noticed the night gown at once. Having deposited the silver sword on my mantelpiece like a soiled trophy, I unfolded the gown, holding it out at arms length. It was long and once it had been white, but now it was yellow with age. When I held it to my face I was comforted by the homely smell of soapsuds and hot irons. I had not worn any night clothes, nor had I sunk into a dreamless sleep, for a long time. I undressed and pulled the night gown over my head.

As the garment fell around my feet, a terrible shrieking erupted inside my head, echoing back and forth from one ear to the other in a blurred rush of noise. I clutched my ears with my hands and shouted, "What is it? Stop!" (When we talked about it later on, Boris insisted that it was I who had shrieked. I retorted that it was not me, but something, or somebody, inside my head. "Well," objected Boris, "if it was inside your head, then it must have been you, mustn't it? It can't have been independent of you and part of you." But I shushed him and told him he was wrong.) The night gown hung on my body like slime; it was as though it had been drenched in pond water. I tried to lift it back over my head, but the material seemed to knot itself around my legs and cling to my body like billowing underwater vegetation. The shrieks still deafened my confused brain; I felt as though I was drowning. I tore the gown off in a frenzy and at once the room was still and warm and silent again.

I stood by the fire, wrapped tightly in a woollen dressing gown and trying in vain to rid myself of the watery chill and the noisome pain in my head. I reflected that this was probably some trick devised by Mrs. Veals. I seized the gown and flung it into the corridor. I found, as I touched it, that it was as dry and sweet smelling as at first.

I did not go to Traumund that night. I sent a bitterly reproachful Boris to tell Joachim and the others that I was ill; that I needed a long sleep and that I would come the following night. I was not ill, as Boris knew, but strangely weary of the whole Traumund business, reluctant to think or act. I wanted to sleep. Consciousness seemed, all at once, a heavy burden.

The following morning dawned foggy and I never saw the sun that day. It did not feel like a day; it felt like a pale night. I had slept deeply and upon waking I was listless. I spent hours persuading myself to rise and hating myself for the idle delay. When, at last, I had shivered out of bed, I took a long, draughty time getting dressed. I did not go down to breakfast, but paced up and down the room instead, fingering my books and flicking through the first few pages of each. I glanced out of the window every now and then, but it was shrouded in cloud and I could see no further than the narrow gravel path that wound its way around the house.

I must have idled away the whole morning in restless meditation, but around noon I was granted a short reprieve. I stood beside the window listening to the clock chime twelve, watching a bluebottle bustle across the pane in fits and starts and as I did so I heard feet crunching the path beneath me. I looked down and saw Fay trailing languidly through the mist. I was surprised by the sense of relief that animated me at once and at the desperation with which I banged on the window (disturbing the fly that blundered against my face) and signalled for her to come and find me.

The prospect of Fay's sunny banality filled me with a grateful sense of the ordinary in my present mood. When she burst through the door with an insincerely warm "Hia, Abigail!", I responded in the same manner, barely refraining from hugging her. We spent an hour or so shaping her shortened hair, as best we could, into a more desirable style, and talked of nothing more profound than our favourite alcoholic drinks and whether, strictly speaking, either of us had ever been drunk.

We decided that champagne was best, that I had not and Fay definitely had.

Mrs. Veals brought our lunch on a tray once again, and lit the fire, while Fay hid inside the cupboard. The substantial spread included, at Fay's insistence and my acute embarrassment (what would he think if he heard, especially as I would appear to be drinking it on my own?), a bottle of champagne in a silver ice bucket. We drank it quickly and Fay was all for ordering another. She glanced at the clock, however, as the idea left her mouth and tottered up with a cry of alarmed laughter: her afternoon classes had begun five minutes ago. I was left alone.

The champagne was pleasant at first, while Fay was with me, but as soon as she left it began to depress my volatile spirits and I became even gloomier than before. I thought I should pull myself together and do something. For a moment I thought I might explore the house, but then that would be an adventure and I felt over-exposed to adventures. I suppose I was missing my magical tree, for what I really wanted was to batten down the hatches and hide, like a rabbit who has been nibbling in the fields for too long and begins to hear (or think she can hear) the echo of a distant shot gun. But, though I was warm and well-provided for, and close to my beloved godfather, I could not settle; I was not at ease. No, for some reason I did not feel safe.

So, from two o'clock (when Fay left me) until four, I sat and stood and paced and read and flung my book aside and began on another. At four o'clock the dark grey day declined by a degree or two, becoming a dark blue evening that pressed against the house and especially against my window, as though a scarf were being wrapped tightly around the eyes of the building. I tried to read The Ghost stories of an Antiquary, but the reader of a ghost story must feel some sense of security or companionship and I only felt fear – my own, unenjoyable fear. I put the book away. I did not light the candles or draw the curtains. I picked Boris up by the leg and twirled him round slowly. I leant my forehead against the window and stared at the outside world, which consisted of nothing but indistinct whirls of white darkness and I imagined that the darkness and mist could crush the stones of this ancient abbey.

Boughwinds Abbey was always quiet, except when the wind tore through its forest walls. Now, under this fog, the place seemed as silent to me as though I was wearing ear-plugs. I began to listen for a sound, any slight sound, anything that might reassure me that life existed apart from me: distant footsteps or voices or, failing that, the scurry of a mouse or a rat, or the flurry of a bird outside my window. Nothing.

There was no light either, except the dubious red light of my dying fire. I began to try and recall my trivial conversation with Fay, as though I was trying to remember words of vital religious comfort.

At last this gathering oppression goaded me to act. I decided I must find Ludovick Montefiore. I would tell him how lonely I felt and at the thought of this pathetic confession I smiled. I turned to the door (still smiling, as I composed his soft reply), only to discover that I was not, after all, alone.

A frail little girl stood, or seemed to stand, between me and the door. I say "seemed", because it was only when I stared fully and steadily that her form possessed solidity. If I took my gaze away then she disappeared and until I stared again, I felt sure that the door behind her was fully visible. In other words, she did not exist in the corner of my eye.

Even when I looked at her properly she was semi-transparent. Her skin was a bluish, icy-white; her eyes were like pearls and her hair was a paler shade of blond than I have ever seen, like weak sunshine on snow. She was wearing a long, white night gown, yellowed with age.

I stared at her, afraid of what I saw, yet more afraid to look away. For a foolish second I thought I was free to break from the dark story to which I had so far submitted, and burst into the mundane sunshine of a comedy. I did my best to muster a tone of lively insolence, but my voice shook. "You're a bit early for bed aren't you?" I said.

The girl looked back without smiling. There was barely any light left in the room, but she glowed faintly white, like a paper lampshade. Then she spoke and her voice, though it matched the movement of her lips, did not pass through the air between us. It existed inside my head.

"I never sleep. I was wearing a night gown when I died. You know the one. Mrs. Veals wanted you to wear it too."

I shook my head vigorously when I heard that independent voice active, though quietly now, inside my own mind. I felt that I ought to be able to shoo it away by my own volition, because surely (as Boris insisted) if it was inside me, then it was me…but that was a dark train of thought. I wanted to cast unbelieving sarcasms at this girl, but I knew that this would only emphasise my own frightened stupidity. I did believe that she was a ghost. I could not help but know it and I could not take my eyes off her.

"I wish you would not stare at me like that," she said haughtily, "as though I was something horrible. I did not ask to be dead. I have not become evil, merely by dying…"

"I'm sorry -" I replied, dragging my gaze away. I felt a little soothed by the irritation in her tone, since it made her seem less ethereal. "I'm just…I've never seen one before. And you're transparent…"

"Never seen 'one'," repeated the girl sulkily, "Well, I am sorry." She crossed her arms aggressively and stared at me as though awaiting an apology. I promptly obliged, since a silent, staring ghost is more sinister than a talkative one.

"My name is Abigail by the way," I added awkwardly.

"I know. My name is Sylvia."

"Suicide Syl..?" I cried and clapped a hand across my mouth as I heard, too late, my blunder. (It is, self-evidently, impolite to refer to the circumstances surrounding the death of a ghost with whom one is engaged in introductory small-talk.) Sylvia replied chillingly, "I am sometimes referred to as Suicide Sylvia. Although in fact, I did not commit suicide."

I felt it would be rude to ignore this information, though I did not want to dwell on it, so I made an interested "Oh?" noise and then quickly asked, "Why are you in my bedroom?"

"I am here to help you. There are things you must know. Allecto and I have been looking for an opportunity to talk to you, but such opportunities are difficult to come by in this God-forsaken place, believe me."

"Allecto?"

"Yes." she replied unhelpfully. "The spies are occupied with a rancid chicken carcass; your godfather is dozing and Mrs. Veals is cooking dinner in the kitchen, so it will never be safer for you to sneak down to the library. We will have to be quick and quiet, but I think we can do it if we hurry. I am good at spotting them anyway – the spies – and if I point them out, then you can swat them."

"Spies? What are you talking about?" A feeling of dread, much quieter and heavier than my fear of the ghost or of the ins and outs of adventure, began to inflate inside my rib cage, slowly and majestically, like a black balloon. "I'm not sneaking anywhere or talking to anyone behind my godfather's back. If I want help, I'll go to him."

Like the most infatuated and unreasoning of enthusiasts, I inwardly proclaimed that blind loyalty to Ludovick Montefiore was my vocation; the one virtue, and the highest, to which I could aspire. Such devotion was of great comfort to me, because it seemed to absolve me from contradictory responsibilities. If only I did not doubt it.

"What are you risking?" Sylvia asked, a pleading tone disturbing her poise for the first time. "Surely you are not afraid of your loving godfather?"

"Of course not!" I scoffed. And then, timidly, "But I wouldn't want to make him angry. Well? Why should I risk that?"

"Because..!" Sylvia wrung her hands. "Because he has not told you the truth. There are things you must know. You must or everything is lost."

"But I trust Ludovick Montefiore!" I exclaimed, (at least I tried to exclaim but, against my will, a whining note crept into my voice).

"You trust him so much that all your curiosity is dead? Would it not even interest you to meet his wife?"

The black balloon kept filling with heavy air, until I thought it would explode inside me.

"Come on Abigail. Come, quickly."

We raced through the abbey, Sylvia flitting against the walls like weak torch-light, while I stumbled along behind her on tip toes. I wasn't frightened at all anymore, or at least, not in a jumpy way. I don't know how I would have explained myself if we had met Mrs. Veals or Ludovick Montefiore, but I hadn't room in my mind for such worries. There was only room for the lead balloon, which was tottering into fullness now and settling inside me. It took all my energies just to be aware of it and to feel it. "Oh no, oh no," my blurred thoughts repeated over and over, with every step. The dark outdoors seemed to have penetrated the abbey, so that all the staircases and corridors writhed with mists and cold, wet breezes.

"In here," whispered Sylvia's alien voice inside my head, as we slipped through a doorway. I knew it, by the unmistakable smells of dusty paper and leather, for the library that I had glimpsed so fleetingly on my first morning. I had not brought my candle and there was no light in the library, except for Sylvia's moonlike glow. I could make nothing out except dark, many-toned walls and black stepladders standing at angles against the shelves. So I stood there, a heap of dense gloom inside the library's airy gloom, wishing I could go back and bury my head under the pillow.

"Come on!" Sylvia whispered inside my head. She held out a papery hand but I did not try to take it. We tiptoed halfway across the room and then turned right into an alcove formed by two sets of shelves. Here there was some light at last: four thin, orange lines surrounding a square of darkness at our feet. Sylvia whistled softly and the darkness swung back to be replaced by a square of brilliant gold that I could hardly bear (though it was only candlelight), because my eyes were so accustomed to shadows.

As the trapdoor opened a hand emerged, and motioned us to come down. So we scrambled down the step-ladder into a cramped hidey-hole beneath the library floor.

The motioning hand belonged to a woman. His wife, I thought. I knew the truth of it at once.

"Abigail. I'm Allecto," she said briskly, without meeting my eye. "Welcome to my...my workshop." I glanced about. She had done her best to make the place homely: it was warm, clean and there were a couple of faded prints on the walls and a green quilt over her iron bed. But it wasn't palatial either, considering that (as it turned out) she lived as well as worked there. There were no windows or comfortable chairs. It wasn't nice like my room.

The most noticeable thing about it was the smell emanating from the large cauldron that simmered over a stove in the corner. It was not an unpleasant smell, though difficult to describe. "Herby" is the adjective that springs to mind, though it is rather a vague one, Indeed there were piles of dried leaves and grasses and roots and so forth piled around the floor and on the table and hanging in bunches from the ceiling. It was a herby smell then: pleasantly warm and heady at first, then, after a while, nauseating. I wondered what she was cooking: sometimes I thought it was something medicinal, but then I thought it must be perfume or bath oil.

I recognised Ludovick Montefiore's wife at once. She was the woman who had appeared in his study the night before with a tray of coffee. He had referred to her as a servant, which – you will recall – surprised me. My surprise was confirmed on meeting her now: evidently this woman did not take kindly to her own downtrodden appearance and her very attempts to dispel the impression lent her a regal air. As for her beauty, even I reluctantly admired it. Allecto was the sort of woman who could dress in bare feet, dirty, ill-fitting trousers, a man's shirt and a scraggy, uncombed pony tail yet still ooze superiority and charm. She was wearing precisely such an outfit when I met her that evening. I was wearing a red velvet dress and my hair was curling down my back, but she eclipsed me. She was fit to be Ludovick Montefiore's wife; more fit than I could ever be. Later that night Boris remarked that Allecto was the sort of person with whom one could become infatuated for no good reason. I replied that she was also the sort of person whom one could loathe for no good reason.

"Sit down!" Allecto continued. I think she was addressing me, though she was watching Sylvia anxiously as she closed the trapdoor behind her. "Sit down please, we'll have to be quick about this."

I did not speak. Boris said later that I had a wary look about me, as if I was waiting for a giant foot to stamp down on me and finish me off. I decided to let him take charge, even though, in the Waking World, he is meant to be inanimate. I had a feeling – Boris himself had it too - that Boughwinds Abbey was not fully connected with the Waking World. I can't quite say how it was: the eerie quietness perhaps, the ghostly presence of Sylvia, the candlelight, the walls of forest shutting us in on every side? Somehow it was more like a frontier of Traumund. I am not saying it was safe for Boris (it wasn't safe for anyone), but I knew that nobody here would be overcome with astonishment if he spoke.

"Could you tell us what is going on please?" he asked imperiously. There was more than a touch of annoyance in his voice, which was meant to make us look a bullish pair. It was I who provoked him though, not Sylvia or Allecto. It was because I had abandoned myself to a cold, glazed wretchedness. I wanted to believe I was not really there.

"We two," Allecto began, "have stories to tell, which you need to hear, even if you don't want to….Hello?"

Allecto bent her head in order to meet my lowered gaze. She was clearly stung by my apparent lack of interest and she continued sharply, "You haven't the faintest clue what's going on, have you? Did you know that, Abigail Crabtree? You're living in a little fantasy world of your own that bears no relation to any reality on earth. I know what your version of events is and I also know what the reality is. Don't you realise that I'm doing you a favour; I'm risking my life in order to set you straight?" Sylvia stood beside Allecto, arms folded and nodded her stern agreement.

I was beleaguered, so Boris pitied me and resumed his imperious tone. "Perhaps you could spare us the self-congratulation and say what you have to say."

Allecto shrugged and smiled. She was too lofty to be offended by the hauteur of a small bear. She leant back in her chair and nodded at Sylvia who now hovered in the middle of the room, casting a bluish pallor over the candlelight.

"Off we go then," Allecto said. "Tell them what happened to you, 'Suicide Sylvia'."

Sylvia's Tale

he silence surrounding Sylvia's voice was heavy like stone.

"Fay, Marcus and all the other pupils who have been here since my time, call me Suicide Sylvia. But they are wrong to do that. That is what I have to tell you.

"I was brought up by my granddad, Toby. You have met him, I know, at The Witch's Broom. I loved him well enough and he loved me, but I did not want to stay with him – more fool me. I wanted an education. I was always reading books and trying to teach myself Greek, but granddad was suspicious of such things. He could never see the point in it. He sent me to the village school of course, but I had vague ideas that I could do better; that there were great mysteries to be learnt about that I would never come close to knowing if I just stayed as I was.

"So when Mr. Montefiore set up a school right here at the abbey, just a few miles from the village, I saw my chance. Your godfather was, and still is, so famous, so lauded in the world of education. I pleaded with my granddad, pestered him, until in the end he agreed that I might take a place, if I could get one. I did get one, so poor granddad scraped all his money together and paid the fees outright for a year. I arrived at the Institute with the same high hopes that you entertained Abigail, three years ago.

"I was quickly disillusioned, as you will understand all too well. People only come here to have their minds stifled and killed by the system that Mr. Montefiore has devised for his own wicked ends. It is true!" (as I made a faint, protesting moan.) "If you give in to it, if you

stop thinking and feeling anything except the things they want you to
think and feel, then life is so cushy and everyone is so pleased with
you. What a relief, when the Institute has laid your mind to rest; when
you know that your beautiful body and your soft, silky hair are the only
things that matter in your uninteresting little life."

I interrupted, though my voice was laden with doubt. "Ludovick
Montefiore has nothing to do with it. Or rather...I mean...he thinks
Institutes are just ordinary schools. He doesn't know what's going on."

Sylvia sneered. "Oh please! How naïve can you be? Mr. Montefiore
invented the whole system. Nothing gives him more pleasure than to
witness the slow, comfortable death of a soul. I won an award once for
a project entitled, "Why thinking is bad for the complexion." No irony
anticipated, naturally. It was your godfather who presented the prize,
Abigail Crabtree. He shook my hand and gave me a bottle of anti-
cellulite gel with his warmest congratulations.

"Of course I went along with it all, outwardly at least – you know
how it is. I doubted myself during momentary lapses perhaps, but deep
down I believed, with increasing fervour, that the Institute was wrong
and my instincts were right. I was not going to give in to it. My head
burned more than it had ever done in its life; burned to read and learn
and to resist that deadly numbness that threatened to subdue it. So I
stole – or borrowed - a hoard of books from your godfather's library.
I kept them under my bed and read by torchlight, when I was sure that
the others were asleep.

"Well, one evening I made my way here - into the library, I mean -
intending to return some old books to their shelves and take some new
ones. No sooner had I entered when I heard a row going on inside one
of the alcoves. Your godfather was shouting at somebody; shouting
so loudly that my ears rang. I could easily have escaped unseen and
unheard, but I was curious. So I scuttled forward until I reached the
alcove adjacent to his. Peering through the rows of books, I found that
I had a perfect view of him and his victim.

"Allecto (I did not know her name then, of course, she was a stranger
to me) was crouched on the floor, her tense arms covering her head as
though waiting for him to kick her. Your wonderful Mr. Montefiore was
frothing at the mouth – really, there was spit on his chin – as he paced
round and round like a bear in its den. He called her all the names under
the sun. I did not realise she was his wife. I supposed that she was an
intruder whom he had caught doing something truly terrible: trying to
set fire to the abbey or abduct one of the pupils or something. But then

she looked up at him through the shield made by her arms and said in a shaky, soothing voice,

"Ludovick, it's only a few books…"

"Only a few books! How dare you insult me! It is your job to look after my books, yet I find that five of them – five – have gone missing! And you have the effrontery, the bare-faced effrontery to tell me that they are only a few books!"

"I'm not saying they're not important. It was careless of me and I'm sorry. But they can't have gone far, can they? I mean they must be in the house somewhere."

"But where?" he thundered. "I want them back on their shelves now! Now!"

"But…"

"Well? Are they back?"

"I…I'm sorry."

"He clenched his fists hard as he paced and his jaw was so compressed that it must have hurt his teeth. I made two surmises. Firstly that your godfather was gearing up to strike her, whether with his fists or with his feet. Secondly, that the five books he missed so badly were in my hands at that very moment. Well, I was tired of skulking about, and if he threw me out of the Institute then so much the better. I did not want to be here, especially if it was impossible for me to use the library. So I stepped into their alcove and cleared my throat. You should have seen them jump – both of them! Mr. Montefiore stood stock still and… just…gaped at me. Allecto looked up in astonishment, then shook her head with such a pitying glare. I did not fully understand her expression at the time, though I understand it now.

"The books you were…discussing," I said haltingly. "They are here. I borrowed them." I was about to add, "I am sorry," but the words stuck in my throat.

"Allecto was the first to move. With a split-second glance at Mr. Montefiore she stood up and snatched the five volumes from my hands. "Thank you" she said peremptorily. "Off you go now and don't do it again please." I hesitated. "Go!" she hissed and shoved me away. Unfortunately, her tone was not sufficient to make me run for my life, though it was sharp enough to rouse Mr. Montefiore from his stupor.

"Wait!" he cried, as I took a few weak-kneed backward steps. "You will wait! I order you to wait!"

"Well, where would I have gone anyway? I stood and faced him.

"Naturally I expected a volley of abuse, even a kicking. Instead I

was led to a soft, leathery chair and invited to sit down. He dismissed
Allecto with a wave of his hand and then perched on a footstool at my
feet. He started to ask question after question: not angrily (far from it)
but intensely. I felt like a vole in polite conversation with an eagle. Why
did I borrow the books? Had I read them? What did I make of them?
Did I often read books? Did I enjoy the Institute system? Did I believe
in its principles? Did I believe in exercising my imagination? Did I
own an imaginary land that I visited at night? What was it like? On and
on he went. He was nice to me and nodded understandingly at every
slight word and every pause I made. Nonetheless, his consideration
towards me was coloured by my memory of that violent scene that I
had just witnessed. I answered all his questions briefly and coldly, even
though he talked of things that were close to my heart. When he tried
to make me talk about Traumund I admitted that I had a land and that it
was mountainous and snowy, but I clammed up when he started fishing
for more details. I even told him that it was none of his business.

"I knew by his narrow-eyed smile that he disliked me, but he would
not drop his pretence of kindly interest just yet. When the interrogation
was over he patted me on the head and said in a voice that made me
squirm (it was all honey), "It seems we have a very special little girl in
our midst. Too special for the Institute's tender mercies, at any rate. I
shall tell Mrs. Veals to prepare you a new room, Sylvia; we can't have
you wasting away in those soulless dormitories. In the meantime, I
hope you will join me for dinner, where we shall discuss your future.
Evidently you are made for higher things…"

"So I went in to dinner, where Mrs. Veals served me soup and lamb
cutlets and trifle, with such a reverential air! It was surreal. It was
dangerously gratifying. After three courses and several glasses of wine
I was ready to like Mr. Montefiore after all – to like him very much
- and I was excited by his mention of my "future". I decided, rather
woozily, that the Institute was an elaborate test, designed to separate
especially intelligent people from the unthinking masses and that I
had somehow managed to prove myself…Oh, I do not know what I
thought. I was drunk or drugged.

"I presumed that he would ask more questions and I was willing to
answer him civilly this time. I even felt embarrassed by my curtness in
the library. But he didn't say a word throughout dinner: he just chewed
his nails and stared, as though I was a problem that he wanted to solve.
His thoughtful glare unnerved me, for all my tipsy amiability, and I was
glad when Mrs. Veals led me away to my new room.

"They gave me your bedroom, Abigail, though they didn't furnish it so beautifully for me. It was quite sparse during the few hours that it was mine, rather as it was on your first night at Boughwinds Abbey. Still, I remember thinking it quite wonderful, because it was grand and atmospheric and, above all, entirely my own. I went to bed thinking how strangely the day had ended for me, and wondering what tomorrow would bring.

"I went to sleep quickly, but lightly: my brain was hurried through labyrinthine scenarios and it protested all the time and demanded to wake up, as though, even in my sleep, I was too tired for dreams. A monstrous figure seemed to lean over my pillow, its moist, smelly breath oppressively close to my nose and mouth. In a moment it lifted me up in its arms and we sped away. For half a second I thought that I knew it was a Minotaur, but then I lost the meaning of the word 'Minotaur', though the sound of it kept banging away inside my head. Walls and staircases rolled past my struggling eyelids as I strained to wake. Half my brain assured me that it was already conscious; the other half remained paralysed and incapable. I think there must have been some slow-acting poison in that dinner.

"We emerged into the garden, where the chilly air brought me round a little more and I saw Mrs. Veals' face against the bright, starry sky, like an unlit moon. I realised that I was being carried in her muscular arms. She could not run under her burden, but she walked, jogged, walked again, panting noisily. It felt as though the real moon, the stars and I were turning inside a giant kaleidoscope.

"We must have reached that rough bit of garden by the chapel, because I could hear Mrs. Veals' feet brushing the long grass. Then I heard their voices.

"You've got the girl?" rapped Mr. Montefiore.

"Yes, sir," replied Mrs. Veals.

"The right girl?" he laughed and twisted my unresisting face towards his. "We might as well do the right one." I felt his fingernails in my cheeks and his sharp eyes sawing quickly, up and down, across my face. When he was satisfied he let go, making my neck jerked backwards.

"It's all ready," he continued. "Now let's be quick about it."

"I cannot remember what happened during the next few minutes, or hours, or however long it took for them to kill me. I can give you impressions of the things I saw and felt when I died, though perhaps they will not convey much. I have never understood them properly myself,and I understand them less and less as time goes on. It was like a dream in two contrasting parts; a dream that made more impression on me than anything I have ever experienced before or since, but that I just cannot, cannot describe accurately – even to myself.

"I must try, all the same.

"First there was…it was like hell. Perhaps it was hell. It wasn't a violent, fiery, active state. On the contrary, it was like floating through a starless, airless, infinite blackness, a void that whistled slightly, like somebody hissing through their teeth. I was fully conscious - I mean I could touch my blind eyes and I could gasp out, "Help me!" and hear my ludicrous words suffocate in the nothingness that was everywhere. I was just afraid at first, then I comforted myself with the thought that it must end soon, and then I began to plead…and then, at last, I realised that it would never end; that I would float like this forever, never even dying, with nobody there. Nobody. That was despair.

"When I had realised this, or rather, when I thought I had realised it, then it ended. If I tell you that I cried for joy, you mustn't imagine a couple of sentimental tears trickling down my cheeks: I croaked and gagged and rivers poured out of my eyes. Imagine being lost in that black desolation and then some music starts up faraway, some tiny lyrical piano notes that you hardly believe in at first, only they swell and swell until they are a great deafening, thundering chorus of orchestras and choirs. And at the same time the air becomes fresh and mild, like the air on a summer morning, and there is a faint dusk somewhere in the dark that your disbelieving eyes seek out and frowningly yearn towards and as the music grows so does the light, until the whole sky is a pale, pearly-grey dawn, streaked with rose and gold. And then, best of all, a warm, familiar hand touches yours and a voice says something lovely in your ear…which I have forgotten… I wish it would come back!"

Sylvia crouched down on the dusty floor, a little flickering impression of a girl, and beat her shadow-fists against her shadow-thighs. "It will come back," said Allecto kindly. "One day, when this is all over, it will come back and you will be in that place forever. I am sure of it." Allecto made as if to put her arm round Sylvia, but there was nothing to hold, so she gazed helplessly and murmured soothing sounds.

"It ended anyway," Sylvia continued after a while, in a matter-of-fact tone, wiping the streaks from her translucent cheeks, "And all of a sudden I came back to earth with a jolt and found I was running fast through the grove of yew trees beyond the chapel, shivering with cold, but also with a sort of heightened consciousness. How can I explain? I was brilliantly awake: I had that energy that comes to you in bed sometimes on sleepless nights, when you feel you could run and run as fast as a cheetah without ever tiring. Only I knew that I really could, and that there was nothing to stop me.

"So I did: I ran for about an hour until I reached a river and even then I could not bear to stop, so I plunged into the water and let the reeds and weeds wind round my legs and drag me down. I was not afraid of drowning and just for a moment I wondered why not, but it did not seem worth worrying about. I just breathed the water as though it was air and that was fine. I was so happy, because the last part of my dream was still with me, that I started to laugh. I laughed and laughed until I was surrounded by swirling bubble pillars that made me laugh even more.

"Hours went by as I swam and ran beneath the stars. But the good dream began to fade. I let my body drift downstream and as I relaxed I tried to think and remember. My joy slipped away as a squalid red dawn spread itself over the sky. I held my hands out before my face and saw how fleshless they were: like tissue-paper cut-outs. When I climbed ashore the water did not cling heavily to my night-dress or drip from my hair: I was as untouchable as the dawn rays that flickered across the river.

"I found myself back at Boughwinds Abbey. I walked into the garden and stopped in the yew grove, because I saw something solid hanging from a branch. I knew, by now, what it was, without need of any closer examination, but I approached it all the same, because I had a macabre desire to look at my own dead face...

"Since that night I have never left the abbey. There is a magnetism that forces me to stay. Nothing is clear to me. Sometimes I think I will be here forever in sort of limbo, sometimes I think I will be allowed to go when I have played my role – whatever that may be. Sometimes I appear before them (my murderers): it does unnerve Mrs. Veals, but Mr. Montefiore merely lifts his cold eyebrows and stares me out. I have never mixed with Fay and Marcus. Allecto is my only friend, but thank goodness for her. I hope...."

Sylvia stopped short with a start. Silence closed round her words and filled her half-open mouth.

Allecto's Tale

araway, in a place beyond Sylvia's silence, the library door had bounced back on its hinges and mannish shoes were stumping across the floor above our heads. Allecto started out of her chair and without a word she whisked open the oven (which was cold) and bundled us inside. She clicked the door gently shut and we sat listening in the semi-darkness, while the cauldron simmered above our heads.

"I'm coming! Who is it?" cooed Allecto, a slight fluster apparent in her voice.

We heard the trapdoor crash open.

"He wants to see you this evening," Mrs. Veals said, without any preliminaries. "Be outside his study door at a quarter to eight with a new bottle."

"So long as he does want me this time," replied Allecto sharply, though nervousness still made her breaths come fast. "I won't be made a fool of again, Mrs. Veals."

We heard a noise like the motion of a rusty saw through wood as Mrs Veals chuckled. "He was not happy, you know, having you burst in on him and his precious goddaughter like that."

"I know," snapped Allecto more confidently. "That is why I made it quite clear to him afterwards that it was your fault in the first place for handing me the tray."

There was silence from above as Mrs. Veals digested this retort.

"How is the girl doing?" continued Allecto, brightly. "Is she proving a satisfactory pupil?"

"Oh, didn't you know?" returned the housekeeper. "He's not having her taught. He has other plans for her."

I stiffened, as though a cold finger was tracing my spine.

"And what plans would they be?" inquired Allecto.

"That, my dear," returned Mrs. Veals in a defensive tone, which suggested to me that she had no idea, "is none of your business. You've made your contribution, that's all you need to know." The trapdoor bounced shut.

Allecto hauled us out before the footsteps had altogether faded. "Sit down again, quickly," she whispered angrily. "This will have to be really quick now I've an appointment, all right?" I nodded, yet she did not begin. She paced about, stirred the cauldron, picked things up and put them down again. Eventually Sylvia spoke. "You must tell them your story as well, Allecto."

"All right!"

Allecto sat down opposite me and crossed her arms aggressively.

"So he's not bothering to put you through the Institute and yet you're still alive and well. What has he got in store for you?" She gasped with coarse, unhappy laughter. I made no reply.

She began again. "Don't you recognise me? I don't mean from yesterday, I mean…" I looked up this time, but my face was blank as I shook my head.

"Ha! Funny that," Allecto laughed again, although there was still no humour in her eyes or her tone. "We've travelled half way across England together, you and I, yet you don't recognise me."

Both Boris and I looked again, with hardened, narrowed eyes. Boris started up from my lap. "You!" he exploded. I felt my jaw tighten and my breathing quicken.

"Quiet!" hissed Allecto in alarm, clamping her hands around Boris's muzzle. "Please let me explain and then you can do as you think fit. Please."

"You are the woman in the veiled hat?" Boris whispered viciously, struggling from her grasp. I noted his obedient whisper.

Allecto's face was scarlet. I couldn't be sure whether she wanted to rage or weep, but whichever it was, she managed to swallow the impulse and continue.

"Yes, I am 'the woman in the veiled hat', as you put it so dramatically. I am responsible for drugging and abducting you and bringing you here."

"You did not bring me here." I snarled. "I came here of my own accord."

"Yes, because I let you. When I realised that you were going to walk straight into his saving arms anyway, I decided to leave you to your own devices. My, but you were keen to get here, weren't you? He allowed me three days for the operation and you made it on your own in two! He hadn't even had chance to get back from London. And I had feared I would have to drag you, kicking and screaming! But all the same, I kept a close eye on you, went to the village ahead of you to prepare a welcome at The Witch's Broom and escorted you to the abbey the next day, though you thought you were alone. Because that's me, the kidnapper, the baddy, the villain of the piece." She did cry now. The tears fell quickly down her cheeks, drop, drop, drop, her breath coming in shudders. She put her head in her hands and her shoulders began to shake. I stared open-mouthed at Sylvia as she laid a weightless hand on Allecto's back and at Allecto as she wept. Without really considering my words, only swearing that I would never soften towards this woman, I half-whispered,

"Yes, that's what you are if all you've said is true. You are wicked! You are evil! How dare you cry?" Then, childishly, "I am not crying!"

Allecto fought for breath and answered me. "I'm n-not crying out of self-pity or at least, I don't mean to. You're right: I am wicked. I didn't acknowledge my guilt in order to hear anybody deny it. But I am only wicked because I am weak. If I were powerful, I mean if I were not trapped, if I had any independence at all, then I could be good. I would be good." She was fighting off her tears now and trying to pull herself together. She looked at me and said more firmly. "I'm truly sorry for what I did. Truly sorry and I will do anything I can to make reparation – though God only knows how it is to be done. Can you forgive me?"

I stared at the table top as though I was sleeping with my eyes open.

"Will you at least hear my story?" Allecto begged, though I could hear a slender strand of ice stiffening and stretching at the core of her melted voice.

I shrugged faintly, so Allecto began her tale.

"There isn't a great deal to tell. I am in my husband's power; that is the long and short of it. My whole story is contained within that single fact."

"I'd like a little more detail however," I interrupted savagely. "When did you marry him? Why?"

"Ten years ago. I was a student on holiday in Paris; he was pursuing some mysterious studies at the Sorbonne, something to do with mythology and the history of magic. We kept meeting at the same café, just by accident at first and then by design – his design. One morning he brought his coffee to my table and began to talk on all sorts of weird and wonderful topics: hang-gliding, legends, Russian literature, coffee beans, Handel, Napoleon…he was so strange, so fascinating and every topic he touched turned to gold so that, whilst he talked, you wanted to make that single subject your life's work, your vocation. I had nothing to say for myself, no fascinating life-story, no originality, no strong opinions. I don't know what he saw in me. I suppose he must have seen something…once? I threw in my degree and married him the following autumn, in the chapel up here at Boughwinds Abbey.

"On his part…I was only a whim. He tired of me very quickly. I wish I could say that I tired of him simultaneously, but it wouldn't be true. It took me years to understand, in my heart of hearts, that he was just mad and bad; before that I had a hazy feeling of self-reproach whenever he upbraided me, as he so often did, for my stupidity, my sullenness, my sheer inability to please him…" She laughed bitterly. "I've managed it at last though. I've finally learned to hate him as much as he hates me."

"Then why don't you do something?" I asked, still dry and unyielding. "Why don't you leave?"

She sighed and rocked her forehead from side to side as it lay heavily in her hands. "You don't understand. He is everywhere; he is all-knowing. He is like a…like a giant octopus. His tentacles reach everywhere: he has minions in the unlikeliest of places…Your Mrs. Lorimer, for example. I mean, who would have supposed…? And he has other, weirder ways…can you believe he trains bluebottles as spies? There are about ten of them in the abbey, presently preoccupied with a roast chicken carcass, please God. He keeps them in an incubator by his bed and talks to them. And he has a bloodhound in his kennels that is specially trained to follow my scent - mine in particular. It isn't possible to hide from him. If I went out and about in the world, knowing that he sought me, I would feel more trapped than I do here in this little room."

"Well then, why does he keep you on? If he is so sick of you…?"

"Because he has found a use for me.

"I studied Chemistry at university, you know. Only two years out of a four year course, but still…When he found this out, some months after our dismal wedding, he was delighted."

"He found out some months after your wedding?" I raised my eyebrows sceptically.

Allecto gave a rueful shrug. "It sounds mad. It is mad, I know, but it's how it was. We never talked about me...almost never. And somehow I didn't mind; didn't even notice it in those early days. Maybe that's what he thought he liked about me.

"At any rate, when he discovered I was a chemist he was delighted; more exuberant than I had ever seen him before. I mentioned it at breakfast one morning. I forget the context, but it was probably some timid attempt on my part to win his attention. He leapt up from the table, grabbed me by the wrist and dragged me into the library. It was the first time I ever entered it. Of course he has books on every subject under the sun, but he wanted me to see the wall upon wall of shelves that he had devoted to witchcraft, especially those volumes relevant to brews, spells and fortune-telling.

""I'm tired of seeing you mope around my house with nothing to do," he said, as book after book hurtled down from the stepladder and landed at my feet. "And at last, just as I thought I would have to ask for my money back, I've found a use for you. You're a chemist, are you? Well then, you can be my witch. You can find me a palliative and then, when you've done that, you can find me a cure.'

"I knew by then that he was ill, I expect that you too have noticed and I was still sufficiently in love to hope for his survival. Besides, I was pretty tired of moping about as well, with nothing to do but stare at the rain and think circular thoughts. I agreed to do my best. The hocus-pocus that he insisted upon involving held no interest for me whatsoever, but I was not in a position to quibble. I needed something to do, however dubious.

"Before very long, with nothing to distract me, I was an expert on herbal potions and after two or three years experimentation I did indeed come up with a successful palliative. That sealed my fate. He was never going to let me go after that, for he believes that I am the only one capable of concocting it properly. Every week I make up a list of ingredients, both for the palliative and for my further experiments, and once a week, as dusk falls, Mrs. Veals goes out into the woods to collect them for me."

"And the cure?" I asked.

"I haven't found a cure yet."

"Why don't you poison him?" asked Boris bluntly. "You would be free if he was dead."

The question did not shock Allecto. "Do you suppose I haven't thought of it?" she whispered harshly. "He certainly foresaw the possibility! Each time a new bottle is required he summons me to his study and forces me to drink the first glassful, while he watches and waits. It's awful stuff; heaven knows what it's doing to me. Anyway, it rules out poison, unless I want to die with him and I'm not that desperate...not yet."

Boris lapsed into a sighing silence for a while. I drummed my fingers on the table. When Boris resumed, I noticed that his tone was resigned, rather than accusatory.

"What about Abigail? What does he want with her?"

Allecto stood up again and paced the cell, her fingers twisting and pulling inside her thick mane of hair.

"I didn't mean to start this thing with Abigail. It was my fault, but I didn't mean anything by it.

"You see, although he despises me, he sometimes talks to me, just because there's nobody else. (There's Mrs. Veals, but her conversation is somewhat limited.) He talks about Traumund, mostly. He learned all about my place in Traumund long ago, of course. I can't say it impressed him much, though he took it away from me all the same. It's...well it was small and very safe and dull. I liked it. You know how it is.

"Anyway, he was always talking about exciting places in Traumund: cliff-top castles, alpine retreats and great galleons that bound across island-dotted oceans. One day, about three or more years ago, he started talking about yours, Abigail. He said, "My goddaughter," (it was news to me that he even had a goddaughter) "has a place in Traumund from which you might learn much, Allecto." Then he described it to me: this tall forest peopled by cannibals and a hollow tree where you lived with your friends. He said that the entrance to your oak was so magically secret and secure that even his royal guard was unable to find it."

Boris and I exchanged looks; aghast, open-mouthed looks.

Allecto continued. "He thinks I'm a fortune teller. I ought to be, the number of fortune-telling books I've been obliged to plough through, but in fact I make it all up. It's always worked fine until now. I just have to keep it vague enough, you know: if you wear purple socks on a Friday then some great misfortune will befall you. That sort of thing. Well, when he started on and on about you and your wonderful land, I decided to incorporate you into my predictions, just on a whim. Just because I was bored of you and your stupid trees. I said...oh I don't know...I said that your destiny was linked up with his in some way. That you were his nemesis. Something like that. He lapped it all up. It was just a bit of private fun.

"A few months later I was told to go and 'fetch' you from your home. It was not for me to ask why: he would never have told me. I suppose it has something to do with my 'predictions'. Or maybe he is using you as a spy in Traumund. But I can't help fearing that he intends to kill you, as he killed Sylvia, because you resisted his Institute system. Or maybe...I don't know...maybe he is really fond of you and wants you as his next wife. Once he's widowed himself, if you see what I mean."

Allecto stood up with a flat, dead-eyed smile. It was nearly dinner time and she would have to go to her husband's study. But I was brimful of terrified questions; it was impossible that we should part just now. Allecto stooped to tidy her hair in front of a spotty shaving mirror, whilst I struggled for coherence.

"Wait, wait. What about...why did he kill Sylvia? Why would he kill me? I mean, I know you said about resisting the Institute...and Joachim too (oh God, Joachim too!) but...but...so what? If we are not model pupils then reprimand us, expel us...But surely not kill us?"

"But that's the whole business of his life," replied Allecto patiently, as she deftly secured her pony tail with a rubber band and dabbed at her face with a damp dishcloth. "Killing children. All children. The one's who do succumb to the Institute system have their minds and souls gently murdered so that, in the end, they are nothing but bodies and robotic intelligences. They are left with no imagination or critical understanding. Fay and Marcus are quite promising pupils.

"Those who refuse to succumb must be eliminated, in the more physical (though perhaps no crueller) sense of the word. That's what happened to Sylvia."

"But why?" I persisted as she wriggled out of her jeans and into a long pencil skirt. "Why?"

She glanced at us briefly as she wedged her feet into a pair of high-heeled shoes. "Have you not made the connection yet? Don't you see? He is intent on emptying Traumund. Murder a mind – a soul - and Traumund loses one proprietor. Once a person's soul is extinguished or has...moved on to another realm" (here she smiled awkward encouragement at Sylvia) "then their land is left unguarded, uncared for and he can march in and take it for his own without so much as a struggle. Obviously it is less conspicuous and more productive to kill large numbers of children by the Institute method, though he resorts to more conventional violence on occasion."

She grabbed a bottle of palliative from the top of the stove.

With a final dissatisfied glance at the mirror she patted her hair and added flippantly, "I'm sorry to dash like this when we haven't even planned anything or discussed what to do. We'll meet again before long, somehow or other. Sylvia will take you back to your room in the meantime. Now I must run. I daren't be late for a date with the King of Traumund." Another trilling laugh. ("Defiant," said Boris later. "Crass," said I.)

We watched as she scurried up the step-ladder and away.

The Scream

flopped, face down on the bed, my faithful bear perched motionlessly at my side.

You have read my story so far: you will tell me you predicted all this and that I ought to have seen it coming. I ought to have known that my idol was false. Well, perhaps I did see more than you think, though not (until now) with comprehending eyes. I would never have idolised him so much if I had thought him angelic. I had allowed him a secret wife for example, and I had thought it perfectly reasonable that he should treat his unfit partner with contempt and lock her away. I had allowed him to commit murder in a vaguely envisaged moment of passion and the agonies of guilt with which he would consequently be ravaged only made me love him the more. I had even allowed him empire-lust, when I imagined him leading armies across mountains and steppes and tapping the flank of his rearing, black charger with the flat of his sword.

I was not prepared for the sordid realness of his crimes. I was not licensed by my upbringing or my inclinations to sanction them, even though I had loved the idea of my love conquering all, when 'all' was still ambiguous. But I had to feel disgust. I had to abhor my godfather's deeds and to resist his influence. There was no other way.

I did not think so coherently that first night, however. In fact, I did not think at all; I only felt. All my awareness was concentrated upon the hole that had been blasted open underneath my ribs and which hurt with a tangible, physical pain, especially when I breathed in.

I lay on my bed for three days. On the first day I was still and silent on my back, like a stone knight on an old cathedral tomb. On the second day I cried off and on throughout the twenty-four hours, until I felt (having eaten next to nothing since the revelations of that foggy night) hollow-kneed. On the third day Ludovick Montefiore himself knocked at my door to enquire after me, since I had not been down to dinner for two nights. I replied that I felt very sick and thought I had better stay in bed. He asked a few more kind questions, reproaching me for suffering in silence, and then he went away. A quarter of an hour later, Mrs. Veals arrived with a murderous expression, a tray, lavender-scented handkerchiefs, green grapes, chicken soup, camomile tea, books and a solicitous note from Ludovick Montefiore. I wrote an inexcusably appreciative reply and sent it back with Mrs. Veals. I accused myself of being a traitor and this led me to ask myself whom was I betraying? My godfather, because I was only pretending to be his friend? Or my true friends, for failing to be properly persuaded against him?

Fay visited me that afternoon. She had gathered, somehow, that I was ill, but though she expressed extravagant sympathy for my discomfort as she burst through the door, she did not seem to think the subject very interesting and she did not ask me any questions. (This was just as well, since I was perfectly well. I might have experienced some relief if my very real misery had chosen to exhibit itself - in pallid fainting fits perhaps or hysterics or a high fever – but it did not.) Fay seemed glad of an audience and her exuberant outpourings did me good.

She told me that she planned to have a career in the beauty business, perhaps in modelling and that when she was thirty she would get married and have two children, a boy and a girl. The maintenance of her family's lifestyle would necessitate the purchase of a London penthouse, a mansion in the home counties and a yacht in St. Tropez. These things, she genuinely believed, would make her happy. Of course my subversive education at the hands of Joachim Larrouse had taught me to sneer proudly at such aspirations and sneer I did, though not wholeheartedly. The truth was that I envied Fay her confidence; her ability to see her own life from the outside like an expensive objet d'art, which, with a touch here and a touch there and a quick polish, would presently be perfected.

When Fay went away vivid certainties went with her and I slumped back on my pillow, picking moodily at grapes and begrudging her (not without a certain glum self-satisfaction) her simplicity. I wished that Joachim had left well alone and that I could have sold my soul in peace to the Institute.

At this point, Boris lost his temper. Poor Boris, he had sat beside my bed for three days while I stared wordlessly at the ceiling or wept into my pillow and during that time he had vacillated privately between anxiety, pity, urgency and exasperation. Later I learned that he had visited Traumund once or twice, in order to bring Joachim and Eyes up to date and to check on their progress (which, by the way, was nil, as the Vulture Men were comfortably camped in small groups throughout the forest and showed no sign of returning to Headquarters). Joachim and Eyes had pressed Boris to bring me along as a matter of urgency, in order that we might form some new plan. I don't think Boris had dared try until now, fearing the stony superiority of my grief. Even tonight, as the third day drew to its close, he began tentatively.

"Abigail?"

I did not move my head, but since he was already in my line of vision I answered with an inquiring stare.

"We must go back to Joachim's hut tonight. You know how things stand: how urgent everything is. And especially since…you know… since Sylvia and Allecto put us fully in the picture. You're not safe, not if he is planning to purge the rebels. Joachim is not safe either. We've got to act quickly or the same thing is going to happen to you and Joachim as happened to Sylvia."

I rolled over to face the wall. I was angry with Boris for his energy and persistence. Why couldn't he just leave me alone? Leave everything alone. My moods were my arbiters of truth these days and I was in the mood to interpret his concern as busy-bodying and his urgency as callousness.

"Oh…look…" I moaned. "Think of a plan if you're so worried. Or just forget about it altogether. What will be will be."

This is when Boris really let rip. I have never seen him seethe with such fury as he did when he whipped the blankets from my face and hurled them onto the floor. I think if he had been bigger or I had been smaller, he would have thrown me on top of them. He called me every name under the sun: coward, traitor, weakling, hypocrite, infatuated moron, murderer, apathetic turncoat. He reminded me of everyone and everything I had once professed to love: my family, Joachim, the tree, the whole universe of Traumund, Boris himself. He asked me whether I preferred the devil incarnate to all these true, reciprocal loves? At one point he leapt onto my lap and began beating on my face with his paws.

I deserved much worse, no doubt, but at the time I felt wronged and misunderstood and though Boris's words goaded me into action at last, I thought it was my magnanimity rather than a consciousness of guilt that made me move.

Later that night I sat at the rugged wooden table in Traumund, unable to meet Joachim's eye with my red-rimmed scowl. Fortunately Eyes was out looking for Vulture Men, so I had only to contend with Joachim's curiosity, for the moment.

"It's good to see you Abigail," he said with stiff, half-suppressed warmth.

"Thanks," I said, glancing at him briefly. I tried to sound matter-of-fact but I merely sounded harsh. "I suppose Boris has told you about the new situation?"

"Yes."

"The man we are plotting against, the King of Traumund -"

"The self-styled King of Traumund," Boris chimed in. He was still descending from the giddy heights of his rage.

"...turns out to be Ludovick Montefiore. Assuming of course that they were telling the truth."

"Oh, they were telling the truth all right!" Boris interrupted again.

I ignored the bear. "So...what do you have to say about that?" I demanded of Joachim.

Joachim was silent, though I felt he had plenty to say. He was afraid of my simmering temper.

"Go on, Joachim." I urged in a tone that was wearier and therefore gentler. "What do you have to say about it?"

"Well...It makes things a lot easier for us."

"Why?"

"Well, because we've found him. If you are agreed, then we don't need to send Eyes out after Vulture Men anymore, because we don't need to find our way to his HQ. We can deal with Montefiore in the Waking World instead. And it's not as if you even have to sneak around hiding from guards and things, he trusts you..."

"Wait a moment!" I burst out of my weariness, refreshed by a rage of my own. "You mean it's easier for you! You mean I can deal with him in the Waking World, because I'm at Boughwinds Abbey and you're not, so all the responsibility falls on my shoulders! But if you think I'm going to murder him or something you've got another thing coming. I'm not stabbing Ludovick Montefiore in the back to save anybody's skin!"

"N-no, of course not," faltered Joachim in a shocked tone. But his tone was a little colder and there was resentment in his shrug. "I don't know. I only thought it would be easier to do something now we have found him. That is if you still want to do something..."

"There is, I think, a way out of this," said Boris with casual relish, "that will not necessitate violence."

"What?" we asked simultaneously, turning to the slumped bear. He sat up.

"Well, we know, do we not, that Montefiore cannot reach Traumund via sleep, as most people can?"

"That's right. Traumund itself somehow...forbade him to come via that route. I don't know how."

"No," muttered Joachim, "But I think we know why."

I frowned at him and continued,

"He builds a square of walls with his grandmother's mah-jong tiles, and then, by some magic that he devised himself, the square becomes a doorway into Traumund. You know all this."

"And in order for his magic to work the mah-jong set must be complete?" Boris asked.

"I don't know, I think so...Yes! Because I almost kicked it by accident and he told me off...well not exactly told me off...but he said the square must be whole and intact."

"In that case, the solution is simple. You must make the set incomplete. You need only steal one tile, and the magic is broken."

Boris shrugged and I could see he was struggling against a smile. Joachim stared at the bear in amazement and then leaned back with a long, grinning sigh. I still frowned, trying, from sheer pig-headedness to find a flaw in Boris's plan. I could not. Yet for all my pleas against violent action, I found it disappointingly easy, like a thriller with an unsatisfying conclusion. Such was the perversity of my mood. I felt as though we had been pouring over a broken machine for months, trying to uncover some intricate reason for its refusal to function, only to discover that we had forgotten to switch it on.

"Boris, you are a genius..." Joachim began, and I could see a joyful confidence creeping into his smile, a joyful confidence that (I supposed, drearily) I would be expected to echo. But I was mistaken. For our collective joys and private disgruntlements were cut short by an uproar.

There was a cry from within the forest; a deep, pained animal scream. It might have been human, but it was impossible, at the time, to say for sure. Just as we were getting to our feet and beginning to voice useless, frightened questions, Eyes burst through the open window like a bullet and pulled up short, circling the room with panic-stricken, feathery flaps. He hardly needed to tell us that the Vulture Men were abroad. The ladder was up in a split second and even before the echoes of that terrible scream had died in our ears we were all crouched in Joachim's loft, peering through pale slits of light into the room below.

We waited, but nobody came. Meanwhile we realised that Eyes was trying to speak, though he was hindered by a combination of breathlessness and an effort to whisper.

"That scream…you heard that scream?"

"How could we miss it?" returned Joachim, adding anxiously, "What was it? It wasn't you was it Eyes? They haven't injured you, have they?"

"Not me…A boy. An actual human – not a Vulture Man. I caught sight of him half an hour ago. I tracked him because he seemed to be heading for the hut. He was sloping along slowly, as though he was exhausted, but he was wary as well, looking over his shoulder all the time and making his way from tree to tree."

"What did he look like?" murmured Joachim, half gripped by Eyes' tale, half on guard, lest a Vulture Man should slide through the door and take advantage of their absorbed chatter.

"He was a complete wreck. His clothes were in rags and you could see all his bones, as though his skin was too small for his skeleton. His hair was long and ragged as though it hadn't been brushed or cut or washed for weeks. He didn't carry any possessions, except for a huge book bound in bright, blood-red leather, which was far too bulky for him to carry with ease. It was easily bigger than this trapdoor and three times as thick. I think it must have contained a map, or something like that, because he paused every now and then to lay it on the ground and open it at a marked page and then he'd study it carefully, tracing a line on the page with his finger,then look around searchingly or with a satisfied nod."

"What happened to him?"

"He was making a beeline for your hut; he was barely five-minute's walk away. He didn't look like much of a threat, but you never know, so I thought I'd better come and warn you. But before I could stir, a couple of Vulture Men burst through the trees. The boy heard them coming and if only he'd acted more decisively he might have escaped them, but he hesitated too long and they got close enough to wound him. One of them was wielding a long sword and he swiped viciously at the boy's chest, that's when you heard him scream. The boy staggered away and I shot off to warn you that they were - "

Crash! Joachim jumped violently and held out his hand for silence, as we all filled our lungs and pressed our eyes to the crannies in the ceiling. The door had burst back on its hinges to reveal a Vulture Man, whose rectangular figure seemed to fill the whole room with darkness. He hovered on the step, half in, half out, scanning the interior with a gimlet eye.

"No!" we heard him call into the forest clearing as he turned his beaked-head from our fascinated gaze. "He's not in here. He must have headed for the stream."

"You think you killed him?" a second voice called from among the trees.

The first Vulture Man screamed with amusement. "He's not going to last for long out there. That wound needs doctoring. If he's not dead yet, he'll be dead by tomorrow morning."

"In that case, we may as well get off and leave him to die in pieces!" There was another screech of laughter, this time from outside, but the first Vulture Man tutted impatiently as he turned away from the house and remounted.

"We can't leave him, idiot! He's got the atlas. Or are you going to inform His Majesty that you allowed a prisoner to steal the priceless book and run off with it?"

"I allowed a prisoner to...? What do you mean I allowed...? We were all responsible..."

Their voices, the clunk of the horses' hooves and the clanging of their harnesses faded into silence; such complete silence as you will only ever hear in a forest. It prickles in your ears.

Joachim was moving and talking before I had even dared to draw breath. "Come on!" he cried, as he swung himself down from the loft. "We've no time to lose. Eyes: go and find this boy. Follow the stream to begin with and then scour the banks, since that's where they're headed. He can hardly have gone far. Boris, you stay here with me: we'll tear up the curtains for bandages."

"What shall I do?" I asked diffidently. Joachim's authority impressed me. I knew that I, in my miserable apathy, would have been content to write off the injured stranger as a lost cause. "What will be, will be," I had thought for the second time that evening, as the Vulture Men discussed his probable fate. Joachim's unhesitating charity, however, had awakened in me a desire, if not to be as good as him, at least to please him and this gave me hope for myself. "Joachim is good; Ludovick Montefiore is bad," I found myself thinking. "Keep that in your head, Abigail, for all its simplicity and perhaps you will recover your sanity."

"Help us make bandages, Abigail. Here, here's a towel, start tearing. And we'll need water to clean his wounds - you can take the bucket if you like; no, I'll take the bucket, you don't know where the stream is. But cram the stove with logs so we can boil it up…" And then fleetingly, fatally, his nerve failed. "Oh God, we're so ill-equipped for this!"

The last words expressed a frustration that was, I thought, akin to my own apathy and I seized on it.

"Joachim…you're flapping and fussing around like a mother hen and for what? We haven't even found this boy and if we do he'll probably be dead; and if he isn't he'll probably die; and even if he doesn't, what use…" I faltered. I had been going to say, What use will he be to us, anyway? I tried to disguise my conclusion by turning it into a teary, weary collapse. "Oh, what's the use? What's the use?" But Joachim was unconvinced. He knew what I had been about to say.

Joachim looked at me. I did not feel self-disgust until I felt Joachim's look. Then I saw myself as he saw me and for a moment I apprehended what I had become since attaching myself to Ludovick Montefiore. I had meant to convey mere weariness; I needed Joachim's glance in order to understand that I had expressed callousness. My only excuse was a wrongful infatuation, whose ins and outs I was not sufficiently sophisticated to explain (even supposing that there had been time to make excuses) and which was not, anyway, an adequate justification.

Stupid, stupid Abigail: the urgency of the situation had still not really penetrated my selfishness. Because all I wanted to do now was to talk at Joachim; talk and talk until I had forced him, by sheer weight of words, to retract his accusing look.

"I didn't mean…" I began, but he was pointedly busy, tearing curtains down and he ignored me. So I swallowed my explanations and apologies. I did not utter another word, but savaged curtains and hurled fuel into the stove, until the night was gone and the Waking World reclaimed me.

Eyes came back to Joachim's house several times during the night, but his reports were dispiriting: the forest was thick with Vulture Men, he said, but there was no sign of the wounded boy.

The Wounded Boy

nce I had returned to Boughwinds Abbey I stayed in my room all day. The silence was not as profound as it had been four days earlier, when Sylvia first materialised at my door. Thin shudders and sighs of wind made their way around the corners of the abbey and between the window frames.

I was so angry with Joachim. The anger coloured my obsession and made Ludovick Montefiore more attractive in my eyes. I stopped calling my godfather '*evil*' and started calling him '*complicated*' instead.

In my mind I composed one-sided conversations with Joachim, during which my righteous, wordy indignation repeatedly floored him and he repented for having misunderstood me; for having underestimated my greatness of soul.

"You think, do you, Joachim," I said, "that by lifting your pious hands and eyes to the skies and making demonstrations of concern for this unknown person who may or may not be our friend, that you are proving yourself better than me? Yes, you think you are better than me and you want everyone to acknowledge it."

He hung his imaginary head in shame.

"But your great talent is for looking good, isn't it? You have all the right gestures and words at your fingertips, whereas, perhaps, I have not."

A miserable nod.

"My God, Joachim! Your naivety! Your impossible naivety! You think that goodness is simple. I know what this boils down to. It boils down to Ludovick Montefiore. You have given yourself a shiny new identity, which bears a direct relationship to him – or what you think you know about him (which isn't a lot). Yes, you are the spotless hero now, because he is the black-hearted villain. You have chosen him to be your foil and he shows you off nicely, doesn't he? But I know, if you don't, that there is no such thing as a wholly bad person. I know that Ludovick Montefiore is not the monster we have allowed ourselves to imagine; he is…he is many things. You are so unsophisticated!"

And, in my mind, Joachim acceded humbly to it all.

The wintry day plodded by, hour after frozen hour and I didn't know what to do or how to think. My conscience must have been at work discreetly though, or, more probably (for all my wordy anger), I wanted to prove myself to Joachim. An idea came to me late in the evening as I began to undress before the bedroom fire. I mused on it for a while, one boot unlaced. It hardly seemed worth doing in itself; there were too many ways in which it might prove useless. But then that was its virtue: a defiant show of zeal in the face of futility would be sure to re-establish my reputation with Joachim. I mused a little longer. Then I re-laced my boot, tucked Boris under my arm and lit a candle at the embers.

I stepped towards the door, through the blades of bright moonlight which sliced through the windows and into my floorboards. The planks creaked loudly beneath my feet. I entered the corridor, where the light was dead and a green chill oozed from the walls and crawled under my clothes. I took a few hesitant steps before stopping and cursing aloud in my frustration. I had been at Boughwinds for days now and still I did not begin to understand the layout of the house. I had made a few wary expeditions, but the place was out to fool and frustrate me: corridors and staircases, pictures and heavy curtains appeared out of nowhere, or disappeared just as I thought I had placed them. I had no hope whatsoever of finding the library tonight. I cursed under my breath. My plan seemed important, all of a sudden.

"Abigail? What is the matter?"

A faint murmur swept along the corridor and into my head: a chilly gust of sound. At the same time I saw a light burnish the wall beside me, like a reflected nightlight, steady and small.

"Sylvia! Will you take me to Allecto? I need to see her, straightaway."

"But the spies?"

"Please?"

Without another word she led the way.

Allecto was not pleased to see me again. It wasn't that she felt annoyed at being woken; in fact she was fully dressed, and her bedspread looked untouched. She welcomed Sylvia's presence with a quick, conspiratorial smile. She didn't criticise me for coming; she understood the emergency straightaway and darted about preparing poultices and powders and bottles of pink, viscous fluid. But she was not pleased to see me again.

We were allies at present and therefore (such was my own naivety) it surprised me that I did not like her and that she did not like me. I often wondered why and I wondered then as I waited for her, offering my tight-lipped apologies for blocking her tight-lipped way as she sought some jar or other from the cupboard behind my head.

I had professed (though only to myself) that I could forgive the kidnapping. I had found her actions, at least on reflection, understandable. And I can't believe she was really offended by my silence. I had been vulnerable and alone; I was sure she acknowledged that and pitied me. She pitied me, and I pitied and forgave her. And yet we eyed one another like cats, flicking their tails on a patch of disputed earth.

"Right!" she exclaimed, when her wicker basket was full to overflowing with medicine bottles and bundles of herbs. Then she sagged and looked at me as though I had been misleading her all the while. "But how am I going to get there?"

"Er…Get there? I asked you if you had any stuff we might use – I didn't know you were intending to come…"

She heaved the basket off the floor. "Oh." She sneered, making as if to present it to me. "And you'll know what to do with all this lot will you?"

"But, like you said, how can you get there?"

She was checked for half a moment and then the look of scared excitement lit her eyes again. She began pulling handfuls of dried flowers and herbs from the ceiling. "You must lie down here, on my bed, now." She lit the stove, placed a small saucepan of water on top and began scattering grasses and petals and powders onto its surface with speedy expertise. "If I, with my basket, am holding tight to your hand as you fall away into Traumund then…well, we'll see. I think it might work."

She stirred the mixture with a wooden spoon, until it simmered. A sweet-scented heaviness seemed to be pushing oxygen from the cell and for a second I panicked, but then the smell took hold of me; wound me in its arms; kissed my eyelids.

"Lie down," she murmured. I lay down on her quilt and breathed the kindly smog. I managed to resent my body's willingness to obey her command; I worried that she should not be allowed into the dream house without Joachim's say-so, but I thought that I knew there was nothing else to be done. When she said, "Take my hand and don't let go," I tried to show my reluctance, but it was all I could do to adopt an expression of pantomime distaste - lips pursed, nose wrinkled – which just made her laugh.

"Now take us to Traumund!" She commanded. "For God's sake start picturing Traumund, or we are going to just fall asleep and how idiotic would that be?" As she spoke she tied our wrists together with a length of string, for her eyelids were drooping too and she was afraid that we would release one another when the dream took hold. For all the self-abandonment which her potion had induced, we drew away from one another as we touched, as though each wished the other to know that this enforced intimacy was repellent. I lay there for a good half hour, my drowsiness checked by self-consciousness and impatience. But at last her potion did its work. As I fell towards Traumund I felt a wrench in my shoulder, my arm burning where the loop of string dug into my skin.

We arrived in the midst of frenetic activity. Allecto understood it all straightaway. She speedily released her wrist. Whilst I stood still, closing my eyes against a faint nausea, she was already stooping over the bloody mass on the table, making soothing sounds and throwing jars and bottles and dressings about. She called for water and bandages, and they were brought by cowed attendants. She rolled up her sleeves and pushed back her hair with an air of one who is at home.

Joachim came towards me with an odd expression on his face. I thought he was angry and I began to justify myself.

"Joachim, I know what you must think of me but I haven't…"

My voice faded away because he wasn't listening to it. He was looking at me and yet his eyes were glazed with anxiety. His hand touched my shoulder and he looked away to one side.

"What's the matter?"

He tried to meet my gaze again, but his eyes would keep slithering away, like live fish in wet hands.

"We found the wounded boy," he said, clearing his throat.

"Yes, I see that."

"He has quite a deep wound across his chest. He might die"

"Oh. That's awful. Do you think -"

"He can still speak though. He told us he was looking for you. He said he was called Prince Constantine."

"...Constantine? ...My Constantine?"

I stood still for a moment and then suddenly I found I was cold and trembling, and that my hands were unable to decide what they should do: they hovered together in mid-air, then reached up to touch my forehead, then came down to cover my open mouth. I pushed forward to the table but Allecto barred my way. I tried to explain that I must see him, but she didn't even hear my words. She closed her eyes and her ears, refusing to countenance any interruption to her work and enjoying the painful frustration which her diligence imposed.

I climbed halfway up the stepladder that led to Joachim's hidey hole. From this vantage point I could see it: the bloody, hairy pile of skin and bones strewn across the table like a macabre, vandalised scarecrow.

"Constantine?" I said, not calling to him, but questioning Joachim's identification with a sense of disbelief so genuine that it sounded like amusement.

The carcass moved and groaned.

"Abigail?" It spoke with a hoarse rattle.

Allecto glanced at me. "Please!" she demanded simply as her red hands worked nimbly over the torn flesh with swabs of red cloth. She bit her lower lip as she worked.

But the corpse wanted to speak. As it called to me across the room, she shushed it and shook her head and glowered at me with eyes of righteous spite.

"Abigail...are you all right?" he spat the words out as though they would not come more easily.

"I'm fine." I replied in a small voice.

"I've found you then. I stole the map – Montefiore's map. You know that he is the King of Traumund?"

"Yes, I know. Don't talk now. It's better if you stay quiet..."

"But I want to talk!"

Allecto shot a furious look at me, as though I was bullying him.

"Sit here, by his head, then at least he need only whisper," she spat, rather as he had done. I obeyed her and stared uselessly at his matted hair while she worked around me, as swift and precise as a humming bird.

The poor body resumed,

"Did you know he has drawn up a map of Traumund – as much of

Traumund as he knows?"

"No, I didn't know that."

"Well it's true, and I escaped and stole it. The red atlas. Look, it's there, by the table."

I looked around and saw a massive volume lying by my feet. It was so big that it would be difficult for a strong man to carry it across a room, never mind a mere boy across countries. It was bound in strong red leather, and its corners were protected by triangular metal shields.

"They found me, Abigail, but they didn't find the others and they didn't find the tree. The Vulture Men captured me in the woods; they were going to take me to his castle. But I escaped, and I stole the atlas. I stole a horse too – not a black vulture horse – I mean I found a horse wandering in somebody's land. But they shot it down three days ago." He took a noisy draught of air.

"And you found me!" I whispered gently, "You managed to find me!"

"Because of the atlas," he replied, "The atlas, Abigail. What a book! We've got to find him now. We've got to kill him…I want to kill him… Aagh!"

He cried out as Allecto emptied the glue-like pink lotion over his wound. She shook out the last drop, and then elbowed me away roughly, as though I had caused this convulsion of pain. She stood in my place, stroking his filthy hair.

"You'll be all right now", she said to him, privately. The ice-strand inside her voice had melted away.

The Rice Bird

stayed in Joachim's house for the rest of the night, but I was no use to anybody there. Allecto was in sole charge of Constantine. I half-leaned, half-sat on the loft steps and stared at the thing that was Constantine and at Allecto's self-assured ministrations. Boris was at my feet, as motionless as a Waking World bear. Joachim shuffled about on the other side of the room, occasionally catching my eye and flashing mournful smiles. It is not often that I am glad to leave Traumund, but I really was thankful when, at last, the scene faded from my sight like a dream.

I was disorientated at first, to find myself coming-to in Allecto's hidey-hole. I looked around for my bed and for the line of light underneath my curtains. Then I remembered. The drowsy smell lingered, but it was no longer alluring.

Boris was with me, but she – Allecto – was yet to arrive. She would be reluctant to leave Traumund I thought, and I decided to make myself scarce before her return. Sylvia was here, leaning against one of Allecto's cupboards with her arms folded and her eyes closed - not asleep, I think, but bored and lonely. She guided me back to my room. It was difficult to follow her through the early morning light. Of course, many of the passages were as gloomy as midnight, but every time we passed a window she would disappear inside the dawn-gleam.

I opened my curtains and flopped onto my bed. It was not an apathetic flop this time, but a thoughtfully curled up flop. I clutched an ankle in one hand and rested my chin on the other. You know that feeling when you wake up one morning determined to do something new and inspired, like read an exciting book or write one, or something like that, but you can't, because everywhere around you there is mess and dust: unwashed cups and clothes, crumpled bedclothes, bits on the carpet, rubbish that you are not ruthless enough to throw away, though you would like to be ruthless. And all this untidiness and dirt saps your happy excitement, until (assuming you cannot persuade yourself to embark upon a massive spring clean) you bury yourself underneath the bedclothes again.

I felt like this, only the mess that paralysed was not around me, in my spotless room. The mess was inside me. I was so taken aback by the whirlwind events of the last few days and nights; so shocked when I considered all that was at stake; so disgusted and yet so further enfeebled by my own weaknesses and misjudgements, that I truly did not know what to do next. But, despite mistrusting my ability to act well, I was no longer content not to act at all. I acknowledged, at last, that a defeatist stupor was not good enough and that my excuses were inadequate. I was, if you like, in the mood for throwing back my bedclothes and starting on a spring clean. If only it had been a case of sorting through boxes of rubbish and running a vacuum over the carpet. I did not know how to begin tidying up my soul.

Boris tried to help me. He talked and listened with me all through the morning, as easily as though we were back in our oak. We went over everything that had happened since that very first night when the Vulture Man came amongst our trees. We cried when we thought about Constantine's wound and about how thin and dirty and ill he looked. We discussed Allecto and agreed that, although we disliked her, we trusted her and respected her dubiously-acquired medical skills. We both agreed that Constantine would pull through and at this point we cheered up. Then we touched on Ludovick Montefiore and though I spoke with difficulty, I acknowledged the truth to Boris. Ludovick Montefiore was our enemy. He had deceived us and caused great suffering to our friends. I could no longer be both their friend and his.

My head was clearing a little and it cleared still more after I rang the bell and ordered Mrs. Veals to fetch coffee and toast.

"I shall tell the master you are feeling better then, Miss Abigail," she said with a derisive smile that was meant to show how little she believed in my 'illness'. I shrugged and said nothing.

I ate and drank greedily once she had gone and we were silent for a while. Then Boris resumed, gently but pointedly, "What do you think he has in mind for you?"

Honesty can be such a bitter thing. Sometimes it seems so bitter that I wonder how it can still be right. Nonetheless I was determined to be honest.

"He knows I won't succumb to the Institute system because I told him so myself, right at the beginning in the King Henry Hotel. I didn't know I was defying him. I thought he was pleased with me! But...I suppose he wants to kill me or keep me prisoner. Why would he treat me any differently to his other enemies?"

"Why has he treated you differently, so far? Why aren't you languishing in a windowless cell like Allecto or hanging from a yew tree like Sylvia? Sorry to be blunt (as I shuddered and frowned) but it's a reasonable question."

I resisted the impulse to flounce away in adolescent contempt of his rationality. I tried to answer in the spirit of his question. "I suppose it has something to do with Allecto telling him that I am his nemesis or whatever. Maybe he's devised an especially horrible fate for me."

"I can't help fearing that that might be true," replied Boris seriously, and as he spoke his expression turned in on itself, as though he was viewing some possibility that he could foresee and I could not even guess at.

"Thanks!" I said, trying to raise a smile, but just then we heard Mrs. Veals' approach and we fell silent. She knocked with insolent lightness and brevity, entering without awaiting my reply.

"A note," she declared, handing over a folded square of my godfather's parchment. I opened it in some trepidation and read softly, so that Boris could hear,

My dear Abigail,
Mrs. Veals tells me that you are well again and I am truly glad to hear it. In view of your convalescence I do understand if you feel disinclined to eat dinner tonight. Perhaps afternoon tea would suit you better? I look forward to receiving you in my study at four o'clock this afternoon.
                    Your affectionate godfather,
                    Ludovick Montefiore.

The last thing in the world that I desired now was afternoon tea with Ludovick Montefiore. It would surely be foolish, however, to snub his cordial, but pressing, invitation. I could not consult Boris, since Mrs. Veals still covered the doorway like a square-shouldered Vulture Man, noting every flicker of expression that passed over my face. So, inhaling a sigh, as though I was about to leap into a cold sea, I asked

Mrs. Veals to wait while I wrote my reply.

Dear Ludovick Montefiore, it ran straightforwardly after excessive consideration.

Thank you for your note. I am very much better than I was (i.e. well enough that he would not question my lack of symptoms, but not so well that he would press me to join him at dinner). *I would love to come for tea in your room at four o'clock. Thank you very much for inviting me.*
>   *Yours,*
>   *Abigail.*

I read the note out loud once I had finished it, glancing furtively at Boris as I pronounced my name. He gave no sign, so I handed it to Mrs. Veals. I feared that her disappearance would be succeeded by a torrent of fury from the bear, who would have seen some painfully obvious reason why I ought, at all costs, to avoid a meeting with my godfather. I was therefore relieved, if slightly baffled, by his reaction. As soon as Mrs. Veals' steps had died away, Boris positively jumped up and down on his chair with glee.

"Perfect!" he whooped, clapping his hands.

"...er..."

"Tea!" he said emphatically, as though I were deaf, stupid, or both, "This afternoon! In his STUDY! Perfect! Abigail you haven't forgotten, tell me you haven't forgotten?"

"...your plan..." I groaned, understanding him at last.

"What could be more perfect? All our problems solved in a single stroke! We can banish the 'king' from Traumund this very afternoon! All you need to do is to pilfer one mah-jong tile while you're in there, slip it in your pocket and bring it back here. Then we'll destroy it and bingo! He's gone! Gone from Traumund forever!"

Boris rattled on, like a fanatic whose first audience is himself.

"There's still the Vulture Men, I know...but they'll fall away eventually, when they realise he's not coming back. It's over Abigail, all over! You will have to escape from Boughwinds of course, but that needn't be a problem. We can worry about that later. It's not as though he need even suspect you. As far as he is concerned one of his tiles has gone missing...that's all. Easily done, with fiddly little things like mah-jong tiles-"

"Boris!" I repeated desperately. I had been calling his name over and over again, with mounting impatience, throughout this breezy speech.

"Boris, how exactly do you propose I steal a mah-jong tile from under my godfather's nose? He has invited me for afternoon tea, not a rummage through his belongings. Do you even know how a mah-jong box is constructed? The tiles, you know, are fitted into draws; the draws are slotted into shelves; the shelves are protected by a sliding wall on the outside of the box! I can't just slip one into my pocket, as you put it."

Boris's enthusiasm was checked, but only for half a second. "Don't worry about that…"

"But I do worry…"

"I'll sort something out. A diversion of some sort. I don't know what yet, but I'll think of something. Just sit tight and wait. You'll know when it's safe to act."

We sat in silence for a long time after that, our thoughts jointly focussed and yet our feelings worlds apart. Boris's face was the face of a disbelieving visionary. I could tell by the rapid twiddling of his paws that he was thinking hard. I was thinking hard as well and after a while I noticed that my forehead was tense and tired with frowning. I had to raise my eyebrows high, as though I was sternly surprised, in order to get rid of the ache. My stomach was crawling with fear.

At last an idea came to me that was coherent and that had an integrity about it that pleased me, and made sense. I felt that it would displease Boris and Joachim, which worried me in a way, although it also hardened my resolve. It made me think that I had a sense of right and wrong that was independent of my friends' magisterial moral codes; that I could act according to my own conscience, rather than merely bending to their wiser wishes.

"Boris?" I said, when I had made up my mind. He jumped, because our silence had been so lengthy and profound. "I've made a decision about something else."

"Oh?"

"Yes. I've decided that it would be wrong for me to keep Ludovick Montefiore's silver sword. When I go down to tea, I shall take it with me and give it back."

"What?" Boris was wide-eyed; struggling to find words to express his outrage. "What for? What for? I mean, for a start that will give the game away altogether! He'll want to know why and…well why? Why do you want to give it back?"

"Because I don't think it's right," I answered inflexibly, "to accept it as a gift when I am actually his enemy."

Boris sank his head into his paws. Five minutes ticked by as he sat there, bowed and silent, in an attitude of despair that seemed to me preposterously melodramatic.

"How can you think like that?" he spluttered at last. "He has armies and a castle; that sword is the only weapon we have, except for Constantine's bow, which was very kind of him and everything, but I mean it's hardly going to subdue nations, is it? We might need that sword Abigail, we might need it to protect Constantine and Joachim and Eyes and you and me and the whole of Traumund against the Vulture Men... Have you really forgotten that, Abigail? Forgotten again? And all for the sake of a sick tenderness? For the sake of chivalrous posturing? You can't actually be on his side, so you have to make him a gesture of – what? – spiritual solidarity? Love that overlooks everything? Some such twaddle. But Abigail, it's misplaced. Why do you dignify him? He's a cruel, petty-minded thief and a child-killer."

"So I should be petty-minded in return? My godfather, who is... all the things you said...gave me that sword in a passing moment of kindness..."

"...oh, here we go..."

"And in remembrance of that..." I stopped, angered by my own pomposity. "...Well, anyway, if he's as bad as you say he is we don't want his stupid sword, do we? And as for how I shall explain myself, don't worry. I've no intention of giving the game away. I'll just say that it is far too heavy for me to fight with and too heavy for my owl."

"Too heavy? For Eyes?" scoffed Boris.

"It's only an excuse - it'll do!" I concluded. "And that is the end of that."

Mrs. Veals came to fetch me at five to four and I trailed through the house behind her with the silver sword in my arms. Boris did not accompany me, since he was to organise a diversion. Mrs. Veals looked askance at the sword but, of course, I did not volunteer an explanation and she made no comment. When we arrived at Ludovick Montefiore's study door, instead of knocking and immediately departing as usual, she knocked, opened the door, and stepped across the threshold. I glimpsed my godfather beyond her bulk. He stood up in displeased surprise when he saw her hovering.

"What?"

"Pardon me for entering, sir," said Mrs. Veals bashfully, her eyes boring holes in his shoes. "Only, Miss Crabtree is here and she…she is carrying a large silver sword."

Ludovick Montefiore laughed and bowed at me as I hovered in the hall. I was embarrassed, trying to hide the sword by pressing it against my jeans. I doubt I could have looked less belligerent.

"I shall take my chances, Mrs. Veals," he said. "Now please show Abigail in with as much courtesy as you are able to muster and then clear off."

Mrs. Veals stood aside and I entered, all elbows and self-consciousness. The tea tray was ready, so that Mrs. Veals' departure plunged us into immediate and total privacy. The silence rendered chatter ridiculous.

This, I thought, is the first time I have seen Ludovick Montefiore face to face and known him to be my enemy. He must not find me altered.

I laid the sword down by my comfortable chair, shyly concealing it in the down-hanging folds of the upholstery. Last time I was there, you may remember, I perched on a footstool. I believe Ludovick Montefiore had brought in the armchair especially for me, on account of my 'illness'.

A blue-bottle settled on the hilt. I tried to cup my hand over it but it rose and zigzagged out of sight.

I had not repented of my decision to return the sword, but the "excuse" had slipped from my mind as readily as it had slipped from my tongue when I was arguing with Boris. Ludovick Montefiore politely – or distractedly - overlooked the subject, passing me a cup of tea. My hand was shaking and the blue and white china cup rattled on its saucer. I stilled it with the other hand and found myself giggling in a petrified sort of a way.

"That illness has hit you hard," said Ludovick Montefiore anxiously. My lungs swelled with hilarity. Laughter seemed to struggle interminably against my own silently horrified protests. "Are you well enough to be here? You can go back to bed if you wish, you know, you don't have to stay in order to be polite."

"I'm fine," I replied, relaxing a little once I had managed to speak normally. The temptation to accept his offer and escape to my room was strong. I tried to focus on my mission and more than that, I tried to make it mine, rather than a task foisted on me by the others. I looked around the room from beneath my half-lowered eyelids and saw the mah-jong set on his mahogany desk. It was, as I had feared, properly shut up in its complicated box.

"Abigail," he said.

My eyes shot to his face, because there was a quality to his voice that told me I must listen. He said my name as though it was the prelude to an important speech, something out of the ordinary, something that would change things. Perhaps, I thought, it would throw my plans awry and persuade me to something terrible. I waited, without answering him; my mad amusement drained away, my hands still.

"I want to talk to you about something," he continued slowly and, I thought, sadly. "It may surprise you and even make you think badly of me – I hope not – but I beg you to listen all the same and not to judge me until you have heard all."

He paused for a long time and then, just as he was taking breath to continue, there came a violent hammering at the door.

"What the…!" he exclaimed, rising from his chair. "Yes?"

Nobody entered and we both stared at the door handle: he, in his exasperation, wavering between movement and paralysis; I stock-still in my suspense. I felt sure that Boris's diversion had arrived.

The hammering resumed. Ludovick Montefiore charged at the door and tore it open. I could see Allecto's face and figure flickering between black and orange in the darkness of the passageway and the light of our warm sitting room.

"You?" he thundered. "What the devil? I thought (with a very slight nod in my direction) I told you never to come into my presence unless summoned?"

"I am so sorry," she replied in a low voice. "And I never would have done it if it wasn't so urgent. Please just a quick word, in private. Please."

He snorted like an angry wild animal, lifting his arms in an expansive, infuriated shrug. She had won his curiosity. I lay back in my chair and gazed demurely at the fire as he looked round at me.

"Abigail, I do apologise. One of the servants appears to have a problem. Will you excuse me for just one moment?"

"Of course," I said faintly and smiled at him. The door closed and I was on my feet, dizzy and directionless with fear.

I tiptoed over fathoms of rug until I reached the mahogany desk. I was stranded by the door now, far from my own chair and mere inches from my enemy. I laid my hands on the mah-jong set and sought its sliding side. The box rattled and creaked as though it was enchanted; as though it was calling out for its master.

I closed my eyes and felt my way around the mahogany contraption with blind fingers. I don't know why this made things calmer and easier, but it did. It also made me listen to the muttered conversation that was taking place on the other side of the door.

"...that bottle," Allecto was saying, "the one I brought you the other night. You see, I've just been up-dating my ingredients-records (I do that sometimes, you know - it's as well to keep an eye on things, as you'll see in a second) and whilst I was doing it, I noticed that I've completely run out of St. John's Wort. Or almost completely. There were a few dried flowers at the bottom of the basket, but nothing to speak of."

"Well?"

"Well..."

"What of it, woman?"

"Well, I've thought and thought about it and the only way I can make sense of it – of being so low on St. John's Wort I mean – is that I accidentally put too much into that latest batch of palliative."

(The sliding wall had come away. Now for the drawer. If only the handles were less fiddly or my thumb and fingers less stumpy and slow.)

"It tasted the same as usual," growled Ludovick Montefiore.

"Yes. Well that isn't improbable. It isn't a strongly flavoured ingredient; not in the small amounts that I use. And I'm not saying I put much too much in, but enough to destroy the balance of the whole."

(The top draw juddered open. Now I had to pick out a tile. But they were so closely packed and my finger nails were bitten so short.)

"Enough to make it dangerous?"

"Possibly. Though more likely it would just make the palliative ineffective."

"Well, what's so urgent about that?"

"Er...it...well it could be dangerous. It could be. But I've made up a new batch and I've brought a bottle of it with me now. I think it best if we swap bottles as soon as possible, just in case you need a dose this afternoon."

"Fine." He said, with a sort of clenched patience. "Wait there and I will fetch the defective bottle."

I heard his hand fall on the door-handle and I saw the oval knob make a quarter turn. "Help me God!" I prayed in a high-pitched whisper as I prised a tile from the pack, slammed shut the draw, leaned the sliding wall against the box (there was no time to put it back properly) and bolted back to my chair.

But Allecto had detained him. "Wait!" she shrieked imperiously, as the door handle turned. "Um…" she continued with a small cough. "Sorry. It's just….would you like me to taste the new one now? In case you need it soon, when I'm not here?"

"No I would not," he snapped and now the door really did open. "Except in exceptional circumstances I only ever take it last thing at night. It is very unlikely that I shall require extra doses this afternoon. You may come here just before dinner and taste it then."

He stalked back into the room. I grasped the tile in my right fist, trying to recover my breath whilst appearing dreamily inert. He brought a bottle out of the welsh dresser and took it to the door. They exchanged the medicines without a word and he shut the door in Allecto's face.

He walked back to the dresser and locked the new bottle inside it. Then he returned to his chair, looking about him with a thoughtful, distracted air as though he had lost something. As he sat he held his hands together loosely and gazed at them, his back bowed. I shifted in my seat and sniffed and blew my nose, but still he did not move. His thick brown tea sat untouched by his feet; I watched it grow cold and bitter.

"Ludovick…?" I ventured after ten minutes had elapsed. My voice was barely audible, as I had never dropped his surname before.

"Abigail!" he exclaimed, looking up at me. His mouth smiled, but his eyes were far away. "I do apologise. Where were we?"

"You were going to tell me something."

"Was I? I can't remember now. No, actually, I was thinking that you still look off-colour. You ought to get back to bed and have some more rest. Or maybe a turn in the garden before it gets dark? Fresh air…you know." He trailed off.

"All right," I said, reluctant to leave him now that my mission was accomplished and the tile safe in my sweaty fist. I was also curious to hear his confession.

He said nothing more. So I stood up and returned my untouched tea-cup to the tray.

"Unless…" he began.

"What?" I looked up hopefully. He seemed to stare, not so much at my face, but at the expression of tentative pleasure that my face exuded.

"Unless you would like a game of mah-jong? I mean, the actual game. I did say I'd show you, didn't I?"

"Oh no!" I said red-faced. "Thank you. I mean…I would like you to

show me, but not now…I'm…you're right, I'm not quite well yet. I've
a bit of a headache. I don't think I could concentrate very well."

"Fine!" he smiled at me candidly and I smiled back with difficulty,
because I couldn't hold my gaze in place.

"Oh, Abigail. One other thing. The silver sword. You brought it
back."

"Yes."

"Why?"

"Oh, it's lovely." (What a stupid adjective for a sword.) "But it's so
heavy. I don't think…I think I'd better just rely on my bow."

I wonder what his expression was as I made my frail excuse. I didn't
dare look and see. We were on the cusp of frankness and I think if I
had met his eye then there would really have been confessions and
revelations. So I bolted. And that, I suppose, was a confession in itself.

I made for the garden, as he had suggested. I needed to breathe
some of that rain-studded air before returning to the stifling comfort
of my room and the stifling questions and congratulations that I could
expect from Boris. It was cold and I wasn't wearing a coat, but I didn't
mind shivering. I hadn't felt fresh air on my face for three days. I felt
like a corpse rising up into the night from a snug, airless tomb.

I walked in the rose garden, which was all spiky stumps and manure.
The path wound round in broad figures of eight and I followed them
abstractedly. I still clutched the mah-jong tile in my fist. I had forgotten
that I could now relax a little; that I had left Ludovick Montefiore
behind.

The light in the garden was low but intense, so that the black valley
walls contrasted starkly with the strong, straining blue of the twilight.
If I widened my eyes then I could make out the design on the mah-
jong tile. It was a Rice Bird. It had no colour and barely any tone this
evening, but I remembered its orange legs, its green wings and its tail
of peacock eyes. My godfather had shown me a Rice Bird tile when
I first met him at the King Henry Hotel. He had given me his address
then and told me to come to him if I was ever in danger. Why did he
do that, only to try and kidnap me? Why did he give me a sword when
I was his enemy? The others would want to tell me that these actions
were mad and deceitful. It was not enough for them that he was evil;
they insisted upon his being consistently evil. Boris was even evolving
a theory (perhaps in an attempt to reconcile himself to its loss) that the
'magic' sword was cursed and that Ludovick Montefiore intended it to

hurt me or at least to fail me in my hour of need. I was alone in wanting the story to be more complex; in wanting my godfather to remain, if not pardonable, then at least inexplicable.

I pushed the Rice Bird deep into my pocket.

There were no lamps lit in the windows of the abbey tonight, so that it, like the valley, formed an unbroken hulk of dense, material darkness against the radiant dusk. With the smoke breathing from its tall chimneys it looked more like a crouching, angular dragon than ever: a dragon that was lying in wait, playing dead, watching its prey. As I stood before it, the prospect of returning inside began to look like sheer madness. I could run to the village, despite the encroaching night, the cold and the spectral trees. I could find John Fogle at The Witch's Broom and let him bring daylight and common sense to everything. Let him shatter my nightmare's meanderings and tell me that I am fretting over nothing. Let him tell me that there is no such place as Traumund. Let him tell me that Ludovick Montefiore is a good, ordinary man.

"Hey!" A familiar voice called from beyond the rose garden. I turned and approached it, drawing nearer, as I did so, to the house.

"How did you get on?" asked Boris, as I reached him. He was sauntering along on his own having, seemingly, abandoned all Waking World inhibitions. I picked him up, nonetheless, and held him in the crook of my arm, like a baby.

"All right," I replied, pulling the Rice Bird from my pocket and flashing it before his gleeful eyes. "Where have you been gallivanting?" I continued quickly, in order to forestall his congratulations.

"I went to see Allecto. I take it our diversionary plan worked?"

"As you see."

We were in the hall, I realised, as the front door boomed shut behind us. I suppose I could have turned round and opened it again, but I did not. We returned to our room, as though directed by the house itself.

There was something wrong.

We both felt it, as soon as we entered. It was colder than usual, for a start: Mrs. Veals had allowed the fire to die right down. And it was dark: there were usually candles by my bed and over the fireplace. But these explanations did not suffice. It wasn't just that there was something lacking, like warmth or light. There was something wrong. Something there, that should not be. A breathing, gloating, hiding evil. It wasn't my imagination: Boris felt it too. I could tell by the way in which his body stiffened and he looked around, alert. I paced the room, holding Boris tightly in my arms. I touched things: the window pane, the wardrobe, the mantelpiece. I could not discover any change and yet I felt as disturbed as though all around me the dragon-house was stirring from its slumber.

"Let's go," urged Boris. "Let's get out of here and into Traumund."

I locked the door. Then I added a log to the fire and as I did so I discreetly thrust the Rice Bird into the depths of the greying embers – using the first action to conceal (but from whom?) the second. I lay down on the bed with Boris in my arms. I closed my eyes.

An hour went by. I could hear my heart thundering in my ears. I no longer dared to open my eyes and look at the room because I felt that somebody was there. My enemy was there.

Two hours went by and my pulse throbbed more slowly. My mind was still uneasy, but its uneasiness was vague. Boris was humming a bear's lullaby, close to my ear, yet far away in another universe. The room was losing its prey. I could see Joachim's hut far, far below me, in a forest, in another world. I felt like an astronaut drifting over the earth, emerging from the black void, plummeting towards home in a flight of panicked joy. The hut came closer and closer. I was nearly there, nearly there. I fell into it with my arms open wide, but I could not fall quickly enough.

I jolted. The hut wavered out of focus and then it came back. I tried to shout for Joachim, but a wind blew up from the tree tops and sucked the sound from my mouth. I tried to stretch out my hands, but I had only one hand. I pulled towards the hut, feeling a great weight at the end of my lost, left hand. Suddenly I saw the abbey clearly, in the weak light of a winter's night: I saw a monster's silhouette loom over the bed and lurch at my flailing hand with a frenzied, clawing grasp. Then the hut came into view like lamp-light in a mist and I flung myself at it. I heard Boris howling, "No! No! No! Too late!" I landed heavily on the floor of the hut, my arm wrenched and aching as though it had uprooted an oak tree.

For a moment I could do nothing but breathe hard against the unvarnished wooden floor. Then I looked down at my hand, because it hurt. But I could not see my hand. Ludovick Montefiore's long fingers were wrapped tightly around it and they hid it from my sight.

The King of Traumund

only had eyes for the hand that gripped mine, so I did not observe Joachim, Constantine, Eyes or Boris while they tried, like me, to realise what was happening. Nobody moved or spoke. Joachim was armed with a short dagger: apparently he saw me flicker into sight during my troubled arrival and, hearing a cut-off cry, grabbed his knife intuiting that something was wrong. He did not use it though, when Ludovick Montefiore lay prone at his feet. He simply stared from him, to me, as though we were beyond his understanding.

Constantine still lay on the wooden table, though he was more comfortable now, pillowed and coddled with blankets. He looked human too and better than half-dead; better, even, than half-alive. Someone had washed him and combed his hair. His clothes, though they were irredeemably beggarly, were cleaned and mended. He propped himself up on a shaky elbow as the commotion of our arrival woke him. He looked at me blankly (sleepily, I think) and then he looked at Ludovick Montefiore with an expression that changed, very slowly, from incomprehension to astonishment. Quite suddenly his astonishment gave way to contempt. He shrugged and lay down again. Like Joachim, he was brave and unconfused. His hatred was pure.

Ludovick Montefiore stood up and blinked away the dizziness of his transition from world to world. My eyes followed him all the time, as though my gaze was a chain and I had fastened it around his face. He shot a fleeting smile at Joachim's knife and then turned to me.

"I'm sorry, Abigail. No, really, that can't have been at all pleasant for you. Is your hand all right?"

He actually stopped to wait for a reply, so I nodded sharply in order (I hoped) to break the net of complicity that his words wove about us.

"Good," he said slowly. I managed to turn away, but I could feel a tug on the chain. He felt that the short exchange would not be finished until I looked at him, but I resisted his will because Joachim was there.

Ludovick Montefiore turned from me to inspect his appalled audience. His voice changed when he spoke to them. It lost its serenity and took on something of that unresponsive harshness that characterised the voices of the Vulture Men. How had I become bad enough - loved enough – to escape it? And why did pride swell up in me as he belittled my friends, even though, at the same time, I felt as sickened as though a blunt knife was hollowing out my insides?

"I suppose you are Joachim?" He said the name as though he was quoting it from an undesirable source; as though it was a vulgar word that he would not ordinarily deign to pronounce.

Joachim nodded, or rather his chin moved downwards by the tiniest fraction of an inch. He stared up through narrowed eyes that seemed fit to burst with power. His hand tightened around the dagger, but his arm remained motionless. He looked like a statue that will never move, even though it seems to possess an inner energy that has been wound up to a tremulously high tension.

"And the Owl. Eyes."

Eyes blinked expressionlessly.

My godfather's eyes swept over Constantine, who gazed unconcernedly at the ceiling. He said nothing to him, or about him.

"Do you know who I am?" he asked, turning back to Joachim.

Joachim levered his chin up, until he could stare down (or, at least, along) his nose at Ludovick Montefiore.

"And – not that it makes much difference - you will not bow your knee to the King of Traumund?"

Joachim glanced at Eyes and Boris with a woefully unconvincing expression of amusement (I only divined its intention because I knew him so well). I waited for him to include me in this burst of fake humour, but he did not.

"I understand that you wish to put a stop to my explorations, and throw me out of Traumund?" continued Ludovick Montefiore in a chillingly chatty tone. "It's all right, you needn't waste your energy on excuses and shaggy dog stories. Abigail has told me your 'plans', such as they are."

"You think we would try to excuse ourselves?" Joachim sneered.

Ludovick Montefiore did not like Joachim's bald refusal to acknowledge fear; his appropriation of equality. In fact, it baffled him. I think he thought it was plain wrong of Joachim; intellectually wrong I mean, and therefore embarrassing. It did not disturb his self-image. Nothing could do that.

At any rate his cheeks reddened as Joachim spoke - in anger, of course, but also with a strange sort of projected shame, as though Joachim had been gauche enough to make any intelligent man blush. He did not resume the conversation, but strode across to the open door. He scanned the clearing and the woodland, and then put his fingers to his mouth and whistled a shrill whistle, like a screeching bird of prey.

They looked at one another – Joachim, Boris and Eyes. I wanted to make Joachim smile at me, so as to reassure myself that I was not a traitor. I said as quietly as I could,

"Joachim?...I didn't mean to let him come."

My words sounded so childish that I thought I was going to giggle or cry. A self-mocking whine started up in my head: "I didn't mean it! I didn't mean it!" I was like a frightened child who has broken a china ornament.

Joachim glanced at me, but he did not smile.

Ludovick Montefiore raised his fingers to his pursed lips once again, but then he paused, and we all heard the soft drumming of hoof-beats. The horses were far away in the muffling forest, and the sound of their coming seemed to encircle the hut with a menacing loop. Louder and louder they came as the loop tightened, though the peaceful evening sunlight still slanted through the branches and lengthened over the green grass. Then at last, just as it seemed that the crescendo was coming, like Sylvia's voice, from inside our heads, there was an explosive relaxation of noise as the Vulture Men burst out of the trees and drew to a jingling, snorting, whinnying halt in Joachim's clearing. Immediately a rancid stench began to thicken the summer air.

We could see them, my friends and I: dozens of Vulture Men drawn up before Ludovick Montefiore, their black hoods hanging slackly around their beaks and their eyes glinting in the velvet darkness. The horses were lined up neatly before Joachim's house, their restlessness subdued. When Ludovick Montefiore stepped out into the clearing they bent their left fore-legs and bowed their glossy necks, and their riders bent their necks also.

Ludovick Montefiore walked over the grass and paced up and down through their lines. Nobody moved. He inspected each rider rapidly, upbraiding one for his torn cloak, and another for his filthy boots. Then he stepped back to the door.

"Is your bow strung?" murmured Joachim through barely parted lips. He was addressing me at last.

I nodded.

"And your quiver is full?"

I nodded again, glad that I could answer correctly and truthfully, but hollow in my arms and legs because I had never even played at bows and arrows.

"And the silver sword?" Joachim whispered sharply. "Where is it?"

I shook my head hastily and returned to the scene in the clearing. My godfather was lounging in the doorway with his back to us, and so it was that we saw (all of us at once I think, because I felt, if I did not hear, a collective gasp) the silver sword itself. He had strapped it to his belt, and the tip of its blade raised the hem of his cloak as it swung by his side, ready for use – ready for his use. I dared not look at my friends.

Ludovick Montefiore was addressing his men.

"Which of you here is most senior?"

A horse stepped forward. Its rider was indistinguishable from the rest, except that the crest on his cloak was worked in scarlet as well as silver.

"And you are..?"

"Captain Karr, Your Majesty, at your service," he replied, as meekly as that shrill roar of a voice could ever permit.

"Captain Karr," resumed my godfather in a low growl, which I strained with all my strength to hear. "How far away is your camp?"

"A matter of minutes, Your Majesty. Most of us were there when your signal came. We all hurried here straight away, Your Majesty."

"A matter of minutes? Really? Then I would be interested to know how this boy here has succeeded in evading capture for months on end!"

"Sire...We..."

"However, that question must wait for the time being. I have more pressing matters to deal with. Listen. I want one of your men to return to camp as quickly as possible, and bring back two fresh horses, a horse-drawn tumbrel, a dozen armed guards, plus provisions. We will be setting off for the castle immediately. You must waste no time."

"Sire!"

"Go!"

"Yes, Sire." The yellow-eyed horse wheeled about and cantered across the front row of riders. The king's orders were passed on to one of the soldiers at the edge of the group, and immediately he raced away through the forest. Then the captain picked a dozen of his freshest horses and men and led them back to the doorway.

"These men will guard you with their lives, Your Majesty," he said, introducing the chosen twelve to their monarch. They resumed their stooping posture. The Captain bowed his head lower than any of them. He spoke quickly and comparatively quietly, as though he feared the sound of his own voice. How terrible my godfather must be, I thought, if he is able to make these carnivorous monsters shake.

Ludovick Montefiore made no reply, but Captain Karr would not withdraw without his king's permission. He waited for a moment before venturing to speak again.

"The other men may disperse now, Your Majesty?"

"Oh, may they indeed? Yes, I suppose they may..."

Captain Karr's whole frame seemed to lift a fraction.

"But you, Captain Karr, will stay. I wish you to form a part of my entourage."

The soldier seemed to fight a paralysing spasm, before bowing low and retreating a few paces from the king's presence.

Ludovick Montefiore re-entered the hut. He turned to me, and once again his voice was the voice I had loved in my daydreams: a voice redolent of firelight, parchment and wine.

"I'm sorry about all this," he apologised, as though he had inconvenienced me in some small way, by slopping tea on my saucer or arriving late for dinner. "Are you all right, Abigail? Are you quite, quite sure that your hand is all right? May I have a look at it?"

Without looking at him, or speaking to him, I folded my arms behind my back. He pulled his proffered hand away quickly, as though I was a favourite dog turned vicious. I felt a small glow of pride in the knowledge that Joachim had witnessed my gesture of insubordination. But most of all (I cannot justify it, but then again how can I be expected to justify something that seemed to fall upon me from outside myself?) I felt shame at having snubbed Ludovick Montefiore. You would think, wouldn't you, that my indignation might be hot enough by now; hot enough to blast such wrong-headed regrets to dust and ashes? But my indignation was very unsure of itself, and some of it had turned against Joachim and Constantine, just because their presence had prompted that show of defiance.

Ludovick Montefiore turned back to the clearing. He bowed his head in thought as I watched him. Before long he seemed to rouse himself, as though impatient at his own self-absorption.

"You!" he barked, motioning one of the guards. The Vulture Man dismounted, and stepped forward to meet his king. The king himself trod across the dewy grass. I could not hear the rest of Ludovick Montefiore's words, I just saw the soldier nod deferentially and then approach the hut.

The stench from his beak was nauseating in that confined space. I tried to breathe as sparingly as possible through my mouth.

"Weapons down on the floor!" he began. "Now!"

His eyes glinted over his exposed beak, which was as long and curved as a scythe, though thicker and cruelly serrated. We cast our arms on the floor, such as they were: my wooden bow and arrows and Joachim's knife.

The Vulture Man stooped, his eyes flickering from Joachim to Eyes and back again. He picked up the weapons and slid the knife into a pouch inside his velvet cloak. Then, placing the bow and arrows across his man's hands he approached me and bowed. He held the weapons as though they were a glass of wine on a silver tray and he was a waiter; a cringing waiter who works in dread of complaints.

"Madam, if you please, His Highness commanded me not to take your bow and arrow away."

Glancing from the weapon to Joachim to Constantine, and finally to Ludovick Montefiore, who now stooped in a listening attitude at the door, I shook my head and blustered in a shrill whisper: "That's ridiculous! Of course you must disarm me! Whose side do you think I'm on? I'm on their side; isn't that obvious? If you leave me my bow and arrow I will be able to use it against you…and I will! I'll kill the lot of you!"

The hooded bird-man turned to my godfather as though appealing for further instructions. We all turned as he turned, but Ludovick Montefiore did not acknowledge our silent inquiry. He stood there with his hands behind his back, like a man who stands at his own back door to relish the evening sun and the simple sounds of birdsong.

The hood turned back to me with a sigh and a diminutive bow. "Forgive me, Madam. My orders were very clear." He laid the bow and quiver in my slack fingers.

He rounded on my friends with a good deal more relish that he had evinced in his transaction with me. "Now then! You scum! Enemies of the king!" he began, resuming his proper volume and tone of voice. "Stick your filthy hands, or paws, or wings out in front of your bodies. You too!" he snarled at Constantine, who still gazed at the ceiling. Despite everything, I smiled. For all his ravaged physique, Prince Constantine only needed a twelve-inch cigarette-holder to complete the image of aristocratic disdain.

The four of them: two humans, an owl and a bear, did as they were told, and the Vulture Man tied their wrists (and the owlish equivalent of wrists) with a jerk of thin rope, so that they all winced, though not one of them uttered a sound.

This was too much. I did not have the capacity to string my bow and launch a single-handed attack on these invading hordes, yet I felt my friends' inner-eyes resting expectantly on the quiver. If I could not deliver them then surely I might be allowed to join them? Desperation overcame repulsion and I seized the Vulture Man's capacious sleeve.

"What about me?" I cried ridiculously. But once again he made me a diffident bow and replied, "You are the king's friend. You are to remain free. My orders, Madam."

The separation that I had already felt as an increasing, though intangible, factor in my relationship with the rebellious four, was now real. I wanted to be maltreated like them, in order that I might join their noble ranks. They were good; they were in the right, and Ludovick Montefiore was in the wrong. I acknowledged that with my mind and my lips, so then why was my position so guiltily ambivalent? To be fully bad, I thought for an angry split-second, would be better than this state of nebulous grey. I felt as though Joachim (for Joachim was the figurehead of this goodness from which I was half-voluntarily excluded) and I were sitting on separate rafts, which he had roped together, and which I had managed to untie. Now that we were drifting apart from one another I could hear that whimpering child again, inside my head. "Oh! I didn't mean to!"

The tumbrel arrived from the camp, and the riding horses too, their saddlebags bulging. As the others were hustled out into the clearing and then hurled, one by one, into the tumbrel, I found my voice and cried out, "Joachim! What shall I do?" He looked at me for a long time, his white lips pressed together tightly. Then he turned away, and the movement of his head betrayed such bitterness. "Oh, you're sure to think of something, Abigail," he replied. "Aren't you?"

Eyes was the first to be bundled inside the tumbrel: a stout wooden cage on wheels, unsoftened by even so much as a blanket or a twist of straw. Constantine was lifted from the table next and dragged to the cart by his arm-pits, his feet trailing stiffly through the dust. For all his stoicism he could not help shrieking with pain as the Vulture Man tossed him across the cage after Boris, regardless (or, more probably, cruelly regardful) of his deep and barely-healing wounds. "Ludovick." I said evenly, like a robot, from out of the stupor that kept me from responding properly to these horrors, "Don't. Stop them."

The king put his hand on my arm and I shrugged it away, following without feeling them the rules by which my morally tepid life had always been run so far. "They are not your friends," he said in a voice that was so certain that a weak mind would be in danger of accepting its infallibility. "I am your friend."

As soon as the four had been locked inside the tumbrel, I sidled up to the bars in order to beg some kind words from Joachim, or to give some paltry comfort, or to prove to them and myself, in some other way, that we were still allied. "Is Constantine all right?" I began in small voice. "Will you be all right, Constantine?" Nobody answered. Joachim's gaze was fixed on the scene behind me. He watched with growing perplexity. Of course I looked over my shoulder then, to see it for myself.

My godfather was standing at the doorway in an attitude that made me think he might be, rather ostentatiously, at prayer (though I shuddered to think what sort of a god he would deign to address). His head was bowed and his arms were outstretched, and he was murmuring strange words in a rapid drone. I say the words were strange, and they were, but at least I recognised one part of them. "AbigailJoachimBoris" he cried, raising the pitch and volume of his voice.

"He's saying our names!" I exclaimed excitedly. "But not Eyes' or Constantine's. What do you think it means?"

"It's magic of some sort," replied Joachim, but there was no excitement in his voice.

"Don't worry," said Eyes, as he wriggled to release his tail feathers, which had become trapped underneath Joachim's left leg. "It can't be a very diabolical spell if he's included Abigail's name."

I walked away.

Ludovick Montefiore's incantation was over. He was all action now. "Abigail, can you ride?"

I had been pony-trekking once or twice, but a round-bellied Welsh pony is a distinctly different prospect to the grass-pawing monster whose reins my godfather impatiently proffered. It reminded me of Miss Konder, because of the self-adoring contempt with which its bony eye-sockets surveyed me from head to foot. "No." I answered decisively.

"Oh well. I'll attach a rope to the bridle and lead you then. You just sit tight. Captain Karr, help my goddaughter to mount her horse."

The Vulture Man gripped my thighs before I even knew what was happening and pushed me over the animal's back. I tried to kick him away, for I hated being touched by him, and though his hands were human, his nails felt like talons, and I could feel them digging through my clothes and into my skin. He held onto me though, for all my vicious struggles, until he had me perched securely. I did not thank him. If I had been astride my Welsh mountain pony I would have urged it away from his presence immediately with a flapping of my legs, but as it was I dared not move a muscle. The horse was convulsed with jitters at the least little sigh of wind, and I felt that if I only sneezed it would sweep me off to the farthest reaches of Traumund.

Ludovick Montefiore mounted his own black horse. He was imposing and, in striking contrast to his minions, handsome. He had lost the stoop and pallor that always seemed to lessen and threaten him in the Waking World; here he was square-shouldered and brown-faced. His clothes were plain yet regal, and they seemed to match the air and earth of Traumund. They were made in shades of grey and blue: different (subtly but decidedly different) from any I have seen in the Waking World. His cloak was long and velvety, like those of the Vulture Men, only his was a thunder-cloud grey, and it was edged with ermine, which was pure white, like a petrified lightning-streak. In one hand he held his reins and my leading rope. Under the other arm he clutched a leather-bound volume. It was the great Traumund atlas that Constantine had stolen; the King had retrieved it. As I watched, he handed it to another rider, with instructions that it was to remain safe and pristine throughout the journey, on pain of that rider's death.

We were ready for our journey to the king's castle. Captain Karr rode in front, followed by the tumbrel, and my godfather and I rode side by side behind that. Of the dozen chosen soldiers, two flanked Captain Karr, four guarded the tumbrel, four rode with the king and me, and another two brought up the rear. Ludovick Montefiore looked about him with unsmiling satisfaction.

"We are all ready, I think...except (and now a smile did give bite to his contentment)...except for Captain Karr." The Captain who was, as

I have said, heading the procession, seemed to shrivel in his saddle. He turned his horse, whose head was now so meekly low that its lower lip trailed in the dust, and ventured within five feet of the king. "Sire?" he whispered, his hooded head bowed.

"I think," continued Ludovick Montefiore, in a voice that was as thin as the draughts that rattle the window panes at Boughwinds Abbey, "that in view of your…what shall we say? 'Inadequate?'… No I hardly think that will suffice… 'Appalling?'… 'Lamentable?'… 'Inconceivably inept?' In view of your inconceivably inept policing of this area, you have a nerve to take it upon yourself to lead this little party of mine. Wouldn't you say?"

"But Your majesty …" the alpine screech was hoarse.

My godfather turned to one of the nameless riders at his right hand. "Make him dismount," he ordered curtly, "and put him in the tumbrel with the other prisoners." The soldier, whether through fear or a genuine lack of feeling for his erstwhile captain (I could well believe in both), followed his orders with alacrity, and my friends, squashed as they were already, were obliged to move over for that hulking, foul-breathed bird.

I did not pity Captain Karr, since I could still feel the bruises on my legs where his talons had pricked me, but nonetheless this incident made me fear Ludovick Montefiore more than ever. The long minutes during which he had waited to spring this trap on his servant, and the self-indulgent toying with words once it was sprung, drove home to me the passionless nature of his malevolence. Before this incident I had hoped that his cruelty – if he must be cruel - welled up from an unreasoning temper. But even this meagre mitigation was now disallowed.

We moved away from Joachim's hut. Joachim watched it, craning his neck and narrowing his eyes against the gloom, until at last it became indistinguishable from the protecting wall of blue-purple forest. I did not look behind me. I was watching my captor, whose hand was joined to my horse by means of a loose rope.

At one point he turned round and caught my solemn gaze. He smiled at me, and if you had seen that smiling face in isolation, in an untitled painting, say, you would have guessed that the artist's model was the kindest and best of men. You might even have developed a school-girl crush on the picture, and invented stories about its subject's life. Ever since I had known to suspect Ludovick Montefiore my sight was prone to seeing things in isolation; I slipped so comfortably into a tunnel vision that flattered my desires and preconceptions. But my reason (thank heaven for it, what there was of it. I valued it very little at the time, since it seemed so distant from what I deemed my real self - the part of me that bubbled with corrupt emotion) forbade me to return the smile; it told me I must fight to be put back on the side of right. So I looked at my horse's neck with a blank face (I could not scowl into his sapphire eyes, it would be like sticking my tongue out at a religious idol of which I understood nothing, but whose power I involuntarily felt) and I asked,

"What was that…thing…that prayer you were doing before?"

"A simple magic spell that will prevent you, and my prisoners, from waking up and leaving Traumund for the Waking World."

"And the spell cannot be broken?"

"Oh yes, it can, it is not very powerful. It can be broken by any superior magic, such as the rare drug Euthusoteria…" (with a short gasp I remembered the cord around my neck and the little bottle with its tiny dose. I wanted to touch Boris's gift, to be sure of it, but I did not dare draw Ludovick Montefiore's attention.) "…and, of course, the death of the spell-worker."

"The…what?"

"You, and the prisoners, will be released from the spell when I am dead."

I did not react outwardly to my godfather's words, though with a jolting pain I understood what was required of me.

"Why do you say, 'you and the prisoners'?" I asked. "I'm your prisoner too!" Again I regretted the childish note in my voice but there was nothing that I could do about it. I continued coyly, almost apologetically, "I mean…I mean I'm not on your side."

"Then shoot me with your arrows," he said slyly. "I won't stop you. Even the Vulture Men won't stop you, you have my word for it. You are free and armed. You are decidedly not a prisoner."

"Why? Why do you trust me?" (Am I such an appalling character, I added inwardly, am I so lost, that you find a kindred spirit in me?)

"Oh, I don't know that I do trust you, as such. I don't have to trust you in order to treat you with dignity."

"And if I plead for them, will you treat my friends as you treat me?"

"No."

He said "No" without the least hesitation or quiver of embarrassment, and I felt, as I had felt before, the mad hope that we (my friends and I) had simply failed to understand. This scenario that Ludovick Montefiore had created, and that seemed so irredeemably depraved in its methods and its intent, was all for the good. None of us could see its validity yet, because we were all his inferiors, both in terms of intelligence and (above all) morality. After all, the very good are always inscrutable; they always talk and act in paradoxes and parables and deep silences. For the very good, imprisonment can be freedom and death can be life, and explanations are never rattled off in a few words, they evolve over days and weeks and centuries. I prayed that my godfather would turn out to be the great paradox of my life, and that we would all thank him one day, and marvel at his benevolent wisdom. But I did not really believe it.

Our horses turned to the right and immediately a salt wind flattened itself against our faces, and I could hear nothing more for a while; nothing but the slapping of cloaks against our horses' flanks and a whistling moan. There was sand in the air, that made my eyes water.

Why didn't I plant an arrow in his back? It would have been for the best. But the idea seemed ludicrous to me then, not just because I didn't know how to string a bow, but also because killing a man in cold blood, which might sound like a reasonable course when you read about it in a narrative like mine, was impossible in practice; impossible for me. I refused in the same spirit as I would refuse to walk a tight-rope over the Niagara Falls.

Besides how could I kill somebody who had invited me to do just that? How could I kill him when my feelings were as ambivalent as they were? I needed hatred and blood-lust; instead I felt curiosity. I wanted to hear his explanations and excuses, and I still possessed a heady hope (a hope I can't have analysed well) that they would prove sufficient. I could not help warming to his flattery, even though I knew it might be part of his giant deception, any more than I could help closing my eyes against the flying salt air. I had heard about his inhumanity, and I had witnessed it, but I had not felt it for myself even yet, and therefore (and this was my monumental failure of imagination) I could not hate him.

We rode upwards, the shrill piping of the wind deepened now by a regular, subterranean pounding that I knew for the rocks and the sea. The quick trot-trot of the horses' hooves turned to a slower plod-plod as the way grew steeper and softer. The trees had thinned away, and now we were riding up light-coloured banks between uneven clumps of long, coarse grass. We crested the slope at last, and found ourselves on the rim of a sheer cliff. There was the sea far, far below us, perhaps a mile below, grey, foamy and chaotic, a picture of certain death. We stopped for a minute to let the horses take breath and I drank in the sight with a sudden, irrepressible joy. The thought that this great cleft of rock, and the seething ocean below us, belonged in the same world as my own little oak tree, filled me with gladness. I felt as though I had been set free from a grinding domesticity. And who had burst the boundaries? Who had freed me, against my will and against my sense of right and wrong, to taste this illicit liberty? I looked at him as he shouted his deafened orders to the leading Vulture Men. We wheeled around on the cliff-edge and continued on our way.

We rode along the cliffs for an eternity. I dozed when darkness fell, slumping forwards in my saddle. Of course I did not really sleep because I was aware all the time that I must remain astride my horse. The deeper my doze, the more urgent this awareness became, and several times I woke suddenly with that heart-stopping sensation that had terrified Boris on the nocturnal flight to Joachim's hut. The feeling, which is unnerving enough when you are in your bed, is somewhat more piquant when you are perched on horse-back a mile or so above the sea.

When I woke up properly it was morning, and the scene that I had so far seen in blues, blacks and greys, was all pearl and pale yellow. The wind still blustered but I was not cold, because a grey, velvet cloak edged with ermine had been fastened around my shoulders.

I looked towards the tumbrel as it rattled on ahead of me. The five prisoners bounced against one another with every bump in the road. They were all drowsing.

Some time after I woke we left the cliffs and edged our way down a steep embankment into a copse, whose yellow-leafed, white-barked trees stood far apart from one another, and where the ground had that hollow, mossy quality that is so comfortable to walk on. Here my godfather ordered a halt and dismounted, motioning for me and the Vulture Men to follow his example. I did so with difficulty, as my legs had turned to stone, but I was determined to do it quickly, without attracting any undesirable assistance. The comparative silence down here was refreshing, after the night's restless winds and thudding waves, and I thought how happy I might feel, if only it weren't for the bird men and the tumbrel.

One of the solders lit a twiggy fire. Ludovick Montefiore rooted about in his saddle bag and drew forth a black kettle, two tin mugs, a frying pan, a loaf of white bread, a packet of tea, and a good pound of bacon. He bustled about on his own, slicing bread and bacon, setting the pan to heat, and filling the kettle from a stream. I was surprised to find him so self-sufficient.

The Vulture Men gathered together beneath a tree and breakfasted upon small dead birds that they drew from beneath their cloaks and tore apart in a flurry of hands and bills.

During last night's sleepy ride I had determined (according to my increasingly illogical and inconsistent system of morality) that I would refuse his food. But the mingled smells of frying bacon, fragrant tea and wood-smoke smoothly overcame my shaky hauteur. Ludovick Montefiore handed me a thick, dripping sandwich and a steaming mug, and I accepted both with monosyllabic thanks. In that moment it seemed better to cry for self-disgust than for hunger, thirst and weariness. I took a bite and a sip.

But then the tumbrel caught my eye and my conscience struck me so hard that I could not resist it. The prisoners were hunched in various states between sleep and hollow-eyed wakefulness. Ludovick Montefiore was washing his face and hands in the stream. I sidled up to my friends and offered them my breakfast.

They (the ones who were closest to wakefulness; that is, Boris and Joachim) barely had time to register my presence, when something hard struck the side of my head. Bacon, bread, tea and I flew several feet and landed at the foot of a tree in a scalding, greasy heap. "Leave the prisoners alone!" I heard a snarling vulture-voice weaving through the blur of my concussion. Then there were pounding feet, incoherent cries and gentle hands lifting me and wiping blood from my cheek. Ludovick Montefiore stood before me, steadying me by the shoulders as I tried to stand.

"Abigail, what happened? Are you all right? No, you're not, sit down again. But tell me what happened."

"I wanted to give them a bit of breakfast, that's all. And one of your guards struck me from behind."

He was only doing his job, I assumed. Following orders. My godfather's wrath would turn on me at last and I could align myself with the others again. I had found a solid cause at last, a cause that could withstand the mountainous clouds of confusion that I seemed intent on pulling over my head. The prisoners must have breakfast. I should hold on to that as my slogan; my credo. The prisoners must have breakfast. Let that come between us.

Ludovick Montefiore was white-lipped with rage. "Which one was it, Abigail? Can you tell me that?"

"It was that one," said Joachim, pointing at a Vulture Man who hovered at the edge of the copse, watching us all nervously and then pretending not to watch. My godfather, though he did not glance at Joachim or grant him a single word, chose to hear him. He strode amongst his picnicking guards. They stood to attention as one.

"Bind his hands," he barked, stabbing his finger against the culprit's chest. The soldier made no resistance as his fellows obeyed their orders. Ludovick Montefiore attached a rope to the Vulture Man's bound hands, a sort of leash that he himself grasped and jerked. He began dragging his captive up the slope that we had so recently descended. Then he stopped, turned round and came back again, the prisoner following, of necessity. "Oh, take Karr out of the tumbrel and bind him as well. I may as well deal with them both at the same time," he ordered. They obeyed, once again, quickly and without a word.

My godfather led his prisoners to the heady coastal heights that we had left behind that morning. He strolled along contentedly, like a man with his dogs: a couple of craven dogs who slink sulkily at their master's heels. When they were out of sight I heard an angry shout and high-pitched yelps.

Five minutes later he returned alone.

On and on we marched, through a flat, green, monotonous country. There was nothing to see but the occasional, distant farm building, or a tree, or a dark grey cloud in a light grey sky. We travelled quickly because we rode along a straight, wide chalky road which, my godfather told me proudly, was of his own making. He was building a network of roads, he said, across Traumund. They unravelled from his gateway, I observed later on, like prying tentacles.

I slept every now and then, and when I woke up I did not know – I really did not know – whether nights had passed, or whether that day was still slowly, coolly burning itself out. The flat land continued on and on: nothing new to see or hear; just the ruler-straight road outstripping our rhythmic horses. Sometimes we stopped to eat, but I was always aware of a gnawing hunger that grew and ached as though rats were chewing through my stomach.

At last I woke up from a doze to find the landscape changing. It was darker and closer and more alive. The grassy plains had given way to ploughed fields that rose up like peat-black waves on either side of the road. The road was no longer so straight, nor so white: it was a soily, snaking track, potholed and uneven. We passed a huddle of sturdy cottages. They were built from a black stone, tinged with yellow.

The air was cold and my brain felt refreshed. I could not see any people or dogs or cattle, only large black birds that swooped and cawed over the harrowed fields.

Then the cottages dwindled away, and the fields became stonier. Soon there were no more walls or wire fences, and the fields were behind us. We were crossing a purple heath, and the night was closing in. I was shivering in my thick cloak, and I could hear my friends' chattering teeth over the rumble of the tumbrel's uneven wheels. Ludovick Montefiore spoke.

"Abigail, look! Straight ahead."

I looked, and I saw an island rising up from this heathery sea. It was closer than I could credit, given that we had been travelling towards it all that time. I could make out very little, since it consisted of nothing more than a hulking silhouette, and yet it was familiar all the same: the shape of it, the crouching threat, or promise, of it; the smoke oozing from its stone nostrils; the crenellations, like ridges along a dragon's spine.

We had arrived at last.

A Traveller's Tale

We entered the castle gates together, but my friends and I separated almost immediately afterwards. The tumbrel turned right and disappeared amidst much clanging of keys and chains, and booming doors. Meanwhile my horse was led onwards through a paved courtyard that was cloistered on all four sides by low, pillared archways. Everywhere there was that distinctive yellow-black stone that affected me strangely. Its very bleakness seemed to ooze a sort of dark romance, so that I failed to protest even as it closed in around me and took away the sky.

Our horses drew to a halt at the foot of a flight of steps. Ludovick Montefiore dismounted. I hastily followed suit when I observed a Vulture Man (not a member of our guard, but one who stood sentry at the door) advancing to my assistance. The king offered me his arm, and I took it. We mounted the steps together and as we did so the doors swung open, and yet more Vulture Men, all of them indistinguishable to me in their full-length velvet cloaks, seemed to fall at our feet, like blades of trampled grass, in homage to our majesty. Ludovick Montefiore ignored them all, and I copied him.

We left them behind and walked together through the castle, along broad high-windowed corridors, through a stripy patchwork of white moonlight and golden lamplight. Before long we came to a green door, prettily garlanded over each of its panels with painted edelweiss. We entered.

The chamber resembled my bedroom at Boughwinds Abbey - not closely, but oddly, in that the windows, door, fireplace and bed were in the same positions relative to one another. But at Boughwinds there was an air of melancholy in my room, as though the place was too

preoccupied with its many troubled secrets to care much for the comfort
of its current occupant. There was always an uneasy chill there, which
rugs, beeswax polish and a roaring hearth could not quite dispel. The
Traumund room, on the other hand, neither meditated nor shrugged me
off. It luxuriated. It wallowed. It lured me in.

Every inch of wall was hung with thick, glistering tapestries.
I studied them later on, while I was dressing for dinner. Its greens,
reds and golds seemed to fluctuate, like stained glass windows on a
day of sunshine and racing clouds, and they showed scenes of such
breathtaking movement: ships lurching over a watery mountain-range;
lions and deer plunging over forest streams through leafy light that was
like a shower of emerald discs; a lightning-storm over a nocturnal town,
where slashes of white blasted the huddled houses and the brave church
spire, like real-sized cannons blazing against a toy town. I recalled
Joachim's hut and wondered. It seemed to me that I must compare
Joachim's art with this embroidered cinema: that I was required (by
my godfather? By my conscience?) to compare the two and choose
between them. It was easier, in every way, to succumb to the force of
my godfather's art, and so that is how I chose. Of course I did; you
knew that.

The room was four or five times larger than my old room at
Boughwinds Abbey, and the furniture was correspondingly majestic.
My bed was so high that a step-ladder, two or three feet tall, had been
positioned on the floor near its head. It was covered in a damask spread,
and it was curtained, like the windows, in a matching dusk-rose cloth.
The wardrobe that stood against the wall at the foot of the bed was
open, and I glimpsed a gleam of queenly dresses. I knew, with a flush
of lascivious greed, that they were for me and that they would make
me beautiful. Before the fire, whose blaze filled a hearth the size of
Joachim's house, there stood a steaming bath on four gilded claws.
Heady perfumes floated up with the steam and filled the room – and
my tired head - with yet another aspect of beauty. As for the rest of the
furniture in the room: the chairs and chests, the footstools and shelves,
and the desk with the curling feet, they were too numerous and intricate
to bear description here. Each article was so clearly an exquisite and
costly work of art in its own right, and each could justify a book of its
own.

Ludovick Montefiore stood in the doorway as the room pulled me
into itself. I turned to him with a sleepy smile, the first time I had ever
smiled at him without simultaneously frowning at myself and glancing

away.

"It would be usual for you to be provided with a maid, or something of that sort," he said, pausing to cough. "You being my goddaughter, you know, and therefore royal. After all, this is a royal castle. But I'm afraid I've no such thing. Only the Vulture Men."

"I don't need a maid."

"Good. Well, if you would like to wash and dress after your journey...then...well....take your time. I'll call for you later; then we can go and have dinner and talk. It's time we had a proper talk."

"Yes."

He turned to go, but as the door glided to I struggled to speak in accordance with the demands of my weakly insistent memory.

"What about my friends? What about...Joachim?" I said. His name sounded ugly and guttural through the perfumed fug. But the door closed with a soft click, and I was glad that he had not heard me.

Later (I don't know how much or how little later, because time was slippery then) I emerged from the bath feeling faint from the fragrant heat, and hungry. I touched the dresses in the wardrobe, but so long as I looked at them I was paralysed by admiration and unable to choose one in preference to another. They melded together in my sight to become a rippling river of purple and velvet and satin and scarlet and muslin and blue, overlaid by golden threads and jewels, like sunlight tracery over shallow water, and flowing away into the darkness of the cupboard. So I shut my eyes, pulled one out at random, and put it on.

The dress was cream coloured, with long, stiff, heavy skirts. It resembled a wedding dress, on account of its colour and its rather solemn elegance, only it was covered from neckline to hem with the most impossibly delicate, coloured embroidery which, like the wall-hangings, seemed to move in the corner of my eye. The threads were in varying shades of green, and a thousand thin inter-linked serpents made up the pattern.

I gasped when I looked at the mirror. I was startled by the beauty of my reflection. I think I must have bathed in liquid gold. I hadn't brushed or dried my hair and yet it fell about my face like satin. My skin was as perfect and pale as a porcelain doll and all my features, although I could not definitely say that one or the other was altered, seemed harmonious and wonderful to look at. My lips were moist and pink, like a little child's. I felt a great confidence in this person that was me and yet not me. I felt that she was intended for perpetual beauty and that I (though I was inside her and could not, therefore, keep a constant check on her) need never mistrust anybody's admiration as I did constantly in the Waking World, where I took much self-doubting care over my appearance. It is a dangerous thing to surrender yourself to self-love, but it is a rare and glorious feeling too: I know because I did it that one time. I stood at my window with my heart drumming at the thrill of being as I was: no longer the wistful disciple of fiction's finest heroines, but their conscious superior.

I thought that Ludovick Montefiore would also be surprised by my alteration, but he gave no such sign when he tapped at the door and opened it. In fact, I had rarely seen him so unfocussed and distracted. He looked hard at my face, yet he seemed unable to register it.

I dragged my whispering skirts through the house until we arrived at the dining-room. I sat down beneath a dripping chandelier and ate platefuls of a strange food that was at once meaty and sweet, like a hybrid of steak and chocolate. I thought it heavenly at the time, and I shamelessly requested larger and larger helpings until my godfather told me I had already eaten more than enough (and even then I do not remember feeling embarrassed). It never occurred to me to ask what it was, and perhaps my ignorance increases the loathing with which my stomach contracts if ever I accidentally recall its flavour now.

When we had finished, Ludovick Montefiore poured coffee from a golden pot and offered me truffles from his golden plate. I ate these greedily as well, as though beside myself with a desire for their flavour. When I had eaten four he took the plate away and placed it in a cupboard. Then he sat down again and said seriously, almost sternly, "Abigail, we must talk. Or rather, I must talk and you must listen. You don't know why I have brought you here, or what I intend to do with you…you know nothing. I am sure that you are dying for an explanation."

His eyes queried my smeared lips, and I felt the first surge of nausea rising towards my throat. I answered in a panicked tone, "No, no! You're wrong! I don't want to know or think anything. I don't want you to explain anything. Please don't talk – not about those things I mean – let's just carry on as we were."

His face still bore a query, which darkened as I answered him.

"You odd child!" he exclaimed; then he broke into a relieved laugh. "You're testing me," he went on, touching my arm with his fingertips as he spoke, as though to soften the sharpness of his tone.

"No!" I answered with tears in my protest, halfway between petulance and fear. "I don't want to know…I'm tired. I want to go to bed. And I feel sick."

"Well that's no wonder," he retorted, eyeing me closely through narrowed lids. "You've been eating like a pig. But whether or not you feel sick you will sit still until I have had my say."

I nodded, because I had no choice in the matter. I knew by now that his will (though his words were kindly teasing, as though spoken for the reassurance of an emotional drunkard) was as binding, as silencing and as dangerous as if he had chained me to my chair and gagged my mouth with his napkin. So he began his story, and I listened.

"I know what your Traumund land is like. I chanced to hear a brief report of it from the Vulture Men, and it interested me so much that I visited it myself, in disguise. I saw you there once, when you were a small child. You were strolling through the trees with that bear and discussing the possibilities of some story or other. So you see, it's a long time since you've been safe from the King of Traumund – a good deal longer than you imagined. I had no particular interest in you in those early years, although I was surprised to recognise you as my goddaughter. Perhaps that added a certain charm to my discovery. But it was your land that interested me and made me look on you...a little kindly, I suppose. More kindly than I am used to look on people. I wished to meet you before I destroyed you: put it like that. I gave your name to the Vulture Men, with orders that, when found, you should be brought before me rather than slaughtered.

"You will wonder why I felt such an interest. After all, your land is by no means the most dramatic or beautiful of places, when you consider that some people choose ice palaces, or sun-soaked, surf-battered islands. In fact your home is rather dingy and commonplace in spirit: a few trees, a mossy clearing, a carpet of mouldering leaves.... But you see, the thing is, it reminded me so minutely of my own land - the land that I began with, I mean, before I embarked upon my travels. Lots of people have forest lands, of course, but none that I have seen are so reminiscent of my childhood place: the thundering of cannibal giants' shouts; the shape and colour and peculiar whisperings of the trees; the oak that you used as your refuge and the magic by which you entered it. I walked about your land for hours, though you never knew it, and I felt sadder and softer and closer to...repentance...yes, repentance... than I had felt for many a year. Then I rode away and tried to forget it.

"The joy of my childhood home, the joy, I imagine, of yours, was in the hiding. It was so exciting to be conscious of the fact that danger,

danger worthy of the best story books, existed just inches away from you in the world outside the tree. And it was so comforting to know that, though it was close, it was still elsewhere, and that, so long as you were careful, you could be invulnerable…but only just. I thought that there was no greater joy, until I took myself into the midst of the danger, and lost, forever, my capacity for such infantine thrills.

"I had a friend called Feathersill. She was an owl, very like Eyes, only even larger and with a snowy white plumage. One day I stood in my clearing and I watched her wheeling overhead in the pale spring sky, like a small aeroplane. There was that sprightliness in the air that comes with the equinoxes and that makes you want to burst out of yourself and act. I had an impulsive desire to share her viewpoint of the land, and to feel that higher air rushing against my face. I called and waved for her to land near me, and when she landed I persuaded her to give me a ride. It had never before occurred to me to make such a request, though she agreed readily for she was my good friend. So I sank into her feathers and we rose off the ground, my heart rising alone, ahead of us, by two or three seconds. And when we emerged from the trees I saw a sight similar to that which you have seen, I suppose: those massive trees just strands of grass in a clipped lawn; mountains in the distance like grey horses asleep on their sides; lakes and fields and the smell of the ocean, and great vistas of sky (for until then my Traumund skies had always been hemmed in by criss-cross branches) with white clouds streaking from one end of the earth to another, as though somebody had wiped a drying paint-brush across the blue.

"We climbed down again before long, and I returned to my home in the tree. But from that day I was restless. I no longer rejoiced to hear the wind howling around my safety, or the cannibals thundering past - I felt impatient, as though my comfort was a cage. I began to walk out in the worst, bough-bending gales, and, rather than flee them, I would make bows and arrows and lie in wait to attack the cannibals as they crashed through my trees. But even as I walked and waited, I was not happy. I could not stop speculating about the people who lived among the countries that I had barely glimpsed, and wondering what further lands might be found over those mountains; what islands or continents lay across the seas of Traumund.

"Every day I begged Feathersill to take me up in the air, and to glide as far as the borders of my kingdom while I gazed with straining eyes, and wondered. Then one morning I could bear it no longer, and I urged her to trespass over my border and fly low over our neighbouring lands, so that I could really see them. She agreed readily, because she was as brave and curious as I was. So from then on we would spend whole days flying across strange territories, landing for rest and exploration amidst dangers from which there was no definite escape; only the owl's wings. I remember clinging by my fingertips to her downy belly once, as she sped from the poisonous, pendulum tongue of a sea monster who galloped towards us through the surf, spitting and bellowing in defence of its master's or mistress's land. We didn't care, we laughed at the thrill of it, and gleefully relived it all that night, at home.

"But, more and more often, we failed to return home at night. Rather than waste half a day on our return journey, we would set up camp in some hostile wilderness, so that we might travel still further the following day. Our expeditions lasted days, then weeks, then months, but my curiosity to see more only burned the stronger.

"Something else was happening to me. I think you will understand. It was as though the ecstasy that I felt at seeing all these new worlds wake beneath my touch was being poisoned by its own excess. I mean, I felt joy, but my feeling was so incommunicable that it was a painful joy and not a pleasurable one.

"Sometimes you feel impelled to do something in response to an event, or a scene, or a person that is dear to you. Say you saw a night-sky that made you feel happy. Wouldn't you want to act in order to prevent it from slipping away and joining all the other forgotten moments of happiness? Wouldn't you feel the need to grasp it; to possess it? Well this was how I felt every second of my travels; it was like a burden of inspiration that I was powerless to fulfil. I tried taking paper and pen with me, and making a record of our day's adventures each evening. I tried fitting my experiences to poetry. I tried drawing them. I began, at that time, to compile the great atlas which you have seen, in the hope that that might assuage my thirst for possession. Nothing worked. I had only to look back on my creations to know that my joy was not alive in them.

"We continued like this, Feathersill and I, for three years, and never in my life have I been so happy, or so wild with pain. Then one day our luck ran out. We had landed in undulating moorland, where the heather was knee-deep and the stones were black and yellow. There we were: I wading through the bristling purple and Feathersill hovering above my head, close enough for us to chatter and laugh together. And then the next moment...disaster caught up with us.

"There was a whistle and a simultaneous thud, and Feathersill screamed and struggled as a wiry net twisted around her body, squeezing a breath from her; stripping puffs of feathery white from her wings and slicing a grid of thin red lines across her breast. I had no time to save her. Before I could see or understand her plight, the Vulture Man had landed his catch and broken her neck with a cudgel. He had three seconds to gloat over his kill before I fired an arrow through his heart. In spite of everything I felt a satisfaction that was new to me when I saw him fall.

"I cut the net from Feathersill's body and caressed her head with my hands and my last tears. I had never envisaged losing her, because I had stupidly assumed that we must die together as we had flown together. Only now, as her heavy head soaked into my lap, did I comprehend my desperate position. Feathersill had been my friend, above all, but she was also my navigator and my steed. I was two months' flight from my home and I hadn't the faintest idea of direction. I was like an astronaut drifting alone through space; cut off from his ship.

"There was no time for lengthy lamentation. I could hear boots and hooves swishing through the heathers all around me, and the unfamiliar cry of the Vulture Men as they called for their dead comrade. I barely had time to dive down amongst the undergrowth before one of the horses trod on my victim's body and reared and screamed, and then there was a great hullabaloo as they gathered around the murdered heap. There could be no doubt as to what had happened, because a long arrow quivered in his chest, and there could be no doubt of the culprit's identity once a yellow-eyed horse had flared its nostrils and nosed my crouching, hard-breathing body. So I stood up and drew my sword (that silver sword - you know the one I think, Abigail - I forged it all those years ago, when my adventure began). I believed that I would die soon enough, a friendless stranger in Traumund, and that I might as well die fighting.

"But no sooner had I risen to my feet and turned to face them, than they began to murmur amongst themselves. Gradually their murmurs turned to whispers, and then one by one they bowed their knees until I, weak little I, found myself standing like a tall rock amidst a gentle sea of conquered Vulture Men. I was utterly bemused by this turn of events, but I wasn't so stupid as to resist its implications. I took it all in my stride, as this seemed the only wise thing to do, and sternly bade them stand up and lead me to a place where I might eat and rest, since my owl and I had travelled so far and met with such a disastrous reception. On my instructions (which were daringly uncompromising, you will think, but instinct told me that my greatest danger lay in an admission of weakness) Feathersill's body was wrapped in a cloak and lifted reverently by four sturdy Vulture Men, while the dead man was kicked and spat upon in turn by every member of the gathering, and then left to rot.

"They brought me to this castle, which had been built many years before by an eccentric Englishman called Sidney Weaver. His escapist vision was this dreary pile in the midst of a dreary moorland, and here his diseased imagination created an army of Vulture Men, whose sole purpose was to obey his dreary command. When he died, several hundred years before my appearance, the only human whom the Vulture Men had ever known disappeared, and with him their entire purpose in life - for having been designed to follow their king's orders they understood, and desired, nothing else. So a myth came into being and flourished, which told how one day a new monarch would arrive in their land, heralding a new Golden Age (though heaven knows, from what I have heard there was nothing very Golden about their first Age, since they seem to have done little more than catch and cook rabbits for Sidney Weaver, and then watch as he ate them in his dismal throne room). When I turned up, of course, they decided to take me for their promised king.

"Well, I had nothing more to lose, and a whole kingdom to gain, so I played along with my subjects' story and installed myself as master of their abandoned castle. I forced them all into hard labour, and they fell to with genuine delight, so in love were they with the idea of their Golden Age, and so afraid (I made very sure) of me. There are few resources in this land, but under my directions they made the castle more hospitable than it had ever been under Sidney Weaver's kingship. They stocked up the larders and warmed the old stones with fires, and constructed such crude furnishings as they were capable of producing. I lived a few happy years here whilst the place was brought to rights about me.

"But once the castle and its modest surroundings began to feel familiarly comfortable to me, rather than daily bettered under the command of my imagination, I felt the return of my old wanderlust. I missed Feathersill dreadfully, not only for her company, but for the freedom that her wings had granted me. I'm afraid I had grown a prisoner to that freedom, and I suffered from its withdrawal like any addict. I brooded away in my new home, remembering my former joy with wonder, and straining my brain to find some new means of flight.

You see, the Vulture Men, though they have bird's heads, and talons, have no wings and cannot fly.

"Then, one wonderful night, as I tossed and turned and fretted for my airborne life, a solution found me. I was struck, as though a shooting star had streaked through my open window and exploded around my head, and I staggered to my feet with a cry of delight. Of course: rather than fly across Traumund, sneaking over its territories like a mere trespasser, I would march across it, slowly and surely, with my army of Vulture Men, as its conqueror. I had enough men, I believed, to take each land one by one: few lands (I knew from my travels) possessed quite so striking a potential army as this one did, and few would be able to muster so much as a show of resistance. And since convention forbids communication between lands, I was unlikely to be thwarted by any serious coalition.

"Of course, marching along the ground would lack the heart-soaring happiness of flight. But as I garnered in my new lands, I would acquire whole stables full of giant owls and other aerial creatures. I would bring back paintings and treasures with which to beautify my castle, and I would make it the most wondrous home ever conceived of. By making Traumund my own I realised that I could at last achieve that sense of possession for which I had so hopelessly striven through my old sketches and diaries and poems."

I raised an objection at this point, in a more belligerent tone than I had ever dared to use against him before. I felt, and probably sounded, drunk; the sentences came haltingly into my brain, as though they had been independently constructed somewhere else, and they issued thickly through my mouth, my tired tongue resenting the manoeuvres that speech required of it.

"You're wrong!" I exclaimed, and I remember jabbing my finger in his direction. "You're wrong you know! Beauty is a...beautiful things die. If something is under your thumb then it's not going to be as beautiful as it was when you first saw it flying past, because... because you'll have squashed it." I sat back triumphantly in my chair, challenging him to answer that if he could.

"Conventional wisdom, Abigail!" answered Ludovick Montefiore, leaning towards me with his fingertips touching. "You know that's just conventional wisdom; you're testing my understanding and resolve. It isn't true! Beauty isn't intangible or transient or any of those irritating things that people say it is – people who are too weak to go out and grasp it for themselves. I know, because I possess it. I already own a fraction of Traumund, the universe of dreams, and I will go on to own more and more. What could be more beautiful than that possession? In all its heights and depths, darknesses and lights Traumund will be mine; its mysteries will not taunt me anymore, because they will be mine. They will not even exist, except by my say so."

"You will run out of desire, once you possess it utterly. And what is the point of possessing the world if you don't desire it?"

There was a flare of impatience in his tone as he answered, though his explanation was as earnestly methodical as before. "I don't want to be forever desiring! What would be the point in that? I want to be satiated at last. Anybody who genuinely desires must hope to be satiated in the end, or their desire is cowardly and false. I want what is now, what is concrete. This ocean, this mountain, this forest. Only actual, specific, concrete things are worthy of desire. Nothing else is worthy; nothing else even exists."

"But Traumund isn't made of concrete." I murmured. "And you do not seem happy."

"Nor am I, yet." He answered. "But I will be. I have my method worked out, and that is more than most people can say. You have only to look at my atlas to see what glories I possess. Have you studied it yet? No. You must. The atlas only really came into its own once I began my march. Since then it has become the richest and most glorious book in creation. It no longer deals in fleeting observations. It is a record of everything that is mine."

As he spoke on and on I remembered the evening of that happy day when my parents removed me from the Institute. That evening was the prelude to so much evil, and yet, to my surprise, its beauty was not sullied by my knowledge of what had happened after. A peaceful evening in a London hotel room shone in my mind as brightly as if it had been the prelude to everlasting happiness. I realised that the memory was a thing, a creation in its own right, and it was among the most precious things I possessed: the least concrete, but the most alive.

My reflections, and our discourse, were fatally interrupted at this point by my being violently sick over the floor. I retched and retched until my body trembled with cold exhaustion. Ludovick Montefiore was very kind all the while, stroking me on the back and holding back my hair, and showing no sign of disgust at the sight and stench of my vomit, even though it spattered his boots.

When I had finished, and he had splashed my face with water, he took me back to my room and waited outside while I washed and changed. I thought that he would let me rest now, since the night was deeply black and chilly, and I was so sick, but as soon as I emerged he took me to yet another room, less brilliant than the dining-room, but just as wealthy in its dusky reds and golds.

"Why have you treated me so strangely?" I asked, when we had sat in silence for a while. "Why do you love me, and only me?"

"Because you are the only person in the world whom I fear," he said, looking up into my green-white face. "You are the Great Liar," he continued lovingly. "I have the key to your softness, your apparent vacuity; I know that you are really made of stone and steel; that you are my equal. You will never be torn in two. You pretend to be timid and weak and to have all sorts of contradictory affections for all sorts of people. But your will is in fact complete, consistent, powerful, and therefore good. You would even kill me – although you love me – if that served your purpose. You are the only one who could kill me without agonies of soul-sapping doubt.

"I know this because I have heard it all from a seer. But I have faith in her words because I have known you. When I first learned that you and I are fatally connected, I decided to destroy you without further ado, and so I sent you away to the Institute in order to sterilise your soul. But you rebelled (of course you rebelled!), and then I met you in London. You interested me enough for me to decide to bring you to Boughwinds Abbey. I thought I would find out more about you and, if necessary, kill you there, at my leisure.

"Soon I began to recognise your peculiar integrity, and to understand your secret; your Great Deceit. You are unable to care for ordinary people. You care nothing for your parents – otherwise how could you run away to Boughwinds and forget all about them and their anxiety? You care nothing for your 'friends' – for Constantine, Joachim, Boris and Eyes – obviously, otherwise you would not have betrayed them and you would not be here with me. And yet they do not comprehend your coldness – this has been your brilliance. You have paraded it, and yet I am the only one to have seen and understood it. They still place their hopes in you; even now they hope in you! It was no weakness in me that I changed my mind and acknowledged that Traumund would be the poorer if my only equal, my worthy partner and heir, were dead."

He seemed to gleam, like a beautiful, arching serpent (I hate snakes, and yet he was both serpentine and attractive) and he held me with his glittering eyes. I wish my eyes could have glittered a self-possessed response, but they were glazed and wide like the eyes of a fascinated rabbit.

"I have sought worthy companions before now – I even married once! But nobody is my equal except you, my dear, and you are here at last. You will be Queen of Traumund and we will be rid of the others, the 'friends' who seek to compromise your love for me, by asking that you love them too, against my interest. You need pander to their usefulness no longer. We will brush them away, like breadcrumbs from the corners of our lips, and then there will be nobody to love except one another. Isn't that how you always imagined love? All-consuming? Our love will consume everything that dares to come within its compass."

I think he sat with me a while longer as I pondered his words. I tried hard to decide whether he had described me accurately. I did not recognise the portrait he had painted so admiringly, but that did not necessarily make it untrue. Cold and deceitful; stony and powerful – was this me? Or was he busy creating a cold, deceitful, stony, powerful Abigail by attaching those words to me; by calling me by these names? With all his charm and magic he was well-placed to succeed.

I don't know when he left me, but I was alone for a long time. I sat hunched and dry eyed while the clocks measured that Traumund night with their fast heartbeats and urgent chimes. As it neared morning I abandoned my meditations for sheer exhaustion. But I remember wishing that all my friends, and family, and past, and memories were dead – non-existent, I mean, rather than slaughtered through my agency or compliance. I wished this, not because I no longer loved them, but because I did. Therefore they stood between me and my happiness like armed angels before the gates of Eden.

The Test

lthough the palace clocks whirred and clacked their way through those Traumund nights and days, they did not help me to keep a measure of time. On the contrary, I believe that time randomly expanded or contracted itself there. I might have been pondering his words for hours or years, but I possessed a dreamlike inability to tell. Sometimes I reassured myself that there was plenty of time to think, or (in my better moments) to plan rescues and escapes. But sometimes I thought, with a stomach-crushing catch of breath, that it was all too late; that my friends must have died in their cells many moons ago.

After that first evening, I never discussed my friends' fate with Ludovick Montefiore. Occasionally, with a sense of relieving numbness, I was able to reassure myself that I had no choice, or rather, that I had already made it by failing to protest as he unveiled his vision of our future. But I was wrong; I knew I was wrong. There was a question mark in the air - it might as well have been emblazoned across the sky – and an expectant hush hung between us at every meeting, even when we were talking.

He was clever, as you know; he did not hustle me, or drop hints, or show the slightest symptom of impatience. No, rather than risk my annoyance, he led me, gently, into his universe, making sure, during all this timeless time, that I read only the books that he left beside my bed, ate only the strange, rich foods that were served at his table and heard no voice except his own. His world seemed to wrap itself about me, strand by strand, until I stood in a new skin. It was like living inside the best book that you have ever read; the sort of book that possesses your mind and invalidates the reality that you lived in before you first opened the volume at page one. But the best books come to an end, and little by little the memory of them loosens its first vice-like grip. My godfather led me into a book that seemed destined to continue for ever and ever, entangling me more intricately, with every line, in its velvet chains and blindfolds.

One evening Ludovick Montefiore told me that we would not be dining in our usual "modest" surroundings (he used the word modest in a totally straightforward tone, with reference to the gilt and crystal room in which I had eaten and vomited that first night), but in the Great Hall. I nodded happily; it was all the same to me. But my godfather looked dissatisfied, and I thought my response must have seemed lacklustre.

"The Great Hall!" I began again, but though he nodded he still looked pensive, as though he felt dissatisfied by his own silence, and yet too afraid to speak. So I invited him into my room. He perched on the edge of a chair whilst I shut out the late afternoon's lavender sky and poked at the fire.

We both began to speak at once, and we both stopped at once. I giggled and said, "Go on, you first." Ludovick Montefiore barely smiled in reply, and he did not (as he normally would) give me precedence. He said,

"This evening will be a grave test for you, Abigail."

His solemnity made my knees go limp, so I sat down beside him on the arm of his chair. I touched his hand, as though to offer him comfort, and then I fiddled with his sleeve, rubbing the material between my tight fingers.

"A test? What, you mean we're going to skip the soup? I'll manage." My light laugh emerged as a hiccup, and this set me off giggling for real.

He ignored my question and went on. "I would like you to wear the dress that you wore on your first evening at the castle – do you remember it? It was cream-coloured with - "

" – with little green snakes embroidered all over it. Yes, of course I remember. Is that the test? Is that all? I thought you were going to say - "

"No Abigail," he snapped, "that is not the test. I am simply asking you to wear a particular dress. Is that possible?"

"Yes, of course," I answered in a small, sober voice, and I realised that my understanding of his character had not progressed during our brief eternity together in Traumund. I had come to feel less shy of him here at the castle, and I had lazily assumed that this was on account of our increased equality. Now I knew that it was due merely to a change in my own perspective; that my understanding of myself, of him, of everything, had wheeled right round to the other side of the solar system, while he – whatever he was – remained static in the centre of things, unchanged. I flushed with embarrassment, all of a sudden, at the thought of our escalating familiarity, but the feeling passed in half a second because I could not bear to retain it, and because I knew that I could never recover my initial reserve.

"Supper will be at the normal time," he continued coldly, standing up and making for the door. "I'll come and fetch you, since you won't know the way."

"Oh wait – please wait!" I cried, inserting myself between him and the door. "Won't you explain what you mean? What is the 'test'?"

"The 'test'?" he replied reproachfully. "Oh Abigail, how can you call it a test when you know it is no such thing? We will be breaking down the final barrier that stands between us and happiness! How can that comprise even the tiniest element of hardship?"

I stood back when he had finished speaking, and allowed him to hurry away. I thought that I half-understood his meaning, and I dreaded his eagle-eye while the half-understanding presented itself in my face.

I should have used my hour or two of solitude to think and plan, but I have already described the degeneration of my mind in that palace of beauty. His words recurred again and again, as though some small part of me was labouring to bring them to my attention, but I pushed them away, and smothered them by talking to myself. I said inane things to myself like, "Mmm, lovely, hot bath," and "Cream shoes or green shoes?" Only when I was quite ready and I paced the room, listening for his approach, did my prattle wear itself out and leave me all alone with no distraction. It was then that I remembered my discarded treasures: the bow and quiver which was Constantine's gift when I left my tree, and Boris's tiny flask of Euthusoteria. I had shut them away in a chest of draws just before taking my first bath in this room.

I opened the drawer now and there they lay: rope, rough wood and mud-coloured clay objects amidst the folds of the red, plush draw-lining. For all their rustic honesty they preened, I thought irritably. They forced me to make a facile contrast between their goodness and the wicked wealth of my new home. I thought that their appeal would be lost on me now, so I touched them with an aloof sort of pity, as though they were mementoes of somebody so long dead, and so remote from my sense of my present self, that it was difficult to believe she had ever existed, and even more difficult to mourn her.

Just then, Ludovick Montefiore knocked at the door. The sound made me jump, and my fingers closed around the bottle of Euthusoteria. My detachment shattered like a broken window, and suddenly, to my surprise, I felt a real, intimate grief threaten to rise into my face. My lips and eyebrows contracted, but they mustn't, they mustn't, I thought, with unaccustomed energy. He knocked again and called my name. "I'm coming!" I whimpered, gaily. Then I looped the tatty string round my neck once more, and stuffed the bottle down the front of my dress. Pausing briefly to ensure that it would not show above my neckline, I flung the door open and took my godfather's arm.

As we walked the corridors together, I wished that I had disobeyed my impulse to retrieve the Euthusoteria from its draw. It felt like a symbol of treachery around my neck – I was sure that this was how my godfather would understand it if he were to discover it – and I was still far from harbouring treacherous feelings against him. When he said, all of a sudden, in an encouraging tone, "Abigail, it'll all be worth it - more than worth it – in the end, I promise," I felt sorry, in case I had given him cause to doubt my solidarity. My love for him enthused me, and I said reckless things as we made our way down the main stairs. I said that nothing could induce me to disappoint him; that I would rather go to hell than leave him. Lovers always say extravagant things, but they rarely expect those things to be put to the test. I knew that my test was imminent and I knew (or I ought to have known) that my loyalties were volatile. And yet, if there can be such a thing as momentary sincerity, I said those words sincerely. Ludovick Montefiore seemed reassured; he smiled happily and the anxious creases lifted from his forehead. But his gladness made me even more sorry than his disquiet.

The Great Hall was like an ice cavern of unimaginable proportions. The walls looked as slippery as ice, and also as varicoloured, as though sheets of emeralds, sapphires, amethysts, silver and gold had been crumpled up and buried deep inside their translucent, polished whiteness. My godfather led me across ebony floorboards to a long, black table weighed down with fruit and cakes, and dishes filled with slabs of that sickly meat which I have described already. We sat close to one another. He patted my hand as I looked down the room.

Our table stretched across the width of the hall, and we sat behind it, looking out across the sable floor. Opposite us, at the far end of the room, a green, silk curtain hung from the ceiling, screening part of the hall from our sight. It billowed gently, disturbed by a draught, and its curling motion seemed majestic to me. I felt a churning excitement as I watched it, as though I was at the theatre, listening to the orchestra's muted hoots and string-tunings, and waiting for the lights to dim. I shivered.

"Abigail, you're not cold?"

"A little bit."

"Have something to eat. Here, have some mulled wine." Ludovick Montefiore reached across the table for a steaming pewter jug. He covered his hand with his sleeve so as to protect it from the hot handle. I almost prevented him from pouring the mist (it seemed to comprise more steam than liquid) into my crystal goblet by saying, truly, that I could stomach neither food nor drink. But I kept quiet instead, accepted the cup and pretended to sip. I noticed that nothing ever passed Ludovick Montefiore's lips, and that, unlike me, he made no pretence. He sat back in his chair with his arms folded and his eyes plunged in thought. Sometimes he surfaced from his meditations, and I would turn to find him looking at me intently, as though I was a vaguely familiar face that he needed to place. The third time this happened I was so unnerved that I had to speak, if only to be sure he knew me.

"Ludovick...what's that green curtain about?"

I waited for him to surface, and then he looked at me as though he knew me, and looked away again at once.

"It's hiding something. Some things, I should say."

This was not illuminating, but at least it was conversation. I dreaded his deep silences. When I existed alongside them I felt a little of what Sylvia must have felt when she experienced hell as a black vacancy. So I blundered on, striving hard for flippancy.

"Oh I see. Now I understand! It was all so mysterious before, but now I know that it's hiding something!"

I waited, but Ludovick Montefiore's attention was wandering even as he forced the corners of his mouth into the shape of a responsive smile.

"Ludovick. What is it hiding?" I asked, slowly and impatiently.

All of a sudden my godfather's mental wanderings ended. It was as though they were brought up short against my question; his blue eyes fired up like lighted gas, and all their energy flared into my face as he answered.

"Deaths."

"…Deaths?"

"Yes."

I shivered more violently than before, and pressed my palms against the hot goblet. I suspected him of teasing me, and I half-hoped he would not hear my little voice as it asked, necessarily but unenthusiastically,

"What do you mean…'Deaths'?"

Ludovick Montefiore shuffled his chair and then explained in a matter-of-fact way. "I have prepared Deaths for your former acquaintances. It is just as we agreed, Abigail, so you needn't look so shocked. Besides, everything will take place behind that curtain, so there will be no need for you to know any more than you wish to know. You needn't witness anything unpleasant. All I want you to do is to run your eyes over the prisoners one last time, and to give your consent to their elimination."

"You want me to see them before they die?"

"Yes."

"And you want me to say, 'They may die'?"

"Yes."

"…This is the 'test'?"

"It is."

I dug my nails into my palms, exasperated by this thoughtfulness; this offensive thoughtfulness that might force my hand against him. If he would only let me drift down the stream in his surging wake then I could absolve myself by deeming myself powerless. But he thought passivity was my mask, and this test was designed to strip the mask away. He expected a blood red murderess to leap out from my heart of hearts and scream for a massacre, but I knew there was only a little sheep in her place: I could hear it bleating and feel the trembling in its bony knees. I was so ashamed of my lurking weakness that I cried. I pretended to cry tears of anger.

"What right have you to test me?" I demanded hotly.

"What right? I have every 'right'," he snorted. "I make up my own rights, just like you, do you remember? I answer to no higher authority."

"Do you doubt me then?"

"Yes."

I felt stung, but most of all I felt surprised, and so I lapsed into silence. He did not interrupt, but watched me until I spoke again, feebly.

"Why do you doubt me?"

"Forgive me, Abigail," he said, with something like his familiar warmth. "My doubts are vague and, I am sure, inconsequential. I cannot blame you for resenting them. But...for one such as you, this is not a difficult test. Surely it is not much to ask? You need only look at the people for whose non-existence you have already felt a desire, and then allow them to be taken away. I could have asked more of you: I could have asked you to talk to them; I could have asked you to go behind the curtain and see their Deaths. But you need only look at them, and then nod your assent, and you will have erased all the lingering traces of my unhappiness. There will be nothing to separate us then."

"What do you mean, their 'Deaths'?"

"Just that."

"What, you mean there are Vulture Men waiting behind the curtain with swords? Or a gibbet all hung with ropes? What do you mean, their 'Deaths'?"

"Do you really want to know?"

"Yes."

"Then you will have to go with them and watch them die. Do so, if you wish, with my blessing. I shall refrain on this occasion."

I sank back in my chair like him, only my arms were not folded, they hung limply at my side, like bodies swaying from a gallows. I felt tired and lost, so irredeemably lost, as though I had been blinded and dropped into the middle of a desert. It made no sense to do anything; it made no sense to wonder what I might do. All possibilities were futile now that I had forsaken the ancient framework upon which my life had been constructed, pulling it about my ears on a lustful whim. I thought, if only I could travel back in time then I could withstand his charm and be as good as my friends had always believed me. But that opportunity was long past, and by now I was so steeped in Ludovick Montefiore's evil that a belated U-turn in the direction of goodness seemed impossibly inglorious. I thought: if it is too late for me to be good then at least let me be consistently bad. I was truly lost.

I shrugged when he asked whether I was ready. He rang a hand bell that stood on the table at his right hand. A Vulture Man appeared immediately behind his chair.

"Fetch the prisoners," ordered the king. His servant bowed and retreated.

We waited in a silence whose character I failed to understand, because I could not tell whether it unified or isolated us one from the other. Was I complying with his plan, or had my internal collapse penetrated his understanding? Such was my helplessness that I looked to him for an answer, but he gave nothing away. He sat by my side, drumming on the table with his fingertips, his features flitting from meagre smile to meagre frown. I watched him.

And then they entered the hall, all roped together in a line, armed guards before them and behind them and chains about their bony wrists. The weight of the chains bent their backs and dragged their elastic arms and wings to the level of their knees. Their ankles were shackled too, and every time they forced one foot in front of the other the chains rattled across the wooden floor like the heavings from a pair of dying lungs. They were hollow creatures. That is what struck me most of all: hollow-eyed, hollow-cheeked, hollow-stomached. When they stood before me and looked at me their gape was hollow: it contained neither gladness, nor pleading, nor reproach, nor defiance. I looked at them all, one by one, with a sort of suicidal resolve: Eyes, Boris, Joachim. They were macabre puppets. I had killed them already.

But where was Constantine? There was no Constantine.

I gazed, appalled, at this undead monument to Ludovick Montefiore's wicked vigour and my own wicked weakness. Where was Constantine? I could not voice the question.

Then, at last, Ludovick Montefiore, briskly businesslike. "Abigail. Come on. It's for you to speak now, remember? There's no point in dragging this out."

In retrospect I might try to put my next move down to cunning; to the scrabbling activity of a late but resolute repentance. Repentance might have been something, but this was only remorse – clueless remorse. I stood up and turned to Ludovick Montefiore with a grimace which was meant for a reassuring smile. I clutched his arm, pinching his skin. If I meant to play for time, it was with no plan in mind.

"I will decide. I have decided. But just wait for me – please wait for me. I need to do something in the Waking World before I send them to their Deaths. I have trusted you, now trust me, please."

If I had possessed a pistol, I think I would have held it to my brains and pulled the trigger. As it was, I had a bottle of Euthusoteria around my neck. I had no capacity for heroics, but I could still desire escape. So I bit through the clay bottle and swallowed my single dose of escapism. As my jaws met through the shards, it occurred to me that I need only grasp one skeletal hand in order to take the chain gang with me. But the thought came too late, and I disappeared on my own, with fragments of clay caught in that honey-like liquid that dribbled down my chin.

Poison

I sat up with a gasp, like a diver bursting from the depths. The world swam around my head in swathes of colour and I let it swim. I did not want to make sense of it. I could already make out my conscious thoughts; they projected from the dreamy froth like barnacled posts. The waves threw me against them and I caught hold of them, necessarily.

Mrs. Veals was in my room, dusting and polishing, and making the place as comfortable as such a housekeeper, under strict orders, conceivably might. Her presence did not have the power to surprise or displease me: she may have been a horror, but she could hardly compare to the horrors I had left behind. My unexpected emergence from the pillows, accompanied by a sharp intake of breath, certainly shocked her, however (I learnt afterwards that I had been absent for three Waking World weeks, which presumably contributed to her astonishment). She emitted a yelp, like a frightened dog. Then she leant against the wall and stared at me. I watched the yellow duster twisting round and round in her thick, tough fingers.

As her heartbeat slowed, so her anger and her old hatred of me solidified. When she was ready, the viciously thin line that was her mouth started open like a trap and she said,

"What have you been doing? What have you done to him?"

I shook my head from side to side, slowly, then I rested my forehead on my hands. I was sitting up in bed, my raised knees supporting my elbows. I felt that inertia and silence were necessary to me if I was to resist a descent into further fragmentation. I was like a broken vase, waiting in trepidation for its glue to dry. Let me grow strong and whole again, I thought, and maybe I will know how to try to salvage something, or somebody, from this nightmare.

It was as I subsided into this state of tense fragility that Mrs. Veals took it upon herself to seize me by the shoulders, shake me till I thought my head might fly off the end of my neck, and strike me across my left cheek so hard that my whole body lurched sideways onto the bed. Then she made a grab at my throat, twisted my collar into a corkscrew - making a hoarse whistle of my wind-pipe - and brought my face within inches of her own.

"I asked you, madam, what you have done to him?"

"Nothing, "I wheezed, but my answer did not satisfy her. The garrotte tightened.

"Nothing!" I insisted, speaking as best as I could in short gasps. "He's alive…he's well…in Traumund."

"And are you going to tell me what you've been doing there together these last three weeks?"

She screwed my jumper round again. I could see her upper lip curling away from her clenched teeth, and then the picture seemed to grow dim, and her persistent voice became echoey and magnified, yet distant, as though my ears were submerged in bubbling bath-water. As I began to submit to the odd peacefulness of this dying she let me go, and I emerged from the depths yet again, and breathed more freely yet again, in an atmosphere that was both life-giving and less kindly.

"I want an answer," she screeched. At first I could do no more than shake my head and massage my throat, then I forced a hiss through my soreness.

"I am guilty." I said confusedly, driven to massage my guilt by confessing it. My confessor clenched her fists. I went on, "I will answer you. But bring Allecto first. I need to talk to Allecto."

"But you acknowledge your guilt?" she said hungrily, and when she opened her palms again I could see that her nails had made bleeding cracks.

"Oh, yes."

"And you will make a full confession, to me?"

"I need Allecto."

"How do you know Allecto?" she wondered aloud, but the point was as irrelevant to her mind's course as it was to mine. "Has Mr. Montefiore returned too?"

"No."

"How do you know?"

"Please, just fetch Allecto, and I will tell you everything."

She wavered, and then, as she was on the point of submitting to her curiosity, and to my command, she realised that she was not, at present, obliged to serve me.

"No more orders from you, my lady!" She screamed victoriously, before grabbing the scruff of my neck and flinging me to the floor. So much for my poise, but though I dully hated her I did not pity myself. My self-justifications had all withered away, and her straightforward reproach relieved me, in a way. At least it made sense, which Ludovick Montefiore's magnificent affection did not – except in its own twisted terms, and they did not hold well in the Waking World, or even here, in this halfway house. Mrs. Veals herself, with her violence and hardness, may not fit into that old moral framework that I had thought abandoned and destroyed - but her accusations did. I was guilty; there was nobody here to turn the world upside down and tell me that actually I was not, and this fact, for all its pain, at least went some way towards dissipating my confusion.

She let go of me, and marched ahead at a soldierly pace, through the unlit, labyrinthine passages and down, down to the dusty, musty library where a slant of afternoon sunlight melted across the floor like a smear of honey. Then, with a warning knock on the trapdoor, we went down again, down the stepladder to Allecto's airless den, where the cauldron churned out clouds of mysterious sweetness.

I saw Sylvia first. She was perched on the lowest rung of the stepladder and she turned as we began our clumping descent. I saw her white eyes survey Mrs. Veals and register disgust; I could only see the back of the housekeeper's metal-grey head, so I don't know how she met the ghost's accusation. Sylvia withdrew to a corner, where she stood against the wall, as still and uncommunicative as the cupboards and shelves that shed their shadows over and through her. She watched though, and listened. I often cast a quick look in her direction, as though to plead for an opinion. I feared, and yet felt an obsessive need for, judgement – judgement pronounced for or against me, I mean, as well as judgement in the sense of sound, practical advice. I feared and needed Sylvia's judgement especially, since she had known both life and death, and her understanding of the order of things might, therefore, be fuller than anybody else's. But she was impassive, and I could get nothing from her except the chilly consciousness of her presence.

Allecto watched us descend the ladder with an expression that turned from bored annoyance as she recognised Mrs. Veals, to alarm as she recognised me. She had been studying a stiff-paged volume; she slammed it shut with a thud and stood up. Discretion kept her from speaking, but I could tell how she itched to make me talk. I put an end to her indecision with a dull, "It's all right. She knows I know you. It's all…I need to tell you everything."

"What's happened? Where have you been all this time. Where has he been? Where are the others? Abigail, tell me what's going on, for God's sake…"

"That's what I've come to do," I said, seating myself at her table.

Mrs. Veals stood beside me, out of my sight. Allecto leaned forwards across the table, so that it was almost parallel with her upper body. She fixed my face with her eyes all the time that I was speaking, and her mouth fell open slightly as though she was sucking up my words and swallowing them down.

I told them everything. I wanted their clear and natural responses above anything else – responses as clear and natural, at least, as they could ever produce in the circumstances – so I did not spare myself. At least their minds need not be clouded by any conscious fictions on my part. I told them my story, from the evening when Ludovick Montefiore and I landed on the floor of Joachim's hut to the moment when, many worlds away from here, I drank the Euthusoteria and abandoned my friends to their Deaths. Neither woman interrupted me, although when I said that Constantine was absent from the prisoners' line-up Allecto shrieked and clapped a hand to her mouth.

"And the worst of it is," I concluded, "that I cannot get back there immediately. Not even your sleeping potions can get me there quickly enough, Allecto. I mean, if he already doubted me before the 'test' how must he feel now that I've run away? How long can we expect him to wait, if we can expect it in the first place? They're probably already… it's probably too late by now."

I had not forgotten Mrs. Veals' presence. I heard her shuffle from one foot to the other and it prompted me to wonder how she was reacting to our mutinous talk. Was she the faithful servant that she always seemed, or did she hate Ludovick Montefiore on account of his harshness? I was surprised, and more than faintly mistrustful, when she said,

"There is a way for us to get there immediately."

Allecto looked up sharply. "Go on."

Mrs. Veals pointedly ignored me; all her words were directed at Allecto.

"The master's mah-jong set was his gateway to Traumund. No doubt he told you all about it in your day – he certainly told her. He laid the set out as usual on his last afternoon at the abbey, but of course he found a piece missing, and he knew at once that she (jabbing a finger in my direction) had pilfered it. "Little Devil," he called her, when he realised what she'd done. I know, because I was with him in his room, tidying away his books. He never let anybody else tidy his books away: he used to tell me that I had a better sense of order than anyone he had ever known. And so that's how I came to be with him on that evening. That's how I came to be with him on many an evening. It's how I came to share so many of his thoughts."

"And what then?" asked Allecto, briskly pragmatic. "Abigail, what did you do with the missing tile?"

I began to enlighten her, but Mrs. Veals waved my voice away. She could bear neither my misdemeanours nor my repentance, my silent presence nor my articulation of a single word.

"It was gone! I searched high and low! He went to her room to wrest it off her – the little thief – and he never came back. There is something she's not saying; she is guilty…"

"Abigail!" Allecto shouted my name, but the blaze of sound was for Mrs. Veals, not for me. Mrs. Veals retreated into her silence like a tortoise ducking beneath its shell. Allecto continued, not angry anymore, but intense.

"Abigail, Ludovick Montefiore hid in your room until he knew you were falling into Traumund, and then he used you as a means to get there himself, am I right?"

I nodded.

"And what about the tile? Did you have time to hide it, or did you take it with you to Traumund?"

"I hid it…well…I threw it into the back of the fire."

"And destroyed it?"

"I don't know. I doubt it. The fire was almost out."

All relevant information was ingested. She turned to Mrs. Veals

"Have you cleaned the fireplace in Abigail's room since her departure?"

Mrs. Veals snorted. "I clean all my master's hearths daily."

"And did you find the tile?"

"No. So the child has destroyed it and – whoops – she has wiped out her friends in the bargain." Mrs. Veals barked with pleasure. "Careless."

"Mrs. Veals." Allecto pursued her course through gritted teeth. "Are you quite sure the tile was gone? There was not so much as a splinter left over?"

The housekeeper shrugged, as if to dismiss these as mean-spirited enquiries. "I wasn't looking for it, was I? It might, I suppose, have slipped through the grate into the ash tray underneath. I generally tip the contents into my bucket without paying a great deal of attention to the procedure. Forgive me. Now I know that I ought to have equipped my self with a fine-toothed comb."

"And the ash, Mrs. Veals," Allecto insisted. "What do you do with it?"

"I tip it over the rose garden."

"Then the tile might still be somewhere amongst the soil. " Allecto's chair scraped across the floor with a bugle call as she stood up in her calm excitement. "And, if it is, we can complete the wall and step inside the castle."

Ordinarily I would have allowed the improbability of our success to swamp my capacity for action, but this time the goal (a passionate urge to pay for the damage I had wreaked) quashed any self-doubt. I was all for scrambling up the ladder and leaping into the garden through the library windows without further ado; it was Sylvia who restrained me.

"I'll go," she said, stepping out from her dim corner. "I'll know whether it's there or not, and if it is, then I'll be able to find it." She darted a barbed glance at Mrs. Veals as she said this, as if to assure her that, as far as she, Sylvia, was concerned, such ghostly sensitivity could not compensate for the loss of mere mortal awareness.

Sylvia had barely left the den before Allecto was presenting us with a new consideration. I was grateful for her urgency; it was in keeping with my feelings. I cannot say that I liked her now, or she me, because the situation left no room for friendship, but we were certainly unified for once, like two soldiers who find themselves together behind enemy lines.

"And what happens once we are there, in his world?" she demanded, urging on our answers with her darting eyes before she had even finished speaking.

"Kill him!" Mrs. Veals fired back. Even Allecto was stunned into a brief silence.

"You say kill him?" she continued at last. "But you…"

"But I what?" Mrs. Veals thrust her head towards Allecto and slammed her forearms down on the table.

"But you were always so loyal." Allecto finished.

Mrs. Veals only laughed a short, cynical laugh, but her eyes were downcast – I would say modestly, if I did not know her better.

"I suppose I was as well...once," added Allecto, and she shook her head sadly as she spoke. They lapsed into a communal silence. But I was displeased by the change in tempo. I did not wish to muse; I wanted to do, do, do. I stood up and paced round and round the table, until I had built up a steady rhythm that was matched by my feet, my heartbeat, my fidgeting fingers and my ticking brain.

"Must we kill him?" I asked at last. It was the best I could do. For my vision, though improved, was not restored. If I disapproved of Ludovick Montefiore's ways I did not therefore disapprove of him. Here, in this place of comparative mental clarity and freedom, I could call him misguided, mistaken and wrong. I could call his actions monstrous. But even now I could not call him a monster; I could not believe him irreparable. You know the sort of love from that I was suffering. It was a life-inverting adolescent passion that cares for nothing except the beloved object. Beside him even good things (and at least now I could agree that there were such things) seem lesser and duller and colder. My brain was in the right now, or at least it was on its way there. The sight of my skeletal, dead-eyed friends, and my consequent cowardice – my desertion – had acted on it like a naked plunge into a cold sea. But my heart, my hot, hot heart: I could do nothing with that.

"Yes, we must kill him," replied Mrs. Veals in a tone of false patience that burst into viciousness as she added, "And we'd kill you along with him if I had my way."

I addressed Allecto, whose dislike of me was dormant for the moment. "Can't we just save them and leave him alone?"

"Leave him?" Allecto replied. Her determined tone was returning. "But leave him to do what? Just think, Abigail, what it would mean to let him live. He would continue to kill; to suffocate souls; to desolate Traumund. You would be the first victim of his disillusion, and then he would finish off the very people whom you meant to save."

"But perhaps...don't you think it's possible, somehow, somehow..."

"That he might change? That you might change him? Tell me, how far have you succeeded in altering his oh-so-pliable character during the time in which you have known him?"

I began to cry, and I was furious with myself for such an untimely breakdown. "No," I spluttered. "The alteration was all on my part. You are perfectly right. But oh God, I wish you were wrong."

"He must die," said Allecto curtly. She was not speaking to me, or to Mrs. Veals, but to the thin air, and to herself. If the finality of her decision did not do away with my doubts, it silenced them, and imprisoned them somewhere deep inside me where they wasted away without any prospect of, or will for, action. I gave my consent with a teary question.

"But how?"

"How? Yes, how?" murmured Allecto, and I could not tell whether she was searching for an answer, or whether she was, like me, meandering away from thought and into vacancy, afraid to face the brutal reality of an answer. Mrs. Veals had no such qualms.

"Poison."

As she said the word she rose and started to rifle through the flasks, bottles and phials that cluttered Allecto's shelves and cupboards. Square, lined fingerprints spotted the moist dust wherever her hands fell.

"Come on Allecto, you must have dozens of poisons here. Haven't you always dreamt of finishing him off with a glass of something potent? Something tasteless and fast, that's what we want."

"Please," Allecto's pale, pretty hand touched the housekeeper's arm in an action that was symbolically, if not actually, restraining. It irritated her to see each carefully placed bottle touched, moved, considered and dismissed. The irritation ran through her whole body like a current. She opened a narrow cupboard, one that Mrs. Veals had yet to search. It was a deep cupboard, and she reached in so far that her arm disappeared up to the shoulder. She frowned at the ceiling as her hand moved against various objects; we could hear a faint tinkle and rustle beneath her searching fingertips. Then her expression relaxed and she drew out her arm, and her hand, and a metal tin that was tied with string and sealed with red wax.

She shut the cupboard door slowly.

We all sat round the table again and watched as Allecto broke the seal and string with a knife, and prized the lid from the tin. Then we leaned forward and peered with a sort of unholy awe at its contents. Wrapped in a coat of fragmented cotton wool there lay a plastic perfume bottle, stoppered with a cork. Inside the bottle there was a brown, powdery sphere, perhaps half an inch in diameter. I have rarely seen anything so momentous and yet so unspectacular as that brown tablet. I felt the same sort of dried-up disbelief that I have felt before in story-laden places, when my imagination fails to corroborate truths: that the names on such and such a monument once attached to real people, for example, or that in such and such a quiet, cow-studded field a bloody battle was fought.

I sniffed. "What is it?" I asked lightly, as you might suddenly feel light during some dark episode, when you are close to waking, and you know that, after all, it is only a dream.

"I don't know that it has a name," Allecto replied. "I invented it… and never worked up enough courage to use it. But it will do the job. It's fast, and very thorough." She too had developed a brittle hardness of manner, as though she was holding this conversation at arm's length.

"And how will we…how will it be administered?" I asked. Allecto looked at me, and at first I thought it was because she was going to answer my question. But she only looked. And then I felt Mrs. Veals hating eyes join with Allecto's gaze. I waited for the silence to end, and then I understood it.

"You want…me?"

"It will have to be you," said Allecto, her eyes falling away as mine rose to challenge them. Mrs. Veals' gargoyle eyes were fixed on me too, but their malice was nourished by my discomfiture.

"But how…?" I tried to worry about practical difficulties: how I would overcome his inevitable suspicions and force him, without seeming to force him, to swallow a tablet of lethal poison.

"Easy!" Allecto tried to laugh. "You turn up in that Great Hall of his, all decisive – you've made up your mind; you can't forgive yourself for ever having wavered…and so on. Then you slip the tablet in his wine – it will dissolve extremely quickly – and you get him to toast the 'Deaths', and the future. Job done." Allecto cleared her throat. "Something along those lines, no? The fine-tuning is all yours, of course."

I tried to picture myself handing him his goblet with a tenderly deceitful laugh, and I dismissed the picture with an irritation that bothered me beyond description. All of a sudden I was like a dog driven wild by its muzzle, writhing, whining and scratching at its own face. I tore at my short nails with my teeth and shouted,

"Why? Why has it got to be me? Why can't you do it, or her?" (glancing viciously at Mrs. Veals). "He trusts me…at least, he trusts me more than he trusts anyone. Can't you see how hard that makes it for me?"

"And can't you see why that marks you out as the only one of us who might be able to pull this off? I promise you, he's never going to be persuaded to clink glasses with me, or with Mrs. Veals…not anymore. He loves you, Abigail, for the moment. He'll drink to you, and to himself…or at least, he might. You've got to try…you see that, don't you?"

I shrugged miserably. Allecto turned to Mrs. Veals, whose silence was palpable. "You agree with me?" Allecto asked.

"Oh yes, it's the only way," came the unexpectedly mild reply. But she seemed so empty as she spoke, so oppressed by hatred and despair, that I feared her more than I had ever feared her yet.

Sylvia's glimmer came among us now, and we all turned to her, our faces strained by conflicting anxieties.

"I've got it," she said quickly, and as she spoke she held out her gleaming palm, and I saw the Rice Bird again. "It's a little bit black round the edges, but that's all. The magic is still intact."

On our way to Ludovick Montefiore's study we met Fay and Marcus. They stood aside as we passed in a preoccupied flurry. I don't think they noticed Sylvia amidst the flashes of broken sunlight and the clatter of our progression.

I remembered later that I caught Fay's eye and looked through it, as though I thought that she, being uninvolved in this terrible business, was beneath my notice. That, I am sure, is how she read my preoccupied expression. In fact what I felt, quite clearly, even at that moment of high drama, was a reverence for her (and even his, Marcus's) cleanliness. I had used to think myself wise beside her shallow worldliness, but now I saw my would-be wisdom as a treacly blackness, and her shallowness as purity. The emptiness of my face was merely a defence against the appalled judgement that I deserved from her, though (I had forgotten) she was ignorant of all our goings-on and could not judge me.

It seemed at that moment – unexpectedly, for I had barely given her a thought for weeks on end – like the final cruelty that Fay, of all people, should be standing at the bottom of the stairs, watching my descent.

The Toast

rs. *Veals lit the candles that stood ready all around Ludovick* Montefiore's study, and the sparse sunlight was augmented with spots of weak light. The mah-jong square squatted in the middle of the floor and we stood around it gazing, just as we had gazed on the perfume bottle a little while ago, transfixed.

Allecto broke the full silence. "Abigail. Do you understand what you must do?" I peeled my eyes from the broken square and rested them dozily on her. She continued, "Keep the tablet in its bottle until you are about to enter the Great Hall. Then tip it into your fist…the rest is up to you."

I nodded. Allecto looked at me and hesitated for the blink of an eye. Then she rubbed and clapped her hands like a second-rate actor who has been asked to play Energetic and Enthusiastic. "We're ready!" She rummaged in her pocket for a long time, searching for the plastic bottle. I wandered round the room, stroking its honeyed surfaces with my fingertips. I almost walked into Sylvia.

She glimmered brightly against the leathery browns and reds of Ludovick Montefiore's study. Hers was an outdoors light, the light of a misted winter sun, not the church-like glow of this room. I felt, as I looked at her, that outside, among the elements, she might disappear and find her home, and that it was the very stones of this place that trapped her and kept her from her peace. I had been about to ask her to hand me the Rice Bird, but my abrupt demand was superseded by these thoughts, so I asked, instead,

"What would happen to you, Sylvia, if he were to die? Do you think you would be freed?"

She shrugged her shoulders. "I have sometimes thought so," she replied. "But then again I wonder whether it would take more than his death to free me. His evil is out; it has spread like an infection. He isn't even in his abbey at the moment, and yet the air, the walls...the people...they ooze his influence."

I blushed, but I was struck by the congruence of our conclusions. Then I said abruptly,

"The Rice Bird...the tile. Can I have it?"

She gave it to me without a word and I took it with a small "Thank you". This was the third time I had ever seen it. The first time I had looked at it from out of the early stirrings of my infatuation. The second time my hand had stolen it like a traitor, but I had still been faithful. This time, the third time, I acted against my love, and in the knowledge that this story must finish without any kisses, but with an act of hard retribution. The burnt edge of the tile left sooty marks on my fingers.

Allecto stood before me. She held out the little perfume bottle and I took it without meeting her eye. Then I gave her the tile. When we stood face to face with those objects in our left hands, I felt that we were complicit, and this was of some comfort to me.

Allecto stooped to place the Rice Bird in the empty slot amongst the tiles. There was something pseudo-religious about the situation, as we solemnly congregated around the mah-jong square with death in mind. I think that Allecto acted as briskly and carelessly as she did in an attempt to vandalise the ceremonial atmosphere. It took her a few seconds to straighten the broken wall. Then the square was complete.

I thought that his magic would manifest itself grandly for us on this momentous occasion; that the wall would take on an eerie, warning glow, or that strands of electricity would wreath themselves around the fragile doorframe. But nothing changed: a wooden square framed a patch of worn, once-red carpet. I cast a look of contemptuous disappointment at Mrs. Veals, and she lashed back with a word.

"Scared?"

I strode boldly towards the square, expecting to demonstrate the inefficacy of our plan. But as soon as I lifted my right foot over the wall an invisible hand rose from the carpet, that commonplace square of carpet, and fastened itself around my ankle. Instinctively I pulled back. The others knew at once that the magic was awake, and they all (even Mrs. Veals, though she tried to hide her fascination) drew closer to that same forlorn carpet square and regarded it with renewed awe.

"Just one thing, Abigail, before you go," said Allecto, her head and eyes twitching as she tried, vainly, to unfasten them from the square and turn them on me. "We don't know where you will find yourself, once you have gone through. Presumably somewhere inside the castle, but further than that we can't say."

"...So?"

"Well, why don't you go on through and find out? And then, assuming you aren't in the Great Hall, or among great hordes of Vulture Men, you can come back and fetch me. I may be able to play a part. I may be able to help you." I glanced at Mrs. Veals, wondering whether she wished to follow too. But she had turned to stone again, and was gazing at the far wall like an Easter Island head.

"Just be discreet." I caught the words as a woven door swung slowly over Allecto's face and the invisible hands dragged me gently, breathlessly down into a grey darkness. I waited and waited for my arrival with a sense of suppressed panic; waited for the jolt that would herald another world of light and material hardness. But I just drifted, on and on, through charcoal air. For a moment I thought I had fallen victim to a plot, and that I was dead. During that moment I did not experience horror. I only felt, with tear-jerking disappointment, what a cock-eyed article my life was, now that I could see it as a completed whole. I felt as you feel at the end of a panicked exam: if only they would give you another hour then you could go back over your paper and make something of it...but no, they are telling you to lay down your pens, and it is too late to think of putting things right.

Then I realised that I was not dead, and I scrambled to my feet in a burst of energy and hope.

I was in a chilly, unlit room, and those unseen hands had laid me onto a flat softness that felt something like a bed.

As soon as I stood up I saw a broken rectangle of mushroom-brown light in the wall to my right, and understood that there was a door. I felt cautiously for the handle and turned it, but the door was locked, or bolted. I saw two breaks in the light where the bolts must be, and I prayed, with an energetically whispered "Please!" that they be located on my side of the door. They were, and they both slid back with silky ease.

I opened the door an inch or two and found myself peering into a deserted corridor constructed, from floor to ceiling, of roughly hewn, yellow-black stone: Ludovick Montefiore's Traumund stone. There were no windows, only three short, guttering candles in the opposite wall. The total absence of daylight, or moonlight, and the heavy, oozing chill that penetrated the walls, and my bones, like an arctic night, suggested to me that I was underneath the castle, inside the cellars. There was no sound, except a faint sputtering of wax.

I prised one of the candles from its stand and returned to the room. I shut the door softly and slid home the bolts. I had decided that, since there could barely be a more discreet entry to the dragon's lair, I would fetch Allecto as she had requested. There is one thing that can be said for me: my cowardice did not hide behind self-deluding visions of heroism; I did not think that my actions would gain in splendour by my performing them alone. I had given up on splendour long ago. I had to go through with this sordid murder or else I had to refuse it, and whichever way I chose to act I would be guilty of great evil. And if Allecto was jealous of my guilt then let her share it. If only she would bear it all.

I managed to balance the candle on the floor, and then I climbed back onto the low bed, or box, and let the unseen hands feel for me and push me away. I was sickeningly conscious as I did so that this might be a race against time, and that time was steadily gaining on our wheezy plans, just as it does in nightmares.

"Well?" I heard Allecto's impatient demand before her face was fully in focus. I hauled myself up, struggling to match her brisk manner. Mrs. Veal's sightless calm was unchanged.

"It's all right," I replied. "I came out in a cellar, I think, underneath the castle. There was nobody about."

"Good!" she exclaimed, and her dark eyes narrowed and gleamed. "I'm ready."

I stepped aside for her.

"You first," she smiled, and I understood that suspicion had made her voice unnaturally light. I felt my cheeks redden as I plunged back inside the carpet-covered chasm. As soon as I was laid down on the pillows I rolled onto the floor and stood up. She followed me.

"Now what? What are we going to do?" I said. I noticed, with some irritation, that when she was there I depended on her.

Allecto raised the candle and moved it round my face in a circle. She was inspecting me, and her conclusions, clearly pleasing to her, were unfavourable to me.

"You look a sight. I think we'd better scrub you up a bit if we're going to try and pass you off as a murdering temptress."

"We haven't time," I hissed. I watched the horrific prospect of leisurely hair-combings and face-cleansings, while my friends were led, one by one, to their Deaths behind that curtain. "We've wasted enough as it is."

Allecto grasped my arm firmly as I turned to go. "This won't take a minute. We'll go to your room and make you look a little less…pathetic. Otherwise he'll be able to tell you've been crying. And there are black marks on your face - heaven knows how - the burnt tile I suppose. And your hair is a haystack. You're supposed to be a champagne-quaffing Queen, not some snivelling teenager. Now come on." I supposed that she was right (she forced that assumption always, on everyone) but nonetheless, if we should be too late?

At least let's keep moving, I thought; even if we run in circles, at least let's keep running. We made our way along the subterranean passage, the little plastic bottle now warm and damp in my hand, hot wax drooling over Allecto's knuckles. We came upon a narrow, upward staircase, glanced at one another, nodded our agreement and mounted the stone steps, plunging first of all into blackness, then winding round and round, up and up, until the walls became a duskier black, then grey, then pale brown, until at last we emerged in a grand, carpeted corridor. The stained-glass windows were dulled by night, but the corridor was lit, all the same, by clusters of golden globes, that hung from the ceiling like static planets.

We ventured along the corridor with a few uncertain steps and then, just as I was about to wonder aloud what on earth we should do next, a Vulture Man emerged from some shadowy recess and blocked our way. I was behind Allecto, and I saw her whole body contract as the monster materialised, but she was too well prepared, and too disciplined, to scream, or even to gasp. I searched furtively for an escape route, swivelling my eyes this way and that, and turning my head as slightly as possible in an attempt to look round. But my nervous twists and turns were arrested by the Vulture Man himself; by his subservience. I realised, just in time, that the play had begun.

He bowed low. "Your Majesty. May I say, on behalf of the entire household, how pleased I am to find you safely returned to us." His eyes remained fixed on the red carpet, so he did not see my cheeks change from purple to white and back again, nor did he see me draw myself up in a shaky bid for hauteur, nor did he see Allecto turn and glare courage at me. He only heard a tight voice say, "Indeed."

"If I might convey these good tidings to the king, ma'am? He has been anxious for news, ma'am, if I may make so bold."

"I intend to announce my arrival to His Majesty in person," I replied, gladly imitating his mannered style, since it was much easier to adopt than a more natural tone. "In the meantime, tell me, has anything occurred during my absence, anything of which I might wish to be informed? The executions in the Great Hall, for example, have they been carried out?"

"No, Your Majesty, the prisoners are still alive. The king will not dispatch them without your consent. He is waiting for you."

"I see. Very good."

I was in danger of losing my way here, since everything inside me and about me seemed to loosen and sink towards collapse. Allecto understood my disarray as quickly as though it was her own. She turned and smiled at me beautifully but falsely, since such smiles did not belong in our relationship. "Perhaps I might…splash my face and brush my hair before you introduce me to the king?"

"Of course, of course." I reconstructed myself and addressed the Vulture Man once more. "I have brought a guest with me. I wish, initially, to conceal her presence from the king. She is…her visit will be a pleasant surprise. Now, if you would be so good as to conduct us to my room, to wait while we wash and to bring us to the Great Hall, then I shall be grateful."

"It will be an honour, Your Majesty," rasped the Vulture Man, stooping to another bow. "Follow me, if you will."

We followed the Vulture Man through passageways and up staircases. They seemed familiar, and therefore welcoming, after that disorientating walk through the underbelly of the castle. I was aware that the castle was straining to seduce me once more, as though it was conscious of a duty to Ludovick Montefiore. Charm seemed to ooze from the walls and slide along my cheeks and down my neck like warm slugs of oil. All my conscious efforts were focussed on keeping my head.

I ushered Allecto into my room and ordered the Vulture Man to keep his post outside my door: this was partly that I might be sure of a guide to the Great Hall, and partly that he might not be at liberty to wander about the castle – perhaps into the king's presence – and be drawn to talk about our proceedings.

We – Allecto and I – both sighed as the door closed upon us, and she shut her eyes. Reluctantly, I abandoned the imperial persona that had demanded so little of my inner self. "What now?" I said.

"Wash your face, brush your hair…come on!" She opened her eyes and the ordinary, capable Allecto reappeared, refreshed. She paced the room as she urged me on, opening cupboards and wardrobe doors and flicking curtains back, as though she was looking for something. If only our common mission had been less urgent I would have resented her presumption, but this was the way with Allecto: somehow circumstances always conspired to justify outrageous or, at best, irritating behaviour on her part, and the time was never right to reproach her, as I repeatedly burned to do.

"What are you looking for?" I asked, as humbly helpful as a lady's maid.

"Oh, I don't know!" She answered, slamming shut a fragile bureau. "Something that might be useful. I don't know, a weapon or something. I mean, you're all right, you've got your plan all cut and dried, but what the hell do I do now I'm here?"

I looked at her anxiously as warm water dripped off the end of my nose and chin and made a grey, damp patch across the front of my dress. At this great moment of crisis I felt afraid of her petulance, perhaps because petulance has a tendency to deteriorate into teary defeatism, and I knew I could not tolerate any defeatism on Allecto's part. I concentrated my powers, such as they were, on placating her.

"I need you as back-up. My bit could so easily fail. The whole plan depends upon his trust in me, and we have no real reason to suppose he still feels any. So I need you to wait outside the hall…as back-up."

"And how, precisely, do you suggest I 'back you up'?" She asked as sarcastically as though I had insulted her. "Do you expect me to barge in and wrestle him to the ground with my bare hands?"   Here, again, I might have justly lashed back by asking why she had been so eager to accompany me in the first place if she had no idea of being helpful; I had not asked her to come. But a prickly tone, it seemed, was her prerogative. I cast around rapidly in my mind, like a nervous schoolgirl at an oral examination. Suddenly I remembered, and I lunged at a drawer.

"I've got a bow that you can have, and a quiver full of arrows." I pulled them out from their hiding place and presented them to her apologetically. She handled and studied them solemnly as I added, "They're not exactly state of the art, I know. But…" I hesitated, "Constantine gave them to me."

She smiled slightly. "They're perfect," she said, slinging the quiver over her shoulder. Then she let it slump back into her despondent hands. "Hang on. They're not going to let me waltz through the castle with a bow and a quiver full of arrows, are they? I mean, what possible explanation could I give? I need something that I can hide - a dagger or something."

"I haven't got a dagger. And anyway, you forget, I am Queen here, or as good as Queen. I am not obliged to explain my actions, or those of my guest, to anybody."

Allecto raised the corners of her lips and then said, darkly, "You might have a bit of explaining to do when they discover you have murdered their king." But she slung the quiver over her shoulder once again, and grasped the bow with her left hand.

"Right, I'm ready," I exclaimed brightly at the plain girl in the mirror, as though her magical beauty might glow out once again if it was sufficiently encouraged by my failing imagination. But then I turned away from the mirror, knowing that the magic was almost dead. I found myself face to face with Allecto.

"You still look a bit of a mess," she said pleasantly. "I hope you don't mind me saying so, but I can't think what he sees in you."

"Ditto…except it's past tense in your case," I spat clumsily, but she ignored my playground retort as effectively as though I had never said it.

"Aren't you going to change your dress? It's very crumpled, and you've managed to acquire a big damp patch right across the front."

I swept my eyes up and down her slim form - its ragged pony-tail, darned grey jumper, jeans and boots – and pretended to disparage her, although she was beautiful.

"No, I am not going to change my dress. The king expressly ordered – asked me – to wear this one, and I will."

"Hmm…strange fabric. Snakes," she murmured, fingering the sleeve, her upper lip slightly raised. "I can't say I think much of his tastes these days. No, not at all."

The Vulture Man bowed as we emerged, a bow for me and a bow for my companion; twice his hood touched the carpet. His deference to Allecto, I thought, was true. He recognised her innate authority, and his whole self, his eyes, his head, his poorly-fashioned soul, submitted gratefully. He did not obey me instinctively or, I think, with pleasure, but only on Ludovick Montefiore's account.

I do not think he would have challenged Allecto's right to carry arms; he simply assumed that, since I approved it, my godfather would too. But I thought it best to clarify the matter now, so as to avoid complications once we reached the Great Hall. I did not even bother to employ cunning; I trusted to his servility.

"This lady, my guest, is a Queen from a distant land. She always carries her chosen weapon…and dresses in the exotic fashions that you observe now." I glanced at Allecto, who rebutted my sarcasm by, once again, appearing not to hear it. My commanding drone was fractured. "She…she…I am posting her outside the Great Hall. I mean she is to wait there. Her arrival is a surprise for the king, a pleasant surprise. You're not to tell him of her coming, not on any account. Do you understand?"

"I quite understand, Your Majesty."

I unscrewed the bottle within the secrecy of my sleeves and tipped the little brown ball into my hand.

So I entered the Great Hall alone, and his eyes were dull with waiting for me. They sprang to life and leapt forwards when they saw me. All the clamouring, dithering excitement that had filled my time apart from him died with an echo and left silence behind. The silence seemed to centre on me. I saw scraggy patches of darkness against the wall; these were the prisoners whom I had come to save. I remembered that I was resolved to do this thing, but all the same I thought to myself that my fingers had only to part by the tiniest fraction and the poison would break apart on the floor and be lost in the cracks between the dark boards. That would not be my fault; they could not blame me. Since when has it been morally delinquent for anyone to relax their fingers? Then I heard my own honeyed voice and it disgusted me, so that while it spoke my heart sank into my feet as though running away from the voice, as far away as it could.

"I'm back."

His eyes smiled more and more brightly. They were like the sea in smooth shallows as it glides to meet a white-gold beach.

"I'm sorry I had to go away."

I turned to the long table and filled our crystal goblets with tepid wine. The tablet fell, intact, into his glass. I saw it disappear inside the black-red liquid. The wine frothed for a second and then it was still. I wheeled round, a glass in each hand. I slopped a little wine over my fingers, because the glasses were full and I was trembling.

I was acting out happiness so well (judging by his responsive face) that I almost began to feel happy. If he saw no menace then there could be no menace, since he was the source of everything that mattered.

"What's this?" he asked, nodding at the goblets.

"A toast." I replied.

"Now?"

"Now." I smiled. "Because I have decided."

"Decided…for me?" he asked, forcing me to lie unequivocally.

"For you. Yes."

"That one is mine?" he asked, holding out his hand. His question affronted me, because it smacked of suspicion. Our happiness was marred.

"What do you mean? Why would it matter? Have whichever one you prefer, if you have a preference." But I offered him the glass from my stinging left hand. He took it, clanged it against mine and raised it to his lips.

"To…" I had given it no thought. "To Traumund."

"To Traumund."

The sound of falling water thundered in my ears as the rim of the glass touched Ludovick Montefiore's lip and his wrist tilted. If I had not slopped it over my hand then the liquid would have risen into his mouth and trickled down his throat. But he did not drink. He paused. My breathing quickened as he lowered the glass. He was looking beyond me. I saw all this in the same self-centred silence that I have already described. Only later did I remember how it all occurred to the accompaniment of threats, screams, pleadings and flurries of movement.

I whipped round and saw Mrs. Veals. She had been discovered wandering through the castle. A Vulture Man had arrested her and brought her to the king. She came struggling and shouting, her stolid voice and stolid body writhing in hysterics. I glimpsed Allecto in the corridor, though she made sure she was invisible to Ludovick Montefiore. There was a helpless fragility in her posture that I had never witnessed before. The bow was strung, and an arrow limply fitted, but she held them low against her side. She stared at Mrs. Veals with a sort of pleading despair, as a marooned desert-islander might gaze at a passing ship.

"STOP!" Mrs. Veals was screaming with a high-pitched terrier yap that disturbed me, in retrospect, by its incongruity with her usual square-jawed persona. "Don't drink it! Don't drink it! Don't drink it!" She made a swipe at the poisoned glass (for she had come close to us now) but the guard caught her arm. "You've been betrayed! She has betrayed you; she's poisoned it, that little viper. I heard her plan it out; I heard it all. She's giving you poison to drink, and if it weren't for me you'd be dead by now. So kill her, kill her, and choose your favourite more wisely next time…"

The words spattered out at speed, depriving her of breath and thought. She was yearning, with all the pent-up energy of her watchful, silent, seething being, to force the king's understanding and sympathy, but he only regarded her with an untouched curiosity, as though she was a hyperactive rodent in a cage.

"What a bizarre interruption, Abigail…I only hope you will consent to find it amusing as well as outrageous."

"You fool!" Mrs. Veals' distraught energies were almost spent, and awareness of this made her still more desperate. "Won't you even bother to check whether I am right or not? See if she will drink from your glass; offer it to her; offer her the venom and you'll soon find out where her loyalties lie."

He glanced at me with a tilt of the head, as much as to say, You decide what happens next.

My voice was shrill and rapid. "If you don't drink it then you must distrust me, and after all I have gladly and freely given up for you…" I petered out and pressed my hands against my forehead. What a flimsy piece of acting. He didn't believe me; I could tell by his veiled expression that he saw through the whole charade. "Oh God." I moaned, giving the game away for once and all. There was a long, long silence. But then he answered me, and his tone was hearty.

"Abigail, ignore that blathering idiot, and listen to me. Of course I will do as you ask. After all, how can I ever thank you for submitting to my stupid test? For bearing with my unpardonable mistrust, and for laying it to rest so absolutely? I would rather have died than lived in the knowledge that you had failed me; that you were not…all the things I believed you to be. And when I say I would rather have died, it is not some rhetorical flourish; I mean it."

I was crying quite openly now, the tears coursing down over my reddened cheeks and distorted lips. I could not look at him.

"After all, when you live, like me, according to absolute values; when you call yourself a Romantic and an Extremist and a King, and when everything you are starts with a capital letter…well, then there are only so many times you can pick yourself up and dust yourself down. I was married once you know; I thought my wife was my heart's desire, but she was a disappointment. I have experimented with others, but I have never placed hope in anyone until now."

He laughed, but his tone was no longer hearty. "One great disappointment is bearable, but two would be…well, it looks undignified, doesn't it? And it hurts too much."

He grabbed my wrist and pulled me towards him. Then he kissed me roughly on the cheek and hissed something in my ear. The words were unclear and breathy, but I thought he said, "This is not the end. For you, perhaps. But not for me."

I pulled away, bewildered and shuddering with sobs. "What did you say?" I whispered wildly. "What do you mean?"

He did not answer, but prised the poisoned glass from my hand. "To Traumund!" he cried, bowing to me with a bitter and knowing smile. Then he drained the wine in three noisy gulps. I could see his eyes watching me through the crystal goblet. They were fragmented by the glass, so that in fact I saw many diamond-shaped blue eyes, each with a dark and seething centre. And all the eyes looked on as he drank to me.

The Queen of the Vulture Men

A s Ludovick Montefiore drained his glass I grew numb, as though he was consuming all my vitality along with the poison. I watched events unfold as if through a wall of ice; everything was muted and blurred. But I must have watched it all – watched it closely – because I see it clearly now inside my head. It unrolls like a film.

Ludovick Montefiore died quickly, though for several seconds I could not believe that this was really death. I mean, I expected him to wear some sort of dying expression; to clutch at his throat, or roll his eyes, or retch. But his face was blank. He just crumpled up in a heap on the floor, like a puppet whose strings had been sliced all at once. The glass fell from his hand and shattered across the floorboards. I stared at him distrustfully; the Vulture Men and Allecto were held back by one giant, unifying hesitation.

Somebody, I think it was Allecto, said "Oh!" in a tone that sounded like mild surprise. It always seems inappropriately comic when I look back at it, that "Oh!"

But then Mrs. Veals started screaming and thrashing around like a wounded seagull. She tumbled on top of him, and shook him. She was crying out all the time; harsh sounds that may not even have been words. When she had finished shaking him, she scrabbled about on the floor for the pieces of his shattered goblet. Then she took the largest shards and licked them ravenously, not caring that they cut her tongue. She died quickly, crumpled up and slavering over Ludovick Montefiore's body. It was like a grotesque parody of Romeo and Juliet.

Allecto took charge once Mrs. Veals was dead. She was incapable of stupefaction for more than a few seconds. ("You can't help admiring her, can you?" as Joachim and Boris always used to say. "She may be a bit…I know you don't like her, Abigail…but you can't help admiring her, can you?")

Well, no, I couldn't help admiring her. She realised that we needed a strident voice; a voice claiming power for itself. That voice, she understood, could do whatever it wished with the proceedings, just like the writer of a story. Perhaps that was why she came with me. The hundreds, maybe thousands of Vulture Men in our vicinity, needed a focus, a leader. If she had not understood this, and acted on it, then God knows which way their force would have turned. They might have thought to mourn for their dead king; to kill in honour of his memory. She saved all our lives.

The first thing she did was to stand over the dead bodies and turn them over with her foot. The king's head had twisted to one side, and the way it was positioned looked…I know he was dead, but it looked like a refusal to acknowledge her. And she was so regal. So she flicked his head over onto the other side with her foot, then stooped and spat on his nose.

Joachim thought she was wonderful. "I know what you think," he said to me later on. "You think her brutal, don't you? I know by the way you watched her…you weren't outraged or hostile, you were just unimpressed. You seemed to stare at her from far away, as though she was a dot on the horizon. But the Vulture Men – they were impressed. They understood her at once. And there was, there really was, something royal about her. When she kicked his face…it sounds so vicious…but there was something beautiful in the way she did it; something monumental, rather than incidental. She was like a marble knight stepping on the neck of a marble dragon." That was how Joachim saw it. I don't suppose the Vulture Men gave much thought to the artistic merit of her actions. They just admired her savagery. At any rate, they had knelt and pledged their allegiance before she had even declared herself their queen.

She took it all in her stride. She understood that the tighter she bound them to her by gestures of power and suppressed any tendency towards directionless freedom, the more they would love and obey her.

As she surveyed her kneeling troops, one of the Vulture Men got to his feet. I don't think it was an expression of insubordination, I think he was merely distracted, or else he had cramp. But she advanced on him before he had fully risen, and struck him over the head with her bow. ("And, don't you see?" explained Joachim later on. "That was the right thing to do!") The soldier cringed and sank down on his knees. The others were watching out of the corners of their eyes, and, as though they were physically interconnected, their hoods sank lower and their cloaks spread about their prostrate forms, until the hall seemed to have filled up with row upon row of black, circular pools.

Allecto put a hand on my shoulder and addressed them. I thought she would free the captives first, but she said, "What has become of the fourth prisoner? The fair-haired young man?"

The Vulture Men were perplexed. They wanted to answer promptly; their eagerness was palpable. But they feared the substance of their reply; they feared her anger.

"If you please, Your Majesty..." The sycophant whom she had struck spoke up at last. "The fourth prisoner...The prisoner to whom you refer...The fair-haired young man...Tragically, and despite all our tender ministrations..."

Allecto snorted, and there was high-pitched savagery in her tone as she said, "So he is dead."

"He has...he did indeed pass away, Your Majesty."

"And his body? What did you do with his body?"

"It...ah...Your Majesty...His remains were reverently laid to rest on a piece of heathery ground outside the castle walls."

"By that you mean his carcass was unceremoniously dumped on a hillside somewhere, for the delectation of the crows."

"And other scavenging...species," murmured the sycophant guiltily. "Yes, Your Majesty."

"Other scavenging...you don't mean...YOU?" Allecto's face contorted with disgust. "Oh, good God." She turned away and looked, with trepidation, into my face. I don't know what she expected or wanted from me. Grief? Revulsion? Sympathy? I gave her indifference. Constantine's death did not move me; neither did his funeral arrangements. It was unreal, like the death of an unengaging character in an unengaging book. I was surprised by my lack of emotion, but I could not, at that time, feel guilty or frightened by it.

Allecto turned back to her subjects. There were tears collecting in her eyes and turning their whites to red. "Go back and collect whatever remains," she spat. "Burn his bones and scatter his ashes over the moor. Do you understand me?"

"Yes, Your Majesty."

"Now free the remaining prisoners." That was her second order. The guilty sycophant was, once again, the most eager to execute her command, as though it was not enough to be shielded from her aggression by anonymity. He had to have her notice, even though that meant another beating. So he rushed towards the prisoners, like an angel of mercy in disguise, and he cut the ropes and unlocked the chains that bound them to one another. They tottered; Joachim fell to his knees.

The soldier stood to attention. He even saluted his new queen as the captives – exhausted and under-nourished - collapsed about his feet. Allecto was enraged by his literalism.

"Well? Help them!" She snapped. "Can't you see they need liquid, food, rest…?"

Immediately there was a flurry of organised activity. Fervent Vulture Men fetched cushions and flagons of wine and soup tureens. Joachim, Boris and Eyes said that they would never forget the soup. It was golden. I don't mean orange or yellow, like carrot or sweetcorn soup, I mean shining, molten gold, and they said it tasted more sumptuous than anything in the Waking World. It healed them as swiftly as a magic potion, which, I suppose, is what it was. It was as though with every slurp they poured liquidised strength into their legs and arms and wasted torsos, where it swelled up and solidified. They said that the torment of their imprisonment became hazy as they drank, like the memory of a bad dream. While they ate I stood over my dead godfather, as though I was guarding him. But when, on Allecto's orders, the Vulture Men came to shift the bodies, I murmured "Sorry", and stepped aside politely.

Allecto climbed onto the dining table in order to address her new people. She looked bored, with her weight on one hip and her eyelids drooping. She spoke to them briefly and harshly – no preliminaries, no introductions, no "Thank you for your allegiance." They loved it; they loved her, you could see it in the way they leaned forward, clasping their gloved hands together in a gesture of reverence.

"Right." She said. "Listen carefully to my orders, because if you fail them in the tiniest respect then I shall have your race wiped out. I'm taking the prisoners away. I may be gone for days, weeks, months… maybe years. That's none of your business. But I shall have my eye on you all the time, even though you can't see me.

"So…first of all you must locate those Vulture Men who are currently dispersed throughout Traumund and summon them back here. Once they have returned, you must never, never trespass outside the boundaries of this land again. That is my first and most important command.

"Secondly, I command that you keep yourselves occupied with perpetual physical labour, except at night when I grant eight hours of sleep, and during three twenty minute periods each day, when you may sit down to eat. There is plenty for you to do: my horses must be exercised, my fields ploughed, sown and harvested, my buildings maintained...and so on. And then of course the palace must be beautified to the highest imaginable standards in expectation of my return."

"If you please, Your Majesty?" a Vulture Man rasped timidly, half-raising his arm. Allecto glared straight into the hood for five, silent seconds, as the soldier's arm and body wilted.

"Yes?"

"If you please, Your Majesty, I only, I wondered, if you please, how you would have us punish any idlers - "

"Idlers? There be no idlers!" Allecto screamed and stamped her foot so that the table wobbled. Then she adopted a menacing softness of tone. "And why? Because, naturally, anyone who disobeys the most trivial of my wishes will be dispatched, at once, by my loyal subjects."

"Yes, Your Majesty. Thank you, Your Majesty." The Vulture Man quivered with frightened pleasure at being addressed, one on one, by his monarch. He looked round at the others with a surreptitious pride.

"My final command is that you engrave this speech – word for word – on a bronze plaque, and fasten it over the castle's outer gates.

"You have your orders. Go. All of you. Go at once."

And they did. They glided from the hall like monks leaving mass, with their hoods drooping forwards and their hands meekly clasped.

The prisoners were quite recovered now, only they regretted having finished their golden soup. I remember how Boris stooped over his bowl and licked the sides like a thirsty dog. But Joachim watched me as he sucked on his spoon. I returned his gaze. I asked him, later on, what he was thinking as he looked at me. He said, "I was thinking... that you had not come back yet. The bodies and the glass shards were tidied away, and the poison mopped up, but you still stood in the same place looking pensive...or were you listening? You looked as though you were straining to catch a faraway voice on a badly-tuned radio."

Joachim came up to me at some point. I remember his hand on my arm, and generous words. He expressed sorrow on Constantine's account, and he reassured me that they – the survivors – were all right. Oh yes, and he congratulated me on the killing of Ludovick Montefiore. I did not respond to any of these kindnesses.

Allecto was speaking with Eyes. We (Joachim, Boris and I)

watched them as they talked quietly, smilingly, with their faces close together. We watched her as if we were all hoping for a royal visit, a kindly handshake and an aloof inquiry after our welfare, which we would answer with blushes and gratitude. That's how we watched her, forgetting that she had abdicated when the Vulture Men left.

Everything happened so quickly after that.

We bid farewell to Eyes, who of course belonged to Traumund, and therefore would not return with us to the Waking World. Joachim embraced the owl fondly, and Boris kissed the tips of his wings. I murmured something inadequate, and Eyes touched my forehead as if with a blessing.

Then Allecto led us to the underground room with the coffin-like bed, where she and I had entered an hour or two before. One by one we stepped onto the wooden box and we were sucked from Traumund.

It seemed too quick – but that is how it was.

We emerged into Ludovick Montefiore's sepulchral study.

All was as it had been before: peaceful, dun-brown and gold. There were the leather-bound books lining the wall, the welsh dresser, the cold fireplace. And there was the magic, the tangible magic; it had not seeped away as I had feared. Joachim felt it too; we talked about it later. The air was thick and sweet: honey vapour; dream air. I shivered and Joachim shivered, and we exchanged looks with one another for the first time in ages.

Joachim wanted to explore, but Allecto needed to get out; she could not escape too quickly from her erstwhile prison. "Out! Out!" she kept urging. There was pure joy in her voice. "Out of this hell-hole! Come on!" Joachim was too polite, and I was too apathetic to disobey her. Joachim put Boris in his pocket and we trotted before her like a couple of harried sheep.

Round the labyrinthine house as dusk fell through the windows and permeated the abbey with its blue-grey chill. Then, as we passed the landing window at the centre of the first floor, I stopped dead. Joachim and Allecto flitted past me, making for the outdoors and freedom. I held back. I stood at the edge of the window pane, my cheek hidden in folds of dusty velvet and my eyes boring through the wavy glass.

Below me, on the gravel driveway, a small crowd mingled and bustled, whispered and called and looked about. I recognised my parents first of all. Mum was turning her anxious head this way and that, while dad talked rapidly at a policeman. Mum was obviously listening to him (or half-listening) because she occasionally interjected with a sharp word or two. The policeman's concerned expression kept lapsing into abstraction. There were other people whom I did not know, and some men whom I recognised from The Witch's Broom. John Fogle was there. I spotted Fay (looking shaken) and Marcus (looking self-important). They stood in the arms of a thin, hysterical woman with pale hair and lobster-red skin. She was recognisably their mother; their lobster-red father stood nearby looking self-consciously manly, his hands wedged inside tight denim pockets.

Then Joachim and Allecto emerged from the front door, and there were louder cries and gasps and little screams. All eyes fastened on them, except my mother's: her restless gaze suddenly found my window. I leapt back as though I had been shot. How they had come here, who had summoned them, I neither knew nor cared. But I knew what it meant. It meant emotional embraces, mutual exasperation, tearful demands and explanations. It meant hearing the name "Ludovick Montefiore" spoken freely and with loathing. It meant life again.

I ran back into the depths of the abbey, and found my way to his study again. The house no longer thwarted me. On the contrary, it seemed to have given me its freedom: corridors opened up when I needed and expected them; doors appeared where I hoped they might. I wondered whether the abbey wanted to keep me now that everyone else had deserted it. I even wondered whether the house had become mine on Ludovick Montefiore's death. Who, I thought ruefully, could be a more fitting heir?

As soon as I shut the study door a massive quiet enveloped me. It was as though centuries of silence had accumulated in that particular room and given it an atmosphere of layered richness. I walked mechanically to the windows in order to draw the curtains against the evening sky, and I found the windowsill littered with the bodies of bluebottles. Then I whisked the curtains to, sat down on his high-backed armchair and cried. I cried quietly, but desperately, for a long time. My tears were not accompanied by any particular thoughts, so I don't know whether they were primarily tears of grief, or guilt, or weariness. They were the tears that a romantic heroine might shed if the author of her story went mad and sent the plot haywire.

When the worst of the weeping was over and my breath was coming in shudders, I thought of Sylvia and I called her name, weakly at first, then more confidently, and finally shouting: "SYL-VI-A! SYL-VI-A!" She never came; there were no cold echoes of her presence in the air.

I thought perhaps she had been set free and had re-discovered that paradise with the dawn, the music and the kindly voice. This gave me hope for a moment, but then I lapsed into despondency because I could not know. I wished for a happy vision such as I had witnessed during my flight through Traumund. I wanted gold, blue and silver lights and Sylvia's voice – a free, wandering whisper – telling me that all was well. But there was no such message.

Some weeks later I learned that her grandfather, Tobias, had died in his sleep on the night after our return.

It was time for me to join the fray.

As I left the room I noticed my godfather's mah-jong square laid out on the carpet, just as we had left it. I slid my fingers over the tiled edges and felt the tug of Traumund magic. I whipped my hand away again as my heart rate accelerated pleasurably. Then I dislodged the sooty Rice Bird tile and, after a moment's deliberation, pocketed it.

The magic charge inside the square went dead. I told myself, reasonably enough, that I was wise to lock the gate between this world and the world of the Vulture Men. But my real reasons for taking the tile were secretive, possessive reasons. I wanted a keepsake.

I left the study and allowed the house to guide me outside. What a wan figure I must have cut as I emerged from the front door.

I looked back as they led me away. My last glimpse was of the abbey's unlit eyes and smokeless chimneys.

Eyes and the Atlas

here followed, for me, a wilderness year. I worked diligently, but joylessly, at my local school. I gave up reading for pleasure and studied only the books that were prescribed by my teachers. (Occasionally, as the year wore on, I was tempted by my parents' dog-eared paperbacks, but I never succumbed: merely pulling one off the shelf made me feel anxious and unhappy.) Sometimes I would sit on my bed and look at the Rice Bird tile, but that only made me sad, so I stuffed it in the back of my sock drawer and tried to forget about it.

I had feared a good deal of emotive discussion with my mother and father, but as it was I got away lightly. I gave my parents the barest account of my time at Boughwinds Abbey (so bare as to be untrue), and they were satisfied – or pretended to be satisfied. Probably they were afraid to probe deeply. They watched me though, and pondered. Sometimes dad broached the subject of Ludovick Montefiore. I think he wanted to say the name, in case it became taboo by being couched in silence. He would speak malevolently of my godfather, though in the vaguest terms of course, since he knew too little to accuse him of much. These conversations – these monologues - never progressed. They made my mother go mysteriously quiet and abstracted; often she would wander away while dad ranted. And of course I contributed nothing.

I steered clear of Traumund during this dead year. If I could have gone straight home to my tree, perhaps...but I knew where I must emerge.

I did have vivid dreams on the very edges of sleep; in the minutes before I woke up in the morning. Most of these dreams involved Ludovick Montefiore, and there were all sorts of weird scenarios, few of which I can actually recall. But I do remember that in these dreams he was often winged. Sometimes he had red, leathery, veined wings, like a devil. But sometimes he had soft bird wings with dun-brown feathers.

A year went by, the Christmas holidays arrived, and Joachim came to stay with us. We had been writing to one another, but this was the first time I had seen him all year, and he looked a good deal happier than he had ever been before in his Waking World life. It won't take me long to explain why.

Rupert Wellington-Grub, Joachim's feckless Putney friend and our go-between, had fallen on hard times. He claimed to have lost all his money on a single race at Ascot, but Joachim thought this explanation suspiciously sensational. At any rate, Mr. Wellington-Grub had been forced, for the first time in his life, to earn his own living, and to this end he had become a music teacher at a boarding school in Dorset. Somehow or other Mr. Wellington-Grub persuaded Joachim's work-absorbed parents to send him to this same establishment as a pupil. His cause was, of course, helped by the fact that Joachim's schooling was a question requiring solution, now that the Institutes had lost their chief benefactor in mysterious circumstances, and were closing down, one by one.

When Joachim talked about his new school, it was always rapidly and with a shining expression. I felt woefully ill-informed beside him, but far from resenting his intellectual superiority I felt wakened and spurred by it. I began to read again. We didn't do much that holiday, except read and talk. He tried to teach me to play the violin. He himself was being instructed by Rupert Wellington-Grub, and he was already (in as far as I could judge) quite accomplished.

One evening we were sitting in my bedroom, looking out across the gloomy winter garden. Mrs. Lorimer and her cats were still in residence over the way, to our joint fascination. We spent hours watching her kitchen window, though as we did so we talked – pointedly – of other things. Sometimes she caught sight of us and waved blithely, and we would duck away with a thrill. Once Joachim waved back, which made me laugh for the first time in ages.

"About last year…" I said quietly, lest my parents should overhear. "…Everything. I'm really sorry."

"I know. It's all right."

That night I dared to revisit Traumund.

The Vulture Men had not forsaken their queen. When I emerged from the castle cellars I met a group of hooded guards as they paced the corridors of a castle that was, I think, cleaner, lighter and more ordinary than I recalled. Even they seemed less frightening than before. That was partly because, for all their superior number and strength, they fell to the ground when they saw me and whimpered at my feet. They thought I was their queen's emissary and I did not disabuse them.

I wonder whether she ever returned to her kingdom, and if so, what she did there. I wonder what became of her Waking World self. But I should not harp on about Allecto. It's strange how my mind returns to her so persistently. Even people whose importance to me is deeper, whom I recall with a glow (even if it is an unhappy glow) – even they do not pester my head as she does. Irritate it as she does. Enough. Enough of Allecto.

I did not feel at home in that empty castle, or in the empty heath beneath its walls. A pursuit of change was underway: there were unfamiliar splendours at every turn, and an air of frenetic, desiring activity. The old air, the old spaces, the old stones that I had expected to meet again if not with a tender nostalgia (that would have been impossible to me by this stage of my recuperation), then at least with a guilty frisson, had all been broken up and carted away amidst the new kingdom's hustle and bustle. I was left cold.

I blamed her alone at first, until it occurred to me that the land, comparatively full and thriving as it was, seemed empty to me only because I had (long ago, as it seemed now) sucked out, vampire-like, all the significance I desired of it. It was not empty, on the contrary it was healthily replenished, only I was sated. This revelation gave birth to some strange and unsettling ideas. I thought, as Ludovick Montefiore had thought before me, that the mindscapes of Traumund are not sacred. In fact, that to treat these lands with delicacy is to abuse them, and to misunderstand their essence. That if your imagination wants to see a whole continent in flames, Traumund exists to provide the spectacle. Beauty, wonder and terror have been compacted into every atom of this second universe, so dig, ransack, tear open every atom, or else it was all made (for it was certainly made, through the colossal union of many millions of wonderful and secret imaginations) for nothing.

I kept coming back to Allecto's land after that first night, but each visit left me cold and depressed – increasingly so. I resolved, when it arrived, that the seventh visit would be my last. But on the seventh night everything changed.

Since it was meant to be my last visit to Traumund, I decided to make a proper gesture of farewell to Prince Constantine. I owed him much, after all, and the memory of him filled me with remorse. I did not know what to do though. I was afraid that a premeditated "gesture" might be mawkish: my adventure had left me with a loathing of extravagant sentiments. In the end I climbed to the summit of a steep hill overlooking the castle, and collected a heap of yellow-black stones, the smoothest and most regular I could find. I constructed a ring, about three feet in diameter, and I wrote across the largest, flattest stone with a piece of chalk. I wrote a line from a John Donne poem that I had learnt by heart for English:

For, those, whom thou think'st, thou dost overthrow,
Die not, poore death

I knew it would disappear with the rain came, but that didn't matter. Permanence was not the point. I sat outside the ring and rested my chin on my hands.

So there I was, alone on a heathery hill in this land for which I felt no desire when, with a thudding, feathery whisper of his wings, Eyes alighted at my side. He had not even spoken, and neither had I, nor had my brain properly understood the fact of his presence (let alone his potential) before I felt, at the sheer sight of him, a prick – a severe stab - of hope. I leapt up.

"Eyes!"

"Abigail."

"You're here?"

"Yes. Well I returned to your tree last year. But then I decided to come back."

"You decided to come back? But why?"

"I decided that I ought to wait here."

I did not ask what he awaited for fear his answer would be antagonistic to my hopes. But his wry, tawny face was hope, and so was his plump tenor voice. He did not know, or he had forgotten, or he chose to overlook, the fact that I was once a traitor.

"How did you find your way back to the tree?"

"I have a fine memory for that sort of thing. And anyway, I consulted

Mr. Montefiore's atlas before I left."

"The atlas! I'd forgotten about it."

"He was right about that, at any rate. It really is a most wonderful book."

We did not say anything else for a while, but knelt (or perched) side by side, looking out across the purple heather. I think Eyes did not like to be still, for he shifted and fluttered constantly.

"Oh Eyes!" I exclaimed languidly after a while, pressing against the back of my head with interlaced fingers. "Now that you've come I feel...I want to get out of here, and to fly again."

"To go home?"

"...Yes...To go home...But in a roundabout way."

"Ah."

"I want to see other lands."

"You'd be following a dangerous precedent."

"Yes...I know."

"You might want to 'possess' them."

"I know."

"You know?"

"Yes, and I would possess them – try to - but not like he did, because I want to get even closer than he did to real possession. Is that wrong?"

"...well... "

"I can't help it. It's true. I want what Ludovick Montefiore wanted. His methods were stupid, that's all. He thought he had to stamp his mark on Traumund in order to possess it. I want Traumund to stamp its mark on me. I want to intrude on its secrets and to have its essence in my memory, but I don't need to reduce or deprive anybody in order to do that, do I? I want to go through Traumund in the same way that I might go through a great book, so that, by the end, I have possessed it and it has possessed me."

"And why is that kind of possession more worthy than his?"

"Well, can't you see why? He wanted to tick each chapter off in order that he could tell himself, and other people, that he had read it. He saw each land as a little trophy and he forgot that it was, in fact, a treasure. That's the terrible irony. He barred himself from Traumund. He wanted so much to grow, and instead he made himself shrivel up and die."

Eyes raised an owlish eyebrow. "That's all very well. But it's not really the done thing, you know, trespassing in Traumund, whether you come as a conquering hero, or with higher ideals."

"It's impudent, I know. And risky."

"We'll get attacked."

"What are your wings for?"

"You could carry a weapon."

"No, I'm no good with weapons. And we'll have enough to carry if we bring his atlas."

"And a cloak. You'll need a cloak to sleep under at night."

"Yes, all right. But there'll be no room for anything else."

"And when I get shot down like what's-her-name, Montefiore's owl? Then you'll be left in the lurch won't you?"

"And I'll die somewhere strange, rather than dying at home. That's not the end of the world."

"No?"

I shrugged.

It was not difficult for me to steal the atlas, since Allecto had set no store by it and allowed it to moulder away in the palace library. The Vulture Men could not care for it if she did not, and nobody understood why, or how dearly, the old king used to prize it.

I entered my old bedroom – my 'chamber' – once again. The wardrobe was still filled with royal clothes. I took a heavy, night-blue cloak with a hood and a silver clasp.

Eyes and I flew into a dark sky. We flew over deserts and oceans; icebergs and jungles; mountain peaks and valleys. We stayed in palaces, castles, town houses, tents and mud huts, or found shelter for ourselves in caves and under forest canopies. We met kind people, strange people, suspicious and violent people. We were scarred, weather-beaten, disturbed and enthralled.

But what is the good of these snapshots? They have told you nothing. Try to understand: what mattered were the things half seen; the snatches of music; the stories. We never reached Traumund's edge and, though at first I yearned to find it, in the end our failure awed and delighted me. For everything we saw we made a mark – a word, a sketch, a sign – on the blank pages of the atlas.

I suppose you might ask why, if I had to write a book about myself, I did not choose to describe these journeys of my later life, in all their extremes of beauty and fearful excitement. Why choose to set down the mere preamble to those flights: the grimy, guilty beginnings?

Well, perhaps those unwritten epics are the more magnificent for remaining unwritten. Perhaps if I tried to describe my trespasses in Traumund they would read like the clumsy synopses of other peoples' books. Perhaps I just like Beginnings best.

I have written this story because it is my confession. I am an old woman now, and the others (all the humans at any rate) are dead. Joachim died most recently. He died four years ago. You don't know what happened to my relationship with Joachim – whether we drifted apart at last, or married one another, or contented ourselves with something in between love and indifference. I won't tell you. I have said enough about the Waking World. You know enough to be sure that my life was not the hopeless, joyless anti-climax that it threatened to be when I left Boughwinds Abbey for good.

I made a promise to myself long, long ago that if I made my full confession before anyone it would be before Joachim. But then he died. Once he was gone my failure of resolve came home to me, and it tormented me like a sore. I wanted him to know, as fully as I could tell it, this story, this one in particular, the one about the beginnings. That would have been the proper way to part. I wanted us to separate in a spirit of mutual understanding. I had come to love my secret story, but now, with Joachim dead, I could barely tolerate it. I felt as though I had handcuffed my wrist to a ten tonne weight and thrown away the key.

So Eyes and I came back to the oak at last, and to my old, old friends, in order to write this book in peace. It was a hard tale to tell, as hard as I had always anticipated, I suppose, judging by my lifelong reluctance to tell it. But my friends helped me – Boris especially – and I feel easier for having confessed, even though Joachim will never see the manuscript.

When I read this book over, and imagine others reading it, I am ashamed and proud of it in equal measure: ashamed to see my inmost self running round for all comers to see, and yet proud of my own adventurous desire to communicate to other people things that are unnecessary, unpractical, intimate and true.

In the woods a mist is rising from the soil and there is a quiet drip, drip, dripping through the leaves. The ground quivers: the cannibals are awake and on the warpath. The clouds and the trees form a grey monochrome of many depths. Inside the oak our fire has caught well: it is time for a story. Boris, Eyes and I sit closest to the flames and the Tree People gather around us.

The light is too dim to penetrate the farthest nooks of the hollow trunk, but I glance out at them now and then with a knowing nod as tonight's tale proceeds. It is in those shadowy folds that my ghosts lurk: the ghosts who have risen with the mists and the moon, and whose presence Traumund, at least, does not forbid.

Epilogue

Dear Reader,

For ten years I have been tempted to consign Abigail Crabtree's manuscript to the fire. It is as much as it deserves when I think of the harm it has done and — God forbid — the harm it may yet do. My eyes need only fall upon that bundle of yellowing papers, and the tell-tale scar upon my throat starts to itch and sting. But I am a scholar, and scholars cannot burn books — not even devilish books. So I have kept it, and placated my conscience by penning this addendum — a warning to be read and obeyed by whomsoever it may concern.

When Abigail died, eleven years ago this summer, the contents of her house were auctioned. We were acquaintances for many years, Abigail and I — acquaintances, I would say, rather than friends — and I attended the sale in a spirit of casual curiosity. In the same spirit I bought a shabby, brown, paper package, containing a solitary mah-jong tile and a handwritten manuscript entitled Montefiore's Goddaughter.

The portrait of me made uncomfortable reading. It is always painful to be thought of as a minor character and a figure of fun. I cannot deny, however, the accuracy of the picture. I was a lazy, foppish fellow in those days, and even when hard times came and money was short, I retained my joie de vivre. I was an old man of eighty-six when the manuscript fell into my hands, but until then I don't think I had ever considered myself old or doomed to die. I was still the debonair youth of Chapter Four.

Well, I read Abigail's story just as you did, and I speculated idly about Mr. Montefiore and Boughwinds Abbey, and I wondered how much of it was truth and how much fiction. One week in late October, with the tale still fresh in my mind, I drove up to Carlisle for the funeral of an old school friend. On the journey home I passed through West Yorkshire, and it occurred to me that, with nothing better to do and nobody to hurry home for, I might just as well see if I could find Boughwinds village and Mr. Montefiore's abbey.

I am no storyteller, and anyway I have no desire to relive the experiences which turned me from a boy to an old man. I think it would kill me to narrate the events of that autumn night, and besides, I have no wish to poison the dreams and waking thoughts of my reader. Suffice it to say that I found the village and took a dram at The Witch's Broom, where I was warned in the most forceful terms to steer clear of the abbey. That I scoffed at the doommongers and swore not only to find the ancient house, but to spend the night there. That I fulfilled my boast — and came away, the next morning, a broken old man with my neck in bleeding tatters and my mind unalterably warped.

Reader, I beg you to heed the warning. I do not write to whet the appetites of the curious, but to prevent fresh horrors. Enjoy Abigail's tale and be lulled by her quiet conclusion. Then put the book aside and forget it. Let that be an end to it. Let there be no more stories. Do not do as I did; do not go looking for Boughwinds Abbey. Mr. Montefiore may be dead but he is there. He is there.

I am your sincere well-wisher,
Rupert Wellington-Grub.

Coming Soon
also by
Elizabeth Brooks

The Murder of Casimir Dudek

Dearest.
Events are overtaking us.
Casimir is dead. Come to me at once. – A.

I nnstood at the garret window with Alyosha's note in my gloved hand. The room behind me was dark, and the gas lamps in the street below were nothing but yellow-grey smudges, muffled by the snowy night. But I did not need much light to decipher Alyosha's handwriting. I knew every inky slash and curl as if I had written it myself.

My attic bedroom was mean and cold, but then I was only the governess. It was, in fact, a wealthy house in the wealthiest district of Mazurka. All the houses were tall along this boulevard, with wide, curving steps spilling down from the front doors to the street. There were five high-ceilinged floors between me and the ground: it was a long, long way to fall. I stepped back from the window and looked over my shoulder. There was only an iron bed and a rickety table and chair. It was a tiny room, yet I could never feel comfortably alone in it. My spare dress, hanging on the back of the door, looked like a tall man in a black cloak. It put me in mind of Abigail Crabtree's Vulture Man.

It was only by reading Abigail's manuscript that I realised this city of Mazurka, with its mountainous hinterland, was my stake in the universe of Traumund. I was the creator of Mazurka; I suppose Abigail would have called me its queen. So you may think it odd that

I contented myself with servitude and a poky attic room. It was odd, but, as you shall see, it was necessary. For the governess's demure grey gown was merely my disguise.

I paced the room with the note still open in my hand and tried to steady myself. I reached inside my cloak for the silver locket that was Alyosha's birthday gift to me, and my fingertips – poking out of the woollen mittens –were like icicles on my warm neck. I had only just retrieved the note from behind the loose brick in the back-lane, and I was still dressed for the outdoors, in boots, scarf and hooded cloak.

I returned to the window and re-read the note. It had not re-written itself while my eyes were elsewhere. I dropped it in the empty grate with a lighted match. Casimir was dead, and I must go to Alyosha at once.

The attic rooms and the wooden stairs were silent and unlit. I could hear faint voices wafting up from the ground floor, and the clatter of cutlery on fine bone china. As I crept from one carpeted landing to the next, I met the rising warmth from the dining-room fire, and the smell of garlic butter. My frozen shoulders relaxed, and my mouth watered.

I pictured the white-clothed table with a mixture of envy and abhorrence. There would be salad and fruit from the hothouse, vintage wine from the cellars, and soft bread rolls. But, above all, there would be meat. Perhaps a joint of beef or venison, served so rare that the gory flesh almost pulsed. Or meats that still looked like animals: bulging-eyed fish, snails, pigs'-heads with gaping jaws. I noticed, as I reached the ground floor and flitted past, that the dining-room door stood ajar. I retraced my steps and scrutinised the diners for a moment. They were an endlessly fascinating trio.

Igor Grinberg sat opposite the door, hunched over his plate and bustling with greed. A gobbet of steak slid down his stained napkin, and another dropped onto his beard from an over-loaded fork. His sweaty face shone in the firelight.

The fire burned behind Kirill Grinberg's chair, so his features appeared less distinct than his twin's, but I could see his dense black beard and the gleaming whites of his eyes. Kirill was not eating. He was sitting back in his chair, fingering his chin and holding up a glass of ruby-red wine. He eyed the wine critically, swilling it round and round, before taking a sip. He seemed uncharacteristically gloomy tonight, and I wondered why.

Sophie Grinberg, Igor's eleven year old daughter, sat to the right of her father. She was a skinny little girl, but she always dressed as though she was an adult. Tonight her black hair fell in ringlets round her shoulders, and she wore a crimson dress which gaped at the bust and revealed an expanse of flat, bony chest. She neither ate nor drank nor talked nor – apparently – listened, though her father cast the occasional guzzling grunt in her direction, and her Uncle Kirill murmured some general remark about the wine. Sophie was my pupil - to our mutual discontent. She was a child and, really, to be pitied, since her mother was dead and her father and uncle were alive. But there was something about her sharp, grown-up face that chilled me to the bone. She always seemed to be looking inside herself – she was doing it now – and thinking malevolent thoughts.

All of a sudden those inward-looking eyes met mine. She did not start or cry out when she saw me lurking in the dark hallway, she simply returned my unsmiling gaze. I leapt back and made for the front door, thankful for the fleecy carpets that deadened my booted footsteps. I thought I saw a ghost running towards me down the hall – a pale-faced figure in a shabby cloak with fear in its eyes. Then I saw that the ghost was framed by gilded scrolls and cherubs, and I recognised the long mirror which hung adjacent to the front door.

At last I was in the street, veiled by the swirling blizzard. I walked briskly, sometimes breaking into a run, and the snow filled my footprints as quickly as I made them. Through the wide avenues with their grand houses and carriages; past the park where leafless branches reached over the railings like fingers and dropped snow showers on my head; down steep streets and dark alleys to the riverbank. Nine bridges spanned the mighty Mazurka; I was only half a mile from the most ancient, the King Alexander, with its three stone arches. The water below the embankment creaked and swayed, semi-solid with ice, but I could hear the thunder of deep, rapid water from the middle of the river, and as I crossed the bridge I peered over the parapet and saw a jet-black torrent, riddled with clashing waves and currents.

Now I had to walk past the university buildings. I looked back over my shoulder many a time as I skirted their walls, and reassured myself that the Grinbergs were dining at home tonight and that they were unlikely to visit their faculty so late and in such weather. The university buildings went on and on, and they darkened the street from one side to the other. I looked up as I passed the medical faculty, and ran my eye over the fancy façade and the tall sash windows with their elaborate metal bars. I looked because I couldn't help my fascination. It was the sort of scrutiny which you would give a notorious prison or a place of execution, if you happened to be passing.

Nobody but the Grinbergs knew what went on in their 'medical' faculty. There was excited gossip, now and then, that the twins were close to some fabulous discovery: the secret of eternal beauty and the elixir of life were both rumoured. The exact nature of their experiments was anybody's guess, Mazurkan society did not speculate, let alone suspect. My employers were respected by all right-thinking people in consequence of their supposed scientific genius, and honoured as pillars of the community.

The innumerable abductions and murders that had plagued the city for years were also popular subjects of gossip, but they were not discussed in the same breath as the Grinberg twins and their experiments. The disappearances tended to take place in the poorer districts; the bodies were washed up down river. There was no connection to be made with the Grinbergs' work, so no one had ever made it.

No one, that is, except Mr. Casimir Dudek, Dr. Alyosha Brodsky and me, Miss Georgia Wellington-Grub.

The Cathedral clock boomed nine as I crossed the square. All the windows in Alyosha's house were dark but one: the curtains of his study glowed like amber, and I could see an anxious face squinting into the wild night. Alyosha's expression cleared the moment he caught sight of me. He disappeared, and a moment later I was ushered inside.

We did not say a word to one another for several minutes. I held my rigid fingers in front of the fire while the snow slid from my cloak and made puddles round my boots. Alyosha poured two hefty glasses of Draconakrov – that great Mazurkan spirit – the very smell of it from across the room was like fire in my nostrils. I swallowed the lot in three grimacing gulps.

"Tell me what happened." I said at last. Alyosha unclasped my cloak and hung it over a chair. We sat down on either side of the fire – I on a low, tapestried stool and he on the floor, his chin resting on his knees. I watched the glowing coals as they collapsed and rustled in the grate. I saw caves and chasms there, plateaus and precipices. But then Alyosha began to speak, and I turned from the fire to study his fierce face.

"I can tell you everything that happened, because I was there. I saw Casimir die and I did nothing to save him. I didn't lift a finger."

"Just tell me." I repeated, lightly stroking his hair.

"Very well." Alyosha spoke rapidly, as if anxious to get the narrative off his chest. "I'd arranged to meet Casimir for coffee yesterday evening; I felt he should know about your discovery sooner rather than later. I sent him a telegram; we were to meet at the Marius, as usual.

"I found, when I got there, that the Marius was closed – it's being refurbished. Casimir was nowhere to be seen – I'd arrived slightly early - so I decided to walk back down the embankment and meet him as he came along. It was gone five o'clock by the time I reached King Leopold Bridge. The dusk was deepening by the minute and there was a mist rising from the river. I was worried I'd miss him, in fact I almost turned back to the Marius, but then I saw him. I'd know that jaunty figure anywhere, I don't care how dark the night or how thick the fog. He was about to cross the bridge. I almost walked on to meet him, but something stopped me."

Alyosha reached for his tray of decanters and filled our glasses with another colossal dose of Draconakrov.

"What stopped you?"

He frowned, threw his head back and drank, as though angered by my question. Then he sighed, and wiped his fingers across his eyes. I noticed that they were bloodshot and deeply shadowed.

"We should pack it all in and go to Zheltydom." He said. "Why don't we, Georgia?"

I was not particularly startled by this non sequitur. Zheltydom was Alyosha's country estate, forty miles to the south of the city. I had never seen it, but I felt as if I had, for Alyosha never tired of describing its beauties: the avenue of birch trees reflected in the glassy lake, and the yellow house, and the way the air always smelt of wood smoke. He was always promising to "pack it all in" and run away with me to Zheltydom.

"Alyosha! What stopped you from walking over the bridge?"

He sighed. "There was a hansom cab at Casimir's back; keeping pace with him. It was odd-looking – no lanterns, and all the blinds drawn down, and the driver so muffled up that I couldn't see his face. The horse was black and its hooves were bandaged up in some way, so that they made barely a sound on the cobbles. I could hardly make it out in the twilight. It was a phantom cab. It sent a shudder through me and stopped me in my tracks.

"Then the door opened and a man stepped down, leaning hard on his cane. He tapped Casimir on the shoulder and tipped his hat, and for an instant there were two gentlemen standing face to face on the

King Leopold Bridge in cordial conversation. The next moment the cane was a long knife and Casimir was clutching his chest. I saw his white opera scarf steadily darken, as though dipped in a bucket of dye. He struck out at his assailant, pulling open the collar of his greatcoat and knocking his hat into the river: that was when I first recognised the murderer."

"Igor?"

"Igor. Of course. Do you think Kirill would stain his lily-white fingers?"

I snorted.

"They were halfway across the bridge by now, where the river flows fastest and deepest. Igor climbed onto the step of the moving cab, clutching the doorframe for support. With his free hand he tried to pull his victim after him. There were no passersby except for me, but nonetheless…the job was not going as swiftly and neatly as planned, I suppose, and he hoped to finish it off within the privacy of the carriage.

"But Casimir was having none of it. He flailed his arms and kicked his legs and spat a mouthful of bloody saliva into Igor's eyes. Both men staggered backwards: Igor fell onto the floor of the cab with a shout of disgust and Casimir toppled, without a word or a cry, into the icy Mazurka. I came to my senses when I heard the faint splash; I ran forward and looked over the parapet but there was nothing to see except ribbons of mist and frothing water."

I viewed the scene with my mind's eye for several minutes. "Isn't it possible…" I began, but I tailed off. A vigorous man, skilled at swimming, would have had no hope. I pictured our tall, bony Casimir rolling downstream, his bloodied scarf fluttering in the currents and his clothes saturated with river water.

Alyosha misunderstood my broken question. He sat forward and clutched my hands. "Everything happened so quickly, Georgia," he pleaded, his reddened eyes gazing into mine. "Please don't blame me. It wasn't cowardice that held me back - "

"Alyosha!" I exclaimed. "I would never blame you! That wasn't what I was going to say."

He squeezed my hands again and sighed, but the look of anguish had not left his face. I knew that he would be re-writing the scene in his head, over and over again, and that every version would end with a heroic intervention on his part, and then champagne with Casimir at the nearest restaurant as Igor Grinberg's body careered downriver.

"Did Igor see you?" I asked.

"I don't know. Probably not. He was too busy mopping the gore from his face."

"And…d'you think it was an unlucky coincidence that they attacked Casimir, of all people?"

Alyosha hesitated. "Y…yes. I think Casimir was just unlucky. The Grinbergs needed a body, and the streets were so deserted, they had to take what they could find. They chanced on Casimir."

We looked into one another's faces for confirmation of these words, but we only found unease.

We sat before the fire until the cathedral clock struck eleven. We made no plans for the future, but we spoke occasionally of our dead friend. I suppose we hoped to find comfort in happy memories, but our grief was too raw for that. Alyosha recalled how Casimir used to pout with concentration whenever he was writing, and how we used to tease him for it. I smiled, but then I saw that comic face resting in the muddy riverbed, and hungry sturgeon gliding through the gloom.

"I must go." I said dully, as the last chime sounded across the square. I hated to leave. My vision of paradise is Alyosha's fire-lit study, and the snow swirling down past the cathedral's golden domes.

"I'll walk you." he smiled, heaving his coat over his shoulders. Arm in arm we plunged into the arctic night.

We parted two blocks from the Grinberg house. We stood face to face for a minute, trying to find reasons to linger.

"Oh! Your locket!" exclaimed Alyosha. I looked down. The necklace had twisted itself in my scarf, and the silver pendant stood out plainly against my dark apparel.

"Oh hell!" I disentangled it and tucked it inside my cloak. I was horrified to think I might have walked through the Grinbergs' house with the locket on display. It was a piece of my real self; the self which Krill and Igor would never know.

"I hope you've put my portrait in there at last?" Alyosha joked. He knew I was too cautious to do any such thing. "A nice little miniature that does justice to my haughty profile and brooding eyes?"

"No." I answered, half-heartedly falling in with his tone. "Sorry. Michelangelo wasn't available."

He smiled and we wavered for a few more seconds. Then faintly, from across the river, we heard the cathedral clock tolling half-past eleven. Alyosha kissed me quickly on the forehead and turned away. When he had gone I looked up into the sky, and watched the snowflakes hurtle towards me through the pale lamplight. It was like falling through space.

Dearest,

I trust you got home safely. The Grinbergs were still sitting up when I got back. Sophie had been packed off to bed of course, but the twins were smoking in the library. I could hear the murmur of their voices as soon as I opened the front door, so I crept down the hall and put my eye to the keyhole.

Igor was pacing up and down the room, biting his knuckles and cursing under his breath. Kirill, in the meantime, was draped so comfortably in his armchair that he was practically horizontal. He was studying a chess board through one unclosed eye, and dropping cigar ash onto the carpet. It wasn't long before Igor tripped over his brother's extended legs.

"Damn it, brother!" he shouted. "How can you sit there, so...so damnably unconcerned?"

Kirill continued to study the chess board. Finally he moved the black knight to a vacant square. At last he looked up at his twin with surprise.

Igor was still blustering. "What a waste of time and effort. What a -"

"Igor, really." Kirill interrupted softly. "You fuss like a mother hen."

"All I am saying -"

"And you are disturbing my game."

Igor was silenced. He dropped into an easy chair and glared at the chess board. He stretched out his own legs in an effort to relax. Then he sat up straight and began gnawing his knuckles again. It was obvious that he wished to speak, but for a good five minutes fear kept him in check. Eventually he spluttered,

"Might we not...might we not recover Dudek's body? Somehow?"

Kirill brought the cigar to his lips in a slow arc. "Dudek's body" he replied, as he took a white pawn with a black bishop and set it on one side. "Is fish-food by now. A slimy, bloated, nibbled-at lump of flesh. No longer fit for purpose. You know that."

"Yes, but -"

"Igor!"

Igor was silenced again. Kirill continued.

"I want you to forget about Dudek. Do you hear me? What you did

was clumsy, it was careless. But you have learnt your lesson and it won't happen again. My dear brother, we can afford the odd mistake. Young men are not so hard to come by in Mazurka."

Igor looked sulky and muttered something about going to bed. I tiptoed away.

Dearest, as a young man of Mazurka, and an enemy of the Grinberg brothers, be careful.

Until tomorrow.

All my love,

G.

I folded the letter into a small square and put it in my pocket. Now to deliver it to the loose brick in the back-lane. It was not the blizzard that made me quail, nor the pitch black lane with its stinking bins and open sewer. It was the prospect of creeping downstairs, over the soft red carpets of this house, for the third time in as many hours.

I had only gone a few paces when a thought struck me, and I returned to fetch my coal bucket. I emptied what shards of coal there were into the grate, before setting off once more.

I was making my way across the hall to the top of the kitchen stairs, when I ran into Kirill. My nose actually touched the paisley silk of his dressing-gown before I saw him, and then I leapt back with a shriek. He watched me amusedly for a moment, before murmuring his apologies. I could just about make him out in the dirty grey gleam from the fanlight. He was leaning against the doorframe which opened onto the kitchen stairs, and thus – whether by accident or design – blocking my way to the back door. Why on earth should he be lurking here at the dead of night, biting his thumbnail in a bored sort of a way, unless he intended to intercept me? It is a good question. And yet he lounged with such a guileless air.

"Miss Wellington-Grub!" He bowed his head, gallantly.

"Mr. Grinberg." I curtsied.

"Are you going out again, Miss Wellington-Grub? I really must advise against it. The weather is atrocious."

Our brief exchanges were always like this. Only ever the most conventional pleasantries, and yet every word and every pause insinuating that we were of greater interest to one another than either of us was prepared to acknowledge.

"I am only going out to the yard, Mr. Grinberg, to fill my coal bucket. As you say, the weather is atrocious, and I find I cannot sleep without a small fire."

"But of course. Those attic bedrooms are bleak on a night like this, Miss Wellington-Grub."

"Indeed so, Sir."

A smiling pause. I felt as those pawns and bishops might have felt, under his absorbed gaze. Then he stood aside and with a sweep of his arm he motioned me to pass.

"Thank you, sir." And then, as a triumphant afterthought, "I trust you will forgive me for disturbing your nocturnal meditations."

"Think nothing of it, Miss Wellington-Grub."

But – forgive me – I am ahead of myself. My story does not begin here.

My story begins on a June morning in the Waking World, with a bored young girl, a shattered old man and a mouldering manuscript tied up with string.